MY COMPANIONS
IN THE
BLEAK HOUSE

MY COMPANIONS IN BLEAK HOUSE

EVA KANTŮRKOVÁ

Quartet Books
London   New York

First published in 1987 by
The Overlook Press
Lewis Hollow Road
Woodstock, New York 12498

First published in Great Britain by Quartet Books Limited 1989
A member of the Namara Group
27/29 Goodge Street
London W1P 1FD

British Library Cataloguing in Publication Data

Kantůrková, Eva, *1930–*
My companions in the bleak house.
I. Title   II. Pritelkyne z domu smutku.
English
891.8'635 [F]

ISBN 0–7043–2705–8

Reproduced, printed and bound in Great Britain by
The Camelot Press PLC, Southampton

For Jiřina Šiklová

This book sets out to tell something
of the reality of life;
nevertheless, any resemblance
to real people which may be
discerned in the stories is purely accidental.

My Companions in the Bleak House was
translated by a friend of
the author who prefers to remain anonymous.

CONTENTS

TO MY FRIEND, EVA KANTŮRKOVÁ

*Preface to English edition of Eva Kantůrková's book, **My Companions in the Bleak House** by Václav Havel*

Ruzyňe is the name of a place on the outskirts of Prague. But when you say the word, Czechs think mainly about the famous prison there. It is a big, dismal structure where most of those who have been accused of some criminal offense in Prague and central Bohemia spend endless months and sometimes even years of so-called "detention" while their case is being investigated and while they wait to be sentenced. (I say "most" because—contrary to the law—only a minority of those under indictment in our country are prosecuted while they are at liberty.) I myself have been in Ruzyňe several times. Altogether I spent more than a year there and so it was with particular emotion that I read Eva Kantůrková's book, *My Companions in the Bleak House*. It made my time in Ruzyňe come alive again. Words, phrases, observations and experiences brought back very concrete memories. From a factual standpoint, I do not think I have ever read a more acute description of life in this prison.

But *My Companions in the Bleak House* is not merely a factual report, a simple document. It is not just so called "factual fiction." It is something incomparably more. It is an account of women in marginalized situations—that is, an account which is universally *human*.

Eva Kantůrková is a Czech author who spent one year of her life in detention in Ruzyně, accused of sedition. She was investigated along with other intellectuals after a French truck carrying foreign literature to Prague was stopped at the Czech border. Hence, she is not a prisoner who became a writer by giving witness to her own life experiences, but an author who became a prisoner and whose time in prison inspired this book.

It is a collection of portraits of some of the other women prisoners, accused of common criminal offenses, with whom Kantůrková shared a single cell. During the length of her stay she had a chance to get to know them exceptionally well. From my own experience, I know that such constant, intimate co-existence (in a certain sense, much more intimate than living together in marriage) reveals a person's identity better than anything else. That is because these are deeply threatening situations, a major breakdown in one's life, a time of profound personal humiliation. I think that Kantůrková has been able to make her "companions" come alive in all their many different dimensions. Although I don't know any of them personally, I have the feeling from reading this book that I know them all very well indeed. If this book were nothing more than that—a collection of a few well-executed portraits of women—it would have been enough.

But *My Companions in the Bleak House* is not just a portrait gallery. It goes beyond this external frame in several ways. I will mention just one. In its skillful compostion based on the individual portraits, the book unfolds into an account of its narrator's one-year stay in Ruzyně, a kind of "meta-story" of her cell, or rather, about her peregrinations through different cells in Ruzyně. This concealed plot captures very significantly, I think, another theme of this book, which is that of *prison-time*, that strange "time/non-time" which offers sharp insights into a more far-reaching enigma, one which touches all of us, that is, the enigma of human time in general. Life in prison (particularly so there) stops in a strange way and at the same time, it becomes denser. On the basis of this drastic "stop," everything we've experienced, everything we've been, is recapitulated and becomes unexpectedly interconnected and in this disentangling all is unveiled and reevaluated. It is as if prison "non-time" would X-ray the "profane" times in our lives. The plotlessness and non-happenings of life in a prison cell cast a new and very peculiar light on the stories and events that have happened to us before, on the outside. This is a moment of truth—the truth of my fellow-prisoners, my truth and the truth of the world in which it has been given to us to live.

So for me, Eva Kantůrková's book is not just about Anna's rum pralines, about Helga and Denise and her other heroines. It is an account of being in prison as an existential, life situation which tells something very important about the human person and about the world.

Imagine a Prague intellectual thrown in prison among prostitutes, thieves and all sorts of social outcasts. Then she writes a book about them. What probably occurs to you first is a question: whether these creatures won't be simply the subject of a coldblooded, somewhat supercilious study, like going to a zoo and making remarks about the various animals? Or else, the author, in striving not to think of herself as something better, will perhaps fall into a sentimentalized self-identification with her heroines because of the intellectuals' bad conscience when they confront "the people"? These two dangers are, basically, just two versions of the same thing: a consciousness of one's own difference.

I think Eva Kantůrková has managed to avoid these dangers and to see her "companions" as quite normal people, as women with whom she has shared a common fate for awhile and who are all different, simply because it takes all kinds of people to make the world. They are not *a priori* better or worse than the author of this book. They're simply *different*—unhappy in different ways, good and bad in different ways. The author herself is in no way judgmental about them. She does not try to make herself out to be better than they are or to condescend to them like a Good Samaritan. She tries to see each one of them separately, as they are—that is, as concrete, autonomous individuals who are responsible for themselves.

I don't know if I would know how to write a book about being in prison. Probably not. But if I could, I'd write it differently. Not just because I'm a different person than Eva Kantůrková, but also because I'm a man. There are situations in this book about which I have a very special feeling. They interest me, they surprise, touch, irritate and intrigue me. Something about them makes me bristle inside, but at the same time, I'm fascinated. I can only explain this particular aspect of my own feelings about Eva Kantůrková's book by the very specific and undisguised femininity of the author's personality and the way she sees the world.

But this is also a great point in favor of this book. Nothing would have been more inappropriate than if Eva Kantůrková had tried to describe her experiences from a man's viewpoint.

VÁCLAV HAVEL
Prague, February 22, 1987

MY COMPANIONS
IN THE
BLEAK HOUSE

1

THE BLEAK HOUSE

A dull brownish building on the outskirts of Prague, it has two shorter and lower wings housing the offices, the stores, the changing rooms, the doctor's surgery, the library, and a long room misnamed the cultural room, which looks like a deserted village hall and is never, in any case, used. The two longer and higher wings enclose the exercise yard and extend beyond it to form a smaller coal yard, where the entrance to the prison is placed. These two parallel wings contain the cells, and even from the outside their function is obvious, for the only distinctive architectural feature are the four rows of barred windows.

A corridor runs the length on each floor, with cells for twelve, eight, six, four, or even only for two prisoners opening off it on each side. All the cells are overcrowded, and so there are three prisoners where there should be two, six where there should be four, and so on. The overcrowding can be observed from the corridor through shuttered peepholes in the doors. The bigger cells have two, an extra one bored through the wall and widening inward to give a clear view, even of the toilet, which is of the oriental crouching variety.

As you are taken down from the fifth floor after interrogation, or out to exercise in the yard, the deeper you sink into the bowels of the building, the thicker and more stifling the prison smell becomes. During my first two months at Ruzyně I passed through this smell four times each day, to interrogation, back to my cell, to interrogation and back again. The prison officer with me unlocked and relocked numerous iron gates, and each time he let me through first—not because he was a gentleman, but because that is what the regulations lay down. He never said "Madame" as he let me pass first, but I always thanked him as I went forward. Once, under the illusion of our common humanity, I said, "We both have to breathe this fetid air." That illusion was totally shattered one sweltering day, on my way up to the interrogation cell; in cells facing south women were fainting in the sickening unventilated air. An iron-jawed, short-cropped interrogating officer, sweating his fat out in the elevator on his way to "work" on me, found the sight of me so amusing that he said jovially, "Some people have all the luck, cooling their heels inside!"

Only once did the prison smell break through my mask of patience. It was a January morning, and we were being herded down the main staircase toward the exercise yard, our hands hidden under a blanket thrown over our miserable track suits to face the cold, our feet in the shoddy prison slippers packed with wads of cotton against the snow that seeped through the cardboard soles. A pane was missing in the corrugated glass of the landing window, and for a split second I glimpsed the glorious shining cold outside while the prison smell rose to choke me from below. My God, what was I doing there? The prison smell clings to your hair, to your clothes, your skin, the mattress you sleep on, the blankets you pull over you; it clings to the floor, the walls, the iron bedposts, and the eyes of the guards. It is compounded of stale cigarette smoke that cannot escape through the tiny windows that are not only barred, but covered with a thick-mesh metal screen that barely admits the passage of air. The smell holds forever the unwashedness of bodies, their sicknesses, the stench of the toilet and the bad food, the fetid moldering smell of air breathed over and over again. The first thing the prisoner's body has to come to terms with is shortage of oxygen. Then you are left with half your strength—and that is what your interrogating officer is out to destroy.

Prison is an abyss filled with hidden threats. The physical center and bottom of the abyss is the exercise yard, where two circles of radiating concrete walls form the cages where the inmates of a single cell of the prison are brought down for air. Each circle rounds a watchtower high above, where the guard is in touch with his commanding officer by an electric signaling system. The watchtowers are roofed over, and the prisoners call them nesting boxes. The guards say they are "out on a limb" when their turn comes round for this unpopular duty. They much prefer to guard the prisoners on their way down the stairs, for "out on a limb" they are expected to see that no prisoner looks up at the cell windows, and no prisoner looks down into the yard. No prisoner, up there or outside, may call out, gesticulate, or remove any garment. From the window of the duty room the officer in command turns his binoculars on the guards, as well as on the prisoners, and so to avoid punishment themselves, they make a great show of punishing the slightest infraction of discipline among the prisoners. The moment the binocular lenses catch the light, high up in that window, the women guards start yelling at their charges, and the unruly get sent back to their cells straightaway. The cages are roofed over with strong wire netting, so that from above the exercise yard looks as though it housed escapees from the zoo— a scene the interrogating officers enjoy from their stronghold on the fifth floor. From the depths of this abyss the prisoner sees only rows of barred windows, and even if some bold soul climbs up to hang on the bars of his or her cell window, longing for a glimpse of fellow prisoners in the yard, from below one sees no more than a faint outline. High above the prisoners' heads rears the water tower in the corner, and here there is a gallery for yet another guard. There was a family of kestrels nesting there, and from the interrogation cell I watched them teaching their young to fly and setting off to hunt in the White Mountain Park nearby. There were gray and white pigeons, too, on all the prison roofs. The abyss is not really deep—a mere six floors on two sides and four on the others—and far above there is the high vault of the sky; yet this is the blackest of Black Holes, one of the assholes of the world.

Here everything works together against the human individual; the system of compulsion rests on a host of trivialities whose implementation robs one of all that makes a human being. You are only on remand (that is, awaiting trial)? You can (theoretically) be sent home tomorrow for lack of evidence against you? You haven't even been brought before a court yet? Don't fool yourself. Once you are on the wrong side of the iron gates of this "Institution for Reeducation," hope is dead.

"You're not in prison," my interrogating officer reproved me. "You're in an institution," and it almost sounded as though he meant "You're in a hotel." If you come in here with hopes, if you think you will still be able to get out again—you are in for grave disappointment. The number of cases in which investigation has been called off for want of evidence is statistically insignificant. Once you are remanded, you can be practically sure you will be convicted; all that is left for the judge to decide, when you are finally brought before him, is the length of your sentence. And even if you are never brought to court, as happened in my case, proceedings are not stopped. You can be legally harassed for years, the only limit being that of the heaviest sentence provided for the offense you are suspected of committing; in my case, ten years. There are many opponents of the regime who are "free" but not "innocent," because the authorities would lose face if they admitted it. And what is more, the state treasury would lose money, because according to the law the state has to pay compensation for wrongful imprisonment.

Hope, then, either turns into despair under blow after blow (Just think how many times I was remanded, again and again!) or else it induces the prisoner to "collaborate in throwing light on the circumstances of the case." Even according to the law, investigation is not aimed at collecting evidence of guilt, but at obtaining a confession from the accused and statements from witnesses against him or her. As the saying goes in prison: admission of guilt is a mitigating circumstance and a guarantee of conviction. The fact that this is the legal attitude to criminal investigation undoubtedly affects conditions inside the remand prison. Prisoners are made to feel isolated and subjected to humiliations, because they must be broken. And hope, unless you stifle it in time, leads you to feel drawn to the person of your interrogation officer: he will lighten your sentence if you confess and if you give evidence against others. Patience is what you need to cultivate in prison, rather than hope.

"The Governor does not regard prisoners as people," one of the officers told me, off the record. She was young, a graduate of the police college, and fairly high-ranking. At college she had studied a little psychology and was prepared to make distinctions between the prisoners. That the prisoner is not a human being, but an offender, is the fundamental principle underlying prison "reeducation," the theory of imprisonment. Daily we listened to the shouts of an elderly drunk, a low-ranking guard waiting to be pensioned off, in the exercise yard below our window: "We'll bloody well educate you!"

Nobody yelled at me, let it be said; they yell and beat up only the worst cases, psychopathic and unmanageable prisoners; tear gas is not often used, nor are prisoners often chained in their cells or strapped down so that they cannot move. The prison system does not work through physical brutality, and as a rule such brutality is provoked by the prisoners themselves. Indeed, there is more brawling among the prisoners than beating by guards. The menace of the Bleak House is subtler: human beings are to be reduced to nothingness. The type of guard who keeps good order and is conscientious in his or her duty toward the powerless though guilty prisoners is dying out. Only once did one of them cross my path; he was quietly impersonal, gave us everything in his power (an envelope, sanitary towels, an extra slice of bread), did not demand circus tricks of us, and did not try to harm us. Decent people who do not abuse their power over the prisoners are no longer considered reliable. The extent to which a regime is civilized or "red in tooth and claw" can best be judged in places where the helpless are congregated: in hospitals, old people's homes, orphanages, and prisons. (And we should not forget that with all its extravagance, our country is too poor to spend money on its prisons.)

Reducing a human being to nothingness, to insignificance

("You think too much of yourself," my interrogating officer told me; he was a brand-new doctor of law, a dandified fellow of about thirty-five) is not at all a dramatic process, but it pervades the whole of prison life. A guard who addressed me as *Mrs.* Kantůrková felt she was taking a heroic risk. It is felt most in those little and rather silly things that go to make up a normal day, a normal life. The inexperienced prisoner still follows the patterns of good manners brought from outside, and so whenever the guards went through my parcels from home looking for contraband, I offered them a sweet or some fruit. They never took me up on it, and in my naivety I thought they were unwilling to rob me of something they had free access to. In fact, besides the distance duty compels them to keep between themselves and the prisoners, the guards feel repelled by them. I realized this when a young and insolent guard was taking me back to my cell from seeing the doctor; I put my hand on the door handle to open it for myself. Another of the vestiges of life outside. Inside, the old hands wait to have the cell door opened for them; the experienced prisoners take good care to do nothing that is part of the guard's job. But I touched that handle, and the guard yelled as though I'd stabbed him. Later on I understood why, when I met one of the more decent guards, with bandaged hands. He'd caught scabies—from a prisoner, who else? We were given a fairly thorough medical examination on arrival, but the doctor only asked about rashes. I said I had none, but what if I had and said nothing? One of the girls they put in our cell had a head full of lice, another had clap, one had scabies and yet another brought crab lice—but luckily that girl was put next door. There they all caught crabs from her and had to have their pubic hair shaved; as they came back to the cell we heard one of them say with grim humor, "Well, girls, that puts us out of business." The defenseless prisoner, dependent on strangers for everything, can easily catch and spread scabies, clap, crabs, and other lice. Who is to blame?

At night, when sleep would not come, I sometimes sat up in my narrow bed bang up against my neighbor's, and let my mind's eye take in the scene of which I was a part. What would I see if I came down the corridor and looked through the peephole at myself? There were six of us crowded in there, although the cell was meant for four; iron bedsteads painted gray, mostly filthy gray blankets, torn and badly washed sheets, sagging beds; the less said about our pajamas the better: of coarse orange-colored cloth, the same cut for men and for women, one with half a sleeve torn off, another with only one leg left, some with no elastic to hold them up at the waist. Our tattered underwear was gray from bad washing. The six of us lying there under our gray blankets looked like mangy parrots nobody wanted. We looked the most miserable human creatures imaginable. Who then is human, in here, and who is not? In civilized countries prisoners wear their own clothes, and in wealthy countries they even have radio and television; prisoners can have their own books, can move freely about the yard, and receive visitors. What are *we* the image of, dressed in rags, evil-smelling and half-starved, our sicknesses neglected?

Let us not judge too hastily. Twice during the eleven months of my imprisonment we were taken out of the cell for a body search. Naively, we thought we were going to have a bath, because it was just before Christmas. Shut in the cells there is nothing to judge from but the sounds outside the door, and we could hear slippered feet slopping along the corridor and the sounds of the next cell being searched. We assumed they were taking advantage of bath time to go through the cells. The guard laughed: "Baths? Sure, you'd better hurry while the water's warm." And she took us all the way down the corridor littered with stuff thrown out of other cells, heaps of letters, underwear, mess tins, spoons, newspapers, bottles of medicine—and instead of the bathroom we found ourselves in a bare cell.

Two women guards ordered us to strip and ran their hands through the clothes we took off; any precious secrets hidden in brassieres or briefs came pitilessly to light. My friend had hidden letters from her lover (not even I had been privileged to hear what he wrote) and now the guard we called Milly started reading them aloud in her drunken voice. "Well I never!" she screeched, "What d'you say to this? If it isn't meant to be a love letter, of all things!" She smirked at us shamelessly. A fat peroxide blond, she was the sentimental sort who certainly spoiled her grandchildren and gave her son money toward a new car.

"Haven't got anything better to think about," the other put in, Potato Face was our name for her. "Like bitches in heat, that's what they are." My friend had to show that the letter had come through the official post and been censored by the prison authorities, although that was obvious at first glance, and proof that it hadn't been smuggled in. Meanwhile, watched by the senior prison officer, another guard had been through our cell like a herd of wild boars rooting in the ground. We kept our little cupboards scrupulously tidy, and now our letters, toilet things, food from home was thrown all about the cell floor, and dirty fingers rummaged through the Christmas biscuits friends had baked for my husband to send me. The beds were tipped up and mattresses, sheets, blankets, and pillows thrown about in disorder. There was no telling which belonged to whom, tables and stools lay overturned in the mess of bread, sugar, soap, cotton balls, cold cream, books, and letters. It was not a cell search; it was someone working off a fury of ill will.

My companion, who was ever ready to tell her fellow prisoners off for the slightest show of cheek or insolence, stood there trembling with fear for her precious letters in Milly's hands. I ought to have taken her part; I ought to have protested and said I didn't want to listen to other people's private correspondence. Yet all I could do was stare, not because I was afraid, you understand, but because the sheer filthy-mindedness of it all took my breath away. In the Bleak House nothing, not even human emotions, are measured by the same yardstick as outside, for the simple reason that if anything so brutal and so desecrating happens there, it happens under cover of other appearances. It cannot happen openly. Outside would anyone dare to violate privacy in that way and even pretend it was his right? If it does happen, it is so rare that very few people have experienced it. But if you create a place where things that should never happen do and must inevitably happen to the defenseless, you have created prison, a world of out-and-out undisguised manipulation, a world it is easy to do anything with.

The experience of prison life is important if you want to understand the mechanism by which people can be manipulated. There is no "unspoken agreement" here. I was present when the guards taking us back from the exercise yard were looking for the key to the freight elevator because they did not feel like climbing all the way up to the sixth floor. The trusty in charge of the elevator lent them the key, although he might just as well have denied knowledge of it, but he was decent. The key must have been a frequent bone of contention, because as the trusty handed it over he very politely asked the guard to return it to him as he was responsible for it. The woman he had been polite and helpful to began bawling him out. Who did he think he was, addressing an officer when he hadn't been spoken to?

He'd better shut his bloody trap. She knew when and where to return the key and would speak to nobody less than his officer-in-charge. Red and furious, she bundled us into the elevator, and the kind trusty knew he'd be in for trouble for having let the key go.

Our things were lying all over the floor of the cell. It was our job to pick them up and sort them out, count how many of the little treasures had found their way to the heap of rubbish in the corridor. It was we who were forced to listen to intimate words of love addressed to another. When a coarse voice yelling at you wants to know who it is on the photograph you've been wearing next to your skin, and you have to utter the name of the one most dear to you in the face of an enraged beast—are you master of the situation? Maybe you will feel you are, later, after you have swallowed the humiliation, chewed it between your teeth, and digested it in your entrails, without throwing up. Are you master of the situation even then? After it was all over we laughed at our fears, but nobody can bring back that photograph thrown out on the rubbish heap, and a thorn remains in your flesh. That thorn is the simple experience and realization of absolute *helplessness*. You may think it is an ennobling experience to savor that last of all things, last before the experience of death; when you realize your own helplessness you can understand anything. It may be so, but the fact remains that this sense of utter helplessness is precisely what those who manipulate want you to feel. In prison you must be brought to accept that you are nothing. You must be made to fear imprisonment.

Another such search took place on March 8, International Women's Day, our very own day. The date itself left me cold, because I observe none of the state-ordained "days," but the others were used to celebrating Women's Day at work, and when they asked Potato Face why they had to choose just that day, she told us, "You're criminals and Women's Day's got nothing to do with you." She celebrated, though, going through our things extra roughly.

We struck a blow for human dignity by refusing to hold our hands behind our backs. When you are taken out of your cell to stand in the corridor—perhaps because a prisoner is fitting a new electric bulb in the cell—you have to stand facing the wall with your hands behind your back. Going out for exercise, the inmates of each cell are taken at intervals, to prevent them seeing the others. You go in single file, you are not allowed to speak—and hands held behind your back. I had a good look at my fellows in their torn track suits, shapeless and usually filthy, staring at a wall with their hands behind their backs; they no longer looked like human beings. And once they have robbed you of your human appearance, they think they have the right to treat you like cattle. We started by asking which paragraph of the prison regulations lays down that prisoners must hold their hands behind their backs, since we could not find anything of the sort in the extremely detailed regulations pinned up in our cell. We put the same question twice, at roll call, and finally the officer in charge of our floor came to tell us what the Governor had said about it at the staff meeting: the Governor has the power (according to prison regulations) to make any addition to those regulations that circumstances demand. This was one of them. Another officer was more astute: when pills began to vanish from their place on a shelf outside the door, she said, "Now you see, that's one of the reasons for making you hold your hands behind your backs." (Later I found out that guards were stealing the pills to sell to prisoners hooked on drugs. In fact one officer was brought to trial for the offense, and prisoners gave evidence against him.)

We stole no pills, but we tried to keep our hands at our sides;

some of the guards posted on every landing and at every turn in the corridor pretended not to notice as we passed them; but one—and it was the man who later got into trouble over drugs— yelled, "Hands behind your backs!" and started using his truncheon. There is nothing dignified about being yelled at or clobbered, and so we put our hands behind our backs, but only to hitch our thumbs in the elastic of our track suits. Our hands were behind our backs, yet they were not behind our backs, like the girl in the Czech fairy tale who came before the king neither walking nor riding because she had one foot on a scooter, and neither clad nor naked because she wore a fisherman's net wrapped round her. Strangely enough, the officers accepted our stratagem—a tiny "unspoken agreement," a minute victory for the prisoners.

One day, I was being taken to the doctor after a fainting fit, not (as I found out afterward) to put me right but because the interrogating officer wanted a doctor's report after I'd refused to answer questions when I felt too ill. I need not say that her report was not in my favor. A female guard and the officer in command that day were with me; he was young and looked intelligent and well brought up, the sort who would give a lady precedence and say good morning politely when he met neighbors in the street. They were chatting, and I—as white as the wall I was trying to hold on to—naively asked if I could catch hold of him if I fainted again. Without replying, he moved to the far side of the corridor. If I fell, and needed to be carried or helped along, they would call a couple of trusties to do the job.

Now whenever I see prisoners in a bus, going to work or to the courts, though I have no idea what crimes they may have committed, and though I find crime more repulsive, perhaps, than those whose job it is to root it out, I feel a wave of that fraternal feeling that is born in places where hope has no meaning. Whoever has been inside is brother to all prisoners, whatever they are in for; this is not just a romantic illusion: whoever has been through the sickness called helplessness knows not only why all prisoners wear a strained look and have fear in their eyes but also why it is no disgrace to be in prison. It is no disgrace; it is a testing time. The conditions in which prisoners are kept make it a testing time, and the disgrace somehow fades out of the picture. The prison system has been thought out, organized, and supplied with human beings, and is applied so inhumanely that at the worst moments you cannot distinguish between the evil that is in the prisoners and that in those who keep them there. Filth, the natural concomitant of prison, exudes from both. And in denial of the proclaimed purpose of those "Institutions for Reeducation," the goal fades away, too. Everyone who passes through prison comes out worse than he or she went in. My turpitude can be seen in that whenever I gaze back toward that hell, I do not turn to stone.

I did not choose the women crowded with me into the space of a few square meters, behind a door with no handle, in a room where we ate, slept, and excreted; where it was cold and there was not enough air to breathe; where it was dark during the day and lit up all night; where there was nowhere to hide from the spying eye at the peephole or from the eyes of the others; where there was no refuge from the stench of other people, from their chatter, their tears, their shouts, their ill manners, their neurotic reactions; and where to make matters worse I was the victim of injust and hate-filled persecution. Outside I might have met some of these women in a cheap restaurant or behind the counter in a shop, if I frequented either, or as a nurse in a hospital if I was sent there. I would know nothing about her, or about her case unless I happened to read of it in the papers, and even then it would only be the judge's or the lawyer's view of it. But when you breathe into each other's face all night long, when you spend long hours of uncertainty together, when you become the chance recipient of painful confidences in nightmare-filled nights—you begin to see many different sides to the same person. The shell, if there is one, cracks under the pressure within. To know is to understand. Not that I condone their deeds (if that is what it was that had brought them there); but I discovered that even if they were caught, unless they were utterly corrupt (and there are very few as bad as that, inside) they were not so much wicked as sad and unhappy, betrayed by life. Guilt is something that retreats to where it can be seen objectively, weighed and assessed, rejected or hidden; one does not identify with it or live with it. What you live with is the sadness; and sadness becomes a bond, a bond as strong as that of the humiliations you have suffered together.

2

MADDY

A cheerful pretty girl with dark wavy hair welcomed me to the cell as though she was at home there; plump, but quick in her movements; not even a prison track suit twice her size could make her look ridiculous. She showed me how to make my bed, and every third day, despite my protests, she took my turn and cleaned the cell. A Gypsy foundling, she was adopted quite small and taken from the children's home. Her father was a retired policeman, her mother a clerk in the local council offices, and for a long time she did not know they were not her real parents. They had come from the country and kept rabbits in the garden of their cottage in a Prague suburb. Maddy was a clever child, indeed she had almost finished the agricultural technical school; she had beautiful handwriting and could express herself very fluently on paper. She liked to read her compositions aloud to us—mostly loving messages to be smuggled to men prisoners. She copied out passages from the books she read, especially pretty verses, and was extremely proud of her manuscript library. Maddy spent the whole day writing or drawing, and so she had two persistent problems: the most important was how to get hold of cigarettes; then came how to get hold of paper. Every piece of toilet paper that we got in the cell was covered in her writing, and she was always begging the trusties for the packets that sanitary towels came in. Whenever I got a new supply of notepaper, she would use the last available corner of the wrapping for her screeds. One morning at roll call I noticed that she was again handing over an "official" letter, but in an unaddressed envelope. God knows she had plenty of time to concoct "reports" on me, I was away being interrogated for most of the day. Then she would smile and tell me that *now* I was sure to be sent home. I would like to know what she, of all the companions forced on me, could find to say about me. You soon learn in jail not to form hasty judgments about people; the true aspect of things may be hidden for good or for evil reasons. Maddy was complying with the expressed wishes of the authorities, and yet she felt the natural solidarity of one prisoner with another. It was not her first time inside; she had done time in a prison camp for young offenders, and the world of prison was already her natural element. She did not feel lost; she could hold her own against her fellow prisoners and against her jailers, carrying on her private war against the world with the weapons at her command, a thorough knowledge of all the rules and regulations that could be turned against her. And I can thank the heavens above that when I collapsed, Maddy was in the cell with me. She banged and kicked the door and got the girls in nearby cells to bang and kick too, until the guard on duty brought a doctor to me. It was a Saturday afternoon, and it was no mean feat to get the doctor to a prisoner in her cell at such a time.

When Maddy had been adopted as a small child, she was

pretty, bright, and eager to please; but as she grew older she felt an urge to find her real parents. And that, according to her adoptive mother, was the first step on the downward path. Perhaps it was a fateful moment when, half child, half adult, she felt the burden of parental authority too oppressive; or perhaps the call of the blood really does exist. When she found her true parents in a Gypsy colony near Kladno, Maddy was spellbound by their vision of freedom—and straightaway she fell head over heels in love. She left home, she left school, and existed from day to day. Her lover lived by shoplifting, and she told us admiringly how he would bring home bags of sweaters, and once he had even brought her a "whole fur coat." The two belonged to a gang that robbed unsuspecting visitors to Prague, in dark streets or in bars. Maddy was the decoy. They were caught at the Central Station, before he had time to get rid of the loot, and that settled it.

The couple who had adopted her, especially her mother, brought her up to respect not so much moral principles as their conventional social expression. From the long reproachful letter Maddy's mother sent her when she was arrested, she was clearly a woman with a strong sense of duty, and Maddy admired her for it; she did not wash her hands of the girl when she went to prison for the second time. She went on trying to improve her, at a distance, with somewhat unimaginative and humorless but undoubtedly sincere moralizing. That was what amazed Maddy: "Can you believe it? She hasn't given me up, though I wouldn't have been surprised if she did!" Yet however hard the admirable woman tried to drive home the difference between good and evil, even if she had loved Maddy as her own child and had forged a real bond of affection between them, she was doomed to fail. The soul is more than enthusiasm, more than the glow of righteousness; it is also conscience, and indeed conscience is what is needed most—that reflection of the world and our actions that we may not clearly understand, whose workings remain a mystery, but that must be alive if our soul is to shine as it should.

From time to time it seemed to me that Maddy did not know what it meant to have a conscience. She lived on the surface, with her skin, as it were, and was absolutely impartial in her attitude to good or evil. She drifted along from one thing to the next without making any conscious choice or considering what she was doing; and only the consequences of her acts brought her either pleasure or tears of anger. That was the only distinction she could make: things turned out well or they ended badly.

"When you get out, Maddy, do you think you'll be able to resist going back to the gang? Won't you go home?"

No answer was needed; smiling, she shrugged her shoulders helplessly: "I know it's not right—but it's so much nicer!"

It is hard to apply the criteria of our civilization to someone who has only heard them as phrases. Maddy "knows," but she does not feel. She had at the tip of her tongue words like fidelity, honor, love, honesty, truth, and falsehood; indeed she would speak them lovingly and in a special voice that intimated she was aware of their weight and significance. Yet it would never occur to her to live by any of these concepts; they existed in her mind, quite distinct from reality. The idea of one trying not to tell lies, purely and simply for the sake of being truthful, would have sent her into fits of laughter. Not that she was always lying; when it suited her she would tell the truth, but she liked to operate with grand words, for her clever little head had realized that symbols like love and honor sprinkled through her speech, like her neat handwriting and polite manners, helped to raise her from Gypsydom to a more advantageous level. Not up to the level of the non-Gypsies (she did not want that) but to the borderline, where she could enjoy the advantages of both Gypsy and non-Gypsy. Maddy had nothing but nice things to say of the mother who had adopted her and brought her up. The reproachful letter from her mother was kept in a place of honor on her shelf, among the poems and touching passages she had copied out of books and magazines. It was her personal bible, turned to at special moments—and it was something that singled her out from the others. Which of them could boast of such high moral tone? Maddy read it to me twice over, dwelling on the things her mother said about her wicked life and the depths to which she had sunk; her mother's reproaches, counsels, and entreaties moved her to tears; they were a moral adornment she wore for effect, like the ring of twisted thread on her finger. The moment their real relationship came into play, Maddy was more prosaic: would Mother please send her some cigarettes and money to buy a few necessities? "You're angry with me too, aren't you, Eva? because I'm so incorrigibly wicked?" How well she pronounced the word, proud of knowing what it meant and how to use it! I could imagine her, if she had grown up with no other influence than home, deftly coping with school and then a job and a dull suburban marriage; those grand words would still have served as an adornment to her person—and nothing more.

The officer in charge of her case was elderly and the nightmare of all the young thieves in the city. He had once served with her adoptive father and had dealt with her first offence; perhaps it was her tears and promises to be good that had moved this strict public servant to get her a light sentence that first time. Now she came before him once more, and this time her mother was brought in. Together the two of them, not using threats or pressure but just repeating how different she was from the others because she had non-Gypsy parents and friends in the police force, managed to get more out of her than even the police knew. Maddy's boyfriend (whom she called her fiancé; it sounded better) was in a cell across the yard, and each could see the outline of the other behind the screen. There was just room for her fingers between the bottom of the screen and the wall, and for hours on end she would explain to him in sign language how dreadfully she had let him down. In the presence of her mother she had revealed the details of their biggest coup, a strange affair she couldn't help boasting about. "I *must* tell you, Eva dear."

I can still see her clearly, with her big dark eyes that looked Southern, rather than Gypsy, her short wavy hair, strong legs crossed under her like a tailor, in her ugly orange pajamas with the fly in front. It may have happened like that, or it may not; prison old hands are like fishermen telling tales of "the one that got away." Maddy wasn't as old a hand as that, yet, but the way she told the story it could well have been true. Late one night, somewhere in the narrow streets near the Powder Tower, she met an elderly man who looked as though he was up from the country for a day, with a well-filled purse. She knew where they could have a good time (I know, too, now, and can tell you which cafés and wine bars it's best *not* to go to). He was the ideal victim, not doubting her good faith because she spoke such good Czech, although she was a bit dusky. He wanted to know if she wasn't Greek, and she nodded, and off they went. In a dark corner behind the big department store the gang fell on him, robbed him, and stripped him naked, leaving him lying on the pavement in a state of shock. Maddy was scared and went back to see if he was still alive. There was no one there! That was what made the affair so strange. Who could have turned up so quickly and taken care of a stranger lying naked and terrified on the pavement in a mess of shit? That was a salacious detail

Maddy had to linger over. "The stink! We had to throw all his clothes into a garbage can." The mystery only deepened when she learned from her police officer that no complaint had been filed.

She virtuously tried to explain away her betrayal of her boyfriend, pretending her mother hadn't influenced her at all. (Later on at her trial she was to say the whole story was an invention.) She wrote him long letters through the prison censor, full of words like love and honor, but it wouldn't have been Maddy if at the same time she didn't deceive the fiancé she *adored* and to whom she would be *faithful unto death*. Her ruin, as her mother called him.

Love affairs in prison are limited to the written, spoken, or shouted word, except for those few bold souls who try to strip in the exercise yard while their beloved watches from his cell. After one such love scene we were all punished by having to wear not only shirts, but track suits as well, on the hottest summer days. The prurient puritanism of the prison authorities went so far that a young guard taking me through the prison to the interrogation cell on a sweltering day bawled me out for having my shirt sleeves rolled up above my elbows as I came out of my cell. Maddy's boyfriend kept begging her to strip for him, but she wouldn't. It wasn't "nice," and "How could I look you in the face afterwards?" she wrote soulfully, laughing all the time.

There was a girl on our corridor who was said to have managed a quick one in the elevator with the kitchen trusty bringing our food up one floor. Nobody really believed her, but on the other hand, guards on night duty had been known to pick out a pretty girl and take her to an empty cell, paying with cigarettes. That was not regarded as love, but as a strictly business transaction. Because it was so restricted, love proliferated wildly. Veronica, in the cell next to ours, had been arrested with her boyfriend who was now in a cell on the opposite side of the yard. As soon as she woke she would climb up on her window, as the ritual of love demanded, and shout, "Johnny darling, my dearest love, good morning. I love you, how did you sleep?" We never heard her Johnny answering, and evil tongues said he was writing love letters to her rival; but without fail a coarse blustering voice would start hurling abuse at her. Veronica had an unpleasantly penetrating voice, and she screeched her morning greeting so vehemently that not a word could be distinguished; a row like that just when you felt like turning over and getting a bit more sleep was more than some could stand. I cannot record those foul expressions, but Veronica was never at a loss to reply, and when men had spent a bad night the yard was soon echoing with repressed passions. Helga was in our cell by then, and as soon as Veronica started up she would take her stand by the window and listen with delight to the abuse flying back and forth. A bit of drama to start the day with; she'd not have missed that contest in lewdness.

Maddy carried on the morning ritual, too, climbing up on a bed to send her message, but she was caught between two passions, and that made life difficult. There was love, and there was profit. Her fiancé over the way meant love; Pierre the illicit money dealer in the cell two floors above ours meant profit. Any young man who was accessible, willing, and provided with cigarettes, meant profit to Maddy. If only her fiancé had been accessible, willing, and provided with cigarettes, things would have been simpler. As it was, she used her fingers to expiate her betrayal in her fiancé's eyes, while she cried her morning love greeting to Pierre, hoping the other would not recognize her voice in the general commotion. Maddy also talked to Pierre through the toilet phone, a fact that shows only how accessible he was and not how profound her feelings were. Talking through the pipe, she would make fun of him, or start a mild quarrel, keeping her more intimate expressions of love for the letters she sent him. Those long epistles written on sanitary towel wrappings or the covers my notepaper came in, describing her love as undying, eternal, faithful, self-sacrificing, devoted, hotly sensual, as pure as a mountain stream—her words were calculated carefully according to the amount of tobacco Pierre was sending in return. That Pierre of hers! His manly self-assurance! But after counting the order in which the cells were taken down to exercise, Maddy clinging to the bars described with horror what she could make out below: her Pierre must be suffering from elephantiasis, hardly able to move his fat ass! Pierre claimed to be the son of a French mother and a Hungarian father. His wife had deserted him, and he wrote so touchingly about his little daughter that Maddy, who expected to be out of jail sooner, was full of promises to look after the child for him—truly a tobacco strategy! To do her justice, Maddy took no small risk for this profitable lover of hers; if she was caught telephoning or smuggling letters, the least punishment she could expect was solitary confinement in the filth of the basement punishment cells on half rations. For the men in the game the day passed more easily, and their boredom was less deadly.

When a friend of mine, jailed ten years earlier for unorthodox political views, described the toilet telephone, I was horrified. What? Talking down a lavatory pipe? If talking was all you had to do! You have to kneel down on top of the sink, which is at floor level, and bail all the water out with your hands, so that your voice will carry. Maddy's fingernails were worn down to the quick from scraping that pipe. Every now and again we'd hear from a window above or below: Maddy, clear the line! Lucy, clear the line! Which meant: get all the water out so we can talk. Maddy's eyes were red and inflamed, and there was a rash on her forehead from the foul-smelling air of the drains. She tried to get me to find a friend the same way; indeed, she was so insistent that I wondered whether that wasn't another job she'd been assigned. But I was not going to give my jailers the pleasure of finding me on hands and knees with my head inside a lavatory pipe; the very idea symbolized the hell of prison.

Nevertheless the telephone habit had one great advantage for me—the girls kept the lavatory clean. And however much the idea nauseated me, I had to admit that it was the bread of life to them. For what other coin have you to get a man with, in jail, but your tongue? Speech is direct communication, speech provokes speech in return. Maddy preferred to express herself in writing, but other girls were not so clever with the pen. There was one in the next cell (we could hear her because we had a common drainpipe) who must have been very good at her profession, for her descriptions of sexual delights were enough to keep all the men happy in six cells above us, and provoke scenes of jealousy among the women on either side. Everybody would stop talking to listen to her: it was the prison version of a sex orgy, a sorry enough version. But some girls talked such filth that the men pulled the chain and filled the pipes with water again, to drown their voices.

Pierre preferred the pen, too. "He's a writer on the side," said Maddy proudly. Most of the time this speculator turned author described his erotic dreams, a stumbling attempt at adolescent pornography, but Maddy was proud of him. Smuggled letters had to be destroyed at once in case there was a cell search, but Maddy kept his under her pillow for at least one night. She would copy out his purple passages.

Letters were delivered "on horseback," the other principal means of contact with your fellow human beings in jail. Letters (or food or tobacco) are rolled up and fastened with rubber rings to make the "horse," hung on a string and pushed through a hole made in the screen over the window. A horse was let down from a cell above, swinging back and forth, to be caught, drawn in, and untied, and then replaced with your own horse. To the shout of "Ready, pull her in!" you pushed your parcel out and it was drawn up in its turn. Lighthearted girls would shout encouragingly, "Geee-up!"

While horses were being caught, untied, and sent off again one of us had to listen at the door, calling out at the slightest sound in the corridor: "Ara! Ara! Bengo!": watch out, a guard! The whole thing had to be done very fast and caused great excitement.

"Hurry, hurry!" Maddy would be muttering nervously at the door while Lucy was swearing and angrily struggling with string that had got hopelessly knotted. At times the excitement seemed more worthwhile than the tobacco itself.

Messages on horseback passed up and down many floors and even to cells far to the side. From side to side it was a rocking horse, thrown upward so as to pass the next window as it went down again; when it was aimed at a lower window the horse was swung back and forth until it passed the right window and could be drawn in. It was an art that needed skill and practice. The string had to be properly weighted at the other end, usually by a sock filled with the powder we were given to clean the toilet with. There were many of us with bare feet in our slippers, because horses would get caught on the lightning conductor or window bars or fall down and be lost for good. There were plenty of these failures to be seen on the concrete or caught on the walls, when we went down for exercise, and an awful lot of socks were used up. When laundry day came round you had to pretend the dirty ones had already been handed in, and ask for a clean pair. It was also an art to hide the "rider" used to catch and rope in the horse. Every day the guards checked the legs of our stools, the wooden window frames, and the mattress underlays in our beds. That was the best material for a rider, because they were made of cardboard, and a piece the right size was easy to throw. Maddy used newspaper for her riders, it had to be *Rudé Pravo* because of the big pages; after use it could be smoothed out again and nobody was any wiser. Horses and deliveries on horseback aroused the bitterest rivalry between the jailers and the jailed; at any moment a voice from the door would yell "Hand over that horse!"—words that meant all had been in vain and the longed-for tobacco again out of reach. The pastime was a regular part of prison life, an expression of the prisoners' inventiveness and their longing for freedom. It brought one human being in contact with another, and at the same time provided fun and excitement. There were sharp eyes everywhere. Sometimes a guard opposite would see a horse swinging, but by the time he had rounded the yard and reached the guilty cell, there would be no sign of it.

Once it happened late in the evening, the guard was sure of his cell and turned it upside down, yelling, "No bloody prisoner's going to fool me!" yet found nothing. By the time he had climbed the stairs and raced down the corridor, the horse had been sent swinging along to the next cell. Some of the cell windows could be seen from the block of apartments where married officers lived, and children would shout, "Daddy, Daddy, there's a horse going up!" Following in father's footsteps, they would note down the number of the cell that could be seen painted by the window. There were times when my interrogating officer would interrupt his interrogation to watch with interest as a horse swung high and silently disappeared behind the bars of a cell window. They caught Maddy at it once, and the horse she pulled in was so big, the guard thought it worth his while to chase round after it. It was a book Pierre had sent her, and the guard found it but refused to believe its educational purpose and sent Maddy to the black hole for her cheek in expecting him to believe such an unlikely tale.

Smuggled prison correspondence is a phenomenon worthy of serious study. If only the prison authorities, instead of destroying it, would hand it over for psychological analysis! Letters very rarely cover plots or attempts to cook up evidence, which is the ostensible reason for suppressing them. They present one theme over and over again: "I love you!" If you have no imagination of your own, you copy other people's letters; some include verses, and some are so well and so aptly illustrated with drawings that the very fact of the time and skill spent on something that is bound to be destroyed shows up the monstrosity of keeping people behind doors with no handles, day and night. The prisoners' inventiveness has found ways of getting round this destruction: letters are written in the way laid down for authorized letters, giving a return address and the prison address of the recipient—and even a forged imitation of the censor's stamp. These smuggled letters were strictly forbidden, and yet they remained the greatest solace for senders and recipients alike.

For about a week I had a woman sleeping next to me who kept up a correspondence with a man she had never seen; she had only heard his voice a few times in the toilet phone. By the time she reached our cell he had been convicted and sent to do time, and every evening this woman carried out her ritual: taking his letters from their hiding place and removing the rubber band. She lay face downward on her bed, so that we should not see what was written in them. Then she laid the letters out on her pillow, one by one, reading them over in a low mutter; although she must have known them by heart, she was moved and uplifted by them over and over again. Yet that forty-year-old woman was one of the lowest, stealing from us in the cell (the worst crime in a prisoner's eyes), and her language was as filthy and primitive as her nature. She had been a concierge and told us how she drove the children out of the yard when they tried to play there. She had used her schoolboy son in her lowdown thieving, only to disown him at her trial because he was "such a bad lot." She showed her evil nature at its worst, though, in her attitude to her own mother; she locked the poor old woman, who was senile, in a room from which she had removed all the mats, curtains, and upholstered furniture, leaving nothing but bare wood and linoleum, because her mother was incontinent. And when she was arrested and her daughter wrote to say it was four days before uncle managed to get the old woman out of the room where she'd shut up with her dog, my neighbor was so furious she couldn't sleep until she'd written an angry letter saying her brother must not be allowed to keep the key a moment longer, because all he wanted was to get hold of the old woman's apartment when she died. And how she praised her own foresight; how wise she'd been to take everything out of the room. "I ask you, what would the furniture have looked like after four days, if I hadn't saved it?" She was the foulest creature you can imagine, yet she lay there sincerely moved by letters from her "dearest Jim" although they had never met and she could hardly hope they ever would. It was not their relationship that comforted her, it was his words and drawings. The written word has indeed tremendous power.

Sign language, the Morse code clapped out or tapped on the heating pipes, the toilet phone, messages on horseback, banging on the floor—all were substitutes for conversation; and if Maddy had not made so many enemies, her prison life could have combined both love and profitable acquaintance. Fighting for your man incites to all the greater cunning in jail, because of the risks and difficulties involved. When one of the girls heard Maddy talking on the phone to Pierre, she told the fiancé about it in sign language, and when another saw her sending him loving messages in sign language, she promptly sent a horse up to tell Pierre about that. Intrigue was the breath of life in the women's cells; love affairs were entangled in webs of intrigue, jealousy, and falls from favor. Screaming, weeping, quarrels, and abuse were always bursting out to rend the air above the exercise yard, the air that lay so heavy between those rows of barred windows. The prison would seem to be heaving with repressed passion. Lies, excuses, courtship, persuasion, assurances and promises fed both love and jealousy, the only two things that could keep boredom at bay. Oh, how often Maddy's enemies held her up to dishonor! She writhed between two fires like a scorpion, swearing at both her men, soft-soaping them, often in tears, protesting her love and threatening to leave them. Maddy's fiancé began sending sign messages to a girl in the next cell to ours—Maddy's grief when she read his loving words meant for another! At such blatant treachery she cut off the lovely hair he liked so much. Nor was that her only physical sacrifice on the altar of love; she was nimble and could scramble up three beds placed on top of each other as quick as a squirrel to reach the window; but she was heavy and had put on weight in jail; at the warning "Ara! Ara! Bengo!" she fell like an over-ripe plum. One day she bruised her thigh and the marks would not go away, as though she had damaged a vein; another time she drove the sharp corner of one of the bedsteads into her foot; and once she damaged a kidney as she fell and passed blood in her water. And since they caught her at the window more than once, she was punished by having her parcels docked. That of course led to even more feverish correspondence. In prison you easily become obsessed by what you cannot have. When the girls got a handful of tobacco—and Pierre was generous when he had any to give—they tore newspaper into strips to roll thick cigarettes, put their feet up on the table, and smoked and smoked until they had none left. I, a nonsmoker but with fellow feeling for their passion although I could neither enjoy nor suffer for it, I offered to save some of their tobacco for them, for a rainy day. No, no, completeness lent depth to their enjoyment. Then when there was nothing left they quarreled over who had smoked the biggest share, and it even came to blows; they started sending appeals up to Pierre again. Thus was love compounded with tobacco. One day Pierre, badly off because the guard who sold him cigarettes was off duty, sent them some tobacco twist. They consigned him to bloody hell: sending them something that smelled like tobacco but wouldn't light! I in my function as technical adviser suggested chewing it, but their passion was not as overpowering as all that. So we tried to pound the twist into smokable form, but you have no idea how hard it is to pound the stuff with the iron leg of a stool, so that at least it would smolder!

3

LUCY

I can't tell you about Maddy without bringing in Lucy; as far as I could work it out, Maddy blamed Lucy for her fall from grace in prison. Before the arrival of Lucy, Maddy had been a good girl—a good girl prisoner, that is: she did not climb up to the window, she never spoke into the lavatory pipe, she never sent messages on horseback, and she never, never shouted at the women guards. For that she was popular with them, but then she disappointed them. She got from Lucy a taste for all sorts of breaches of prison discipline, until she had lost all the privileges of the good girl: the right to receive parcels and the right to spend her money on purchases from the prison shop. When I was brought into the cell it had a bad reputation for behavior, and the girls told me the prisoner who preceded me was always complaining about them until she managed to get herself moved to another cell. One of the most spiteful guards—they called her Specks because when she came silently up to the peephole, which she did more often than any of the other guards—her spectacles caught the light as she looked in. She was unkind enough to return Maddy's parcel to sender. And so Maddy found herself more and more dependent on the prison food and on her men friends, on the telephone, on the window and on smuggled messages; she was caught in a vicious circle. She let herself be corrupted quite happily, though, for to be a good prisoner only gets you deeper into prison boredom. There is nothing to do in jail all day; the books are torn and dirty, and anyway the sort of reading available aroused derision rather than interest. The only game allowed is snakes and ladders, and it takes a very low I.Q. to stick at that all day. There is nothing happening, nothing to talk about; girls like Maddy are only interrogated once, and then kept on remand until the state attorney sets out his case and they are sent for trial, which may not be for two, three, or four months. Justice is sometimes unjust, but it always takes a long time about it. Prisoners must amuse themselves as best they can. And they need contact with other human beings.

Lucy had her Tony in the same cell as Pierre, but he was more of a friend than a lover, and the erotic talk she gave him was good-natured teasing rather than provocative. He was not a young man, a thief who had frequent convictions; he may have been married, but he was certainly the father of children, because he wrote about them in his letters to her. Unlike Pierre, he was a prudent man and often tried to tone Lucy down, as though she were his younger sister. That was strange, because it was Tony, and not Pierre, who was always getting into trouble with the guards, and once he was tied down in the "bearhug" for several days. During his last term inside, he had got a fellow prisoner to tattoo a colorful Mexican eagle all across his chest; what it was meant to symbolize I couldn't find out, but I imagine it was strength, rather than freedom. He often drew pictures of it for Lucy. If he really had his chest and belly tattooed with what he drew for her, it must have been a sensuous sight. Tony and Pierre would draw and make up crossword puzzles for their girls, thus demonstrating their intelligence. But Lucy could hardly put a simple sentence together, and Maddy wrote her letters for her, so that she could copy them out in a childish hand, her tongue between her lips. Lucy preferred the toilet phone, and her voice rang out many times a day: "Tony, telephone!" Her language was inventive and she had a natural wit.

During the time I was on remand, Lucy managed to pass through the prison twice. She was not yet eighteen and should have been in a remand home for juvenile delinquents, but there is no such thing in Czechoslovakia, whether for lack of funds or lack of interest, I do not know. On remand, these youngsters—some of them just turned fifteen—share cells with old hands, experienced thieves and prostitutes, the veterans of many a prison. The offenses of the youngsters could be dealt with by a magistrate in police courts, instead of their spending three or four months in jail, waiting to be tried. It is only after conviction that they are sent to special juvenile work camps, and many of them have already done their time on remand. Lucy was perhaps predestined for prison life; her mother was serving her third or fourth long sentence, this time for a pub brawl in which she attacked a member of the secret police. Lucy admired her mother, and the only time I saw her cry was when she got a letter from her, a letter that had wandered from one prison to another before it reached her. Her mother would probably never have written, but since Lucy was still underage, her mother was called as a witness in her case, and so she got the news that her daughter was also in jail.

Lucy had been only six months old when her mother was first jailed, along with her father. Lucy's mother had started a brawl and been beaten up, and when Lucy's father found her lying injured in a ditch, he went off to avenge her. Lucy and her elder sister were placed in a children's home. The mother's prison term had ended only the previous autumn. Her mother was home from the prison camp only a few weeks before she was back in jail again. She couldn't help getting caught up in brawls, and her sentences were heavy; this time it was for eight years. Lucy's short visit with her mother was only long enough for Mother to equip Lucy with all she needed to know about how to get along in a prison camp. It was from Lucy, just turned seventeen, that I heard all about the different ways a woman can get sexual satisfaction in prison; there is no limit to the inventiveness of the human mind in restricted conditions, but I would rather have talked to Lucy about less shameless things. I do not mean that the ways and means she described were necessarily shameless; they might be, but they need not be. What was shameless was hearing it from the lips of a seventeen-year-old. Lucy was sorry she was still a minor and would have to go to a camp for juveniles; at eighteen she could have joined her mother in the work camp.

Lucy was "wrong in the head," but she had no certificate to say so, only a permanent prescription for sedatives. She would fly into uncontrollable rages, and warn Maddy, "Leave me alone, stop it. You know I'm not right in the head and if I kill you it won't be my own fault." She was angered by ridicule or mistrust and would calm down with kind words and admiration.

One day I washed her hair for her, it was all messy from telephoning down the waste pipe; I brushed it into a fringe over her forehead and lent her my spectacles to catch a glimpse of her reflection in the glass: "Look how well it suits you!" The look in her eyes was like that in our dog's eyes when his master praises him. She had a clear strong voice, pleasantly resonant, and a good ear, and when I told her that, she spent hours singing and making plans to take singing lessons and become a professional. She was a child with no one but herself to fall back on, and what child can bear that burden without coming to harm? Her physical strength was amazing; she told us how she'd stopped a runaway bull when she was helping her father on the farm where they worked. When they saw the bull running about the garden they all fled to safety, and only Lucy waited till he came near enough, took him by the horns and led him back to his chain. She was only thirteen then.

Until Lucy was about ten she and her big sister lived in the children's home; she liked it there because her sister was with her. Thanks to those years she spoke well and grammatically, with no trace of dialect; her Czech was certainly better than that spoken by most high school girls in Prague—but she had never heard of Christ. Although Maddy had been brought up in an atheist household, she was able to explain things like that to Lucy.

Lucy had not wanted to leave the home and kept going back to that moment as to a fateful change in her life. She and her sister were dressed in their best clothes, nobody told them why, and then their father came to take them home. Lucy tried to run away but finally went with him because her sister did. It was not long before her sister left home to be an apprentice, boarding in a hostel. The household was ruled by her father's second wife, and Lucy found herself looking after the younger children and putting up with her stepmother's unkindness. She became belligerent and would beat up any child in the village who laughed at her. Once she even set on her stepmother. "She ought to leave me alone," was her answer to all reproaches.

She ran away to find her grandmother in Prague and stayed

there, admiring the old lady for standing up to her father. "She boxed his ears for him once!" she told us admiringly. Granny did not laugh at her or hit her. For her low level of intelligence Lucy was sent to a school for defectives, and the second fateful turn in her life came when she was sent to work on a truck farm. Her job was looking after carnations; they were two or three apprentices to a big greenhouse. If she had been put to digging and trundling wheelbarrows of manure, she might have got used to being a gardener, but she got no fun out of nipping carnations. "Can you think what a bore it is to do nothing but nip carnations all day long? They grew along a sort of net, so they wouldn't break their stems, but I broke plenty."

Lucy ran away from the carnations with a gang of boys— herself more boy than girl. They stole a truck and had driven half round the country before they were caught. The first time, she spent about three months in Ruzyně prison before being sentenced to a reform school. When she ran away from there she found herself back in Ruzyně again, still underage, but already marked by vice. I ran into her in the doctor's waiting room when she came back that second time. I did not want to believe my eyes: it was no longer the rather silly girl with a sniff, wild but amenable to kind words. Once when I reproached her for something, she told me, "Just you wait till you come up against a real tough girl!" She did not think of herself as tough then, but when I met her at the prison doctor's it was a wolf I saw, with a coarse expression on her face and wary eyes. There was nothing of the woman about her and even less of the girl. She glared at me wildly, and then looked sheepish; she still remembered that she had once felt affection for me. Her bed was next to mine, and every morning she had an arm or a foot under my blanket, or else her head on my pillow—and then she would apologize, "You see, you remind me so much of Granny." The conflict within those abandoned children brought up in institutions is a tragic one. They long for affection but they have none to give, and how could they have? The emotional vacuum is filled only too easily by meanness and vice.

Lucy had lesbian tendencies and was more than a bit butch; she was dimly aware of this even before it came out into the open. She was proud of her tomboy ways and of her physical strength, and she never put on a skirt—she wore nothing but jeans. One day, when she was talking about learning to sing, and I said it would mean learning to dance as well, she roared with laughter at the thought of herself in a long dress, going to dancing lessons. She knew, too, that her appearance was boyish, but that was something she was sensitive about. In prison, and probably in children's homes too, girls like to be made the object of sexual advances, without necessarily being lesbians; it is the result of their surroundings and the opportunities presented. It is also partly due to fashion; homosexuality is a popular attitude among these young people. In jail of course it is the older women who go for the young girls. Lucy would have had no difficulty finding a "mother," she would not have far to look; the older woman would have nosed her out and then loved her, protected her, done her laundry for her, stolen for her. Lucy's own mother, the idol of her life, was not a lesbian, and Lucy swore loudly that she'd beat up any dike who dared to touch her once she got to the prison camp. Her lesbianism was still latent—but only waiting to burst out.

Before sending her to Ruzyně the first time the police had her examined in the VD clinic. There in the closed ward through which every girl suspected of prostitution is forced to pass, Lucy fell in love with Evie, a very beautiful Gypsy. It was a platonic enchantment, as Evie would not have permitted anything else. Nevertheless, it was a strong infatuation and probably her first, for up to then she had always been in the company of boys. Evie had arranged with her gang to bring a car one night; the closed ward is on the second floor and the windows are barred, but the girls had found an unguarded window in an unused passage. They left it ajar and used it to escape. Lucy forced them to take her along; following her adored Evie around like a little dog, she had somehow sniffed out their plans. If she hadn't joined their planned escape, who knows? she might not have landed back in jail. Evie broke her leg jumping from the window; the others dragged her into a coal shed until the hue and cry died down; then just as someone passed the shed, one of the girls sneezed. And so they were all sent to Ruzyňe, and as luck would have it, Evie was put in the cell facing ours. Every time the door opened for us to hand out mess tins or dirty washing, Lucy slipped into the corridor hoping for a glimpse of her idol. And every day she begged Maddy to call Evie "through the door" for her.

There are always a couple of guards about during the day, although the women's cells are not guarded and controlled through the peepholes at regular intervals, like the men's. Nevertheless the corridor is always under observation, and prisoners can only call "through the door" after nine in the evening, when the officers on night duty retire to the guardroom and only make their rounds once an hour. During this time every sound from the cells and the corridor is caught by microphones and transmitted to the guardroom, but no great risk is involved because by the time a guard reaches the corridor the business is over. There were a few guards who would silently unlock the gate without a key rattling, wait just inside until they heard voices, and then catch one of the girls lying on the floor, calling through the slit under the door. Only the real tough girls called "through the door," and Lucy was not yet one of them. Maddy used Lucy's need to call her idol as one of her forms of black-mail: You won't give me any? You won't do this for me? All right, then, and I won't call Evie for you. Lucy tried to talk to Evie on the toilet phone, because our two cells shared the same waste pipe, but they were too far apart, she couldn't hear Evie answering; maybe the others refused to call her. If there was one thing Evie did not want, it was bothering with that crazy Lucy. Leave Evie alone, everybody told her the same thing, but Evie had become the dream of Lucy's life, an obsession. "Did you see her?" she asked me, all lit up, when I got back from the doctor's. "She's a beauty, isn't she?"—hanging on my answer. In some way Evie reminded Lucy of her older sister, the center of her feelings as a child; at the same time Evie was her sexual idol, her first sexual infatuation. Lucy behaved like a lovesick schoolboy. Evie really was lovely to look at, but she was inaccessible, and not only to Lucy's attentions. She was a proud girl and resented Lucy's adoration which she thought made her look ridiculous. Lucy was incapable of realizing how ridiculous *she* looked. "You do love me, don't you, Evie, darling?" she shouted joyfully into the waste pipe, her mind forever arrested at the level of a small child's. "Evie! Answer me! I can't hear you! What did you say? Do you love me?"

It was Maddy, the jealous and treacherous Maddy, who brought the romance to an abrupt end. Moved primarily by jealousy but perhaps also out of some deep-seated need to do mischief and create wild scenes, Maddy began provoking Lucy, who was soon beside herself with rage. "I'll laugh at you as much as I like. I'll laugh and laugh and laugh . . ." That was all Lucy needed to set her off. There were times when I felt Maddy really needed physical pain, and their fights gave her the bruises she asked for.

"Just you leave me alone," Lucy would crow as Maddy felt

her injuries tenderly. "You know I'm not right in the head." This time the sly digs, the insults flying back and forth, the ridicule followed by curses ended in such a murderous onslaught as I had never even imagined. Lucy, her physical advantage growing as she got madder and madder, was taking her revenge on Maddy's body; the victim screamed, yet at the same time masochistically continued to incense her assailant. Maddy took heavy punishment; Lucy's fists pounded her at will as she leaned against the door, banging with all her might and shouting for a guard while still goading Lucy with screams of laughter and "Clot, moron, weirdie!" They tore at each other, gasping for breath, Maddy used her nails on Lucy and blood mingled with their tears, chunks of plaster came off the walls, the table and stools were overturned and I shrank into the space under the window, partly shielded by beds. Then Lucy picked up one of the iron stools and hurled it at Maddy, missed, and almost hit me. Then she went for the heavy table.

At first the woman on duty just peeped through the spy hole enjoying the scene. There were several guards in the corridor— it was the time when women were being taken to the doctor— but they did not open the door until Maddy began screaming she was being murdered. Lucy was using both hands and feet, scarlet and sweating with the effort. The door promptly shut again as Lucy hurled another stool at the guard, who sent for one of the male guards. He was a long time coming, and by this time Lucy had Maddy on the floor, banging her head on the stone. And that was the fateful moment: the male guard opened the door and yelled, "What's going on here?"

Maddy slipped out under his arm, Lucy threw the last stool at him—and there in the corridor was her adored Evie, watching scornfully as Lucy raged. The inmates of her cell were being lined up to be taken to the doctor, at last Lucy could see her beautiful haughty idol close up, but only to hear the contempt in her voice: "What a sight! I wouldn't have thought it of you, Lucy!" as she turned away.

In that split second before the guard, fearing another attack, slammed the door shut, Lucy realized two things: that Evie had seen her brawling, and that Maddy was laughing at her from the door of Evie's cell. The door clanged shut, and I was left alone with a girl almost out of her wits and now despairing into the bargain. She was so dazed by the shock that she obeyed me at once when I thrust a rag into her hands and told her to start clearing up the mess before they came to investigate. Her tears flowed as she swept up the scraps of plaster from the floor.

"Evie will never forgive me. Evie can't bear girls scrapping." She told me about a fight she'd got into in the VD ward (Why? Because of Evie, of course!) and how Evie wouldn't speak to her afterward. When Maddy, the hussy, came back to our cell, which had been tidied up, she was full of news about Evie: she'd plenty of cigarettes at the moment, and her broken leg was healing fine. Maddy was sly enough not to say Evie was disgusted by Lucy's behavior but told how horrified she was at the sight of Maddy's injuries.

Lucy was overcome with grief. Maddy had seen Evie; Maddy had been talking to Evie; Maddy had spent over two hours in Evie's cell—and all at the time Evie was so angry with her, Lucy! The poor girl went down on hands and knees over the toilet and penitently told Tony all about it. "She won't ever want to see me again, Tony, what am I to do?" Tony's advice was no good to her. How could she just put Evie out of her mind? And then that hussy, Maddy, her ear pressed to the door that evening, described what she could hear going on in the corridor. Lucy couldn't hear a thing, because though she had a good ear for music, she was always half deaf from a cold in the head.

"Shhh! Stop rustling things. They've caught someone with a horse."

"In Evie's cell?" Lucy was horrified.

"They're taking her away." Maddy went on with her commentary.

Dazed by her unattainable dream, Lucy would believe anything if Evie's name were brought into it. Maddy said she thought from the voice that it was Evie they'd caught, and Lucy did not need more convincing. Evie was being taken to the punishment cells! She was down on her knees over the toilet again, asking Tony's advice. She wailed, "What am I to do, Tony? Evie's been taken down to the hole!"

It was an unwritten law that if you were taken to the punishment cells, you were never sent back to your previous cell, and so it was likely that Evie would be put in a cell somewhere else. She might never see her Evie again! Evie would be lost, far away! Lucy's sense of guilt and her longing were so entangled ("I've got to tell her what really happened, why I was fighting," she told Tony.) that she deliberately provoked a row with the guard and earned a term of solitary confinement. Maddy looked on with the ingratiating smile of a child anxious to please. "Pack up your things," said the officer, and Lucy glowed with the hope that her cell would be near Evie's in the basement. Then they could talk! And she'd scrounge cigarettes for her Evie. You have certainly guessed, rightly, that nobody had sent Evie into solitary.

It was Nan who told me the last of Lucy. Nan, the most womanly of women, as I shall tell you when her turn comes. She met up with Lucy in the transfer cell, in one of the filthiest parts of the prison. Nan had just been arrested, and so had Lucy, but for the second time. There were three of them in a cell meant for two, Lucy sharing a bunk with another girl, while Nan lay with the blanket pulled up over her head to shut out the horror. Lucy was trying in very inexpert fashion to practice her lesbian desires—no longer latent—on the other girl, who tried to put her right: "Ouch! you're pushing on my pisser." Those words summed up the nightmare of jail for Nan; if she had met Lucy on the street afterward she'd have started to scream. It only took half a year for this young girl, still a minor, to become a menace feared throughout the prison; she was no longer a lost ugly duckling but a big bully who would hit out without warning and be proud of it. Lucy was at last a real tough, ready for what life had to offer her.

4

THE FAIR
HELEN

They took Maddy off and brought in the fair Helen, a woman
of carefully guarded secrets. She was fifty-eight and looked
forty-five, proof that mental activity ages you faster. At that age,
she was still beautiful, with regular features, wavy chestnut hair
that needed no color rinse, long slender legs, a good figure with
only the suspicion of a rounding belly, and lovely breasts. She
was what you call a well-preserved woman and I did not dare to
ask her how she had kept her beauty, whether it might be the
result of sexual restraint. She looked ridiculous, a poor thing, in
her prison track suit; and since it was cold in the cell she
wrapped a blanket round her like a burnous, with one corner
trailing along the floor. In better times and well dressed, I could
easily imagine her sitting in one of the fashionable cafés, ele-

gantly sipping her coffee. After she came in, her case trickled out drop by drop, with a sincerity that made it sound completely convincing. She had come to Prague from Terezín, where she had been staying for a while in a home for the elderly, a sort of better-class pension. She was going to visit her son, a waiter in a big cafeteria, and at the station she got into a tram, where she picked up a purse that somebody had probably *dropped on the floor*. This honorably acquired purse contained about two hundred crowns and a hundred hard-currency coupons, or else it was only fifty coupons and three hundred crowns, I've forgotten which; but in any case, at the official exchange rate it didn't come to more than five hundred crowns. For thefts of less than five hundred crowns you don't get sent to jail, but she had a plausible explanation: she had no identity papers on her, she "just took it into my head to drop in" on her son. And afraid the police would ring up Terezín and they'd know in the pension that she had been taken to a police station, she had promptly torn up the doctor's certificate allowing her to be out. This of course made things much more difficult, because it made the police suspicious of her unproved identity. She couldn't have known that the purse lying on the floor of the tram belonged to a woman passenger, who dragged her out of the tram and took along a witness against her, but the police did not believe her innocence.

The woman and her witness hustled the fair Helen to the police station, where they accused her of stealing the purse. I wasn't clear who had hold of the purse while all this was going on, but the two of them had a firm hold on Helen, one on each side and both hurling insults at her. It never occurred to her to try to get away, as they dragged her down the crowded main street; she was just dazed. And she really looked dazed as she told us the story, dazed and defenseless. Her eyes wide and staring, so upset that she was trembling, dribbling, twitching her lips and sticking the tip of her tongue in and out; she couldn't sit quietly and moved about the cell like a trapped animal. Luckily I had some cigarettes, and with long hungry draws, sending narrow spirals of smoke from her nostrils, she became calmer. That first night I was alone with her in the cell, and I was afraid to fall asleep. What would so disturbed a psychopathic woman not be capable of? Later, when Helen read the diagnosis "psychopath" delivered by the forensic psychiatrist, she asked me what it meant. Not wanting to hurt her feelings, I said it meant her habit of moving her tongue and lips as she did when upset. Gradually I pieced together the story of the purse found on the tram floor, and after separating the probable truth from what she had invented, that is to say, from what she adopted to shield herself, I realized that I need have felt no fear. It was she who was afraid, in a panic of annihilating fear. Prison crushed her like a rock. Time also proved that she was not at all aggressive and was incapable of more than a tearful protest. She was taken to see the psychiatrist the second day, and from then on she took psychopharmaceutical drugs every day. And being an experienced patient, before going for interrogation, she dropped her daily dose down the drain. Even if she hadn't, her terror would have unhinged her.

The fair Helen belonged to a well-known family of traveling amusement-park people; once when I came on a newspaper article about western Bohemia, where the village fair was described in idyllic terms, her name was there. "Yes," she said, "that's our family, but they're talking about Uncle. We worked a different route." Uncle traveled from fair to fair, from one patron saint's day to another, from Easter to Martinmas. He worked the southwest corner of Bohemia, while Helen and her mother were farther eastward. Uncle owned a bump-a-drome, grandfather worked a puppet show, mother had a flying chair round-about, a switchback railway, and a shooting booth. They brought fun to the villages; mother took the money and the fair Helen handed out the air guns, five shots for a crown. Mother must have been doing well: when even fairground business was nationalized, she handed over to the state two tractors, three vans, and all the fairground equipment; and she lived many years with Helen and her sister on the compensation paid for it all. That's the truth, just as everything else Helen told us was the truth, so long as she didn't happen to be lying.

As the days passed, Helen's lies were elevated to the status of an imaginary painting peeled off, the gilt of the fairground flaked away, leaving the rough truth of reality, with an inexorable dynamism that even I, who worshipped truth, would not have wanted. The fair Helen was utterly dependent on her surroundings for everything; all she was capable of, herself, was enjoyment, a pleasant life (and handing out air guns). She repaid us for her dependence with scattered mites of information we did not ask for but could not help noting.

Although she was a dependent person, she was not without will; the fight she put up in her own defense was a stiff one. She carried on a vast correspondence with the authorities, much bigger than my own (and they were always sending me notice of this and that). It looked as though letter-writing was not only a way of defending herself, as though that might not even be the main purpose she was pursuing; letter-writing lifted her out of the miserable conditions in which she found herself. Indeed, letter-writing seemed to be a hobby of hers. Such a passionate hobby that in the pension in Terezín they had issued a regulation especially on her account, forbidding her to keep writing complaints to their governing body and bringing controllers down on their heads. In prison her efforts were not restricted in any way; although private letters are only allowed once a fortnight, official letters may be written as needed, and for those prisoners without the means to buy them for themselves, the prison authorities are required to provide paper, envelopes, and even postage stamps. Nor do these letters pass through the censorship. At least twice a week Helen would ask for paper and envelopes at roll call. However it was, defense or hobby, she could not write her letters without help, and since she needed a scribe, and the scribe had to ask for details in order to make her arguments convincing, thus she was forced to let fall bits and pieces that filled in a mosaic she did not want revealed. At first I wrote her letters for her, and later it was Helga. We wrote to the state prosecutor, to her defense lawyer, to the judge, to the doctor in charge of the Terezín home, to the psychologist at the home, the forensic psychiatrist, to all of them over and over again. Then we helped her to think of other people to write to, and all the time we tried to prove one and the same thing: that she was innocent, and that she could not be brought to trial because she could not act *sui juris*, that is, on her own behalf, that she was not competent to handle her own affairs.

That was the truth of it; the fair Helen was certified "not right in the head," and *non sui juris* adorned all the letters written in her defense. Alas, she had been certified incapable of managing her own property apparently at the request of her family, but she was responsible for her conduct. The prosecution had no difficulty in proving her responsibility in criminal matters. When he asked her if it was right to steal, like a lady of good breeding she answered that it was wrong. He took that as proving that she was aware that what she did was wrong and that she should be sentenced accordingly. The fair Helen could not grasp this legalistic distinction, could not see why she was responsible for some things and not for others. She simply did not accept it, and after she was sentenced she wrote her last letter, this time directly to the President of the Republic. Somebody had advised her to write to him, and to ask for pardon; but as she wrote the letter she decided to make it a complaint. This was the only letter she wrote by herself; I did not want to compound my "crimes" with that of encouraging a person not responsible for her actions to ridicule the head of state. Helga refused for a different reason. I did not even read the letter, but Helga said I had missed a good laugh. I did see the envelope, though, addressed to "Myster Presydent Husak the Rypublyc the Casyl." The fair Helen seemed to find "y" a more elegant letter than "i" or "e." (The prison officer never sent the letter, anyway.)

Besides being passionately fond of writing letters, Helen had to keep talking. She did not confess her misdeeds; she only told me the story of finding that purse because she was suffering from the initial shock of imprisonment and never referred to it again of her own accord. Indeed she said little about herself, and then only when we asked her directly. She spent hours walking up and down the cell in a brown study or lay on her bed pretending to sleep. But when she was in a good mood she demanded polite conversation—and there are so many suitable subjects! Her favorite was food. She liked indulging herself, and food was the center of her world. And the way she savored her cigarettes—I could well imagine her sitting on the steps of her van, her long hair carefully brushed with a part down the middle (every morning she asked if her part was straight), her hands well cared for, lacquered nails, eyebrows carefully darkened and eyes half-closed with pleasure, nostrils flaring as she drew on her cigarette, a long deep draw. She always drew twice, first a short sharp one, enjoying the smoke as she breathed it out through her nose, and then a long one to fill her lungs. Her cigarette was gone in a moment; it took Helga twice as long. And how she loved her cup of coffee, something unattainable in jail. Dreamily she told us how they would sit on the veranda of the pension after dinner, sipping their coffee. The other old ladies had plenty of money, she said, and would send her out to buy cakes; but she didn't eat cakes, coffee and cigarettes was what she'd sell her soul for. On the days when she had nothing to smoke you could see her physically suffering; her face grew slack, her body trembled, and those horrid lip movements came back.

She was greedy, too, and would eat everything there was, even our leftovers, but in her anxiety to get the best she could, she was not very clever. For instance, she asked to be put on a diet. There were two, one without salt, which meant the same food as the others, only unsalted, which made it absolutely uneatable. The other was a light diet, which meant fairly decent food with plenty (by prison standards) of milk, meat, cheese, and eggs. To stop her bothering them, they allowed her the unsalted diet; you are not allowed to have salt in the cell, and so we threw her meals down the toilet and asked for a second helping ourselves, so that she had at least that to eat. As she ate the unappetizing food, she would lovingly recall the good things she had eaten, and where; but the places she had spent her life in were so few that before long we had a complete survey of the different camps and prisons she had passed through. This lady of good family involuntarily talked about prison camps as though she was at home there. She didn't enjoy her food in Pardubice at all, and the queues were so long that by the time you got your mess tin full the best bits had been taken and the stuff was cold. In Opava, now, they'd once had roast chicken! She confessed that her favorite dish was a fowl boiled in its soup—and again I saw her on the steps of the van, with a fowl cooking in an iron pot hung over an open fire. She would beg me, "Please, dear, tell us about your social life," and being quite without interest or ambition in "social life," and realizing that what she really meant was "Tell me the good things you've eaten," I invented when my memory gave out. The poor creature wanted colorful descriptions, full of luscious detail, and so I went into long evocations of a thoroughness worthy of Balzac. When a well-known name came up in connection with dishes that she knew of, she would smile dreamily as she saw herself at some famous table. She did envy me once, though; that was when I said I'd eaten prawns in Alexandria, and she had never even heard the word. Since her dreamy mind registered the world mainly through words, and not from direct experience, she added the new word to her vocabulary. Later on she "remembered" that she had eaten prawns, too.

And so she went on betraying her own secrets. One day, in her sweet way that both moved and disarmed one, she greeted one of the guards who occasionally took Saturday and Sunday duty; he handed our mess tins in through the door, and Helen said happily: "So you're working here now?"

"That's Tony," she confided, delighted to have gone up in the world so far that she now had friends in the Ruzyně remand prison. Before that, her Tony worked in the closed ward of the Bohnice psychiatric hospital and left because he thought guarding normal convicts would be more bearable.

"Always wallowing in their shit." Helen told us how kind he'd been to them in hospital. In Opava, too, she'd been in a prison psychiatric ward, and from there she'd been sent to Terezín, not to a comfortable home for distressed gentlewomen, but to enforced confinement as a psychiatric case. It was not prison, but neither was it possible to leave when she felt like it. That was why she said she'd destroyed the doctor's certificate allowing her to leave (but she'd had no such thing). In fact, when she was released from Opava the authorities had been kind to her, allowing her the minimum pension to cover her expenses in Terezín, although she had never been employed; she had worked in prison, of course, but you never earn a decent wage there. She destroyed every official communication that arrived for her, because each revealed another miserable crumb of fact, and her imaginary life story was firmly fixed in her mind to shield her from admitting the grim reality. Although she did her best never to give herself away, the spray of truth sometimes splashed the pretty picture she tried to present. And most merciless of all was the affair of the purse on the floor of the tram, as bit by bit the veil was lifted.

The fair Helen presented me with a complex sociological and philosophical question: Does a person partly become what he or she pretends to be? A fairground beauty, I thought, and where will you find a good old-fashioned fair nowadays?

I spent four long months shut up with her in a very small space, breathing each other's breath—and in spite of all the doubts her words sometimes aroused in me, there was one possibility that never entered my mind: that she was a notorious pickpocket. We thought she'd simply been unlucky in the tram that day, picking up the purse when the owner was close at hand. That was what we thought, because Helen made such a defenseless, helpless impression. She could never have consciously stolen anything. She was just as awkward in the tram as she'd been about getting put on a diet—ineffectual, that's what she was. She had a gentle voice, and though she'd grown up among rough people she was never coarse in her behavior. Once when we'd refused to use the toilet to talk to the men in the cell above ours, and they retaliated by throwing buckets of filth against our window, spattering some on her, she cried angrily: "Elephants!" It was the worst word she could think of, although the whole atmosphere was thick with low vulgarity. I can still hear her voice squeaking with indignation: "Elephants!" That was the only time I heard her try to swear at anyone. She made such an innocent, fragile impression. And yet she lied as often as she opened her mouth, lied as naturally as she breathed.

I have no way of telling how far she adapted her ways to fit in with Helga and me, but that is not important. The fundamental element in her was the gulf between reality and her dream. Lies were the only defense she had against her helpless subservience to her dream. How she longed to be a fairground beauty! And she made us behave as though her imaginary self was her real self. In my heart of hearts, I wonder whether we would have found it any easier to live with her if we had known the truth from the start. How could she live in accordance with her dream, when the only ways she knew of and was capable of using to get the means to that end were dishonest ones? If only she'd had a shooting booth! If only she'd had a van and a tractor to pull it! If only she had youth as well as beauty, and a watchful mother in the background! Driven into a corner by grim reality, she pretended that what she longed for was real. The full grimness of her reality did not burst upon us until she was convicted.

The prison officer entrusted me with the job of helping Helen fill out the questionnaire you are given before the "execution of your sentence"—a charming term—begins. There it lay on the table, four pages of it with printed questions. Poor thing, it was so obvious that she wanted to fill it in herself and looked cross with me for having been told to help her. Not that I pushed myself forward, but she simply could not cope with it. If only she had been less beautiful and less stupid! She took the papers over to her bunk and turned her back on me and Helga, muttering the words to herself. She did not know what the individual questions meant, but she knew from experience what the questionnaire itself meant. We had no idea what was required, or what drama was going on in her soul. Then she gave in. I was surprised at the fascination the paper held for her; but she must have known that it did not pay to lie when filling it in, and she dared not refuse to answer the questions. And so she was forced to tell me what to say, and I had to write it all down: that she had never been married (despite her descriptions of her husband to us in great detail); and that she was not a widow, as she virtuously pretended (Why is the idea of widowhood so interwoven with that of virtue? Are widows more faithful?); and that her dear little boy was illegitimate. Her sister was her legal guardian but did not want Helen in her house. And her mother was not much to go by, both *her* children had been illegitimate too. In her old age her sister was making a living as a charwoman in some government offices ("My sister works at the Ministry" was a favorite aside in our polite conversations). The sister had looked after Helen's boy ever since he was a baby. In that family, the fair Helen had been the one who was above work. The chinchilla that had kept her warm during the war, the Dior scent she was used to—none of that had existed, though I must admit that she knew the proper names for them. And when we reached the questions: "How many previous convictions?" and "Where did you serve previous sentences?" it hurt to hear her voice grow smaller and smaller. The case of the purse "picked up" in the tram was the eighteenth, that is to say the eighteenth proved case, the eighteenth conviction. When Helga and I came to work it out, we found that since coming of age the fair Helen must have been convicted every second year.

Although she was going on for sixty, was not *sui juris*, and could not get through the day without tranquilizers, she was sentenced unconditionally to a year's imprisonment for attempting to steal a purse containing less than five hundred crowns, which the owner had succeeded in guarding. She certainly worked harder in her own defense, with all her letters to the doctors and the prosecutor, than her court-appointed defense lawyer who did not even turn up at her trial. It was a very thorough trial, with a forensic psychiatrist present, as well as several witnesses; besides those concerned with the purse, the psychologist from the Terezín home came to give evidence against her—that pension that served coffee on the veranda after dinner and such good food as chicken soup! The psychologist said that Helen had sold bed linen from the home to people in the town; she sold sheets to have money for cigarettes. I soon realized that Helen was not defending herself against the accusations nor against her sentence. Crime and punishment were immaterial to her, because accusations can always be denied, and at the worst you can resign yourself to punishment. Her conscience did not trouble her: the simple truth was that she was fighting for a decent roof over her head in the years to come.

Her family, that is to say her sister and her son, had had enough of her. After she finished her last sentence, it was they who had had her put away in Terezín, refusing any responsibility for her actions. Now she was not wanted back there, either; although the psychiatrist tried to get the doctor in charge to change his mind, he had failed. So long as the old doctor was there, the one Helen remembered with such affection because he was understanding about her need for occasional trips "to see her son," things were better. He had died of an infarction the year before, and the younger man who took his place was a stickler for regulations and had taken the first opportunity offered to get rid of an awkward patient. The psychiatrist then tried to place Helen in a psychiatric hospital but could find no bed for her. It was left to the prison authorities to send her somewhere; and so she got a year "unconditional," after which she would be somebody else's problem. Once she got over her fright at the sentence (up to the last minute she had hoped to be sent back to Terezín), Helen began to spin new hopes. She was old and sick and so they wouldn't send her to a work camp with the young girl convicts she was so terrified of, but instead to a prison ward. The last time she was sentenced she had been certified sick and did not have to work to the normal scale (the job was threading beads for costume jewelry) and so this time maybe they wouldn't make her work at all. And so she began to dream again: once in the Opava psychiatric prison they'd even had roast chicken for Sunday dinner! And Opava was where women with long sentences went, the prison aristocracy with plenty of money from all sorts of rackets. They always had plenty of cigarettes and they weren't mean. Life is never as grim as it seems.

All that she had was prison for a home, an unsatisfiable longing for pleasure, and her dreams. Dreams! Pretenses become real values if you can persuade those around you to believe in them. She was penniless but never without cigarettes. At first I bought them for her, although I don't smoke myself. Don't think I was doing my good turn for the day: I just did not want to be bothered by her, and unless she had something to smoke she got into such a state, trembling and mouthing, that I felt afraid rather than sorry for her. She was so contented when she could sit on her stool, one leg elegantly crossed over the other, and puff greedily at a cigarette.

Then domineering Helga arrived in our cell, and took it upon herself to supply Helen's drug. With a magnificent gesture she even repaid me (in chocolate and biscuits) for what

Helen's cigarettes had cost me, although I had not asked for recompense; she paid Helen's "debt" to me in order to have her all to herself. Nor was she a disinterested benefactor; she fell for Helen's tales—especially the one about all the things hidden in her Prague flat, where her son was living. (In reality, of course, he lived with his aunt.) Helga fell for the piles of good quality things Helen's husband had left her. This nonexistent husband was said to have been a traveling salesman who went from village to village selling cloth, underwear, and knitted goods. He had died of a heart attack when Helen was forty, that meant eighteen years ago. His inventory must have been enormous, if Helen could still find sweaters and brassieres to sell today; her last customers had been the nurses and wealthier inmates at Terezín, and her first conflict with the authorities had been over sweaters. When her husband died she tried to make a living by selling from door to door in a Prague suburb, but somebody gave her away and she was accused of robbing the state by concealing goods that should have been handed over. With an experienced eye she assessed Helga's bosom, saying with an air of unshakable credibility, "You take an eight, or perhaps a nine. I've got a few tens left, as well, made of good strong lace; and the sweaters are all pure wool, not the artificial stuff you get these days."

I was thinking back to the bras we wore eighteen years ago, especially those you could see at village fairs, but I said nothing. I was fascinated by the magnetic fascination this dream of prosperity had for Helga. She did not see Helen as a penniless creature who could not afford a cigarette, but as a wealthy woman whose stocks she would one day take over, just as she now took over responsibility for supplying Helen with her nicotine. Thus the dreamed-up husband and respectable widowhood were transformed into greedy puffs of cigarette smoke. They smoked like sisters, taking turns on the same cigarette; but early in the morning, before Helga woke up, Helen would steal a secret smoke. Helga shared all she had with her. Helen had arrived with only a remnant of face cream in her tube, but she kept that for a rainy day and used Helga's, plastering her hands with it although it was an expensive cream, genuine Dior.

Helga's fury when she discovered that this wealthy past was a fiction of Helen's imagination! There were no brassieres, no eights or nines, no bales of silk and pure wool cloth, nothing but a family that does not want to have anything to do with her, nothing but legal incapacity that could not touch those sweaters even if they existed. Helen's family showed very pointedly their anger at yet another police court case. Her sister had the conscience to send Helen a parcel, but she did not write. But Helen's son gave no sign of concern at all. Helen wrote and asked them to send more parcels, but nothing arrived.

"They've dropped you for good," the disillusioned wealthy prisoner stormed at the poor but sly one, "it's no use denying it, your son couldn't care less. Your sister doesn't care either, the two of them had you put away and now there's nobody left to take care of you. Don't you go imagining things. Nobody's going to give you a penny, and I'd like to know who's going to repay me all the money I've invested in you."

The kindness she had been tricked into showing Helen had miscarried, and Helga put all the malice she could muster into convincing the poor deluded creature that she was indeed all alone in the world. In her perverse desire for vengeance Helga, too, cast her off, refusing to share anything and even throwing her fag ends into the toilet so that the poor woman could not roll them in a scrap of newspaper to smoke.

"I'm not going to keep you in cigarettes. Who's going to pay me back, I'd like to know?" Her indignation was understandable, but she need not have been so cruel. Helen was made of more generous stuff. When that first famous parcel from her sister arrived, she took the sweets out in handfuls, happy to have something to offer us for a change.

"Take more, go on, do take them. You wouldn't want to hurt my feelings, would you?"

At this time Helga had only just arrived in prison. She had nothing of her own, smoked my cigarettes, and was anxiously waiting for her own first parcel. Assured of her own wealth, when Helen's bounty arrived she took a good half share of the smoked meat, the salami, sweets, and smokes. Together they downed a kilo of smoked meat at a sitting, eating it alone without bread. They cut chunks of salami off at a time.

Later, when Helga had turned against her, Helen regretted the ham and salami that had been guzzled away and turned vindictive. It really looked as though her family had consigned her to oblivion: there were no letters, no parcels of goodies. During that last month Helen, broken, did not even exercise her right to write home; she was visibly shrinking and her trembling and mouthings were back again. By that time it was Andy who shared the cell with us; at first Helen let herself be persuaded to sing in her high childish voice. She knew all the popular songs of prewar years. One day Andy said passionately, "You're not to sing that one about the little dark-haired boy!"

"Why ever not?"

"It'd make me cry."

The song is about a dark-haired boy complaining to his mother that the other children won't play with him. They wouldn't play with him because he had no father. He was a bastard child.

Sometimes, though, the world looks up from the ruins of justice and remembers the lost. In the end our fair Helen rejoiced in the triumph of home and family. It was her last day in the cell, and she knew she would be taken that afternoon to the transfer cell, and thence, who knew. We could only hope that it would be to join those wealthy women convicts in Opava. She looked dreadful, having had nothing to smoke for a week; she could only sniff the provocative smoke of Helga's cigarettes, puffed out deliberately to torture her. It was a terrible week; I was helpless because my lawyer who might have helped had not been to see me, and the prison shop would not be open for another ten days. We had no relations with men prisoners and couldn't beg cigarettes off them. It was past dinnertime, and all hope seemed lost. I had already given Helen my chocolate and my soap, so that she had at least something to take with her, and then half an hour before she was due to leave, the officer brought her a parcel. Salami, smoked meat, cigarettes, and sweets fell out of the box on to her bed. She didn't say, "I told you so!" She said nothing, just threw herself on the cigarettes and started chain-smoking. And to make her triumph complete, the astonished officer brought her yet another parcel. The family had suddenly received two parcel permits at once and had responded by sending two parcels. I had to give her a plastic bag so she could take her riches with her. If only she hadn't stopped writing to her sister, she could have hoped for more. But with two, three, four parcels in view, no longer abandoned but overwhelmed and beaming joyfully, she not only refrained from paying her debt to Helga, but gave her a bad name in the transfer cell: "Don't trust that woman with the big breasts, she's stingy. She's got plenty to smoke but she never shares."

That finished Helga. She calculated that Helen's imaginary wealth had cost her at least four hundred crowns. And from that time on, everyone Helga met in jail had to pay for her misjudgment of Helen; she became an incorrigible miser. "Nothing for anybody" was her motto, and she castigated me for irresponsible behavior when I handed round good things I got from home.

Being a creature of dreams, existing in a world far removed from the dirty everyday world, Helen felt close to the supernatural. One morning she sat up in bed and announced, "I dreamed of salami hanging on hooks; that means good news." That same afternoon her first parcel arrived, bringing her cigarettes, smoked meat, and salami. After that joyous coincidence of dream and reality we began to tell her our dreams.

Fresh water, that means happiness; befouled water means trouble; floods are a warning; white foam on water means sorrow, and so do white dresses and especially a wedding dress.

"To dream of turds brings wealth." That was Helga's dream; I was always drowning in floodwaters. Fire is not necessarily a danger sign in dreams; but it is good to see the dead, because it means they have come to relieve you of your troubles.

The fair Helen did not really take to me, and I sank very low in her eyes when I failed to make our Gypsy Andy the cell servant when I had the chance. I was much too much of a democrat to qualify for her idea of a gentlewoman. Helen had not been in the cell more than a day or two when she slipped and fell on the toilet sink, breaking her arm. That prolonged her time with us, because they waited for the bone to set before she was brought to trial. It was her left arm, so that she was able to smoke and eat, but could not make her bed or take her turn to tidy the cell; we helped her to dress and supported her down to the exercise yard and back. I cut her nails and washed her hair for her. And when they took the plaster off her arm, in my democratic way I handed her the floorcloth—not respecting the lady in her—and told her to do her bit.

She complained to Helga: "In Opava the others took my turn at cleaning the room, and they called me Milady. They did my washing for me too, even my panties." I objected that I took my turn at cleaning the toilet, and anyway, she needed to train her arm by doing light jobs, and wringing a floorcloth out is a light job. After that she took her turn, saying coyly, "It's Wednesday today, my room day," but she did not forgive me for making her do it.

She was so greedy that she had to get everything we did, and when we were given a laxative she had to ask the doctor for the same tablets as we'd been given. She was taken short in the exercise yard, and we all suffered, because there was no escape from the stink. They refused to give her a change of underwear, and so she had to wash her things in cold water, with only one hand, in the cell. We washed her ass for her. Besides pills and cigarettes she had another drug: snakes and ladders. Helga played with her, but I refused absolutely to take part; there are limits to what one should undertake, even as a good deed, in jail. It is a game for imbeciles, and to play it is to make yourself at home in prison—there are even tournaments, in the hope that stupefaction will dull the sensibilities. I cut up chocolate boxes to make cards, and played rummy with Helga. We invited Helen to make a third, but even a childish card game was beyond her. She cheated slyly at snakes and ladders, getting a six whenever she wanted one, and moving extra squares if the number she threw was too low for her taste. An insatiable and passionate player so long as she was winning, she got bored and gave up once Helga started checking on her moves. She did not forgive me for giving Helga the chance to play cards, for Helga then had less time for her. Helga was a real gambler; we manufactured a board and cardboard money, lots of it, and on a Sunday morning when the guards were lax, we turned my bed into a gambling den. Helga held the bank while Helen and I placed our bets, I won and she lost four thousand cardboard crowns. She never forgave me.

For me she was a character in a story with an open end, and as Helga and I put together the jigsaw puzzle of what her life may really have been like, and laughed at ourselves for being had, she went on the next stage of her pilgrimage, half-doped, with bags of salami (that means good news!), to try her luck once again in the shelter of her dreams.

5

ANDY RUM CANDY

For about a week the three of us, Helen, Andy, and I, were a sight to behold, such a miserable looking trio that we gave our jailers plenty of cause for malicious laughter. As we came in from the yard, the one we called Scooter jeered down at us from her vantage point on the landing, "A fine bunch you are!" The sarcasm was meant for me, but instead of feeling insulted (for who was responsible for my state?), I had to laugh at the picture we presented.

It was a critical time for me; after hours of interrogation I returned daily to the stresses of the cell; after my first collapse the doctor prescribed some pills that the guard crushed and sprinkled into my palm every morning. Nobody told me what I was supposed to be taking, and until I knew for sure, I was not going to risk being made sluggish and pliant for my interrogators. I had to put the stuff in my mouth before she went away, and then I spat it into the toilet. I felt it was safer to be without treatment; but that meant that I dragged myself about on the verge of fainting, while Helen staggered along at my side dopey with tranquilizers and nursing her broken arm in its plaster. She found it difficult to manage the various parts of her body, especially her feet. She barely stumbled along, and behind us came Andy.

Andy! The door of our cell opened and there stood a young Gypsy with an enormous bruise across her right cheek and one eye filled with clotted blood. A terrifying sight. She looked so villainous. You don't get a bruise like that through no fault of your own, and my first thought was: Heavens! what have we been blessed with this time! But Andy was smiling diffidently with the rest of her face, as she put her prison outfit down on the unoccupied bed—a dirty blanket, two sheets and a pillowcase and two blue towels—and waited shyly for us to tell her which stool she could sit down on. That first bad impression faded away when the guard who brought her in said grimly, "Mind your heads," which meant, "Beware of lice." Andy did not take this as an insult, did not start calling the woman names as soon as the door shut on her, but simply put her head down on the table for us to examine it. *She* was the one who was afraid she might have caught lice in her beautiful hair, in the filth of the cell where she'd spent her last night.

Not many guards make it easy for new prisoners; mine was not disagreeable, it was a woman officer who let me take a long shower, but the man who received Andy did not even let her go to the bathroom. It is the done thing, in prison, to make the newcomer welcome. Nothing can make you feel so lost as when your new companions turn their backs on you with indifference. Prison is a hail of horrifying impressions. You fall into a dark pit full of unknown snares; keys rattle; iron gates clang shut; the corridors are gloomy; and the rows of locked doors with their peepholes are grim indeed. The prisoners in the cell you are taken into are the first human beings you meet, and so the rule is: Welcome, newcomer! Time will show what sort of a person you are. I was no longer a greenhorn ignorant of my rights, and since the guard was so careful about lice I asked her for warm water for Andy to wash her curly hair. Then with hands modestly over her private parts, she stood on the flat sink of the toilet while I poured water over her, a make-do shower.

She remained pleasantly diffident, quiet, and retiring; I would have called her well-bred, if it were not for the shocking state of her face. She was neither brash nor saucy, speaking only when we spoke to her, or rather when I did. The fair Helen was aghast; she'd had bad experiences with Gypsy girls and was scared of them on sight. At the same time she looked down on them. She watched jealously as I offered Andy a cigarette. Andy accepted it as a gesture of welcome but said she had some of her own (she had about five of the cheapest). She offered them round; Andy accepted kindness graciously, as if to give you pleasure. And when she found that her ears had not been deceiving her, and I really was addressing her with the polite "you" and not the patronizing "thou," overcome by this display of equality she instituted herself my protector.

And so as the three of us were being taken back to our cell from the exercise yard where I had almost fainted, Andy who came no higher than to my shoulder half carried me, my arm over her shoulder. Her cheek was still bruised and swollen, with one eye hidden behind clotted blood, while I was as white as chalk, and behind us stumbled the doped Helen like a guard of honor. We looked so ridiculous that even the most stupid of our guards, the one we called Potato Face, managed a witticism at our expense: "Look like they've lost a battle, don't they?" Who is to say which battles are lost, and which are won? . . . Potato Face seemed to feel real class hatred for me. One day, when both my companions had been sent to court, I was alone in the exercise cage; I would willingly have shared it with women from another cell, but I was strictly isolated, although before my arrival our small cell had always been taken along with one of the others. It meant that my companions were now worse off because of me; to share a cage gives you some chance to pass on news, cigarettes, and other things. And that day, as luck would have it, I was in the biggest cage of all; Potato Face, on duty "out on a limb," jeered down at me: "Fancy yerself, don'tcha? Like a duchess, that's wot." The Duchess of Prison Cage! Potato Face was often outraged by what she found among my things. I had the privilege of an occasional visit, and my husband brought me a lot of valuable things—valuable, that is, in prison terms. He was especially generous with toiletries, bringing more than I could ever consume, and when Potato Face peered inquisitively into my cupboard one day, she almost dropped. She'd never been so close to such luxury soaps and creams in her life.

"Look at this 'ere," she yelled, "wotcher say to this for 'igh living!" The first time he was allowed to see me, my husband found a beautiful way of protesting my imprisonment: he brought me five orchids in transparent wrapping. We stood them in a plastic vase and Scooter opened our door twice just to convince herself that she was looking at real live orchids. Then she calculated how much they must have cost him, and I felt sorry for her; gossip said her husband beat her up frequently.

I could feel Andy's defiant strength as she half dragged, half carried me, a strength that would not let me fall. And like Maddy before her, she put me to bed and cooled my head with wet towels. They had just changed my interrogation officer and assigned me to a conceited young dandy very proud of his high-speed doctorate (from one of the Czech schools where a degree can be obtained in six months by the "politically reliable.") He was anxious to show off his literary erudition. When he was surprised that my health did not stand up to prison life, I asked him whether he had ever seen what prison was like inside, since he and his colleagues were holding me there. That had nothing to do with him, a police officer; prisons were run by a different department, the Ministry of Justice. He was charmed to learn, though, that I shared a cell with a psychopath and a Gypsy. At that time I was allowed to lie in bed during the day, and Andy sat by me on her hard stool and watched over my sleep between interrogations. That horrible eye was fixed on me, and there was a smile on the undamaged half of her face. Whenever I opened my eyes she was there, giving me a motherly smile that was all the more moving for the black and blue bruised cheek above it. Once she said, "Eva, dear, prison camp will finish you; you're not made for this life. Don't worry, though, I'll look after you."

Another time she told me, "Don't believe a word anybody says in jail, don't trust a single soul," and added softly, "not even me." What was that, Potato Face, a lost battle? I lost a lot, though, when I lost Andy.

At seven in the evening, when all the prisoners were allowed to lie down, she set her bed up in the middle of the cell, close to mine, relegating Helen to outer nothingness. Then Andy sat on her bed cross-legged and began to talk. I was tired and sleepy, hardly able to take in what she was saying and needing above all to think clearly about the traps my interrogator might lay for me next day. Andy talked relentlessly on and on as she plaited her thick hair for the night. Seven o'clock was her time, and whether what she said was true or made up, whether it had happened to her or to somebody else, she was a wonderful storyteller with a wealth of tales, boundless imagination, and a talent for vivid description. She talked and smiled and talked, her smile throwing doubt on the strict truth of what she was saying. She narrated piecemeal; what she did not complete one day would be finished the next, and she did not bother to make clear who was involved in which event. She was a modern writer, leaving it to the reader to work out things for himself. I was a hollow tree where secrets could be whispered, and I was a willing and attentive listener. All Gypsies were enchanted by the popular film of the moment, "Gypsies on Their Way to Heaven." The theme song had become the Gypsy anthem, and Andy sang it, too. When she discovered I was a writer, she took even greater care with her stories. I think she felt some kind of affection for me, too, because when she was with me she could let herself go. She had a soft attractive voice, deeper than most girls', and just a bit husky when she talked Czech instead of her throaty Romany, a voice as soft and as rough as a horse's mane that clings as it streams in the air. It was a lovely singing and speaking voice, rippling through the cell. She taught me some Romany, but it seemed to me to have a desperately small vocabulary. And in that fascinating voice she told me not only why she was in jail, but all about her life.

Everything had been fine so long as Poppa was alive. They had their own cottage in East Slovakia, with animal pens and a garden, close to the woods and the river. They kept a pig, hens, and a goat; and her mother gave no trouble, but a malicious aunt put a spell on Poppa and bewitched him in a chimney. This is how it is done: take a clean rag and wrap it round a lump of clay, and stick it to the wall inside a chimney. The bewitched victim starts getting fatter and fatter until he's the size of the chimney; the broader the chimney chosen for the spell, the fatter the victim will get. That was what happened to Poppa, because his sister had chosen a very wide chimney. The family knew he must have been bewitched, but they didn't know which chimney it was, or they could have torn the rag out and broken the spell. It never occurred to them that the evil one was their own aunt, and that it was the chimney in her cottage. As broad as a chimney, Poppa was taken to hospital and there he died. The children were alone with their mother who took to bad ways, and soon they'd got nothing left and their aunt made nothing out of it, either, the sties, the cottage, the goat, the pig, and the hens—it was all gone. They left Slovakia for Bohemia, at the mercy of a bad mother.

For Andy, her Poppa was the living incarnation of affection, protection, and an orderly life. She told me how he killed a snake—a good story for psychoanalysis! It was an enormous creature, as long and thick as a man's arm; there were snakes like that where she came from, lots and lots of them, hiding where the wild strawberries and the raspberries grew, and sometimes sunning themselves on the flat stones by the river when she and her mother went down to do the washing. This long fat snake got into the goat's pen and spread itself all around the walls so that nobody dared to go in, and it sucked the goat's milk. The poor goat was bleating with pain and fear and Poppa knew he had to kill that snake, but it wouldn't come out. So he opened the door just a crack and drove the prongs of a pitchfork into it and killed it. Then he had to light a fire and burn the snake, because even dead a snake is capable of working evil, if it's big enough. The snake was burned on a bonfire and fat was dripping from it, or blood or whatever. Poppa put a pot to catch it and rubbed it in the children's hair—snake dripping makes your hair grow beautiful. When the snake had been reduced to ashes, Poppa found a nest of baby snakes under a stone against the cottage wall, and killed them too; but he didn't have to burn them because little snakes can't harm you once they're dead. Andy was Poppa's favorite, and he showed it when he died. They brought him home from the hospital, dead, and laid him out on the cottage door, taken off its hinges and placed across the backs of two chairs. He was dressed in his best suit, and hat and boots as well, lying on a white sheet. All his friends and relations came to bid him farewell, and whoever could afford it brought money toward the cost of the funeral and the wake. They all put their coins by the side of the body: her mother, her brothers, and her sister. Only Andy put her coin into Poppa's hand, and he closed his fingers over it. He gave her a smiling glance out of the corner of his eye, under the brim of his hat, so nobody else could see it. They couldn't force his palm open, and he was buried with Andy's coin, he loved her so much.

Left with her mother, that was when Andy's life started going wrong. Her mother turned bad, though Andy didn't say exactly in what way. Her two brothers went to southern Bohemia to work on a farm, and the younger was drowned in the river. (It must have been the Veltava; its level raised when the Lipno dam was built.) "They'd been drinking," Andy said, "and he didn't know how to swim, Evie dear. They dared him and he jumped into the water from the bridge, and then they stood there laughing to see the Gypsy boy drowning. It was miles down the river that they found the body." Andy and her mother came to Prague, she must have been fifteen or sixteen then, and her mother married her off to a bad Gypsy; he was thin, lazy, and brutal, a bony creature she never got to be fond of. He was her husband, though, and she meant to keep him; another Gypsy girl started flirting with him, following him to where he was working as a bricklayer. Andy went to see what was going on—she was pregnant and nearing her time—and when the two girls started a fight, the other knocked her down and started hitting her in the belly with a brick. "It hurt something terrible," said Andy. Her big belly was in the way and she didn't have a brick in her hand to defend herself with. So she used the only weapon she had: her nails, those terrible long curved Gypsy nails like eagle's claws, hard and unbreakable. A Gypsy girl in prison will let you cut her hair off before she'll let you touch her nails, tended as a thing of beauty as well as a weapon. Andy wanted to get her fingers into her rival's hair and twist out a handful, but her nails went lower than she meant them to, and she gouged the girl's eyes out. That was where her wanderings from prison to prison began. She was taken to the psychiatric hospital in a state of shock, and woke to find herself in a cage in the closed ward. Because she was underage, and because at her trial the blind girl said it was an accident and Andy hadn't done it on purpose, she only got four years. They let her out to have the baby, and six weeks later she went back to jail, leaving the little girl in an institution because she was not normal. Andy was convinced it was because of the blows with that brick.

She liked to think back to her time in the prison camp; she was in Pardubice, and from what she said I guessed she'd been there more than once. The first time she must have been with the juveniles. But many of the things she described could only have applied to the women's quarters, like the lack of a place where the lesbians could be together, the dinner queues, the newcomers' scut work (fetching breakfast and emptying the slop pails in the morning), the stealing that went on when each had only an unlocked case under her bed—in short, the pleasures of prison life. She related even the worst things with a smile of resignation. But what did she regard as the worst, and what would have seemed the worst to me? You had to be on your guard with Andy, not to interpret her experiences in the light of your own. She was always ready to stick out her claws, and yet there was an age-old primitive resignation in her, an acceptance of fate: What else can we do but use our human skills to hold fate at bay, to fight it or at least cheat it? She was not predatory, and she knew pity. Andy said she didn't mind work, and I believe her, for she really liked keeping the cell clean. She could fit in anywhere, and so in the camp she hadn't minded the amount of work required of her. (Just about this time there was a girl in the next cell who had come from that same camp; she was so terrified of having to work that she had swallowed some pins, and now she faced trial for self-mutilation with the intention of not serving her sentence.)

For a time Andy made valves for electric meters; then she was put on to setting tiny bits of cut glass to make brooches. Fiddling work that probably only prisoners can be made to do. She told me how difficult it was to smuggle a brooch from the workshop into the camp, where you could barter it for food. Yet the women made presents of brooches to their relatives on visit, and took them home as souvenirs when they were released. I did my best to understand the system of payment for work done in the prison camp, but it made no sense, and not only from what Andy told me. There was a standard production norm, but responsibility for keeping to it rested with the team, not the individual. That meant that those who worked hard had to work even harder to make up for those who did not pull their weight. Sometimes it meant working late, so late that they missed meals, and sometimes they had to make up time by working on Saturdays. Their pay was calculated by an overseer who was also a convict and who did pretty much as she liked. There seemed to be even less sense in the official payment of wages earned: a certain amount was set aside to cover alimony where it was due, another sum was deducted to cover living costs in the camp, and at least eight hundred crowns had to be put to the prisoner's account for when he or she was released. The rest was the prisoner's to spend. Yet even convicts who fulfilled their production norms thought eighty crowns a month was big pocket money! Looking at the prices asked for costume jewelry in the shops, and being told in the papers what a successful export article it is, I have often thought what a goldmine our prison camps are.

Andy's description of life in the camp was not without its wisdom. Once she was declared a model worker; it was on the occasion of some state holiday, and when after the usual speeches the commander of the camp read her name in the list, she wriggled with pleasure on her chair, and was presented with a little banner. She hadn't been working for the honor of it, not in the least; she wanted to earn pocket money to buy tea, a lump of salami, a tin of meat, and some cigarettes, and the bonus for model workers was fifty crowns! She was already counting what she would be able to buy for her bonus, and as she left the hall some of the others started a fight, doubtless the feckless who envied her the money but not the work she put in to make up their idleness, so that Andy would seem to be involved. The commander saw her as he left the hall: a model worker caught up in a brawl? On the very threshold of the place of honor? There was no fifty crowns for Andy, and instead she went to the punishment cells. "Life's not a bed of down"—her favorite saying.

The camp was not only a place where envy and malice thrived, though. On Sunday afternoons, the only day they didn't have to line up and march in columns round the barracks square fully dressed in long cotton stockings and prison uniform buttoned up tight, in rain, frost, or sweltering heat, the women would make up for those deadening roll calls and hours of marking time, by fun and games of their own choosing. Once it was a mock Gypsy wedding—Andy's idea—with all the traditional songs and ceremonies. She sang the songs for me in the East Slovakian dialect that she cherished in memory of home, her home with Poppa. Andy played the bride, and it was the loveliest wedding she could remember. Dressed in white sheets and colored curtains, with a wreath on her head, she "looked wonderful." They got ready in the washroom, where there was a mirror. They had a job getting hold of civilian trousers for the bridegroom. The wedding guests drawn up in two lines sang as the bride and groom passed down between them; two girls played the part of the two fathers, two were mothers, and there were bridesmaids to carry Andy's train. She liked to be the center of whatever was going on. "It was lovely," Andy sighed, "so lovely that even the guards came to watch."

There was something so clear-cut, so individual in Andy. Other girls talked about the Pardubice camp too, of course, and we listened avidly to know what we could expect. The one thing they all talked about was the TV and the radio. Each of the huts had the radio turned on full blast in the morning and left on until lights out—a nightmare thought! When the girls had time off they could watch the TV in the clubroom where there was nothing else but a few hard chairs, the box, and a couple of bare tables. Andy did not mention the radio or the TV; everything interesting and special came from within her own self. There was one thing in the camp that enchanted her, though—the bachelor flats with a communal kitchen, intended to help women coming to the end of long sentences to prepare for life outside. They learned to cook meals, to do their washing and some housework, to use knives and forks again, to manage a stove. "There was a lovely electric stove there." Andy was enthusiastic. "And curtains. And everything was so clean!" She had seen the flats soon after they were built, when she was sent to clean them.

If there was one thing Andy liked better than telling stories, it was singing. She would sit cross-legged on the floor, in a corner, humming all day long. She was happy, because her songs took her wherever she wanted to be. She sang Slovak songs that I had never heard, as well as innumerable Gypsy songs. Her childhood must really have been happy for her to sing with such abandonment. She gave all the tunes a mood of gentle melancholy, with her warm, moving voice. She was the only person for years—and for many years to come—who got me to sing without a crowd to hide in. As her bruises receded, her beauty returned and her gentle, friendly smile took over the whole of her face. The cell seemed to be a place where she could rest from the ups and downs of her turbulent life. Andy made me realize that the written word is not the whole of literature. Her tales were often fragmentary; and looking back I find there are a lot of pieces missing from the puzzle that was Andy, making her a mysterious figure only partly revealed. She had a great sense of atmosphere and not only described scenes vividly but could convey all the emotions involved as well. I remember so many of the lively pictures she conjured up for me. And yet one day, when I had written a letter for her to send to the home where she was in arrears of payment for her children, and gave it her to sign, she first begged me to sign it for her. Not until it dawned on her that I really would not do it, did she awkwardly pick up my pen, and turning her back on me to hide her shame, wrote her name in clumsy capitals. She had never learned to write more than that, and she would not let me see that signature. There must have been literacy courses in some of the prison camps, but Andy had learned so little, so very little. We dropped the subject hurriedly.

Growing up with a bad mother, in bad surroundings, and then in and out of prison, it must have been thanks to that happy childhood with her father that she had very firm principles and highly cultivated standards of behavior in some things. She liked to wash, turning the procedure into a solemn ritual, significant of what? I often wondered. A well-ordered life? A victory over something she despised and hated? She scrubbed her skin in icy water until it glowed—bodily cleanliness was the central tenet of her creed. She plaited her hair every night, knowing even without a mirror that she would look nice. I have already said she was not afraid of hard work and that in itself was unusual. She never begged, even with a glance, and she never asked for anything. It wasn't pride, it was dignity. She would wait for hours until I got back from interrogation and *offered* her a cigarette, although my cigarettes were lying on the table and Helen smoked them all the time. I might have thought she was trying to behave like me; Gypsy girls are often oversensitive about their race and readily take umbrage, but they do not take pride in it. However it may have been, Andy was remarkably consistent in her courtesy, down to the smallest details. There was much in prison life that was easier for her than for me, because experience made her an accurate judge of the possibilities of any situation. She generously shared her knowledge with me, something not every prisoner will do. Her good manners were in marked contrast to Helen's sloppiness. There was no room for three to eat at the table, and so I took my food to a small stool by my bed. Three times a day Andy suffered a double trial: she had to watch Helen messing with her food (she'd end up with gravy all over her) and she had to struggle with her inability to hurt the older woman's feelings by moving

80

away and coming to sit with me. She asked me what to do: Should she leave Helen alone at the table and squeeze in by me? I said she should if that was what would make her happier. No, she couldn't, what would it look like? She was not greedy, and she knew how to do without—a sign of true cultivation, whether by upbringing or the experience of a hard life. The fair Helen would watch my things greedily but never Andy. Yet she had nothing, not even the hope that someone might send her a parcel; she had nothing but what the prison provided: a toothbrush and comb, a paper mug and a cake of cheap soap. She had been wearing jeans, a shirt, and a sweater when she was arrested. In the cell where she spent her first night was a girl who was being sent home next day, in nothing but a sleeveless dress because it had grown colder while she'd been in jail. Andy gave her the warm sweater. "What about you? By the time you come up for trial it'll be winter, and you've nothing but that shirt." She laughed it off—that's life, it's never a bed of down.

Andy hated the Olashi Gypsies; she said they were nomads from Rumania, still wearing long brightly colored skirts and black aprons, and their mouths were full of gold. Everybody agreed the Olashi were very rich, and it was a fact that all the Olashi Gypsies I saw in Ruzyně had gold teeth, wearing their wealth where it could not be stolen, but accessible in case of need. When an Olashi opens her mouth to speak, to say nothing of when she smiles, it's like lightning flashing. They had shrill voices, and even Andy could not understand their Romany. When they started screeching through the door in the evenings we had to cover our ears. They were like clucking hens. The guard would throw open the door, finding an Olashi woman lying on the floor talking to her daughter in the next cell. After taking her by her bodice, and she would still pour out voluble instructions, until, realizing she was caught, without stopping to take breath, she would go off into a hail of curses at the man. Olashi women put all their money into gold "but don't know how to use a knife and fork," said Andy scornfully. She told me how the non-Gypsy women had turned the Olashi out of their hut in the Pardubice camp, but let the other Gypsies stay. "Olashi don't even know how to use a lavatory, just go anywhere along the fence."

A moment later Andy revealed how thin her own veneer of civilization was; I asked where the Olashi got all that wealth from, and she told me how they worked. A beautiful Olashi girl finds a lone man (Wenceslas Square at night is their favorite hunting ground) and when he follows her and starts playing around, the Olashi men come up behind and "punish him," beating him up and robbing him. It shows how primitive they are, according to Andy, because they "work" in the open air, going with a man on the street or to an empty lot. The woman who was screeching advice to her daughter had been caught stealing a hen; civilized Gypsies would never stoop to poultry stealing, and their working methods called for a wine bar or at least a pub. Andy had done her share of waylaying lonely men at night: she told me how they'd got a drunk nicely "worked up" in the park by the Main Station when she and her confederates heard a police siren. They ran and ran until they were out of breath, and still there was the siren at their backs. They thought the police had heard the man's shouts, and all the time it was only an ambulance taking the victims of a car crash to the hospital. Andy was not shocked by *how* the Olashi got their money; she despised them for not using it to make life pleasanter. Now *she* would know what to do with her money, you wouldn't catch her stuffing it into her mouth. Maybe she'd buy that lovely electric stove, or curtains and a carpet, or bedspreads. And she'd bathe in rum—Wouldn't she smell good?

She gave me good advice for when I felt like making money that way: "Get good hold on his hair, Eva, dear, and bang his head on the pavement, that's the safest—bang it good and hard on the ground."

Andy had a dramatic tale about a man with wads of money she and a friend took up with in a wine bar; when they got him outside they found he wasn't drunk at all. The other girl cleared off in a fright and Andy was left alone with him. They were in a dark alley, by a pile of timber, and although Andy knew which pocket he carried his money in, she couldn't get at it because he held her body so close to his, like a leech. If there'd been the two of them, one would have played him along while the other picked his pocket, and they'd have got away together. Now she couldn't get his money without giving him what he wanted, so she grabbed a log and hit him over the head. And told the story as though she'd been in the right all along.

"That wasn't fair, Andy," I said reproachfully. "You offered to go with him and then just robbed him."

"If he'd been decent he wouldn't have gone with me, would he?" She was quite sure of herself. "He wanted a fuck, that's all, and serve him right."

It is part of the professional code of the non-Gypsy prostitute to serve the customer first and take payment afterward; that's what makes prostitution an honest business. Andy did not consider herself a prostitute; she was a decoy. Indeed she was very self-possessed in view of herself as a woman. "We give pleasure in ways white girls have never even heard of," she told me; but do not think her sexual arts were on sale to all comers. She was not on the streets; she was out for robbery, and her logic was unshakable: a decent man would never get himself caught like that. Her victims were all the same: they wanted something they'd no right to, and what they got served them right. Her

83

explanation shows the fundamental line of Gypsy thinking: we know what we want, and we take advantage of your stupidity to get it.

Andy did not always get her money so brutally; she had another technique, subtler and more refined. She invited a young girl to a drink; her customers were already there in the bar; as a rule there would be two men. It all looked so natural, the four of them chatting and drinking a little; the younger girl thought she was seeing life, and would readily agree when Andy suggested going on somewhere else. In the street the men found a taxi, taking care it was a small one, for driver and three passengers. After arguing a bit about which of them would follow with Andy in another taxi, things so worked out that Andy was left behind while the men carried off her young friend. It had never happened that the girl tried to struggle out of the taxi; for one thing, it didn't occur to her that she'd seen the last of Andy for that night, and then, she was more than a little drunk. None of them had ever made trouble afterward; she chose her "friends" well. How much Andy got for her services, I was not told.

For really hard times, Andy had something to fall back on. "Everybody has her old man or two," said Andy; and "old" was apparently the right word. "I never went to see him when I'd got money, only when I couldn't see any other way out."

The old man wanted no more than to look at her and caress her lovely young body. She found her old man when she went to help a friend steal his money; but he was so poor, and his rooms so shabby, that she was sorry for him and sent her friend away and stuck to the old man. He'd been pensioned off because of a bad heart, and he didn't have much to spend. She didn't go to him often, knowing he'd be good for five hundred crowns when she really needed it. "He was good to me," said Andy.

During those endless nights with a bare electric bulb glaring overhead, a shutter clicking every hour as an eye spied on us, Helen groaning in her sleep, no air left to breathe—somewhere a restless bird chirped—Andy led me into a terrible universe, a universe peopled with human beings yet dark and seemingly boundless. Andy moved with the light step of a gazelle between the idea of killing and that of keeping her body clean. Cultured on the surface, she was quite sure of the rules determining what one may and what one should not do. If I were to say, "Thou shalt not kill," she would promptly give me three reasons why she must kill, reasons based on those fixed rules. I wondered when and how a person is born to freedom. How would Andy, with her sensitivity and her imagination, have developed in surroundings where spirituality was the goal? What have the realities of our life to offer the Gypsies, torn from the patriarchal society that embodied the most sacred of their concepts? The state tries to replace the paternal authority they have lost by the pressures and restraints of our civilization, but as with one hand the state teaches Gypsy children to clean their teeth and speak broken Czech, with the other it drags them by the ears not to a more cultured level of existence but to homes for children where they never learn what affection is, and then—by the logic of the process—to prison. It occurred to me that man had first to learn fear before he began to long for freedom. They ought not to try to force Andy and people like her to be afraid of their fellows: all they achieve is more and more primitive behavior. An unbeliever, I found myself thinking heretical thoughts about the need for religion when I reflected on Andy.

When she was released from the prison camp, Andy knew how to sign her name in capitals, and she was not afraid of hard work; from the point of view of the authorities and the bureaucrats, that meant a fair start in life. "Work, the mother of human progress. . . ." Andy got a job washing dishes in a big cafeteria on Wenceslas Square, and she felt she'd gone up in the world. "Everybody liked me there," she said. She had the messy tables wiped in a trice, her plates and glasses gleamed, she was earning money, had enough to eat, and sometimes enough to take home as well. Best of all, she could have her little boy with her, her second child. She could feed him there, she was not humiliated by the staff, and she was happy. It was her husband who spoiled everything. Pretending he'd got TB while he was in jail (what he was in for I do not know), he refused to work although no doctor would certify him for sick pay. As soon as he got out of bed in the morning he followed her to the cafeteria, standing round for hours scrounging food and drinks and giving her a bad reputation. He ought to have been at work and not living on her, and Andy was ashamed of what the staff and the customers must think of him. Not to be saddled with that good-for-nothing, she left the job and had never had another since.

At times I thought Andy's loathing for her husband distorted her view of herself as well as of the world, but there was one period of her married life that she talked about in friendlier tones. That was when her mother-in-law was still alive. She was kind to Andy, and Andy gave her the affection she could not feel for her own mother. Then the old lady got a bad leg, it had to be amputated, and though she was given an artificial limb, she was too old and fat to learn to use it. She just sat at home all day, Andy did the shopping and the housework for her while her mother-in-law did the cooking, happy to have company. "She had such long hair," Andy told me, "and it hadn't been washed for ages. I did it for her with shampoo and dried and brushed it out nice." She enjoyed telling her good deeds. Sometimes she heated water and gave the old lady a bath. But the good fairy who watched over Andy's marriage died, and the wicked one took over—her own mother, who was always on the side of the no-good husband and was unjust to Andy.

If I understood right, besides the poor little first baby, Andy had another girl, making three children in all, but the only one she really loved was the boy. She was always talking about him. For a long time the two children were in a home, either because Andy was in prison or because she didn't take proper care of them, and one of her favorite stories was how she had kidnapped them. Andy and her sister-in-law went to visit their children in the same home one Sunday morning and took them to a pub; there was nowhere else to go in that little town, except the station waiting room, and it was a cold day. The children were so happy to see their Mum, especially the boy.

Andy smiled her most beautiful dreamy smile as she told us: "They were so happy!" She bought them chocolate biscuits and a glass of rum each; they sat at the table nicely, a four-year-old and a six-year-old who didn't yet know that rum was the best of all good things. Andy could manage to live without cigarettes, but she missed her rum terribly. We tried to work out ways and means of smuggling a few drops of her nectar into the cell. Using a shampoo tube seemed the best idea, but it takes a long time to arrange things like that, and Andy was moved out of my cell before it could be done. She dreamed every day of the moment when she would be released: the first pub she found would offer her rum—a liter, that would be her first drink. Hence her nickname: Andy Rum Candy. At last her children knew how sweet life was with Mum; the drink warmed them and they cuddled up to her, kissing and being kissed, until the gush of reawakened mother love was too strong for Andy and she took them with her on the next train to Prague.

"Don't do it, Andy," her sister-in-law called after her warn-ingly, but Andy wouldn't listen. They were her children and she wanted to have them with her, especially the little boy.

"He's so lovely," she said.

Andy's children were fated to influence her life. Because of the first baby, battered before birth, she had had to get married and then found herself in prison. Because of the boy she had to suffer her husband and found herself in prison again, and more than once. After the kidnapping, Andy was in trouble with the authorities; it was probably a court decision that had taken the children from her in the first place. When the local social officer said they would have to go back, Andy insulted her; it was "an attack on an official in the performance of her duties," but the scene was an eloquent one.

"Have you got children of your own?" Andy asked her.

"No," the woman answered, not seeing what her barrenness had got to do with this impertinent Gypsy's case.

"Then you're not fit to decide."

The official insisted nevertheless that the children must be in a home, and so Andy scrambled over the desk behind which the woman was entrenched, taking decisions about other peo-ple's children, and beat her up.

She certainly went to jail for that aggressive outburst, but before long her children were living at home, the love of her life. Yet another disaster for Andy: if she wanted to be near her children she had to live with her husband, and she just couldn't do that. Her children were a source of joy and a source of suffering. The boy had started school and was doing well—and it was he who had trapped her the last time she was arrested.

Andy went to see him when she was a fugitive, running away from yet another disastrous source of joy that I'll come to in a little while. She hadn't seen the boy for a long time, maybe a year or more. How long can a great passion last? Perhaps she was hoping for a reconciliation with her husband and her mother; or perhaps there was nowhere else she could hide out. Who knows? Andy herself never analyzed her own conduct. In fear and anxiety she ran to her old address, and the child begged her to stay the night.

"He started to cry so when he saw me," she said. The boy proudly showed her how well he could read and write, and she lay down on his bed, caressing him and comforting him with that marvelous smile of hers, until he fell asleep. Unfortunately she fell asleep too, and meanwhile her own mother had given her away to the police. They came to her husband's home and took her away from her little son's bed. Early in the morning she heard suspicious sounds, but there was no escape because she was in a little room off the kitchen, where she could hear her husband telling them, "She's in there!" The police stood over her while she dressed, and the boy started crying for his mother as they took her away.

Andy considered aloud all the possible reasons for her arrest; there were so many of them! The last time she left her husband he went to court and forced her to give him support money for the children, and he seems to have gone to court again when she stopped payment. She did not appear in court on either occasion; they did not even know where to serve her notice since she left no address, but that did not invalidate the court's decision, and so she may have been wanted for nonpayment of maintenance. The police who arrested her said something about a warrant being out for her. But she might just as well have been arrested for assault, if one of the gang's exploits had come to light. Andy remembered a taxi driver who gave evidence he'd taken her from one place to somewhere else. The most obvious reason, of course, was that without fixed employment she was living as a parasite on society. It was how she earned her daily bread.

There was yet another reason, however: she had almost killed her love. It was late one night when she told me the story; Helen was gurgling in her sleep and Andy's voice rippled softly round the cell. She was sick at heart and her barriers were down (at least that was what I felt) and she was revealing her deepest and closest secret because she could no longer bear it alone, because she had to tell someone. In the cell she never stopped talking about the man for whom she had deserted even her children; such wild passion horrified our fair Helen. But to reveal how she had almost killed him, she needed the dead silence of night in a prison cell, a silence that keeps you awake, a blanket of helplessness that envelops you like a living tomb. Oh, how passionate was Andy's love! The bruised face, the bloody eye, and (as it turned out when she no longer had any sensation in half her face and half her teeth) a torn nerve—all that came of love, whether it was her lover who had struck her in a fit of jealousy, or her husband who had first beat her and then given her up to the police.

"It's Valdice where the real men come from, Eva, believe me," she confided, and she had found one in a Prague pub, driven out the girl he belonged to, and taken him over. Let's say his name was Kamil; he was a bricklayer or a road repairman, and wore filthy denims held together under his belly by a single button, a sweat-soaked shirt and the same dirty windbreaker summer and winter. He did not even wash when he came home from work; his hair was thick with sweat-caked dust. But "it was such beautiful hair, Eva, so fair and thick and wavy." Kamil was *the* man of all men, but because he came from Valdice, there were some things he had never learned. "He was greasy, and he stank," she said. "He was so handsome, but how he did stink!"

Occasionally she would succeed in warming water to wash her beloved, but there was one time when she had warm water ready in the basin, and clean sheets ready in the bed, and he went and pissed in the cupboard where she kept her clothes. He never put his one and only windbreaker anywhere but over a chair. It took all the power of her great love not to let him see she had to hold her breath when he was near, he was so filthy.

It was a passion like an unfathomed whirlpool, like a peaceful spreading lake, like a deep clear pool, like an overgrown pond. Kamil preferred Andy to her white rival—white girls can't make love like Gypsies can.

"The things we know about love!" Andy gave her secret smile and Helen hid her head under the blanket, for Heaven's sake, the Gypsy hussy was going to describe her goings-on! and Andy swayed a little, like a cobra full of mystery. Andy was provocation and submission, she was tenderness and subtly held distance. She was complete absorption. Not a clinging plant, neither ivy nor bindweed, but salt that dissolved on her man's body. Kamil drank, of course, and if Andy was Rum Candy, he was a beer barrel. He went straight from work to the pub and drank his earnings away, then staggered home and into bed, to sleep until it was time to start the same round again. Andy once let slip that they didn't make love often; he'd come home drunk with the flower of his manhood wilted. Sometimes he brought home a bunch of soaks from the pub who drank and ate up everything she had in the place, and when they staggered out he'd be lying there, in his piss or his vomit or worse—a swine. And one day she found him lying spread-eagled on the table dead drunk, his arms and legs hanging over the edge, and by him there lay a long, sharp knife, a churo. Andy had the knife in her hand, ready to strike and have done with it all, when Kamil opened his lovely blue eyes, and she couldn't do it.

"Andy, you wouldn't really have stabbed him? I thought you loved him?"

"You don't know the first thing about love, Eva, dear," she replied. Love means blows, blood, bruises, battles. Her Kamil was furiously jealous, although he was a wilted bloom and every penny he had went to drink. He would not let her go out to work, he wanted her at home, to be waiting for him and to look after him—he was keeping her. But he didn't tell her where to find the money for food and clothes and the rent, when he left the whole of his pay in the pub till. So she did her best not to let him know how she managed, and he was often attacked by violent fits of jealousy. Where had she got the money for a goose? Where had that new skirt come from? Those new shoes? His love was so overwhelming that he hit her over the head with a log of wood one day just as she was coming in with a bucket of water from the well, and she slipped on the icy doorstep and hit her head on the stone threshold. Dazed, and with blood pouring from the wound, she stumbled in.

"But you should have heard him asking for forgiveness," she said proudly. "He was so afraid he'd lose me." He would have done anything for her then. He brought his pay packet home and handed it over for her to go and buy herself whatever she wanted.

Alas, Andy had her enemies in the district. For example, there was the girl she'd stolen Kamil from, still hanging about the pub. Andy would sometimes go into the bar where her lover sat with his friends—her enemies—and have a rum to steady her nerves, but she never made a scene; often enough his love for her survived only because she waited for him outside, by the lavatories. The landlord was another of her enemies. Karel was his name and he'd have liked her for his girl. But he wasn't good enough for Andy, thin and with a black moustache, and he took his revenge by emptying Kamil's pockets so there was nothing left for her.

Kamil enjoyed her cooking so much and she kept the place so clean; sometimes even he would comment on it. She'd have washed his trousers for him, even. And she loved his body—fat and potbellied from all that beer, it would have disgusted her had it not been tattooed. The Valdice tattoo marks made it beautiful. Andy had a beauty spot tattooed on her face, too; the shape of the beauty spot tells which camp a girl has been in. Kamil must have thought his Andy the most beautiful thing in the world, because in a frightening burst of jealousy he tied her down on the table—the same table where she had failed to stab him—and shaved her. Scraped every hair off her body. When Andy washed herself she tried not to let us see her shame.

And that melancholy night, she confided in me, she had stabbed him. The churo came into its own at last. The wound didn't bleed much when she pulled the knife out. That outburst of fury on both sides, that wild throbbing emotion, brought them together again, and next morning Kamil went to work. But the wound wouldn't heal, it turned yellow and then green, and he couldn't work properly for the pain. His belly was running with pus. She begged him to go to the hospital, but he wouldn't. Then the pain got worse and the wound turned black and she called a doctor and ran away. That was what she told me: she ran away into the night, sure the district would have it in for her now, and not knowing where to turn. That was when she thought of her other great love, her little boy. Now, in prison, she did not know whether Kamil had gone to hospital or not, whether the doctor had been to look at him. And if he was in hospital, had he told them it was she who had stabbed him?

"He wouldn't do you a bad turn like that, Andy."

Andy just sat there smiling, her voice rippling on. Life isn't a bed of down. And she started dreaming out loud: she'd go to that pub, maybe that white girl would be sitting there with Kamil, but it wouldn't matter because Andy had a new pair of shoes and her hairs had all grown curly again, and the moment Kamil saw her he would get to his feet and brush the white girl off, hoist up his trousers under that belly with a wound that had healed; his shirt unwashed for God knows how long would send the smell of his sweat through the room. But Andy wouldn't mind, she wouldn't even tell him off because the white girl had left her nice kitchen in such a mess. She would just smile and Kamil would go to the bar and order her a double rum. The rum would taste wonderful, the first she'd had for so long— she'd saved the great moment for when they were together again. "And if you're out too, Eva, you must come and see me there." I promised her that if I could find her, we'd drink a bottle of rum together, whether she was with her Kamil, or with somebody else.

All of a sudden Andy was moved away. In prison you never have any warning of such things. A guard opened the door and said, "Get your things ready." Andy did as she was told, and I am not sure—in her fear of what was going to happen next— that she even managed a smile. They only moved her a few cells down the corridor, though, and whenever she passed our door she knocked or called out. I never did find out what she was really tried for. And I am amazed at the strange way time works: there are people you know for years and never spare a thought for; I only knew Andy those three weeks.

6

HELGA (1)

They took Andy away to make room for Helga. It is quite an experience to be moved from your cell. "Get your things ready!" An officer comes into the cell, says those four words, and bangs the door shut.

"Ready" means rolling your blanket, pillowcase, sheet, pajamas, spare socks and undies, and your towel, and tying it all up in the second sheet. Anything personal you may have with you, food from home, letters, your own comb, toothbrush, cream, or soap (I even had a bunch of flowers), all has to lie beside the bundle, and you wait. Your bunk, hard and narrow but till now your own, yawns nakedly. You are ready, but unless you are going to the punishment cells, or you've been sentenced and know you are going to a prison camp, you haven't the faintest idea why you have to leave what is at least a known evil; nor do you know where you will spend the next night. There must be mystery to create dread. At times they seemed to move prisoners round simply to show their power over them. One girl asked, "Where am I going?"

"To the execution squad," was the "joking" answer!

And so it was "Get your things ready!" for Andy. She wrapped her prison issue in her sheet, and an avalanche of flesh poured into the cell. I still feel the shock of that moment, deafening and threatening to overwhelm me. It was not the flesh and bones that created the impression, it was the thundering momentum of Helga's arrival. The cell, which had been crowded before, now seemed to be bursting at the seams. That shapeless mountain of flesh sat right down on my bed, a piled-up blond hairdo at its peak.

"Just think!" the woman burst out, "I'm a magistrate, and they have the cheek to put me in jail!"

A magistrate? Just who can be a magistrate in Czechoslovakia in 1981? And what could "their" creature have done to land in prison? It takes much less than that to put you on your guard. And my God, of the hundred and forty women in that wing, it had to be this full-breasted Fury who took the place of Andy with her charming diffidence!

The woman went on and on about the world's ingratitude, while *my bed*, the only place where I could put my feet up, rest my back against the wall, look out at a patch of blue sky, and forget for a moment where I had to live and breathe—*my bed* was groaning and creaking beneath the weight of her huge buttocks. Bed! The doctor is as grudging about the right to lie down during the day as he is about pills: for one day, for two days, for three days. The prescription "bed" hangs on a hook by the door, so that the warders know who has the right to lie down and who has not. The tragic film hero, taken to a cell where he falls in despair on a bed, would be envied by the prisoners in Ruzyně. All they have the whole day long is an iron stool with no backrest and no crossbar for your feet. The only place you can lie down is on the bare floor. The first week in prison I put my pillow between my back and the chilly wall, and the Deputy Governor himself bawled me out: your pillow, with your sheets and blanket, must be in a neat pile on the lowest of the three beds put away for the day. By the time Helga arrived I had a prescription allowing me to lie down; it hung in the corridor, beside our cell door. My bed was therefore standing in the cell instead of being hooked up with the other two, and it was the most comfortable piece of furniture in sight. It angered me to see her make straight for it. If there hadn't been so much of her, or if she'd said "Do you mind?", or if I hadn't been so upset at losing Andy, or if I hadn't been put on my guard by her amazement that a magistrate . . . As it was, I said, "You have to have special permission to sit on the bed. There'll be a row the moment they see you." And I felt disgusted with myself for not being able to say outright: "Get off that bed, it's mine," and for invoking (out of perverse politeness) a regulation I myself considered shameful. And so I went on more gently, "That's my bed, you see; yours is over there." The bare mattresses on the lower bunk still gaped hungrily for Andy.

She stopped short in her expostulations and got up. She did not know her way about, she was new to jail, and she could only believe what she was told. She was set on making a good impression and, as I realized only later, was someone who took what life had to give but did not beg. So she was not hurt by my remarks although she had certainly expected curiosity, admiration, and questions from us and not a prisoner ready to fight for such a trivial thing as a bed.

She reacted with a hardness I could respect, because she was hard on herself. We all broke the rule about lying or sitting on beds during the day; Andy crawled into the narrow space between the piled-up beds whenever she could, while I shielded her from the eye at the peephole. When the guard on duty failed to count three inmates as written outside, he banged on the door with his baton and yelled, "Out of that dump!" A sleepy Andy would scramble out, only to crawl back again as soon as we heard the iron gate clang behind him. The right to lie in bed was something to be fought for unremittingly, yet Helga gave up at those few words. We were together in that cell for over four months, and she spent her whole waking time on the spot she took for her own that first day: an iron stool between the piled-up beds and the table. From there she had a view of the door and the window. There was just enough room for her to sit squeezed in like an African queen on her throne, stiff and immovable, breasts and belly drooping over her thighs, feet planted firmly on the floor, her back against the wall, one elbow wedged against the bunks, the other on the edge of the table. When it was cold, she did not move to the lukewarm radiator but wrapped a blanket round her body and went on sitting there. At the end of those four months her elbows were rough and chapped, and one day in the shower room she found her buttocks narrowed to a calloused ridge like a monkey's ass, deformed by her prolonged immobility.

Instinct warned me not to obey the prison code of decency toward newcomers; I was ashamed of myself, and yet surprised that Helga changed her role so quickly. She had burst into the cell like the goddess of revenge and suddenly she turned skittish—there is no other word for it, because she was too overweight to be girlish. In a clear fluting voice several notes higher than her opening outburst, she introduced herself, "I'm Helga," and held out her hand in a charming and refined gesture. I pointed to Helen, who had understood nothing of what was going on, merely watched Helga's impressive performance timidly from her corner. Seeing it was her turn, she murmured politely, "Helen."

"I'm Eva," I said then, and Helga burst out as quickly as if she was trying to get in first: "Eva Kantůrková!" and her round blue eyes, her best feature, seemed to be embracing me.

Nobody is ever told who is going to be in the cell when they arrive. Nobody is ever told anything, so that you cannot make demands or protest in advance. "They'll tell you all you need to know," the guard will say as the cell door clangs shut, and "all" means how your bedclothes must be folded so you aren't bawled out at roll call and when your turn to clean the cell will come round. The newcomer has to find out for herself things like how the post works, when and how to get a parcel sent from home, how to get to see the doctor, and all the other things that make up the day.

"How do you know my name?" I asked.

"So it's really you!" Helga's enthusiasm rolled over my question. She might just have seen my name on the card allowing me to lie down, but I had noticed that while other cards hung openly, mine was always turned face to the wall; no prisoner on her way along the corridor was to read my name. Instead of an explanation, Helga began a long and breathless tale about a man in the apartment house where she lived who was arrested with the same group of people as I was. Bursting with sympathy, she described the day-long police search, then the arrest at night. She claimed friendship with him and told me intimate things about his family life that he would never have confided in me himself. Her recital left me with the strong impression that she was piling on the details in an effort to be believed. The woman was like a grenade that starts exploding in your hands and round your feet, and you wonder how soon the thing's going to blow up.

I had not talked about my case to anybody. As soon as my companions learned that I was accused of something far more serious than they were, and with the added distinction of political secrecy, they tactfully accepted that it would not be talked about. Even Lucy managed to restrain herself and did not tell Tony the news on the toilet phone or through the window. Her way of indicating the mystery delighted me: "We've got a lady here who's not well."

I replied to Helga quite loudly and clearly, "I did not know I was in a group."

She passed this over, too, with her cries of joy. Wasn't it marvelous that way we'd been thrown together? Her words poured out, her blue eyes shone, and she started off again about the house where she and my friend both lived, and what a sensation it had been when the police came. All at once in that spate of wonderful coincidences she let drop the name of her defense lawyer. Naturally he was my lawyer too. That was certainly a coincidence, but its very innocence made me wary about the rest. This woman knew who I was, said she sympathized with me, was friendly with a man implicated in my case, shared the same lawyer and now the same cell. Before long we'd be finding we were second cousins! It was too good to be true, or to be a good thing. Enthusiasm is a bad counselor even for people who are otherwise cunning enough. In that first conversation Helga had said things that would normally take weeks to emerge.

"I hope you don't mind my asking . . . Don't take it personally, you can't choose who you'll be eating with and sleeping with in jail, but I *would* like to know how you got this cell. There was no empty place here, you see, and they had to move Andy out to make room for you."

"All that fuss about a Gypsy," Helen said fretfully. "You might as well know she's a nigger lover."

Helga explained what had happened, so reasonably and without taking offence. That night in the transfer cell she'd overheard two girls talking. They'd slashed their wrists and there must have been a third who'd died, because when they were taken out in the morning they were joking with their guard about whether they'd be let out for the funeral. Their wrists were bandaged and they looked rough and shameless. "I was terrified, so I asked to be put in a cell with decent people."

It sounded so plausible, except that it is the prison office that allots cells; and as I found out when I checked up later, no officer had ever been known to change that decision. It involved a great deal of paper work. "A guard changed your cell?"

"I don't know who she was; a blond, standing on the stairs. I told her about those two." Soon she was able to point the blond out to me, one of the lowest-ranking women, serving guard duty only and without any contact with the cells.

"So it was she who told you my name?"

She grabbed at that broken straw. For their own sakes officers are very careful what they say in front of prisoners, indeed more so than the prisoners in front of their guards. The staff know what a jungle *their* prison life is.

"And did she tell you what I'm accused of, as well?"

And Helga answered with an emphatic smile that seemed to reproach me: "There is only one Eva Kantůrková!"

There are some things that give you gooseflesh. That woman was making one blunder after another. She could hardly have known anything about me; she may have lived in the same house as my friend, and the police search and his arrest may have aroused her curiosity enough for her to listen to a foreign news bulletin. Our names may have been given in a broadcast from the West. I knew that quite a number of us had been arrested. Why should she have remembered just my name? Curiouser and curiouser. And her overeager friendliness only increased my suspicions. My first impression was not false; instead of Andy's songs and stories I was in for months of unrelenting tug-of-war, a battle of wills locked in unavowed contest. I lived through a drama with Helga, a drama that dragged on for most of my time in prison, a stifling drama with no catharsis.

From the outset Helga took possession of Helen; but in any case the poor woman was of little account in the cell. She worried about how to satisfy her appetites, drugged herself on tranquilizers, with snakes and ladders enough to occupy her mind, and she did not care who she belonged to so long as the relationship brought with it the right to smokes. She was just a big baby needing someone to fuss over her, to comb her part straight, cut her nails, wash her back and her hair under the shower, and to stop her breaking bits of the plaster off her arm. As an ally she was no good at all. No prisoner can help revealing something about her case, and Helga must have told her something, because one day as she was searching through the Penal Code for the relevant paragraph Helen said helpfully, "It's paragraph 250 you need."

Helga snapped angrily: "Shut-up, you stupid clot!" Paragraph 250 deals with fraud. That was the last time Helen intervened.

Describing other people, I try to see them as they see themselves, but it is difficult to see oneself as others see us. I must have looked ridiculous, doing exercises every morning, standing on my head like a yogi to relax during the day, not bothering about the things that mattered to the others, like meals, but washing several times a day in cold water, keeping silent when they chattered, reading whenever I could—and writing. Helen was suspicious of my writing until she made sure it was only a long letter home, in daily installments. I am reserved rather than outgoing, and most of the time absent-minded as well.

For the common criminals, the political prisoners are both obvious and mysterious. That they are "agin the government" is obvious; it is something that makes them popular and earns them something like silent admiration and respect. "What are you in for?" I was asked at the dentist's by a girl with a long list of housebreaking offenses; "Hell, I wouldn't change with you, however much you paid me," was her reaction. In many ways, though, political prisoners seem mysterious. For instance, every morning I was taken away for interrogation, returned to the cell for the midday meal and taken away again after that. The others spent their entire day sitting in the cell; Helen was not questioned at all, the police station scene seemed to have been enough. Helga was only taken for questioning four times in all. Before leaving them in the morning, I rolled their cigarettes. Neither of them knew how to do it, and for the moment they only had loose tobacco. I never talked about what went on during my hours of questioning, coming back tired out with nothing to say, not even curses.

From our cell I could see the window of the interrogation cell, and when it was open I knew they would be coming for me. Helga watched with excitement. How she would have loved to encourage me in a swearing match! My things were at their mercy now Andy was no longer there to guard them for me; and later, when Helga had turned against her, Helen told me the other woman had read through all my papers while I was out of the cell. That did not distress me, for my letters had been read by my interrogating officer before ever they reached me, and there was nothing there to hide. The case of the French couple who came to spend Easter in Czechoslovakia was well known. At the frontier, the police, obviously alerted beforehand, found books and magazines hidden behind the lining of their car. Some of the parcels were addressed to individuals; among the books were some of mine that had been published in the West, and in some of the magazines were articles I had written on Solidarity and Lech Walesa. That was why I was in prison: Paragraph 98, subparagraph 1: plotting against the state, sedition. Penalty: from three to ten years.

Once when I came back from questioning in an angry mood, Helga was so happy—at last! She described her own interviews as loud and angry quarrels, and said she had called the officer an idiot. I had my own opinion about my interrogating officer, but he was certainly no idiot. My reticence angered her; but even outside I had never indulged in cheap abuse of the regime and all the less so in jail. I did not laugh when she told jokes against the regime; at most I reacted by telling her to be more careful, for the cell was certainly bugged.

Deafened by the impact of Helga, a few days afterward I collapsed again; they were bad attacks, as though my overloaded nerves had blown a fuse. Nerves have their own way of getting back at you. Unsuspecting and unaware of what was happening even during the attacks, I passed out, and came to myself lying in an ungainly heap on the cell floor, feeling like death. Maddy said my eyes were open all the time I was unconscious, and so she thought I was dead. Again it was a Saturday when it happened, undoubtedly because of Helga. It needed Maddy to get the doctor to me, or Andy to put me to bed with damp cloths on my head. Helen was not in a state to notice anything, and while Helga watched me with close interest, she did nothing. I complained to the guard in charge of our corridor that I felt ill, and all he said was, "You're allowed to lie down during the day, so put on your elegant pajamas and lie down." Those elegant pajamas had no elastic at the waist and big holes torn over the thighs. Thus appareled, when the trusties brought our meal round I demanded the doctor, barely conscious of their contemptuous glances. The doctor did not come, and Helga was loud in abuse of the way the prison was run. It was Sunday morning before he came, and all that time she kept up her noisy tirade. She did not soak my towel to relieve me, though. Her feigned indignation was wearing me down, and I realized that whoever she really was, I was going to have a tough time with her.

Reticent as I am, I was forced to accept that Helga was creating a spate of details to build up for me the desired picture of herself and her case. She was like a river in flood or, perhaps more precisely, like a tank driving straight at me. From time to time I would wonder whether I wasn't imagining things; surely I couldn't be worth all that trouble? But she wouldn't take such pains to impress Helen, and there was nobody else. Was she inventing the story for her own sake, I wondered, so as to fit in with me? There are people who involuntarily adapt to those around them, with no conscious intent. I felt that perhaps Helga was too ambitious and too domineering to be able to admit the simple truth about herself. It was this faint hope that her need to make up stories would turn out to have a natural explanation that restrained me from using what I suspected as a weapon. Then, too, the atmosphere in the cell was heavy enough without my sparking off an open conflict. How could she have gone on living side by side with me, literally, if I had let her know that she had given herself away? And in any case, it was interesting to see how that sort of thing was worked in prison.

Helga had a real gift for invention, and she was good at it. The story she made up for my benefit did not have too many gaps or illogical twists; with her cunning and insistent eloquence she could have got it past any average TV producer. Andy liked making things up; practically everyone in jail does it to some degree, either in self-defense or because they have no sense of truth or of reality. While Andy made up stories that let her live a life of love, Helga's inventions served her practical goal of getting on in life. Not a work of art, but what artists call potboilers. Helga's potboilers were effective. She was an old hand. Even if she *had* invented them because she was ashamed to show me her real self, she gave herself away by the very kind of story she made up. It was a strange contrast: I could give myself up to Andy's fairy tales without stopping to wonder where fact ended and fancy began; it didn't matter, because she was still Andy even in her poetic fantasies, just as Helen was herself in the dreams she wove.

With Helga my suspicions were constantly alerted. If she had only felt ashamed (or pretended to), she could have said she'd cooked the accounts of the pub she ran, or that she'd knocked a child down driving her car. She laid the politics on too thick, in order to put over what she thought I would expect; but whoever had told her what I expected had not done a clever job. If she had pretended to be a small-scale embezzler, I would not have paid much attention to my suspicions and would probably have believed her. But her tales so neatly put forward the things she wanted us to talk about. We simply *had* to have friends in common (all the people she asked me about! that she lived in the same house as a man I knew was an added bonus for her); she *had* to tell me a life story I could sympathize with; our conversation *had* to come round every day to subversive matters. (Was I to give away to her the things I managed not to say during those hours of questioning?) I watched her trying so hard to get me to play her game that I felt sorry for her, though she sickened me at the same time. It reminded me of a story by Jan Beneš about a political prisoner sharing a cell (in Ruzyně!) with a simple-minded countryman who told dirty stories and tales of village life in thick dialect and said he was in for rape. When the hero came up for trial, who should be there to testify to his subversive views but the "rapist," shorn of his dialect and his countrified ways and no longer half-witted. In real life things are not done so blatantly, but there is not a single political prisoner who has not experienced something of that kind.

It is hard to say whether Helga's inventions were her own; I was fascinated by her picture of the last thirty years of our history, which could have been taken from any of the novels and magazines published today with official blessing. The family story she gave me was the quintessence of that literature, with no enlivening detail, no original touch. It taught me that even the grimmest horror can become a dead stereotype when deliberately misused, in literature and elsewhere. Poor Helga! If she had told the truth about herself, she would have felt better; and she might have won me over. I might even have joined her and cursed a bit.

Her story: she was of a good family—good, that is, before 1948, a family with strong Masaryk traditions. Not that she knew much about Masaryk, except that the portrait of the Father of his People hung on their wall; I would have said her philosophy of life was too amoral for a follower of Masaryk; it was closer to that of the reactionary manufacturer class of his day. Her father had aristocratic Polish blood on his father's side (strange how Poland kept cropping up, just when Solidarity was fighting for its existence). His father, her grandfather and the husband of that Polish countess, was a headmaster. Helga's other grandmother was a sister of Švehla, leader of the land-owners' party whose estate was not far from Prague, in the little town where grandfather's school was. Mother had come down in the world when she married Father (apart from that aristocratic Polish blood!) but it was a love match. She lived in the manor house studying singing and the piano and had fallen in love with the schoolmaster's student son, seven years her junior. Now she was seventy-six and he was sixty-nine.

Helga's mother was well over thirty when Helga was born; she had not wanted to sacrifice her career as a singer by having children and changed her mind only because of exceptional circumstances. Although Father was no more than the son of a schoolmaster, he had risen to be a diplomat, and in spite of the right-wing affiliations of her mother's family, he was one of Beneš's close collaborators. At that point, if I were the TV producer, I'd cut something, either Švehla or Beneš; both together would take too much explaining. To continue: after Munich her parents went to London, the mother's operatic career was forcibly interrupted and so two children were allowed to appear; both Helga and her brother were born in London. At the end of the war, by then with the rank of ambassador, Father returned home with President Beneš and was sent to Yugoslavia. He helped to put together the Little Entente. Helga was not quite sure whether he did that before the war or after, but she knew it had something to do with Yugoslavia. I was almost sorry she made that mistake in history. At the time of the Little Entente, her father could not have been more than seven years old. Indeed, I wished she would not give me so many chances to trip her up.

After the war Father worked with Jan Masaryk and knew plenty about his mysterious death. After the Communist takeover in 1948 Father was one of the first to be arrested. He was tried at the same time as Dr. Milada Horáková, a leading right-wing woman politician executed for "treason" in 1948. He was lucky to get twenty years and not the death sentence. He served fourteen. Helga didn't know exactly whether he was arrested in Belgrade or in Prague, but she was sure he was wearing diplomatic uniform at the time, because that was what he had on when he came home fourteen years later, emaciated and ridiculous in that finery. Helga was still friendly with Dana Horáková, Dr. Horáková's daughter. Mother sang in opera; she was a fantastic success when they put on *The Bartered Bride* for the Americans in Pilsen. They had a house in an elegant part of Prague, there was a nurse for the children, and Helga went to ballet classes. The concrete floor of the cell thundered as she demonstrated the difference between *fouetté* and *entrechat*; she could stand on tiptoe and had she had ballet shoes in jail, she would have shown me how to walk *sur les pointes*. She taught me the five positions and showed off her leg-raising at the *barre* of a prison bed. She walked like a ballet dancer, and though she must have weighed more than two hundred pounds, the fat on her was all round the breasts and belly, and she was dignified rather than ridiculous when she performed. The grace of ballet lingered in her movements as beauty lingers in the face of a once lovely woman grown old. She said that when Mother was singing in the National Theater she was in the corps de ballet and sometimes got a small role, like the girl dancer in the traveling circus in *The Bartered Bride*. When Father was arrested Mother had to go out charring, but their faithful old nurse really kept them; as the children grew she was first housekeeper, and then mainstay of the family. Mother's people dropped her, and they were turned out of their nice house. But it was beyond me how anyone in that situation got allocated that large flat where they were still living. Mother managed to save her piano but could only sing at home. The first time Helga saw her father was when she went to Mírov prison to get his consent for her marriage, at eighteen; the arrogant mother made a scene, and Father burst into tears.

Helga managed to get accepted at technical school and then at the Railroad Engineering Faculty. By pure chance I knew something about the railroad project that she said was her first assignment after graduation (she could not have guessed any connection); when I asked her to draw the incline for me, it was not a deliberate attempt to test out my suspicions; but I was sadly disappointed when instead of a technical drawing she produced a childish sketch of two railroad lines. When Father came home after the amnesty he was first employed as a stoker and then as a night watchman. Mother could devote more time to her singing but still only at home. She practiced whenever she could, singing even folksongs in operatic style.

Yes, I know it sounds absurd, but the absurdity is not my fault; it lies in the odd scraps from which her portrait was built up. Reality is often made up of odd bits and pieces, but they are credible.

Once Helga started depicting Mother as an opera star, the thing became a caricature. Mother used a lot of makeup and a lot of perfume, dressed extravagantly, and was altogether a lady inclined to extravagant behavior. Especially the way she told everybody exactly what she thought, and then the family had to step in and smooth things over. She made a dreadful scene at the local council offices when the social service officer refused to send her for spa treatment. Father, on the other hand, was kind, and the soul of honor; truth and straight dealing was his creed. In one of his letters he wrote: "Bear up, my girlie, be brave!" Helga showed me the letter, written in a clumsy, labored hand, and that fitted, for in fact Helga's parents were the cleaners and concierges of the house where my friend lived. Father's spelling was all right, but his style was definitely not that of a retired diplomat. Nor had he ever been in prison. Nor was Dana Horáková the daughter of the executed Milada Horáková.

Helga told me she was first married at eighteen, with her father's blessing bestowed from the Mírov prison. She had a little girl, but her husband left her and later emigrated. She got married a second time, in style, the patriotic style she was so fond of assuming. Another miraculous coincidence: the wedding took place on August 21, 1968! Early that morning they heard the news of the Russian occupation, and Helga put wide sashes of red, white, and blue across the chests of the bridegroom, herself, and all the wedding guests, and marched in a proud procession to the New Town Hall, past the Central Court of Justice and round the Soviet tanks on guard there. (If I were that TV producer, again, I'd go to the Town Hall and check whether there were any weddings at all that day.)

"You must come and see the photographs," she said in her skittish voice, fondly. Her marriage was a happy one, her husband tolerant. When she stayed out too late, drinking with friends, he would come and pick her up; once she came home dressed in nothing but her slip, and he didn't mind. She tried to get me to reciprocate with stories of that kind and was chagrined to hear that my husband and I went out together when we wanted to celebrate. For her part, if her husband got drunk she'd go and help him home. Once he rang up and said he was in such and such a place, on such and such a square. It was cold and he hadn't got much on. She set out at once but could not find him. Imagine, there are two places of that name, each with a square named after the same man, but at the opposite ends of the city. What a joke! They were always having fun like that. Her husband was easygoing, but Helga liked new ideas, changing the furniture round, papering the walls, turning a cubbyhole into a boudoir. She drew me the floor plan of their flat: it was a good-sized apartment, her parents living in half the rooms, her daugther in the sitting room, and herself in the bedroom with her husband and their dachshund bitch. Her husband wrote two or three letters to her in jail, addressing her as "kitten" and describing how the dog missed her, lying on the bed wrapped up in Helga's nightie. Then for a long time there were no letters, and together we loyally cursed the censor. Her letters had not been held up; her husband deserted her and did not even come to her trial (there was only her father present). The man was not her husband anyway, and there had been no wedding on August 21. Gradually even her father's letters became fewer; her brother, who was very dear to her, did not write at all, merely adding his name to his wife's. Her daughter was the only one to write cheerful and affectionate letters. Helga said not a word about the things that really made her anxious and unhappy. How could she, when she had woven such a web of falsehood around herself? At night I heard her sobbing quietly, but she was not the type to ask for pity, and I admired the way she kept her troubles to herself. Helen could take refuge in her fantasies, but Helga's cold mind must have found the gap between the fable and the reality a painful one. She was almost likable, the way she bungled her attempts to dominate other people and life itself. She had the overweening self-assurance of those strong characters with calculating minds but no gentle feelings. They are incapable of seeing themselves as they are, unhappy people whose bold schemes never succeed for that very reason. Now she had been left alone to face the consequences of her scheming.

The way she presented her case to me was this: she was the

engineer in charge of the Holešovice railroad project, which involved accommodating the railroad lines to the overpass system being built for a new highway. She had been arrested at work on a Saturday, when she was directing a volunteer shift. She'd been questioned at police headquarters in Bartholomew Street without respite, over Sunday and into Monday.

"Didn't they take you to the cells for the night?" She did not even know there were cells there.

"You mean they questioned you all night as well?"

"Yes, all night, both nights."

"And they didn't bring you anything to eat?"

She was brought to Ruzyně on Monday and that was when she had her first bite of food. I would not like to praise our security police, but I can say with a clear conscience that what she said was impossible. Nor had she given sufficient thought to explaining why her arrest was so urgent that they had to question her so pitilessly. The reason she gave for her arrest was not so serious as all that: she had signed a subordinate's application for leave and then given him permission to extend his holiday. But he and his wife and family had defected while in West Germany. She was suspected of knowing his intentions and covering up for him. So long as such cases do not involve robbery, murder, or the betrayal of state secrets, they are dealt with summarily, outside.

In time she realized that suspicion of involvement in somebody else's defection was hardly enough to make her case as important as she wanted me to believe it was. (In fact, her real case was so notorious that guards came to get a glimpse of her through the spy hole!) And so she described how the terrible weather had turned her into a saboteur. It really did pour with rain all through July, and Ruzyně itself was flooded; the drainage of the Holešovice site was not finished and it soon resembled a bog where the railroad lines would not hold up. The papers we got in the cell were full of the damage caused by the heavy rain, including reports on the state of Holešovice, and she read the weather reports avidly as day by day the rain augmented her guilt. The bogging down of the railroad project was of course due to the way things are run on every building site in the country: the builders want their annual bonus, especially those at the top (whose bonus is fatter); the inspector for the state investment office closes his eyes to all the shortcomings (he wants his bonus, too) and together they agree on a date by which everything will be put right. The final handover is signed, both sides have fulfilled the plan and get their bonus, while the figures go to swell national statistics and everybody is happy, right up to the government departments concerned. In this case the shortcomings were not made good during the first three months of the year because you don't mix concrete at 25°F. below zero; in April there was no labor force available, and now Helga was in jail for letting someone go on a holiday that had turned into emigration. Now her colleagues were cunningly blaming the "sabotage" of the Holešovice project on her and she couldn't defend herself because she had no access to the documentation. One day she came back from questioning in a good temper: she had insisted on expertise by someone from the Ministry. Then the next time, she came back furious: she had been confronted with a man who had been trying to get her job for years and was taking this heaven-sent opportunity to give evidence against her. And so here she was, with sabotage added to the crime of helping others to defect. One more wonderful coincidence: I came under Paragraph 98 of the Penal Code (sedition) and she under Paragraph 97 (sabotage). What could bring us closer together? She was so inflexible that after her preliminary appearance in court (an experience that is bound to shake one), she gave me a long account of the proceedings that bore no resemblance to what actually took place. All for my benefit: what the prosecutor said and what the witnesses said. The case had been adjourned for defense counsel to put forward expert opinion. In fact, Helga had really worked in a builder's office, as a draftswoman, and Helen admired the calligraphy when Helga wrote letters for her.

There was one feature, though, that was common to both the real and the imaginary Helga: her philosophy of life. She was violently anticommunist and violently patriotic; in both cases her words were loud but her actions tame. Her "national" politics were a caricature in solemnly pronounced commonplaces. When people take to drink, the nation is going to the dogs. Theft and bribery are everywhere. The nation is corrupt. The family is the mainstay of the nation. All her views were generalities tacked on to the word "nation." She disapproved of people who emigrated; they betrayed the nation. She hated Gypsies; they were pushing their way into the nation. The nation would only be saved by people of enterprise. She herself showed enterprise enough, wherever the regime left an opening: her daughter went to high school, so of course Helga was the chairwoman of the Parent-Teacher Association, arranging outings for the pupils and nights out for the staff. Besides that, believe it or not, she was a member of the executive committee of one of the noncommunist parties. Invited to join the Communist Party in 1970, she had joined the other, just to spite them. In a dizzy political career she became the most popular member of the executive committee. The papers had written about her; she organized a trip to Poland for the committee as soon as Solidarity was formed and was one of her party's candidates for election to the All-Party National Council. And she was a magistrate, hearing traffic offenses. That last claim may even have been true.

"Why on earth did you do that, with your opinions?"

"Don't you see?" she replied loftily. "To help people!"

Help them to what? Help them to go scot-free when they'd caused an accident? She said she'd helped her now-defected subordinate to get his driver's license back without waiting for the court to sit, so that he could take his car on that holiday from which he did not return.

"Things will go better if we have our own people in the right places." Yet, illogically in view of the "help" she gave to offenders, she was indignant about the bribery that goes on in the courts of "justice." The cases of corruption she talked about quite openly were truly shocking, but I refrained from comment. I had no intention of bribing my judges. One day she used the fact that she was a magistrate to convince me, quite cleverly, that what she had been telling me about her case was the truth.

The mail was brought round at four in the afternoon, and as the guard drew nearer the shutters went clang, clang on cell doors. How miserable it was when the shutter did not open! How hopes rose when it did, how anxiously each of us listened for her name to be called, and how those hopes fell when there was nothing more than an official letter announcing a further remand. That day Helga got a writ to appear in court, a form that can be recognized at sight; she just glanced at it and said: "So here it is! I'm going to be suspended from office," and explained that she could not be tried in court so long as she was a magistrate. She spoke with such authority that I was shaken; I do not know what the law says about the prosecution of magistrates. They are publicly elected and perhaps they really do have to be suspended by a court of law before they can be tried in one. Together we talked about how she ought to behave when her colleagues, whose sins she knew so well, sat in judgment on her. She wondered who was likely to volunteer for the shameful ceremony; who would manage to avoid it; and who would maintain a benevolent neutrality. By the time the day came round, I was as excited as she was. Prisoners who are to be taken to court are waked up by the night guards half an hour before the siren goes in the morning. We were both awake the moment the trolley rattled into the corridor with bread and rye coffee for those to be tried that day. The shutters in the cell doors rattled and you could count how many cases were coming up that day. The trolley came nearer and nearer—and passed on. Helga cursed furiously all morning: they were unfrocking her behind her back! After all the work she'd done for them! The hours she'd spent in court! Her case was timed for eleven; the shadow of the bars on the cell windows opposite ours was our sundial, and at eleven Helga kept a minute's silence in memory of her office. Fraud is an art, dear readers! The woman never stepped out of her chosen role. The bare truth of the matter was that she was accused in a local court of embezzling tens of thousands of crowns, and the writ form had been used to inform her that her presence at court was not necessary, as she was already in custody.

I said that I lived through a drama with Helga, but for the first two months I kept my suspicions to myself and the possible conflict between us was well hidden. It worked silently in her anger at me for not playing along, for not behaving as she expected me to, and in my constant care not to be taken in by her. Reasons for conflict were piling up and there was no knowing when it would break out. Helga devoted all her energy to building up the tension; not a day passed without some sort of a trap being set for me. By being careful not to be caught, I got the upper hand; and it was up to me to decide whether the conflict should come into the open, and if so when.

If our drama had had an audience, an unperceptive on-looker would have been bored with our uninterrupted idyll. To all appearances we were very friendly; except for that drama below the surface, our relations were indeed as ideal as can be in a prison cell. We helped each other, shared our goodies, chatted, and joked. Helga was sociable and amusing. We told funny stories about things that had happened to us, falling over ourselves with laughter. Helga had an infectious laugh and I enjoy a good chuckle; Helen sniggered shyly, never quite sure what the joke was about, poor thing. Shut up together, we might as well be cheerful. In the evening we pushed the beds together and sat with our backs to the door, the sheets rucked up to hide the cards, and gambled—Helga played passionately. We had pretty cards cut out of chocolate boxes, and when the cell was searched or when we went out to exercise, we hid them under our clothes. I was slowly getting used to Helga's appearance; when bristles began to appear on her upper lip, she would lie down on Helen's bed and the beauty salon opened: with two crossed matches I tweaked the black hairs out one by one, working downward over her chin and neck. It must have been a painful process, but she bore it without flinching. I plucked her eyebrows and tended her hairdo. We made curlers out of news-paper and scraps of absorbent cotton. They were put in every night and every morning she brushed out her thick curls. In return she massaged my aching back. In the corridor, in the cages, in the shower room, we looked like the best of friends. Ours was a "nice" cell and we gave no trouble, younger women guards would stop for an unofficial chat; the trusties gave us the best bits of soap and kept the torn sheets for other cells. Helga rewarded them with cigarettes, I handed out chocolates. Occasionally we persuaded the guard to give us books with no pages missing, and we were even taken to the shower room out of turn, along with the "shampoo girls," the trusties who cleaned the prison building and had their own privileges. Helga said our excellent behavior in the cages, and our tip-top cleanliness in the cell had earned us an extra permit for a parcel from home, but she had been told that "that writer" was not allowed privileges. The atmosphere was so idyllic that she didn't even blame me over the parcel (unless of course it had existed only in her imagination). As for the threat of our drama breaking out into the open, I must admit that I used the idyll to deceive her. For a long time she honestly thought I believed her tales, while I was secretly hoping the conflict could be avoided.

We had two soul-shaking experiences that could have brought us together. It was in August, and Helga had just come back from questioning. She, Helen, and I were moved to the smallest cage of all; it was also the worst because it was right under the water tower and the sun never reached it. You could not even see the sky, only rows of barred windows. No breeze ever reached that corner, and the bloody spittle on the concrete floor made it even more horrible. It had been raining, and while Helen soaked her cardboard slippers pattering about in the puddles, Helga and I kept to the dry patches.

Helga was terribly upset because her only real friend had testified against her. She had often talked about this woman, well-educated, efficient, with a good job, and an interesting woman into the bargain. She had fallen madly in love with a foreigner, a man who let her down because he was not the Hungarian he pretended to be, but a Gypsy. He deserted her after she had sacrificed her marriage (leaving her flat and all she had) and finally her position as well, because after he left her she took to drink and lost her job. With two children on her hands, she did not know where to turn. As we walked round and round that filthy hole, Helga told me without a hint of reproach in her voice how she had taken her friend in and helped her with money, fed her and the children, and helped out when the children needed clothes. Helga's own family had warned her not to trust the woman, but she had her own way, because she believed friendship was something precious, something that went deeper than family ties. She thought it was the drink that had made her friend betray her, selling herself for money to get more of the stuff. What Helga told me about her friend's evidence was pure invention—she had testified that Helga knew of the proposed defection beforehand—but her pain at being let down was real and unfeigned. It was in a rare moment that she let me see she was suffering. At that moment nothing stood between us. The concrete stank of filth, vague outlines of men's bodies could be guessed behind the bars, the guard "out on a limb" yelled, "Get away from that window or I'll have yer guts!" In the next cage Gypsy girls were singing, and Helga talked on softly and insistently, so softly that I couldn't catch every word. At that moment I imagined I could forgive her betrayal of me, and we could laugh it off together.

The second occasion was at night, and it was the terrors of prison that brought us together. We had been up pretty late playing cards and could not fall asleep. Helen was snoring quietly, and Helga talked in a low voice not to be overheard by the guard. That was when we both heard the sounds: whispering voices, quiet steps, stumbling feet, the rustle of clothes. They turned everybody out of one of the big cells near us, the women were standing in the corridor. That happened when a guard caught sight of a horse swinging from one window to another and came to search the cell, but there was always shouting and swearing, the guards cursing and the girls pro-testing. This time it was all unnaturally quiet. We pressed ourselves against the door, Helga with her ear to the gap by the floor. There was something menacing in those quiet voices, those dragging steps, the scraps of sound we couldn't piece together. Then we clearly heard a girl say, "That's a photo of her grandmother." She was speaking to someone in the cell, and that meant a guard was looking into their cupboards.

In the confused hum of words, whispers, sighs, quiet steps, we picked up, "Why did she do it?" Then we heard them dragging something away along the corridor, slithering horri-bly over the linoleum like a dead body, or someone unconscious. The gate clanged shut, guards came and went, and the women were still shuffling in the corridor. A man's voice said that was a bloody mess to make of things, the crime squad would have to be called in.

"You'll stay out here until they come." There was no protest-ing from the girls, nothing but inaudible whispering and shuf-fling. It was terrifying. Then the women were let back into the cell, and we never learned what had happened that night, or whether we had been reading more into those mysterious sounds than was really there. The horror we had felt together, the long slow unnatural sound of something being dragged along the corridor, that stayed with us both.

I found out the truth about Helga in the banal prison way. Even the least of offenders receives official communications in jail: the need to remand him or her over and over again is certified by the police, by the state prosecutor, and—if you appeal—by the High Court itself. The prosecutor and the judge can both prolong your remand in custody; the prosecutor may send you his case against you, you may get a writ, you may be told your sentence. Delightful correspondence. Your fellow prisoners measure your sincerity by what you reveal or hide about this correspondence, about your case. Friendships and even love affairs can grow from such revelations. "What are you in for?" is the formula of introduction to prison society; everybody has the right to ask. You need not answer, you may tell lies, but if you do lie, you bear the consequences.

The paragraph in the official communications that specifies what you are in for is your membership card. Nobody minds you telling lies about the facts of your case; indeed, that is the best way to prepare for your trial. But you will be ostracized if you make your case out to be morally better than it is. And if anyone wants you to have a bad time in jail, he or she has only to start a rumor that you are in for something more reprehensible than you admit. A woman, for example, will have it spread around that she has killed her own child.

Official papers become a fetish for most prisoners. Our fair Helen tore the essential part of the document off and flushed it out of sight, but she never destroyed the whole thing. Perhaps the prisoner feels that official correspondence gives one more weight, or perhaps one is simply afraid to throw it away. The inexperienced read those official letters over and over again, arguing with the writer as if that could change what is unjust in the document. I met an elderly prisoner everybody called Doctor, carrying a string shopping bag crammed with official letters; he was not on his way to court, or to interrogation, but to the hospital. Even those who tell lies about themselves keep their papers carefully, and whoever wants to find out the truth about them has plenty of opportunity. This is not inquisitiveness, a trait rarely found in jail; it is natural to want to know whose body you are so close to, whose breath you are breathing.

Helga (1)

It is not regarded as impolite for someone to look at your documents when you are not there; it is a way of forcing you to accept the prison code of honor. At the same time nobody has any illusions that what is found in your documents is the real truth about you. The whole business is purely formal—like other social conventions.

Helga kept her official correspondence in a large envelope, mixed in with personal letters. Alone in the cell one day when Helen was at the doctor's and Helga was being questioned, I read her official correspondence, careful not to disturb the order of the pages. It was not an honorable thing to do, and Helga reproached me bitterly for it, later. I already knew a great deal about her from other sources, without even trying, for it is a paradox of that most secret of places, prison, that it is impossible to keep a secret there. And the biggest discovery I now made was not about Helga, but about myself. Knowing so much that I did not want to accept, I had denied myself the exciting pastime of comparing Helga's fables with the reality. Something that might have fascinated me as a novelist, at home, although even then my interest would have been short-lived: she was such a clear case! In the same cell, her inner conflict was constantly before my eyes, and that was perhaps why I did not immediately note all the discrepancies. Although my mind registered them, and my feelings were upset by them, my instinct warned me to remain neutral. I did not want to create either disgust or hatred of her in my own mind. I wished I did not know, and so my subconscious suppressed my knowledge for a time; I "forgot" what I had read in her official documents, let it fade into the background. While I continued to be wary in front of her, for my own sake, I left her case to the gods. That way we could go on living side by side. If it is of any interest to the reader, Helga was a large-scale swindler who had wheedled huge sums

123

from unsuspecting victims. The Sunday papers were full of her and the "Wanted" TV program broadcast her photograph, after which many more people had come forward. Their additional claims formed the "expertise" for which her case was adjourned.

The conflict erupted unexpectedly. A guard came for Helga on Friday afternoon, and she was away at least two hours. When she brought her back to the cell the officer said significantly, "Now you'd better ask the doctor for a parcel permit." This was meant to show me that Helga had spent two hours convincing the authorities that she needed a parcel of fruit. The argument was one I had started, since the prison regulations allow prisoners to buy fruit, but the prison shop doesn't have any. Therefore, I argued, extra parcels of fruit should be allowed from outside. When the officer in charge of our floor told me a parcel of fruit was only granted as a reward for good conduct, I complained to the office of the State Prosecutor (responsible for holding me in custody). My complaint was never forwarded, but the Governor decided that rather than have complaints to his superiors, he would allow anyone in custody for more than three months to have a parcel of fresh fruit each month, subject to the doctor's consent. This had been agreed on Thursday, so that there was no need for Helga to argue the matter for two hours the following Friday. She was clever enough to see that the officer's remark was misplaced. So she told me she'd been taken for questioning.

"On a Friday afternoon?"

"Yes, just think!" she replied in disgust, what are things coming to, they won't even let you alone on a Friday afternoon.

"Your interrogating officer is hardworking, I must say. Why didn't they send one of their guards for you?"

"They didn't have time, I suppose," she replied carelessly.

Taking a prisoner for questioning is an official matter. Guards employed in the prison, which comes under the Minister of Justice, hand the prisoner over to the interrogating officer, who is an employee of the Ministry for the Interior. The interrogating officer (and the defense lawyer who comes to talk to his client) have to fill in a form giving the prisoner's full name and date of birth; the guard who accompanies the prisoner writes up all the details in a book on the prison floor where interrogation takes place, and the interrogating officer signs that he has taken the prisoner over. It is also entered into the book that the prisoner has been released from interrogation. There is complete evidence of the movements of a prisoner between his cell, his interrogating officer, or the court where he is tried.

"Our guards can't take us for interrogation just like that."

"She only took me to the corridor gate."

Should I go on asking, or should I let it go at that? I might have if I had not been so sure of myself, or if she had not been so provocative.

"Who took you over?" If she had said that the special guard was waiting for her there, or that our guard was on her way to the other wing and saved the guard coming for her, I might have swallowed it. In her unaccountable self-assurance she lied: "I went by myself!"

"By yourself?" Now I was in the saddle—a horse against a tank—and I did not know whether to be glad or sorry. If she had not made that mistake, I might have been silent much longer. It was such a terrible mistake, a mistake that could not be passed over in silence, unless I was to give in completely.

"What's funny about it?" She was angry, already aware that she had made a fatal mistake.

"How did you get through the gate?"

The law has it: if you do not correct your first mistake, you are bound to add more and more.

"The gate wasn't locked," she said shortly.

"The gate wasn't locked?" To get from the women's ward to the interrogation cell, she would have to go by the elevator or the main staircase; but in any case she must have passed three guarded and locked gates. "They unlocked the gates for you?"

"How can I be expected to know?"

"Nobody stopped you? Nobody noticed you were wandering about the prison without a guard?"

"I didn't see anyone."

I was forced to say, "Helga, you haven't been taken for questioning."

"I was, so what?"

"You couldn't have gone through the prison alone, unless you were not a prisoner . . ."

She felt I was doubting her, insulting her, and refused to reply.

"Don't forget we have a mutual friend. Don't you care what I say about you when I get home?"

That helped her to admit the truth, and she overcame her feeling of defeat, and became friendly. We said no more about the incident, because our world was overpowered by another wild force, by name Jitka Paterka.

7

PATERKA

Our fair Helen was taken away, happy with her bags of food. Nobody knew where she was going, but we all hoped it was Opava. She was old and sick, and there she wouldn't have to work. She'd be in a closed prison along with long-term prisoners who had plenty of cigarettes and even the occasional cup of coffee for her.

A short-cropped juvenile took Helen's place, yet another child with beseeching eyes . . . a neurotic, depraved but clever enough to find mitigating circumstances in the declarations of the institutions responsible for her: her father was an alcoholic and therefore his daughter had the right to be depraved, and to expect the authorities to take care of her. She was so affectionate that it was frightening; she tried to get as close as she could, a hungry little louse, on Christian name terms from the outset. She told us a hectic and not too well thought out story of grand passion. Her lover was a ward cleaner in a sanatorium on the Sazava, and out of jealousy, one of his friends had given her away to the police. She had been arrested one night in the woods near the hostel. Helga and I decided that she probably belonged to a gang that robbed weekend chalets in the Sazava Valley, because she had already been arrested twice. She was so sweet that it set your teeth on edge, and we did not know, as yet, that she was already the terror of the Ruzyně prison. You only had to say: Paterka! and the guards crossed themselves: God help us! It was enough to say her name and everyone in the cell shrieked: No, no, not here, please, please, we'll be as good as gold if you put her somewhere else! Paterka relied on psychopathic performances to obtain her release; but she had not been professionally trained, and so her performances were not successful. Helga was one of her first victims.

Fate is malevolent. Paterka had to meet our fair Helen in the transfer cell, and impressed by Helen's wonderful clothes she was only too eager to repeat what she had been told, "Beware of that full-breasted creature; she's got plenty of cigarettes but she won't share." Helga was still smarting under the knowledge that Helen had not repaid her debt, and then she had to listen to insults heaped on her by a parasitic creature who first of all looked over what we had in our cupboards and then sat down and ate up all the bread we had in reserve. O.K., if I'm miserly, so I'm miserly, and Helga hardened her heart. Paterka soon smoked all the fag ends she'd collected on her way to the cell and started begging cigarettes. Helga said, "No!" I was amazed at her firmness.

Paterka begged, wept, threatened, offered her extra fat ration (she was under age). She went down on her knees, but Helga threw her fag ends into the toilet and flushed them away, so that Paterka could save nothing to smoke. No! her voice was like a whiplash. It was the same psychological process as when I moved her off my bed, the day she arrived. No means No. No pity, no soft-hearted neighborliness. Paterka told us how men prisoners put all they had together, and everybody in the cell smoked so long as they had anything. No! Paterka told us what happened to prisoners who wouldn't share out in the prison camp: they'd be beaten up and robbed. No! Paterka tried to soften Helga's maternal feelings: her father was a drunk, and so everybody ought to help her, the victim, corrupt in spite of herself. No! Then Paterka went directly: Helga had just got a letter from her daughter and was in an impressionable mood. Paterka said: "Just imagine if your daughter were here, instead of me, and she'd be dying for a cigarette and nobody would give her anything." Helga's No! was accompanied by a flow of curses.

"You've no right to bring my daughter into it! How dare you compare yourself to my daughter! My daughter would never be here, in prison!"

"You're here, aren't you?" was Paterka's cunning reply.

"A miserable creature like you, and my daughter!"

"So I'm a miserable creature, am I? What d'you mean, miserable?"

"Miserable is just miserable. I don't have to explain."

"Shop-soiled, you mean? Just you wait till I tell the others. They'll give you shop-soiled. You think you're the only lady round here, don't you?"

That was the first time I saw Helga lower herself. "Don't you start threatening me, you . . ." and so on.

Tempers were high on both sides, when as luck would have it, Helga got a parcel from home. As always, it was packed with cigarettes, the best under-the-counter brand, and Paterka started trembling like an addict. She begged me to plead for her, "She'll listen to you, she'll do what you say," she flattered me. I pleaded for five cigarettes a day for Paterka, just for peace and quiet. I promised Helga I'd pay her back as soon as shop-day came round.

"I've only got Spartas, though," she said, "and you can't get such good cigarettes here, so you couldn't pay me back."

And so Paterka went thieving at night. When we woke up the air in the cell was thick with smoke. Helga threatened to beat her up and took all the cigarettes to bed with her. Paterka started howling like a dog. Helga stuffed absorbent cotton into her ears. When the guard on duty looked through the spy hole to see what was going on, It's only that Paterka! and passed on. So we sat up for the rest of the night, Helga guarding her cigarettes, while I listened to the howling. She was like a dog howling at the moon and kept the performance up till morning.

On the third day of unrewarded howling, while we were trying to make up for our lost sleep, the girl worked out a diabolical plan. A plan such as only an uninhibited creature could have thought up, a cunning plan by which she not only took her revenge on us, but demonstrated how very wrong in the head she was. We kept the flat surface of the toilet so clean, scrubbing it five times a day, that on Sundays we could light a fire of newspaper there and toast our bread ration; Paterka did her business there, instead of into the drain, and then crouched over her pile of shit and poked about in it with a splinter of wood. Thinking over what to write about Ruzyně and what to leave out, I decided to leave nothing out. Human misery is infinite, and it is good to take pity on misery; in prison I saw no misery that deserved pity, all the misery was despicable. Why, I do not know; perhaps prison deforms even misery. If my grossness stinks, the reader can turn the page.

When she came to our cell Paterka told us proudly that she had swallowed a hair clip; she would forget about it while she ate. She must have been half-starved, she gulped down food as

long as there was anything about—even the jam they gave us, an
artificially colored mess of turnip bought in twenty-pound cans,
and the two stale doorsteps of bread we each had each day. We
used to eat the crusts and throw the rest away, but Paterka ate it
all. We asked for more so she could go on eating, even second
helpings of watery soup. Let prison fatten her up! In between
meals she would finger her belly to decide where the clip had
got to; the intestines, it had certainly left the stomach, her
stretcher-bearer boyfriend had given her a smattering of anat-
omy. She said it was the large hair clip, and was opened out full
length when she swallowed it. We decided that swallowing even
a small clip, closed, would have meant that if it remained in her
intestines then she wouldn't be here either. There was no point
in arguing with her about it though; when she started on the
subject her pupils dilated.

Paterka had told the doctor about the clip, when she came to
Ruzyně, and she waited every day to be taken for an X-ray. The
last time she'd been in prison, she'd swallowed a pin and showed
us the ugly scar where they'd cut her open. The prison doctors
didn't mollycoddle their patients, especially when dealing with
self-inflicted injuries. Paterka was grubbing about in her shit to
find the hair clip, because if it came out then she'd have to cancel
the X-ray; because if the X-ray did not show the clip, she'd have
to pay for it and she hadn't any money. So she grubbed on. I can
think of pleasanter nightmares.

The air in the cell was motionless. The window was high up
by the ceiling and opened only the thickness of a hand, made
the air circulate quite differently from what we had learnt in
school with a lighted candle to demonstrate; cold air sinks and
hot air rises, cold air comes in and drives the hot air out. The
five-meter-high cell was divided somewhere above our heads; in
summer, when the air outside was warmer than in the cell facing

north, the fresh warm air that came in circulated above us, and to breathe it we had to climb on the piled-up beds, while the dank cold air stayed immovable round our bodies below. In winter it was the other way round. The little warmth from our breath and the central heating rose to the ceiling and escaped through the window, while the icy air from outside sank down to our level and made us colder still. Helga and I tested the circulation with lighted matches, and wondered whether it was an accident or deliberately so planned by the architect—a new prison building with medieval dungeons instead of cells! How could we get rid of the stink in our dungeon? Helga and I sat on my bed, which was separated from the toilet by a thin partition; all barriers between us fell away as we faced this new threat together, and we held eau-de-cologne paper sachets to our noses. My husband put them into every parcel he sent because we were not allowed bottles of scent. Our eyes exchanged mute proposals: Shall we kill her? How? Or shall we just push her face into the shit? Before we could decide, she flushed the mess away.

She repeated that performance three times, revenging herself on us completely. The stink hung in the air over our heads and would not go away. At roll call I reported her troubles with that hair clip, and Paterka listened avidly, hoping to be sent to hospital. The guards said grimly that young girls were always put into cells with reasonable women, it did them good. I objected that I was in custody and not employed as a governess.

She promised that Paterka would calm down; she'd been quite good last time, with a reasonable woman in the cell. Paterka remembered the reasonable woman with affection— but because the reasonable woman had shared everything with her. We were locked up again with the Paterka creature and Helga refused to be "reasonable." To give or not to give, that is the question in jail. It's not only that if you don't give of your own accord it will be stolen from you anyway; it's an existential-ist rather than an existence question, the question of how to maintain your own standards of decency, in conditions so far from decent. The decencies, perhaps, rather than decency, because they add up, while lack of decency grows in mathematical progression. Decency is sometimes strong enough to annul lack of decency. Everywhere you can find people who return decency with decency, even in jail.

"Nonsense," Helga objected. "Just remember how that old liar repaid me, spreading lies about me!"

At last they moved the Paterka creature out, but that was not the end of her. My old friend Lucy, a few cells down the corridor from us, noticed one day that the trusties who came for our used mess tins had not closed the shutter behind them properly. She pushed it back and tried to reach the doorknob. It wasn't locked! She only had to press the handle down, and the door opened, she was in the corridor, free! There was no guard in sight, not even in the office at the end of the corridor; she could go right up to the iron gate. Lucy ran up and down, dancing and shrieking and looking through the spy holes into other cells. Then she tried other doors. Helga had heard me talk about Lucy and was scared to death. The Paterka creature was in a cell opposite ours. She hated Helga, and now she had the chance to get her own back, helped by mad Lucy. Bessie was sharing our cell then, another wealthy woman—between them they had stacks of cigarettes.

At first Lucy just ran wild; when the others realized what was going on, some of them told her not to be a fool, while others begged her to let them out, too. Helga, listening with her ear pressed to the door, was sure that Paterka was shouting the loudest. If Lucy let her out the two of them would go for Helga. Helga's eyes were wide with wild, unfeigned terror. She and

Bessie started building a barricade across the door, piling the stools on the table and pushing their two beds up against it, one on top of the other. There was nothing feigned about their distress: Lucy and the Paterka creature would steal all their cigarettes! Maybe they'd beat up Helga as well! Lucy had opened more doors, there were girls wandering about the corridor, but they soon went back inside—freedom is a dangerous thing! Lucy tried to find the keys to the iron gate in the office. If only she could get out on to the stairs and down to the yard! But the keys were not there. Lucy began to try the cell doors systematically, and Paterka was banging and shouting to be let out. As Lucy came nearer Helga said desperately, "Those two mad creatures will kill us!" and she really meant it. The danger subsided a little when Paterka wailed her disappointment. Her cell was firmly locked.

"She can make Lucy mad at us, though." Helga was still anxious, straining her ears to catch the sound of a guard coming round, oh, if only they'd come and put the handcuffs on crazy Lucy. "What shocking carelessness," she was disgusted, "leaving cells open. They're paid to keep a watch on us. No discipline even in prison. What are things coming to, I'd like to know?"

I'll willingly confess that I was on Lucy's side and was looking forward to her bursting in on us. The barricade was absurd—the door opened outward. Ours was locked, though, and Lucy only banged a greeting. The "riot" fizzled out. Suppose she was caught in the corridor? She had had enough freedom and shut herself in her cell before the officer returned, wisely pretending that all the doors were locked. "There you are with your decency," Helga lectured me as they cleared the barricade away again. "If you don't hit first, you'll be beaten up."

The Paterka creature moved from one cell to another, creating unbearable situations wherever she went, either beating up the others or getting beaten up herself, until she swallowed the handle of a spoon and was taken to hospital. If they cut open that old scar, I wouldn't care to see the new one. It was not enough to prove she was a psychiatric case, though, and about Christmas time she was back in the cell next to ours. We heard the row that first evening: the girls there were real hard cases, and Paterka got beaten up. She threw one of the iron stools at the window, tore a piece of broken glass out, with the wire embedded in it, and started cutting her wrists. Some of the girls shouted about the draft coming through the broken window, the others screamed in terror at all the blood. They banged and kicked at the door for a long time before the officer came, and then we heard her taking Paterka past our door, "You should have cut your head off while you were about it."

Paterka was sentenced to a few months for "parasitic living," but she had served practically the whole of her sentence in the course of these wild exploits. When she was released from the prison camp, there was another writ waiting for her at the gate: a woman guard she had thrown a stool at, and injured, was suing her. Nan heard her telling this latest affair, in the transfer cell. Paterka was back in Ruzyně, and I felt like saying: God help us!

8

BESSIE THE HUCKSTER

They relieved us of the Paterka creature, and brought in Bessie, blessed Bessie. If our eyes were not dazzled, our ears were certainly humming. Not a young woman, older than me, small and thin; she reminded me of the little girls in fifth grade who were always either whispering and giggling in the corner or playing hopscotch or tag. I wasn't far wrong: one day when we were all three desperately bored, with nothing left to read, even Helga's passion for cards had flagged, letters home had all been sent off, and the cell was icy cold—Bessie drew lines on the linoleum floor and we played hopscotch. It was fun, especially with Helga's figure. Bessie was "a little nipper" and her agility helped to cover up the contrast between her real age and her little girl ways. She did everything at top speed: she ate fast, talked fast, tripped round the exercise cage instead of walking, hopped and skipped on the stairs. She was like lightning, and fastest of all were her hands, hands that were never idle. Bessie's hobby outside had been making rugs on patterned canvas. As soon as she got home from work, she dropped into her armchair, and her husband brought her a cup of coffee, and away flew her fingers on the rug of the moment. She didn't even switch on the TV. The rugs sold at two and a half thousand, and she made tapestry pictures as well—"Prague Castle" and "Stag at Bay" sold best.

When she wasn't restlessly hopping about or climbing or dashing to and fro, Bessie liked a good cry. Her tears came all of a sudden, for no apparent reason. Tears rolled from her short fair lashes like strings of beads; crying didn't leave her eyes red, it just washed them like a tiny shower of rain and made her feel better. "I like a nice little cry," Bessie was smiling again, wiping the tears from her cheeks with the edge of her hand, "then I feel all right again. It's better to get the sadness out of your system. It only brings on heart attacks and stomach ulcers."

Even better than having a good cry was a heart-to-heart talk. Just opening her eyes in the morning was the signal to begin, and she did not stop until she fell asleep. She slept well and would wake up refreshed from the night, light a cigarette, and start talking. She talked to herself until one of us woke too, and that gave her good enough reason to go on talking. Her technique was the inner monologue: whatever passed through her mind was on the tip of her tongue. You might think spoken words are much slower than thoughts, which spin wordless, leaping from one idea to another like signposts; but Bessie was still at that happy stage of childhood when the human mind was not yet burdened by thought, but simply registered sensations.

"Now I'll sit down and shuffle the cards. Ow! The stool's so cold it's freezing my bottom, and it's hard, too, the beastly thing. Would you lend me your pillow? Thank you, now how many do we deal? Thirteen? I always forget, two, two, two, four, four, four, I can smell something, burned onions I think. I smell the smell of goulash soup. It's Friday today, isn't it, that means soup for supper, mmmm, nice goulash soup. Can you smell the onion? six, six, six, what's that? it can't be eight, when did I deal five and six? Here, let me count my hand, one, two, three, four, five, six. Yes, you're right." And so it went on all day long.

Bessie dashed about, rummaged, chattered and lit cigarette after cigarette; smoking was part of the fun, and sometimes she had two going at once without noticing it. Could I object? Could I beg for mercy? Tell her there were three of us, the cell was tiny, what if we all . . . it was hopeless. For her to have mercy somebody would have to hit her on the head first. Only once did I try to stop her talking: I forbade her those long descriptions of her excretory processes. She gloated over them with puckish delight and was offended when I said, "It's bad enough to have to stink each other out; talking about it only makes it worse."

She pouted: "What's wrong with it, I'd like to know? You're too fussy for words. At home I leave the loo door open so Willy can help me. 'Push properly, Bessie,' he says, 'spread it nice and wide and push hard, dearie, you'll soon feel better.'"

"Willy's your husband and he loves you, that's different." Even Helga was on my side, although she and Bessie had taken to each other at once.

Bessie had no clear idea of herself as a person, and she would have been incapable of working one out. She simply caught on to every subject that came up in conversation and added something from her own experience. I still cannot decide which is worse: descriptions of excretion or words as the excretion of the mind. Body linen is dirty, the sweat and pus of life clings to it, our evil deeds, our humiliation, and we each try to wash it silently with our spittle. Bessie had no idea that anything she chose to say might seem dirty. She lived without context, never judging her actions, simply taking each moment as it came. She would pass judgment on others, while convinced that she herself could never have acted otherwise than she did. She was therefore never in the wrong; the fault lay with other people or with circumstances. Perhaps that was why she was so sure she could reveal anything and everything. Perhaps it was not just that she was stupid. Immaturity confers a strange kind of self-assurance, and the self-confident victims of circumstances are so hard to shift because they can always find something or someone to blame.

Until she was thirty-seven or thirty-eight, if my calculations are right, Bessie had a hard life. Her mother gave her no affection when she was little; she was a domineering woman who wanted all their father's love for herself. There were two children, Bessie and a younger boy, and they were happiest not at home with mother, but at the neighbors', a childless doctor and his wife who spoiled them a bit and let them play. "They treated us like their own children," Bessie liked to remember them. Sometimes the children even spent Christmas there.

Not that mother had no time for them; she did not go out to work and her home was easy to manage, but she was interested only in herself. Daddy loved his children, especially Bessie, but he was henpecked and scared of his wife, and unlike her, he had no time to spare.

He worked in the postmortem lab of a hospital, a good job, putting the corpses back in shape for the coffin. He helped out in the wards as well, and except for the head doctor, he had worked there longer than anybody. Daddy was proud of his job and used to work late and even on Sundays; he knew more about sickness than the head nurse, and more about corpses than the pathologist. When patients didn't want to bother the doctor, they'd come to him for first aid and even for medicines. He brought lots of useful things home, things the dead left behind, and what the bereaved gave him, or patients who were lingering on. He was certainly highly respected.

Bessie's parents had a little house, two rooms upstairs, three down, with a small garden, but both children left home early. Bessie married against her parents' wishes; daddy did not approve of his son-in-law, though mother was perhaps secretly glad to be rid of her daughter. Bessie broke off relations with them and for years they did not know that they were grandparents. Bessie was too obstinate to speak up first, and her mother did not care. It was only daddy who sometimes helped Bessie out with money. It may not have been for love that she married in the first place, but as a protest, out of spite. All her life Bessie jumped at the first thing in sight, never complicating things by waiting to see what . . . She longed to get away from her mother, and what else could a girl do than get married? And so Bessie took the first man that happened along, and ever afterward blamed her unhappy life on her mother.

She and her husband went far away, into the border regions where life looked promising. The Germans had been driven out and their little businesses were taken over. The newlyweds were given a photographer's shop to run, complete with laboratory, the only one for miles around. Not a bad beginning. Those were the early days of ascetic socialism, but Bessie did not see it that way. She discovered what it was that made her tick, her talent, and her salvation: she was a born businesswoman. She might be as stupid as you can imagine in everything else, but when it came to enterprising ideas or the energy to put them into effect, no one could beat her. If she had had a more satisfactory husband, she might never have discovered her talent; but he was a lazy good-for-nothing womanizer who drank. Her family life fell apart and so she clung to the only thing she could, the studio. She may have inherited the property instinct from her mother, so proud of her house and furniture, linen, silver, and china; or it may have been the stream of daddy's "gifts" from grateful patients and sorrowing relatives that made their life so much easier. Whenever she could, Bessie locked the shop and took refuge in the mountains. The firm's books balanced thanks to identity card photographs, weddings and funerals, children of all ages and high school notice-board snapshots. What she photographed up in the mountains was her own private business. She contracted with the managers of ski chalets to photograph their dances and ski parties. Who wouldn't like a picture of himself or herself on skis? It was terribly hard work, scrambling about ski slopes all day and looking on at dances in the evenings, then going down alone in the dark, through snowdrifts and in biting frost. Coming home late at night, she sat up developing and printing, to get the shots back up to the chalets before lunch next day, before her customers left for home. "It was good to see them happy about their photographs. I could have sold far more than I was able to make in one night."

"It's a profitable line," Helga said knowingly.

"I enjoyed it."

"Was it taking the photographs that you enjoyed?"

"No, that was an awful bore and even worse was getting the prints out right. I was good at it, but I didn't enjoy it. What I liked was the fun of the thing, not knowing whether the shots would turn out, whether the customers would like them, and whether I'd get up there in time anyway."

She enjoyed her own skill too in managing the firm's material so as to have enough left over for her private commissions. Making up the firm's accounts was a monthly adventure. How much of her mountain successes should she credit to the firm, and how much could she keep for her own pocket? Unaware of her pioneer role, at the very birth of our socialist economy with its policy of deliberate destruction of private initiative, Bessie helped to set up that subsidiary economy, that underground system of small private enterprise within the closed state economy, ever more in demand, indestructible because forever flourishing. And in any case, it was much more fun going up to the chalets than sitting in the shop waiting for the occasional identity card customer, or newlyweds who wanted to hang evidence of the fact over their beds.

What about her husband? Her son? Her husband was away for days on end; and when he did come home, he was drunk and hit her. It would have been a cheerless existence without those expeditions. A neighbor took care of the boy when she was out late; once he set out to meet her, missed her in the snow, and by the time they found the child asleep in a road repair crew's shack, he might have had frostbite.

"Some nights when I got back it was dark, the street lamps were lit, and he'd be standing there in that vast square, such a tiny figure. . . . He was so frightened, the sight of him drove me mad, he was so pitiful. He had a terrible childhood, terribly unhappy."

"Couldn't you have left your husband?"

"Where could I go? It'd have been the same anywhere else. Alone with the boy I'd still have had to leave him like that."

"Did you have to go so far away, up the mountains?"

"What sort of a life would we have had without it? Sitting at home and crying because my husband was a drunk? I had to make money for the child as well as myself."

"Couldn't you have gone back to your parents?"

"To be laughed at? Never on your life!"

Grown up now, her son reproached her for that unhappy childhood, but Bessie thought he was downright ungrateful. What else could she have done? "He ought to be sorry for me, not for himself. I worked my fingers to the bone for him, not him for me. I was the one that suffered."

"He was only a child. He couldn't change things."

"I was taking care of him, he ought to be grateful to me, and not the other way round. Now's the time he ought to repay me for all I did."

Bessie was far from thinking, as most mothers do, that their lives should be guided by what their children need. She thought the child should suffer with his mother, put her needs before his own.

She had another son, but that was after daddy had died of cancer. Mother was lonely by herself in the house and agreed to take care of the child. Robert, the older boy, continued to stay with his mother in the rooms behind the photographer's shop, with a father who was getting more and more dangerous. One night when he caught the curtains on fire and Bessie had to escape down the lightning conductor with Robert in her arms, to prevent her husband killing or maiming the two of them, the neighbor who gave her shelter called the police.

"Daddy, Daddy, don't kill my mummy," Robert is said to have screamed. Surprisingly enough, as soon as he was old enough Robert took to drink, too. For a long time Bessie heard no more of her husband, except for rumors that he was a wino, hanging round pubs and begging. Perhaps Bessie had been his only link with normal life, because after she was reconciled with her mother and divorced him, he drank so much that one night he froze to death. "I should have waited," she said, "if I hadn't divorced him, in a couple of months I'd have been a widow."

And then came her great stroke of luck—lifelong, overwhelming, the one and only: he wasn't much to look at, a short man with a rounding belly and half bald, about five years older than Bessie, full of jokes and real good fun. She had taken his photograph once, on a ski slope, and then by chance they met in a restaurant. He recognized her and they had a drink together. Bessie was in a hurry to catch her bus home. He had come to order stuff for his small-town pub. "Isn't that funny?" cried Bessie, "I've been here placing my orders, too." Their next meeting was no matter of chance. Bessie was nearing forty, and the passion aroused in her, the first in her life (you cannot count the illusions of childhood or short-lived moments in the mountains), this was IT. Even more magnificent compared to the wastes of her life before, roused by the loving caresses of her man, new horizons opened before her. Still immature herself, she had not known how to give love to her own children, but her heart opened wide to love from a real man. Bessie's arms were stretched wide; she grasped her love and held it tight. Few women have the luck to satisfy all their passions in one man—there is always either too much or too little—but Bessie found her perfect partner. Her one passion to date, that of selling and buying, buying and selling, was echoed in him. And he brought new ideas and his perseverance to that passion, and manly prudence as well. And it was he who opened up for her the second passion of her life: erotica!

Bessie left the studio and the two of them led a free life for years, until they were arrested. Her first husband was dead, the younger boy was being looked after by her mother, the older boy was in an apprentices' hostel, learning to be a cook. Bessie and Willy went hand in hand with no other responsibility than to each other: you love me and I love you. From one shop to another, one pub to another, Bessie changed her profession as need demanded: she sold vegetables, was a cashier, a pub manager, a waitress, a hotel manager, ran the kitchen, served the customers, carried heavy crates of vegetables, and all because love sanctified her labor—love that was greedy, insatiable, restless, affectionate, and lewd. At last she was a complete personality. In the shop or behind the bar she was enterprising and cheerful and in her private life she was at last a WOMAN. What woman does not experience the moment when the neuter in her gives way to the feminine?

Her husband's love revealed to Bessie the beauty of her own body. She had surely sinned here and there on her mountain trips, because she had always had a weakness for the male sex. One day she let drop to us that her mother had driven her from home because Bessie was too familiar with her father. The doctor's wife, too, decided one day that Bessie had better stop visiting them; she was "growing up" and the doctor's liking for her was a bit suspect. Sensuality is one thing and the form it takes is another. When we met in Ruzyně, Bessie was well over fifty; but in her sexuality she felt twenty, and her behavior was that of a twenty-year-old. "You are as old as you feel."

I sketched a portrait of her. The lines were not difficult, but I did not omit the wrinkles by the mouth and the nose. She threw my sketch down angrily: "I'm not as old as that!" How could she be old, if she was still loved?

"My poor dear Sweetie Pie," she wept, "what is he doing now?" Everything served to remind her of her husband. We were given a horrible mess of boiled carrots and noodles for supper, something Helga and I poured straight down the drain, but Bessie was so happy: "A hot meal twice a day! My Sweetie Pie can't complain about the food." Bessie was not much of a cook; when she wanted to send her son the traditional parcel of goodies on military service, she had to order the cake from one of her customers. So long as they were running a pub, it was Sweetie Pie or the cook who did the meals. When they were managing a shop, they went out for lunch and in the evenings Bessie cooked a packet soup with some noodles. On Sundays, before she got up her husband would go in the car and fetch a take-out dinner. Bessie enjoyed prison food, licking her mess tin clean like a soldier. She had been so keen to do business that by the time they shut shop, there was nothing worth eating left in the local restaurant. When they ran a pub themselves, either there was nothing left after they'd served their customers, or else they sold the best portions to take-out customers. And now Sweetie Pie was in jail and had two hot meals a day!

Sweetie Pie patted her bottom affectionately in front of the customers, what do you say to that, ladies, just fills my hand nicely, doesn't it? and Bessie squealed delightedly. Bessie was proud of the attention her womanhood was attracting at last, full of the grace of love.

The very first day in prison she started looking for him in the labyrinth. They had been arrested together and spent the first night together in a cell in the local jail; they had been driven to Prague in the same car and in the transfer cells they were close enough to throw cigarettes. Then they were separated; they did not know that Ruzyně was such a vast place and had arranged that when Willy was in the exercise yard he would cough under her window. Hundreds of men and woman shuffled past under our window every day; there were a hundred and forty women on our floor alone, and there were eight other floors. It was cold in the cells and everybody had a cough. We sat below the window listening carefully for a cough that sounded different, then Bessie would climb up to the window and try to pick out Sweetie Pie. Of course he could just as well be coughing under the windows of the opposite wing, or he might have given up when he realized how hopeless it was. Then Bessie broke the rule we had made for our cell, and started shouting out of the window: "Hello, Hello! This is Bessie. Who are you? Is my Willy with you?"

There were plenty of willing voices raised in reply. Bessie recognized several young men from the same town, and her womanhood was flattered even though she had not found her beloved.

When Bessie talked to any man, from the guards to those twenty-year-olds, her voice took on coquettish overtones. Whoever the man was, she acted like a woman aware of her sexual value. It was amazing, because she was not at all attractive: bony, with sticks instead of thighs, no front teeth, a shrunken mouth, thin hair with no sheen that came out in handfuls, so that she did not wash it for fear of losing it altogether. Only Sweetie Pie could have seen any attraction in her, but the woman in her did not realize that. "This is BEssie," the siren called from our window, "B-E-E-E-S-S-IE-IE-IE" she lovingly dragged the syllables out. She was incapable of learning the deaf-and-dumb alphabet, and shouting was not enough; so she had us cutting out capital letters from newspapers. Helga and I put them together to form words, and Bessie pressed them against the window screen. Once there were six young fellows in a sixth-floor cell just facing ours, and they could see right in; Bessie got to know them and in the evening when the lights went on and it was time to wash, they would start singing. We held a blanket up to make a screen behind the toilet, and Bessie danced in front of it, naked. She felt so happy to be a woman; the love which came to her late in life had driven out all that was neutral in her.

Pubs and hotels are hotbeds of eroticism; Bessie and her husband ran a beautifully restored old inn, in a popular beauty spot, with rooms to let and an erotomaniac as cook. A fine figure of a man, he needed more than one woman a day; and all his women loved him and wanted to keep him. The staff had far more trouble covering up for the cook than they had running the hotel. They had to stand guard when he was upstairs with one woman so that the next on the list would not find out. He was sometimes imprisoned for hours because his next appointment was already sitting in the bar, and then Sweetie Pie had to cook lunch and everything was at sixes and sevens.

"Wasn't that bad for business?"

"The cook was worth it."

In the evening, when the guests had eaten and drunk and gone to bed, and only the locals sat on in the bar, the cook would invite them to join the staff in the kitchen, buy everybody a drink, and start the betting. "He put his cock on the table," Bessie related. "I didn't know what was going on at first, and why they were all crowding round. Sweetie Pie said, 'Don't come over here, Bessie, you'd get a fright.' Then I heard the cook say a hundred crowns if you touch it and five hundred if you kiss it."

"Did it scare you?" Helga asked.

"Well, it was a sight when he got the horn, all purple it was, everybody was amazed at the size of it."

"Did anyone win that hundred crowns?"

"Men don't like the idea, they just looked and looked, but the waitress always got her money. She was a good-looker, about thirty-five, a real hot piece of goods. She'd done time for trying to murder a man, but nobody ever mentioned it."

"Didn't she try for the five hundred?" Helga was all curiosity.

"She was a clever bitch. She laughed and said yes, but only in her room. The cook whacked his big cock on the table and undressed her with his eyes, all het up. He was a stallion, all right. And he sent our sales up. Those village oafs would have sat there drinking all night, better than the telly, they said it was. In the end they got so tight we had to throw them out."

Out of season Bessie let the rooms upstairs for secret lovers' meetings; it was a quiet spot, married men would bring a woman (usually married too) by car and be let in at the back door. There was one regular couple, an official from the town, with his secretary. Bessie had a hole bored in the door of their room and the staff took turns to stand on a chair and peep at them in bed. The cook said the man was hot stuff, but Bessie described the erotic scenes in a disapproving voice. She would never do anything of the sort herself. Her Sweetie Pie made love to her properly, decently.

"Did you know the couple?"

"Of course, and I knew his wife and her husband, as well."

"Suppose they'd found out they were being watched?"

"That didn't worry us. That's the sort of thing nobody ever tells."

"Somebody might give it away without meaning to."

"So what?"

"They felt safe with you, and they paid for it."

"It was the room they paid for."

"And your discretion."

"Why shouldn't I look if there was anything worth watching?" and she chuckled.

Then letter day came round, and Bessie had to decide who she'd write to. Not to her mother in the hospital. Mother wouldn't mind getting a letter from prison, but the nurse who brought it to her bedside would find out. She'd had to pull strings to get mother into the hospital, and that might spoil it. Where could mother go if they turned her out? She wouldn't write to her older boy, either, because if his wife found out they were in jail she'd make him go and steal stuff from their cottage.

And she couldn't write to the younger boy because he was on military service, and she didn't know his address because Willy always wrote; and a letter from prison would get him a bad name. And so there was nobody else left but Sweetie Pie. Letters from one prisoner to another are always sad affairs, helplessness calling on helplessness, and the intimate thoughts are read by so many eyes. Her letter would pass through the hands of our head guard, her investigating officer, and the head guard of Sweetie Pie's corridor.

Bessie wrote: "My dearest Sweetie Pie, I miss you so much, I'm sad all alone, I want to come to you, even in the cell, that wouldn't matter. I'd just catch hold of your little pecker and play with it, I miss it so, I can't tell you how much. I'd play with it and don't think I've forgotten how, my Sweetie Pie, the little dicky-bird must be missing his pussy too." And on in the same vein for four pages. Then she signed her letter: "Your loving Bessie, take care of that little pecker, don't forget it's mine!"

She was laughing happily as she wrote, reading the best passages aloud to us over and over again, and then declaiming the whole four pages, amused by her own wit.

My sense of responsibility is often greater than my common sense, and so I said as tactfully as I could: "Don't you think . . . Won't your husband mind? . . . You don't know what kind of men he's got in his cell . . . and there's his investigating officer."

She was hurt. "You worry your head too much. What would happen if we were all like you? It's not a nice way to talk, either."

And so she sent her letter off, and after the requisite interval for all those censoring eyes to read it, our head guard on night duty, warming up on beer and on the fun he was going to have, started shouting the best passages of her letter into our corridor. Eros is indeed a mighty god: Bessie didn't mind in the least. She laughed and called back, "Jealous, aren't you?"

Bessie the Huckster

Bessie's case was not a complicated one; she and her husband were accused of receiving smuggled goods, but Bessie could not get the figures right, the way the prosecutor calculated them. Either there was a man's leather jacket too many, or there were twelve floral-pattern shopping bags too few, and the color TV sets didn't fit in anywhere at all. Bessie wanted to work out how many years they could expect to get, since it's roughly one year per ten thousand crowns, and so she sat at our little table, spectacles halfway down her nose. Whichever way she added the things up she never arrived at the sum the prosecutor put forward.

"For Heaven's sake," Helga was losing patience, "you must know how much stuff they found!" Sometimes it looked as though their joint effort was getting somewhere, and then Bessie would remember artificial flowers or something of the sort. But since she was a queen, since she was Helen of Troy and Cleopatra all rolled into one, she just put the papers away and left it all to her husband. She was so sure he would get around the district officials who had good reason to be grateful to him; and of course they'd help to get the two of them out of this mess. That irritated Helga; she was the masculine type, running both home and job with a firm hand, and she found Bessie's light-hearted womanliness all wrong. "Your husband won't be able to give your evidence for you when you come up for trial," she expostulated. "You've got to think things out properly beforehand."

The day for the final write-up of their case arrived, and Bessie was taken to hear her husband's testimony and the evidence brought against them by the prosecution. Helga was dreadfully anxious to find out the real facts about those leather jackets and color TV sets before Bessie got back. She found a hopeless muddle and cursed the investigating officer for not clearing the mess up. After the midday meal Bessie came danc-ing in, hopping and skipping like a little white goat, flushed and in the seventh heaven.

"I've seen him!" she cried as she came in at the door.

"Who?"

"Willy, of course, my own dear Sweetie Pie."

"Of course you saw him. You both have to know the case against you. Well, now, what has happened about those leather jackets? That was the biggest item, if you don't count the TV sets, and it doesn't look as though they're going to prosecute for those . . ."

"The minute I saw him I just threw myself at him!" Bessie was glowing with happiness, her gray complexion pink, and a beatific expression that made her face almost pretty.

"Who did you throw yourself at?"

"He was sitting at the table when I came in and I shouted and rushed to him. Poor thing." Bessie wiped away a sapphire tear. "He'd got such a torn track suit on, his knees showed through. Their guard's a real beast, hitting them all the time. They only have to open their mouth and he starts knocking them about. He's on the second floor but his cell doesn't look into the yard, they're bang up against the watch tower, the bengo up there can see right into their cell, they can't even get away with a fart. He's got terribly thin, too."

"Did you agree on what to say?" Helga was insistent.

"He's been sick, caught a cold and had a fever. They didn't have a bed for him the first days and he had to lie on the floor on a mattress, in a dreadful draft all night. The doctor gave him aspirin, but there's an awful rough Gypsy in the cell with him, walking about with his prick hanging out all day just to show off; and he snatched Willy's aspirin because why should the whites have all the pills and a poor Gypsy can't get high on anything, so he swallowed it paper and all, and the warder wouldn't give Willy another, said he ought to take better care, so Sweetie Pie couldn't even cure his cold, he did look awful . . ."

"Was the officer there all the time?"

"He was sitting at the next table, reading something." Bessie skipped round the cell. "I jumped straight into Sweetie Pie's lap, I wasn't the least bit shy about it." She flung her arms round my neck to share her joy. "And I didn't half make a fuss of him, I kissed him and petted him . . ."

"Did the officer let you talk things over?"

"I told you, he was reading and didn't bother. I had such a good time with my Sweetie Pie!"

"Now look here, Bessie," Helga was beginning to suspect the truth, "what were you doing all that time?"

"Sitting on his lap and cuddling up to him!"

"Did you read what that woman said in evidence against you? The one that gave you away?"

"I didn't read anything," Queen Cleopatra declared and Helen of Troy nodded assent. "I was so happy to be close to him again."

"What about your husband, didn't he read anything?"

"I didn't give him much chance, he was trying to read over my shoulder but there wasn't much he could do."

"Did you come to some sort of understanding, though?"

"There wasn't time. I'd got my Sweetie Pie in my arms! The officer was enough of a gentleman, when he saw what was going on, to go away and leave us together."

"That was real clever of you," Helga was intent on her purpose, "so then you settled everything. It would be a great mistake if your husband were to mention the leather jackets himself, at your trial . . ."

"There was no time for that," Bessie trilled happily.

"You had time enough for other things!" Helga got up from her stool, disgusted, majestic, and scornful.

The unattractive woman smiled dreamily. "I wouldn't say we'd had time enough, we hadn't, but I wouldn't say we didn't have enough time, either . . ." She sat leaning forward at my side, her bony knees pressed together and her clenched hands pressing down into her lap.

"Now what do you say to that!" Helga's astonishment knew no bounds. "Their officer goes out and gives them the chance to get together over their evidence, and all they can do is canoodle!"

"Don't you worry, we did more than just canoodle," the ugly loved one assured her.

"Did you ever hear anything like it?" The strong helpless one was flabbergasted.

Bessie and Willy were an ideal pair. They started from nothing; the first place they took was a broken-down country pub that nobody else wanted—a couple of old men for beer in the evenings and the stray tractor driver for sausage and pickles at midday. The inn itself was really old; Bessie discovered wooden marionettes in the attic, three feet high, genuine carved antiques going back to the days of the national revival a century and more ago. She kept the skeleton with the scythe, to put inside a cocktail cabinet when they got a home of their own. Anybody going for a drink on the sly would get a real shock! The pub barely paid its way, but they left it with a reputation for hard work, and then during those few years when small private enterprise was allowed to put out shoots, Willy never wanted for ideas. Then economic rigidity clamped down again, and they decided to stick to orthodoxy; but the supermarket they got wasn't a good thing. They couldn't keep pace with the customers' thieving, and so they went back to the pub business.

To that hotel with the erotic cook. It was a good place: in the summer there were people out for a day in the country, and it was a favorite place for wedding breakfasts.

One of Bessie's best stories was about a wedding. Willy got the date wrong, it was the staff's day off, and the two of them were still in bed when wedding guests started arriving. There was no meat prepared, no cakes baked, they hadn't even got clean tablecloths back from the laundry. They tried to cover up; then Willy made a clean breast of it, and all the kindhearted ladies went to help in the kitchen and the husbands took over the bar, and in the end it was one big family party. The climax of their career was a new motel on the motorway out of Prague. By that time Bessie was thinking of buying a home of her own, and she'd got piles of sheets, blankets, eiderdowns, crockery and cutlery, glass and china, tablecloths, linoleum, carpets. (She told us the trick they used to get these things without the firm's name stamped on them, but I'm ashamed to say I can't remember it.) Mirrors, too, and plenty of money—but the joy of possessing was second to the joy of acquiring it. Bessie could spend hours talking about how to make money.

Plain stealing is not a good way to get rich. Make no mistake about it, thieving gets found out. What you have to do is get rich while taking good care of your reputation. The business must always be a flourishing one: their food was first class when they ran a restaurant, the goods they stocked were first class when they ran a shop. The last had been a greengrocer's. When tomatoes came in Bessie picked them over, threw away the bad ones and wiped the rest, singly, with a cloth, before putting them on the counter. Where did they make their money, you ask? Restaurants do well on weddings, bus tours, and week-long study groups. When a bus poured fifty people into the motel's private dining room, and fifty people ordered fifty schnitzels and potato salad, you had to make money, and one party was hardly out of the door when another bus would roll up. Bessie did not let her customers linger; there were always others waiting in the lounge to take their places at the tables. It was hard work, a rush in the kitchen as well serving the tables, but it paid. A greengrocer makes on the big regular orders for school dinners, nursery schools, and hospitals; the stuff comes invoiced as Grade B but appears on the school bills as Grade A. Neither the children nor the patients suffer, because they are only sent the poorer stuff, anyway; it is the state that "suffers," paying out of one pocket into another, robbing Peter to pay Paul. And the bribes you have to hand out! To the truck drivers and their mates, the warehousemen, and—the inspectors. Bessie was full of good advice about how to get around inspectors, advice handed on by one manager to the next as a trade secret. You can't fool the drivers or their mates, though; they're the real bosses. If you don't grease their palms well enough they'll take the better stuff to other more generous shopkeepers. Sometimes it's money they want, sometimes just your signature to shady deliveries that are well underweight or below standard. And no questions asked. You trust me and I'll trust you. Willy presented their district manager with a smuggled color TV set, and Bessie always took the office girls coffee.

As soon as you get a reputation for business, others of the same ilk will gather round. Sometimes something goes wrong somewhere and somebody lands in jail, but that's all part of the game. You can make money on anything that is in short supply but in great demand. Country people keep pigs and hens, but corn for fattening is very hard to get. So someone who works on a cooperative farm will make a private deal with the district retail manager to deliver a sack or two to one or two of his shops. The corn need not necessarily be stolen from the farm's stocks;

it can be part of the man's pay in kind. The delivery does not appear on the books, and the profit is split three ways—and the customers are happy. I learned how to stretch gravy so it stays thick and creamy even if you've added water more than once; how to warm up three-day-old potatoes so they taste freshly boiled; how to stretch the local hard drink with pale tea; and how to adulterate wine. Bessie told us a story about that pale golden liquor. As the pub changed hands, successive managers took over existing stock, counting the rows of dusty bottles on the top shelf but never opening them; clean newly delivered bottles are pleasanter to handle. Until a nosy inspector took one down and got a drink—of cold tea. There's an easy way to make a profit by buying liquor in a retail shop and reselling it at the higher restaurant prices, but it's a childishly simple trick. Bessie managed alone with Willy, however hard the work was, because a third pair of eyes is one pair too many, even if a cleaning woman doesn't do anything in the shop. Bessie worked her fingers to the bone, but it pays to have the reputation for hard work. In a pub, though, you need a real team; if there's just one who doesn't fit in, you'd better give them all notice and take on a new staff. And it's a good rule not to stay in the same place longer than three or at most four years; it gets too easy to see what's going on.

Bessie's lectures revealed the narrow range of what interests people in a consumer society further deformed by socialist poverty: to get hold of anything, you have to be able to offer something in return. When Bessie got a delivery of that rarity, peaches, she kept back the finest so that she could slip across to the butcher's with them and get better quality meat under the counter, and then around the corner to the shop where winter boots had just come in. She needed them to offer in return for a tea set that a neighbor wanted and had promised to get Bessie something else . . . and so on ad infinitum. In the first volume of all lived there, but then Willy had to sack him; Capital, Karl Marx explains that social conditions bear a direct relation to the level of the system of payment. Payment in kind is what a society falls back on in conditions of material poverty and backward production relations. Czechoslovak consumers have to track down what they need like the old woman in the fairy tale: she must find grass for the cow before she will give milk for the cat, and milk for the cat before she will catch the mouse. . . . In the story all ended well, but Bessie and Willy were given away by the woman in the haberdashery because they didn't supply her in time for All Souls' Day with artificial flowers smuggled in from Poland.

And so one passion was played off against the other, and Bessie's life took a disastrous turn. She had acquired plenty of possessions, but lost her husband for those last few years when she could still have played at being twenty. As for her possessions: she had carefully packed away all the blankets and bed linen, all the stuff she had acquired in the course of business; but her husband told her that after the police search everything had been left lying about, and if she didn't get back soon, the mice would get at it. And how she feared for their money! An enormous sum; she didn't even know how much. "Willy didn't believe in savings banks; he didn't want any strangers knowing how much money he had. He carried it round with him, well, not all of it, he buried quite a lot in the garden."

"Do you know where?"

"No, I don't. I never bothered about things like that. But I do know he'd got a packet of five-hundred-crown notes on him when he was arrested. Do you think they'll have confiscated it all?"

"He could say it was what he'd got for the house."

"If it occurs to him."

"Come on, he's a sensible man."

"We didn't get as much as that for the house. And then we bought the other house."

"Well, he's not going to tell them that if they don't know it, is he?" Helga tried to calm the other woman's fears.

Ah, those houses! Now we come to the house game. Bessie and Willy, those free-living birds on the wing, had decided it was time to settle down under their own roof. They bought a tiny cottage off an old woman in a delightful idyllic village. Bessie drew the floor plans to show us. There they installed the skeleton on guard over the drinks. But a cottage is only a cottage, and Bessie wanted a house. Mother still had hers, where she lived with Bessie's younger son, while Rudolph, the elder, lived upstairs with his second wife. Bessie and Willy decided to sell the house and buy something more stylish. They managed to get an apartment in town for Rudolph, but the daughter-in-law refused to move. She wanted to live in a private house. The argument dragged on, and Bessie hated her for it. The story of the houses became entangled with the story of Bessie's family relationships.

Rudolph had married a Polish girl, had a son, then turned her out because she was sluttish, and she went back to Poland. He would not let her take the little boy; lonely, he took to drink. Bessie liked her Polish daughter-in-law, she was good-hearted and easy-going. Willy took Rudolph on as assistant cook in the motel, and they all lived there, but then Willy had to sack him; he was always drunk and couldn't be relied on. Rudolph went back to his grandmother's, with little Rudy.

"He was working in a bakery, and poor little Rudy was all by himself at home, he didn't get proper meals and he was sick. Granny was too old, she could hardly look after herself, and the child was too much for her."

"But you are Rudy's granny."

"We got a place for him in a really good children's home. It's ever so hard to get a child in there, you need connections. Then Rudolph refused to send the child away, said he'd rather Rudy died than go to live with strangers. He might just as well have let him go to Poland with his mother, he said."

"Couldn't you . . ."

"Have you any idea what it's like, running a motel? You can't guess the trouble it is."

"Couldn't you have paid someone to look after him?"

"Why me? Rudolph wouldn't listen to me when I told him what he ought to do."

Rudolph met his second wife at a dance; soon she said she was pregnant, and they got married.

"The brat isn't his, you can see that right away. She squints and she still dirties her pants, and she's two. I warned him not to start anything with a woman when he was drunk. She got her claws in him all right. We made inquiries and people said she'd been carrying on with soldiers."

Rudolph's second wife looked after little Rudy as well as her own child.

"Yes, and when we went to see them and I took Rudy some chocolate, and she took it away from him and divided it between the two of them. Then her brat ate his share as well. You're a big boy, she's only little. That's what he has to put up with all the time, because of that little bastard."

"And you only brought presents for Rudy?"

"That child's not our Rudolph's."

Bessie found a young couple with a house in the country who

wanted to move to the town where mother's house was and would even pay a good bit extra. When mother died Bessie's brother would inherit half her property, so Bessie found a way of doing him out of it. Mother made her a present of the house, stipulating that Bessie would look after her until she died. The notary public registered the transaction, and Bessie promptly pulled strings to get mother into a hospital—she had had a stroke in the meantime—and sold the house. The new owners agreed to let Rudolph and his family stay on a while, till they got ready to move into that town apartment.

Bessie had all sorts of plans for the house that was now their new home. They wouldn't do anything to change its ordinary appearance from the road, not to rouse envious talk, but inside it was going to be a paradise. There would be a greenhouse in the yard, so they could sell their own fresh vegetables all the year round. The roof of the garden shed, up against the house, would become a terrace and winter garden, and Bessie would be able to sunbathe there naked. Downstairs there would be a place for mother, with her own entrance.

The keys were to be handed over to them when the new owners moved into Bessie's old house, but Bessie and Willy were kept late at the shop and left it till next day. Mother's things had been moved out of the ground floor, so that the new owners could move in. The hated daughter-in-law would open the place for them. Next morning, when Bessie and Willy went to get the keys to their paradise, there were no keys, there was no Rudolph or his family. The keys had been handed over (why not to the son, since his mother was not there?) and the family had moved out and into Bessie's new home, taking advantage of the empty moving van at the door.

"The bitch! The dirty slut! What do you say to her cheek? She moved in as though the place was waiting for her and hung her curtains at the windows and called the plumbers in and even ran off to register her new address at the police station."

"D'you mean to say you let her get away with it?" asked Helga.

"Willy doesn't like rows. And she's always being sent on training courses, it's politics, and he's afraid of what she might do. She spoke up right away that we'd just bought that cottage ... you know what that means, illegal speculation in property . . ."

"When did all this happen?"

"Just the week before they arrested us. Mother doesn't know her house has been sold; we didn't want to upset her." Bessie borrowed the Penal Code from the prison office and tried to find a paragraph that would enable her to prosecute her son for breaking and entering.

"You wouldn't take your own son to court?"

"He's just under her thumb, the poor fool." Bessie's life was like a spindle twisting around a single hated figure. In childhood it was her mother, then her first husband, and now her daughter-in-law. "They had a washing machine of their own but saved it and used Mother's. When I moved Mother's things out I couldn't find her extra eiderdowns, and there's a lot of her china missing, too."

"Yes, but Rudolph's your son, and you sold the roof over his head."

"It was my roof, wasn't it? I've got that gift contract registered—that's law. The flat we got for them cost us plenty. It's me who's paying all along the line, and it's me'll decide what I'm going to give him. He can like it or lump it, and if he isn't satisfied he'd better do something about it himself."

Now Bessie is in jail and has nobody to write to outside, nobody she can send her parcel permit to. I offered to have my husband send her a parcel, if she let him have the permit—it wouldn't ruin him—but she suspected me of trying to wangle something and refused. While she was cuddling her Sweetie Pie there was one piece of evidence she had read, after all: her daughter-in-law's. This charming young woman admitted that her mother-in-law was a criminal and proved it by handing over to the police a smuggled leather jacket that Bessie had given Rudolph for Christmas. "I don't want stolen goods in my house," said this right-minded student of political training courses.

"She doesn't want a jacket that cost me plenty in the house she's stolen off me," said Bessie in a moment of grim humor.

She was happiest when she and Willy moved about from one place to another. She had never got used to possessions and did not know how to enjoy them. "I never had an easy time, we just slaved and slaved." She never wore the nice things Willy bought her; her cupboards were full of clothes: she had five coats and two fur coats, skirts and blouses and sweaters galore, all neatly put away in plastic bags with the shop tags still on them. In summer she wore a thin jumper, in winter a track suit top, with a change of trousers and blouse. In the shop she wore a pinafore over her trousers. Once Willy bought her a beautiful silver fox off some Polish tourists in need of money; she sold it right away, at a good profit. Selling and buying, buying and selling, it was a mania, a disease. As soon as the things we ordered from the prison shop were brought round, Bessie would start bartering.

Playing at shop. Perhaps she enjoyed the sight of new things, untouched. One time Helga and I both ordered salami, a whole kilogram, because Helga said meat would keep our strength up. When it arrived, instead of one kilogram of decent salami there were two of horse sausage, for the same price. It would keep her strength up, so Helga overcame her prejudice and ate it, but I couldn't. I gave chunks away to the trusty who came to put a new bulb in our light, to the trusties who brought our food round, and still I had a whole long sausage hanging there from the window. I gave it to Bessie, who, although she adored horseflesh and would take pieces of Helga's sausage and fry them over a fire of newspaper on the toilet, would not touch her own. Her eyes looked it over lovingly every day until it went bad and had to be thrown away. Fashionable philosophers these days set "to have" against "to be," but when I think of Bessie, the antinomy does not seem so clear. Bessie did not know how to *have*; possessing gave her no joy, not even the pleasure of giving, and that was what was wrong with her. Sad as it is, Bessie did not know how to live.

It was Willy, her Sweetie Pie, who rescued her from prison. His final statement declared that she knew nothing at all about any of the things they were accused of. He took the entire guilt on himself. He bribed somebody, because Bessie told us he had decided he did not need his beautiful new delivery van, but he did not manage to get himself out of the mess. He had already been involved in an embezzlement case, and this time he would get several years in jail. So the guard appeared and once more said, "Get your things ready." Bessie was so happy she almost touched the ceiling. "I'm going home! I'm going home!"

It was Denise in the cell with us then, and she whispered, "Listen to her, not a word of pity for her husband. All that matters is herself. She's going home!"

"She'll miss him when she gets home."

"That creature?" Denise was scornful. "Unless she starts digging up the garden to look for his buried treasure."

Prison no long existed for Bessie, although she was still within the walls. She had forgotten it, forgotten it so completely that she never thought of the husband she was leaving there. All she said about him was how lost she'd be, because he took her everywhere in the van and she didn't even know how to buy a bus ticket, and how ever would she get back to their hometown? She didn't even have a doorkey; Willy always had it, and who should she ask in the office, when she left, so they'd get the key out of Willy's locker?

She asked me for a plastic bag to carry all her cigarettes off. She would still have a night to spend in the transfer cell, and asked the guard whether the cigarettes would last her. She had at least five hundred left. Bessie had been lucky when she came to our cell: they gave her a clean almost new blanket, still thick and warm. It was late in the year and getting cold. A prisoner going home or passing on to a prison camp will always leave her better things for those left in the cell, and give up the worst, dirtiest, and most torn at her release. Denise's blanket was worn and thin, and filthy. "Won't you change with her?" I asked Bessie.

"That I won't," she snapped. "I've got to sleep in this place another night. Why should I sleep under a dirty blanket when I've got a clean one?"

"You'll have your sheet under it."

"Hasn't she got a sheet, I'd like to know?"

That evening, when supper came round, the guard asked us, "Did she really take all those cigarettes? Didn't she leave you any?"

"Her?" Denise said scornfully. "That huckster?"

That word made everything clear to me and freed me from the mixed feelings that had been worrying me.

"Of course she's nothing but a huckster, and I don't see why you feel ashamed because you didn't like her."

9

HELGA (2)

It was not a good thing for Helga that Bessie was put in our cell; at least, that was how I felt about it, though Helga might not agree. It is depressing to watch a prisoner gradually turning into a convict. The prisoner does not accept prison and tries to preserve herself from its effects, but the convict accepts and adapts to it. That was a difference I felt between some of the prisoners I met. And Bessie was the first to break down Helga's rejection of imprisonment—a rejection we had helped each other to sustain. In the era "before Bessie" (time is so compressed in jail that a few months can figure as an era) Helga was totally absorbed in the cultivated impression she was out to make. She had a clear idea of dignity and was proud of her highly civilized attitudes, which she herself considered superior. Indeed, the big swindler needs more than talent; he (or she) must do more than dominate other people and force his will on them, must do more than simply abuse their confidence. His "art" includes a wide knowledge of the world. He must be attractive and (to women) charming. Swindling has a style of its own, and in a way this style is cultivated and sophisticated. It is also the prerequisite for success: nobody will fall for a primitive con man. Helga wanted both to win me and fool me with her cultivated ways, but at the same time she needed them herself. They bound her to her daughter, her father, her brother; they were her path back to decency. So long as we were discussing Kazantzakis together, she could feel she was above the dirty foul-mouthed prison and not so far removed from her good-looking daughter and her social ambitions as we vied with one another to read Stifter's dull novel, borrowed from the prison library. Later she would be able to boast: when Eva Kantůrková and I were reading Stifter, who d'you think finished first? You'd never guess—I finished it and Eva gave up.

Helga had common ground with Bessie in all that was most vulgar in her. They whispered together at night; Helga confided to Bessie things she could not tell me or was ashamed to. They competed in describing Dionysian orgies, but while Bessie was content to have been a mere onlooker, Helga had to take a leading part. When she described her evenings out, to me, Helga stopped at the point where they were all drunk, having great fun, or the moment when she discovered in the taxi that she was going home in no more than her underwear—and had to carry it off with dignity. What she told Bessie went much farther: that last evening, for instance, she had danced naked on the table; the men were beside themselves and she let them paw her. And there was plenty of flesh to paw, no doubt about it.

"Look what I've got to offer," she boasted to Bessie, needing both hands to lift each massive breast. Her bosom, her ticket of entry to cheap sex; almost all the guards looked admiringly at her bust and more or less furtively tried to touch her. It is hard for a woman to judge, but I think a sex orgy with Helga must have been worth it, if only for the amazing carpet of pubic hair she presented. If I wanted to describe cheap sex, that would be it.

Bessie couldn't help herself and had to pass on to me whatever Helga confided. "Piles of money hidden away; so much that she's scared stiff someone will find it, hidden in a used tire warehouse somewhere. And she doesn't know whether to send a message home about it." She was afraid to tell them, because she knew how they disapproved of her way of life. "She cries at night because her brother won't write to her," Bessie revealed. "She built him a house—Isn't she clever?—she paid for it but it's not in her name. There's nothing they can confiscate even if they do convict her, not even her car. And the apartment she lives in belongs to her parents."

Bessie changed the balance in our cell, and I felt Helga moving away from me; she no longer talked to impress me with her mother the singer and her father in diplomatic dress. In jail a friendly ear is everything. To Bessie Helga could sob out that her father had stopped writing to her, while to me she had to pretend her family looked up to her with admiration. She no longer talked about her "sabotage." She did not spend much time reading, playing cards with Bessie instead. She had decided to stick it out, and collaboration with Bessie made it easier to deceive me. With her, Helga began to accept prison. She still criticized Bessie for shouting out of the window, and for her shameless coquetry with the men in the cell opposite. She was angry when Bessie tried to smuggle a letter to one of them; it was intercepted, and we lost our privilege of extra bath time because we had done nothing to stop it. But Bessie's calm acceptance of guilt was wearing down Helga's resistance to it. Bessie gave her the example she needed; she saw that there are other ways of living in jail than the one the two of us had worked out together. In time, of course, other fellow prisoners would have achieved the same transformation, and Helga would have come to accept prison conditions as natural and inevitable; but it was Bessie who dealt the first blow. And so strange are the ways of the world, that while Bessie went tripping back to her houses, to her piles of banknotes buried in the garden, her eiderdowns and never-worn fur coats, her skeleton on guard in the cocktail cabinet—the Helga she left behind was very different from the avenging magistrate-goddess who had descended upon the two of us not so long ago.

Bessie acted as a catalyst on me, too, and I began to feel I couldn't stand the couple much longer. Even a whiff of drains in passing can make you feel sick with revulsion. The blame should not lie solely with Bessie. In a liberal society she would have been a hard-working market woman with a big stall and plenty of customers—of whom I would regularly and gratefully have been one. If she were running a hotel, the only thing to watch for would be knots in the wood of the bedroom door. The economic conditions she lived under drove her halfway to thievery, while at the same time they made her the master of both market and consumers. "Business is business," she retorted when Helga the patriot angrily objected to Willy's bartering with Soviet officers of the occupation army, subject to no customs restrictions, and bringing in TV sets to get chandeliers and carpets to take home. And when I objected that I thought a civilized country was one where you could get what you need in the shops, and that I disliked the idea of bribing shop girls for anything at all, Bessie said rudely, "Just try it, try getting hold of anything without tracking it down and paying just to get it. You'll not get a decent meal together!"

"I will, don't worry, better than you with your dried soup packets."

In time, prison gets you down with the submarine complex, and I was becoming less curious and less anxious to understand my companions. Bessie's everlasting chatter was tiring, and Helga's obvious purpose too pressing. Her attempts to peep into my world had been almost enjoyable. In the morning when we heard a plane taking off she said knowingly, "Half-past eight, the Munich plane." It might just as well have been a ten o'clock plane for Zimbabwe, but that didn't bother Helga. All she wanted was an opening so she could tell me how she always used the eight-thirty plane to Munich when her brother was there. By four in the afternoon she was flying back with the marks that her brother wanted smuggled in so he wouldn't pay tax on them. I was then supposed to say unsuspectingly: "Yes, I know, whenever I get money sent from Munich . . ."

The way she tried hardest to trap me was by talking about Poland. That was when Solidarity was fighting for its life, and she found plenty of ammunition in our communist press, which was mainly concerned just then to attack the working class of Poland. And so where would Helga's brother be then, but in Poland? On a dance tour: she was his impresario for both West and East. When she came back from Warsaw she brought cases of silver cutlery with her, the poor Poles were selling whatever they could; but she also brought Solidarity badges. The colleague who wanted her job and was giving evidence against her had wheedled a badge out of her—and now produced it as proof of her guilt. "Can you imagine what I felt like? He put his hand in his pocket and took out that badge. My interrogating officer was jumping for joy."

I did indeed have a Solidarity badge at home for a week or two, brought me by someone passing through Poland at a time when even the traffic police there were sporting them. Somebody saw it who should not have, because I gave it away and the police could not have found it when they searched our apartment.

"What does the Solidarity badge look like?" I asked curiously.

"Round and red, not very big."

I envied Helga her self-assurance: the badge was oblong, white, and the only touch of red was on the Polish flag. To reassure myself that I hadn't been unduly suspicious of her, mistaking coincidence for intent, later, I asked a friend who knew her case, whether the Solidarity badge had played any part in it; my discreet friend laughed outright.

While the general strike lasted in Poland, planes were taking off over our heads every night, far more than in "peace" time. From cells looking south prisoners could see the taillights; every plane that soars away makes them sad and frustrated. The roar of the engines during the Polish strike filled the cell and throbbed through our sleepless nights. We were cut off from the world outside, and if they so wished the authorities could deprive us even of the meager news in the local papers. All we could do was wonder what the noise meant: Were the planes flying *there*? Or only to the frontier and back, as a warning?

The dull roar of the engines reminded me of the night of August 21, 1968. My husband was away with a TV unit, making a film about worker democracy, and my son and I sat huddled together listening to flight after flight passing overhead. The same fear flowed over me again in Ruzyně jail, on December 13, when General Jaruzelski clamped martial law down on Poland. In the mood of those days, it hurt doubly that Helga was using the lost struggle of the Polish workers to drive me up against the wall.

She was also inordinately inquisitive about "Georgina," as she called her. There are quiet ways political prisoners find out the things that matter to them, and although my interrogating officer took great care not to mention any names, within a few days I knew who had been arrested along with me. I did not mention any names in the cell until after the case had been closed and the state prosecutor's summing-up arrived, with all our names clearly set out. From the outset Jiřina ("Georgina") was cited as the head of our "conspiracy," but the newspapers that were so busy flinging mud at us never gave her name: she was "Dr. J." and that was all Helga and I had read together. From the way the newspaper campaign was running, it was going to be a major political trial, and Helga asked me, "Have you seen Georgina?"

I actually did see her once, when the midday meal was brought round just as she was coming back from questioning; her guard made to hold her back and she said, "Why not?" and came on down the corridor. At the end of that long, high-ceilinged passage she looked small and frail, with cropped hair and lively eyes, and her track suit fitted her; she could have been training for a race. My guard pushed me hurriedly back into my cell. Interrogation cells were all on the same floor, and it must have given them a lot of trouble to prevent us all meeting.

"I've no idea," I replied to Helga's question. "You see, I don't know her, so even if I did meet her I wouldn't know who it was."

One of our guards let fall the information that there were only two small cells on our floor, both overlooking the yard. I reasoned that if I was in a small cell, so was Jiřina, and counting the windows from below, and calculating the probable size of the cells, I thought she must be two cells away from me. By that time I knew my way about and could work out what risks were worth taking. If it hadn't been for Helga I would have tried to phone Jiřina. At questioning I denied that I even knew her, and so I couldn't very well explain that I knew where she was. My greetings had to find another way.

There was another occasion when Helga's presence affected my honor as a political prisoner. About six months earlier a young laborer, Jiří Gruntograd, had been arrested, questioned, and later sentenced for copying verse and prose written by forbidden authors. One day when I was passing through the gate of our "chicken-coop," our exercise cage, there was a moon daisy carved on the doorpost, and by it: "For EK from JG." It was a wonderful moment. Helga never left my side when we were out there; she noticed it too and asked: "Is that meant for you?"

"Who could it be from? I don't know anybody whose initials are J. G. except Jiří Gruša, and he's living in West Germany now." And so I couldn't return the greeting. I found a suitably sharp stone, but either Helga was always with me, or we were taken to different cages. What would she do if I started scratching a message on the cage doorpost? I am still unhappy to think I could not show him how moved I was by his lovely thought. I wrote to him as soon as I was released but could not let him know at the time the inestimable joy he had given me. In time Jiří found out that there were more of us and added the words "and all of you." Honzy Ruml was able to get an answer to him.

In jail I recalled all the advice passed on by friends who had been through the same experience: 1. Never let them catch you out. 2. Name no names. 3. Dictate your statement yourself. 4. Stay calm and smiling. 5. Never say more than you need. 6. Don't let them get you down physically. 7. At least once a day, rise above the banality of prison life. That last wise counsel came from a priest who in a prison camp had prayed devoutly every day for years. It was perhaps the most valuable of all, because cool objectivity is not enough to overcome the evil of prison life.

My instinct suggested a Machiavellian ruse, and after it was all over I was amazed at the cold-blooded way I could set an intrigue in motion; one's instincts are always subconscious. Helga was preparing for her second appearance in court and could expect to be sentenced. We managed to get some warm water for her to wash. I plucked the black hairs from her chin and upper lip and put her hair in curlers, and she took up her habitual African queen pose. She did not speak, she barely touched her food, she smoked one cigarette after another and did not even want to play cards with Bessie. But she said not a word about her coming ordeal.

"What a stink there is in here," Bessie complained just before we went to bed. One elbow on the table, the other on the bedstead, her feet planted firmly on the linoleum, Helga was sitting there in a pool of sweat. Poker-faced, she was sweating her terror out through all her pores.

Next morning we got her ready, hair nicely brushed, eau-de-cologne paper hankies in her pocket. When a prisoner is taken to court she is first given the clothes she was arrested in, just as she took them off: torn and dirty from a pub brawl, long evening skirts after a dance, a sleeveless summer mini dress on a winter's day. And then there is a ritual in the prison yard: in the presence of the Governor each prisoner is solemnly handed over to the commander of the bus making the round of the courts that day.

Helga was hardly out of the cell when Bessie began to pour out the secrets they whispered night after night. She could not wait to pull Helga to pieces for my benefit.

"Why don't you say things like that when she's here?"

"I don't like making bad blood."

"What if I tell her?"

"You?" She laughed.

"Why do you smile at her if you don't really like her?"

"You have to get along with all sorts when you run a pub."

"Why didn't you tell her you saw her photograph on TV in the police program? It might have helped her to answer their questions."

"Why should I? Her case is nothing to do with me."

"Then why are you telling me about it?"

"Well, we can talk freely now she's gone for a while . . ."

"Bessie, my dear, when I'm away, is that the way you and Helga talk about me?"

"Of course. What did you think!" and she laughed heartily.

And so I did what I did: I went to Helga's cupboard and took out the envelope where she kept her private letters mixed in with her official correspondence and spread it all out on the bed. Like a greedy mouse Bessie flipped through the papers; and as efficient as a calculator, she worked out how many hundred thousand crowns Helga was being prosecuted for. She was indignant.

"Cheating the government's all right, but swindling people like me!" Helga had wormed one hundred and forty-five thousand crowns in one case alone, the total life savings of a couple of old-age pensioners. They would never get a penny back, because in the eyes of the law Helga had no property. Even if she were sentenced to make regular repayments, deducted from her earnings, she would find a job that barely brought in the accepted minimum. "She's got it all thought out!" Bessie realized at that moment that if she got too close to Helga, she might be the next victim.

"Bessie, you'd better not tell Helga we've read her papers. It might upset her to feel ashamed she'd never told us the truth."

When Helga got back from court she was less distressed than when she left in the morning. She told us excitedly how one of the guards, a handsome bearded fellow who had always been casting eyes at her bust, took time to listen to her trial and told her admiringly in the bus on the way back to prison, "I'd no idea you were such a big case."

She told us practically nothing about the trial itself, and the word sabotage was never heard again. Sentence had been postponed, which Helga thought was a good sign. Time was on her side. There were others in the case with her, and her gamble was that the longer it took, the more blame she could shift on to them, lightening her own. Her lawyer thought she'd get five to seven years, and was trying for the lower figure. A five-year sentence is served in Grade I prisons, where good conduct can mean release halfway through the term. A sentence of over five years means serving at least two-thirds. Helga's proven swindles amounted to almost a million crowns. If they released her after two and a half years in jail, it would have been a profitable venture.

That night I was wakened by whispers; the two of them were sitting in the corner smoking. Next morning Helga did not speak to me. She kept it up all day and then burst out in the evening: "I didn't think you would lower yourself to that! You have bitterly disappointed me. Reading other people's letters is the lowest anyone can sink."

"You are right . . . I've never done it before."

"I'm through with you! Don't speak to me and don't touch my things."

"How can you be through with me when we haven't started anything yet?"

"I forbid you to touch my mess tin."

Helga (2)

The only duty I had agreed to perform was that of handing round the mess tins when food was put in at the door of the cell. It was not a particularly pleasant job. For one thing, I naturally took the poorest helping for myself, so nobody could accuse me of abusing my position. The metal bowls were greasy and messy, too hot to hold comfortably. It wasn't an appetizing sight, either, to see the trusties' dirty fingers in the gravy. Still, it was less obnoxious than the duty of reporting at morning roll call. Then I could stand negligently in the background while somebody else made a fool of herself in the prescribed manner.

"All right, you can get your own mess tin."

Bessie advised me to apologize. "I told her I was sorry."

"You've got something to be sorry for, after you'd promised not to tell her. There's bad blood in the cell now, with a vengeance."

"I didn't mean to tell. She wormed it out of me."

"How did she know what to get out of you?"

"I hadn't thought of that."

I did not apologize. "You are a strong-minded woman, Helga, you know how to take things as they come. And I was getting tired of your game of hide and seek."

She was furious. She fetched her own mess tin from the door, and every gesture, every look, every word she said to Bessie, all expressed the most profound scorn for me. Bad characters who are conceited at the same time are remarkably thick-skinned when it comes to their own shortcomings.

For another whole day she continued to ignore me. Then she was away from the cell for about an hour, and when the guard brought her back there was not a trace of her angry scorn. She behaved as though nothing had happened, and thanked me prettily for carrying her scalding mess tin over to her. But something *had* happened, and that afternoon the guard who had smiled at her so meaningfully when she took Helga for "questioning" came in and said, "Get your things ready."

"Me?" Helga was visibly frightened.

The guard took her away. Was it chance, or was it deliberate? They put Denise in her place, a girl whose physical condition demanded a small cell. But they could just as well have moved Bessie. Helga was in Ruzyně for another three months, and all the time she was in a cell with seven other women. That was a real comedown in the prison world, for up to then she had been privileged. She certainly thought the transfer was due to me; if I hadn't let on that I had seen through her, maybe they would have left us together. I would not swear it was so, but like Helga, it occurred to me, too.

I had often wondered what she would do when the truth came out. Would she attack me? Hate me? Insult me? Treat me with scorn? She was furious in her hatred of the people who produced proof of her guilt. Her urge to deceive had a good deal in it that was immature; she was like a cheeky schoolgirl who goes too far. Found out, the child is not ashamed, but angry and frustrated. Helga must have hated me, and she could well have looked down on me. If she really got into her chosen role of patriotic heroine sacrificed on the political battlefield, she could see my revelation of the truth as an injustice. And if she felt any desire to be like me, then I had torn that tiny baited thread she flung into the waters of decency. I am not sure that I feel guilty about spoiling that corner of her soul, if it was really there at all, but I am sorry that I never learned how and when it had happened to her: the moment when a genuinely talented person puts all at the service of evil, when a soul goes sick, when a mind becomes so arrogant that there is nothing it will not turn to. Perhaps it was Helga's body that determined the path her life followed, as one of the friends in jail at the same time thought. The man in a woman's body. A full-blown woman with the heart of a man. That full-blown body was not all feminine; the hips, the legs, the hairiness, all suggested the masculine. What trouble Helga had to find a man, and how readily they left her in the lurch when she did! Her mind was enormously ambitious, and her abilities could have been put to such good use. Yet life kept slipping through her fingers.

10

DENISE

At last! We have Denise with us in the cell. Small, delicately built, with long hair, as pretty as a doll, she was a courageous woman flinging challenge after challenge in the face of life— and for the moment, crushed. She called up all her strength of will not to give in. When I failed to get her a shower, she was grateful for a bucket of warm water poured over her on the toilet; she washed her lovely long hair and looked at her surroundings: one gray iron table, three gray iron stools, three gray iron bedsteads, gray blankets, gray lockers up on the wall, yellow linoleum and dull green walls, bits of cheese stuck to the ceiling bearing witness to someone's protest at the food, bars on the window high in the wall, and a metal door with no handle but a peephole. So this was the end of the road. She had known hopeless places before, psychiatric wards, screens round the beds of the dying in hospital wards, but nowhere was there less room for hope than where she was now. Not a trace of this showed: the worse she felt; the gayer and chattier she became.

She drove her fears out of sight and hid them beneath a cloak of playfulness. Just before Christmas, which is the saddest time of all in jail, she made a Christmas tree out of crumbled bread, decorated it with silver paper off our chocolates, and we put each other's presents round it. It was she who invented the game of trying to hit a soapdish floating in the washbowl, using pellets of bread dried hard on the radiator. The one who got in most shots would be the first to go home. She had no luck, and so she changed the rules; nothing must spoil the fun. A few minutes of peace were blessed to me but those minutes were such a strain on her that she granted me very few. I taught her to play rummy; I found it a boring game, but she played happily by herself, laying out sets and sequences on the bed. All I had to do was leave my book now and again and go over to admire how she was winning. She was extraordinarily lucky with dice— made out of bread, of course—she cast them with long elegant movements, and her figures worked out easily. Yet she was lucky in love, too, and played dice with Jaroslav, the great love of her life. I very soon found out that it was difficult not to like her but extremely demanding to love her. When she liked someone and was afraid of being let down, she could be aggressive.

"Eva, do you love me?" I can't remember any chance acquaintance ever asking me that.

My crazy mother, who has been dead for years now, when she felt menaced by the loneliness she had brought upon herself, asked me more than once: "Evie, you do love me, don't you?" Denise said the words in a teasing voice, her pride made her turn the question into a joke, but ask she had to. She could not bear to be in doubt.

I answered in the same joking tone. What can you say to such a question? The way you behave is your answer. "You bet I don't."

"Take care, Eva," she warned me, "don't make me mad, or you'll be sorry!"

There was an inexhaustible fountain of love in her, love was her way of life, love that was crazy, fanciful, purely feminine—and the love of a friend, a daughter, a mother, a sister. A creature living for and by love alone, she gave herself without reserve, with all the exuberant vitality of her wide-open heart, to each moment as it came. It is love, if it IS. Whence follows that what is, IS. And what IS is all that matters. The consequences? Oh, how far away from the present moment are its consequences. Yet, overflowing with love as she was, it was the disastrous consequences of love that she constantly had to cope with. In prison her love became a torment, the tormenting fear of loss; prison was the worst of those disastrous consequences of her love.

Women who live for the moment, spontaneously, are generally thought of as hussies; they certainly get more emotion out of life, more love, more of what the moment has to give; more than those heavily serious people with a sense of responsibility, who see the present as a transition from the past to the future; and more than those calculating minds whose lives and emotions are carefully worked out beforehand. Not only would I hesitate to call Denise a hussy, I would refuse outright to use the word. For each moment as it came, for each new emotion, her heart was pure. She gave herself without reserve, with no ax to grind, simply for the joy of the moment. Such people are said to live like thunderbolts; hers struck several times a year, and the consequences made one long roll of thunder.

Shortly before a kind fate sent Denise across my path, the prison librarian, pushing his rickety truck along the corridor once every ten days, handing out books haphazardly according to the number of women in each cell, gave us a book about

Sumer. Here I found the epic of the goddess Inanna, a fearless young woman who stole fire from her divine father, for love, and gave it to man. A gardener had planted a tree, and Inanna sat down in its shade and fell asleep. She was so lovely that the gardener violated her.

> Dawn came, the sun rose, the woman gazed around her in horror, Inanna gazed around her in horror. What disasters has not the womb of woman wrought, what disasters did Inanna not wreak through her womb. She soaked the thickets and the gardens of the world in blood, the slaves gathering firewood drank only blood, she filled all the wells of the earth with blood, the girl slaves who came to draw water filled their pitchers with blood. With blood they filled them.

The repetitive parallels drive the images home and give the narrative a broader setting, placing the poetry on more planes than one. Whenever I think of Denise, I remember Inanna. The Sumerians put facts side by side, capable of perceiving but not of generalizing; repetition was the only way they could give depth to their verse. Sumerian civilization evolved neither religion nor philosophy; in their epics the gods mingle with the human actors. Denise, too, lived in this world, and the poetry of Inanna enabled me to see how she, and most people, look at their own lives. Denise clung voraciously to what is NOW, and that did not make her any less honest than Sumerian poetry is delightful.

Denise perceived only trivialities, and she lived with trivialities. What seemed to me a mere detail was for her an installment of a novel. She saw the insignificant things that go to make up life and was blind to the fundamental significance beneath, the pattern of reason. She was not a shallow person, her capacity for genuine emotion preserved her from superficiality, and though she did not look for deeper meanings, could not have defined them, and indeed would not even have been interested in them, yet her life was motivated by them. However often I felt defeated by her trivialities and looked down on the fabric she wove from them, I had to admit that if one is so absorbed by generalities that the tiny threads of day-to-day concern pass unnoticed, one loses something fundamental, something of the firm ground one has to stand on to view both the heights and the depths. The fundamental exists in a stream of trivialities and is carried along by it. Great matters rest on a host of contemptible trivialities that nevertheless are the substance of everyday life, life as we have to live it. One need not be able to define good, in order to be a good person: that was what I learned from Denise. I got to know the women I shared a cell with, got to know them very well, seeing them all day, every day, talking to them, listening to them, defending myself against them, helping them. We went through a lot together. I knew a good deal about the trusties we saw several times a day, and something about one or two of the women guards. Everybody knew that Vera, the Gypsy trusty with the long hair, was not in jail for the first time, and was back again because drunk, she had allowed her husband to rape their little daughter—it was even said that she had held the child for him—and then desperate with remorse had carried the bleeding, torn child to the hospital, where she died. Vera was cheerful, helpful, with a misty look in her eyes; she had several more children at home. The smell of that terrible death of a little child seemed to cling to the bread she handed in at our door. I knew that one of the guards had a husband who was unfaithful and beat her, another was divorced and lived with a growing daughter but had as many men as she felt like because she was still attractive; yet another had a crippled husband. I was not particularly anxious to know more about the male guards, because that would make them seem more human, it would bring them closer, and that was something I did not care to have happen.

Denise put her romances together from a word heard here and there, from chance meetings in the doctor's waiting room (the only setting for social life in prison and functioning something like a small town post office), from what other women shouted from their cell windows or under the door across the corridor. She gathered up her facts and linked them to people she could only have glimpsed or heard at a distance, yet she knew more about those girls, those women, than if they had come to her in the confessional. The slightest murmur was enough for Denise to be on the alert; nothing escaped her notice, and her memory never let her down, so that in a week or two she was quite sure, "That Milly, you know the one I mean, Eva, the one with the long hair, we were in the same cage with her once, you must remember, you said her irises were enlarged and she had that faraway look as though she was high on something, you must know the one I mean, she's the girl that boasted the trusty had fucked her in the elevator, only that's not possible, the elevator isn't all that slow, for heaven's sake. Don't you remember her horse falling down when she tried to send her papers to the lawyer they call Perry Mason? And the convicts mending the roof on the other wing picked it up. . . . Can't you remember the one I mean? Well, I must say it took you long enough. Now what I wanted to tell you was that she isn't as innocent as she looks and she isn't a teacher, either, she only pretends to be better than the rest of us. Yes, she did work at a school, but only helping out at lunch-time . . ."

Another time it was, "Eva, don't be so stupid, you're mixing up two different people, no, three, really. Vlasta is the one who sings, she's the beautiful girl in the cell next to ours; you said yourself she's a beauty, the one who holds her towel in front of her in the shower room, you know, the lesbian that was sent to see the psychiatrist.... Why can't she have a son? She's a lesbian, O.K., but she was raped, wasn't she? And that's why she hates men, and anyway it's her mother looks after the kid.... Eva, use your head, she's the one that belongs to a gang; they break into weekend bungalows, remember? It was the boy that beat up that old woman; he gave them away.... For heaven's sake, Eva, you've mixed it all up again; the boy that gave them away was Mike. Vlasta got him away from Irene; Irene's still calling him every night across the yard, but Mike sends cigarettes to Vlasta.... Remember the horse that passed our window yesterday, and Vlasta saying, 'thank you, Mike' afterward?.... Why should anyone tell Mike Vlasta's a lesbian, what she needs are cigarettes, for heaven's sake, Eva, have some sense.... Now, Ilona's Vlasta's girl, only she doesn't care for her much any more. At least, she makes out she doesn't want her.... Ilona always talks to Milly under the door and Vlasta's always trying to get her back ... you're all wrong, Eva, it's not Ilona that sings. It's Vlasta, and Vlasta sings for Ilona ... Ilona's the tall thin woman, thirty-five if she's a day, short cropped hair and a scar on one cheek. You went to the dentist the same day, can't you remember her? She'd got letters for the other wing ... it was at Ilona's that they caught Vlasta, and now Ilona's furious because if Vlasta hadn't gone to her place that night (the police must have been following her, see?) they couldn't have got her for sexual assault on a minor.... Why shouldn't a girl have a baby when she's underage? Eva, what sort of a world do you live in? I've been midwife when a girl of eleven gave birth ... have you got me?"

Tiny, pretty, a plaything, a doll, Denise had enough vitality
for three lives, and she managed to live three lives at once. You
might think this impossible, but she was ready with tales of all
three lives, wide open to anything that might come. "Now watch
me, Eva, we're in a pub, O.K.? and if I get up *like this* in a pub,
and kick my chair back, *so*, then things are going to happen. I'm
out for a fight." Her pub was right by the station—I've been
there—it's mostly local but Saturday and Sunday the weekenders come in; the river bank is lined with bungalows. There's
a soccer field behind the pub, and in summer the locals (Denise's husband is both captain and trainer) play the weekenders.
Cold beer tastes extra good after a match. It tastes good, too,
when you get out of a crowded train, and Denise often dropped
in for a glass on her way home. Saturday night was the best time.
We're all brothers, we're all friends, the old hikers' creed. The
locals accepted it, too, lawyer, doctor, bricklayer, we're all friends
and equals . . . but Denise was the uncrowned queen.

And it was early one Saturday evening, the mood relaxed
because the whole weekend lay ahead, that a made-up doll came
into the pub. She hadn't been coming long enough to know the
local rules, and while she probably dismissed Denise scornfully
as a loud village flirt, she made a set at Denise's husband.
Marital relations may be of all kinds. Everybody else knows
what is going on, but there is one unwritten and immutable law:
if a married couple come to the pub together, they belong to one
another, and only one of the two concerned can break that
bond. Denise's husband was not interested at all in that painted
doll; he was busy setting up next week's team, and so when the
painted bird went to the toilet Denise pushed her chair back *like
this* and her friend took the hint and went with her. The other
girl held the doll's head under the tap while Denise washed her
paint off. They didn't do anything to hurt her, and the poor girl

ran out, wet, weeping, smudged and tousled, to the jeers of the locals. Much later, when the girl had learned the law of the village versus the weekenders, she told Denise that someone had put her up to it. "I thought it was him that was unfaithful to you, not the other way round!"

Enemies! Denise made enemies as easily as she breathed. There was one who had her nose broken for her. They were sitting happily in the pub, Denise with her rather loud mastery of the situation, something she could afford, with her position as uncrowned queen never threatened, and they were singing— not that Denise could sing or had a good ear, but she liked to join in. It was a fine noise, glasses tinkling, feet shuffling, a guitar in the background, and half-drunk voices—and at the next table an enemy said something about Denise and her limp. That dot-and-carry-one, a lame duck, who's she to lay down the law round here, can't stand on two feet, or something of the sort.

"There's nothing wrong with my hearing, Eva, when I needed to rest a bit, on night duty, I could put my head down on the table and snooze but the minute Sister came along I heard her, and she *did* know how to walk quietly. My kids? when I'd boxed their ears for them and they were grumbling in the next room I always knew, even if they had the tape recorder on loud. Nobody can fool me. I can hear what's going on round the corner, and I heard what that bit of fluff said." Denise had just had one hip joint operated, she was always lifting patients, changing their sheets, putting them to bed when they were wheeled back from the operating room, and it was the one thing that drove her mad. If anyone drew attention to her disability she lost her head. She made trouble in Ruzyně when a young guard who was said to be suffering from leukemia and scared stiff of dying, and who took it out on the women he had in his charge, told her roughly that she ought to stay in the cell if she couldn't move faster, holding up everybody else. She shouted back at him and then she put in an official complaint to the Governor—something unheard of, and it took her lawyer to smooth it over. That day in the pub, though, she was still at liberty, and she kicked her chair back *like this*, and the chair rattled across the floor, and everybody round grew quiet because they knew what *that* meant, and my tiny, pretty little doll, with one hip still painful from the operation, flung herself on the sneering creature at the next table. She did not need to use her stick; she left that hanging from the table. She just grabbed the girl's hair at the nape of her neck and banged her face down on the table.

"There wasn't a thing she could do, Eva, the blood was running. She was a mess, all right. Her nose'll never be straight again." That time the police were called in, the fight spread, because both girls had their friends with them.

Marvelous days, straightforward characters. Denise met the sallies of fate with strength of will and an invincible sense of humor. She was not afraid of what life could do to her, and so she often had to suffer for it. "I was something, Eva, when I was a kid . . ."

That was when she hadn't yet had a child; her daughter was eighteen, Denise was thirty-six or thirty-seven. "Twenty-two inches around the waist, the biggest size in bras, can you imagine me? My breasts just cut the air away in front of me. When I had a low-cut blouse and a narrow skirt, or jeans just right for my hips, and high heels, there wasn't a man wouldn't turn to watch me when I went past. I used to dye my hair, long and blond with my dark eyebrows and brown eyes. I must have looked a bit cheap, don't you think?"

"A bit provocative," I said.

"No, just bloody silly," she answered. And she told me how her provocative beauty had done her a bad turn. She used to come to Prague to work every day by train, a local that serves as much as a social meeting place as a means of transport. Everybody knows everybody else, you keep seats for each other, have a bit of a gossip, the ticket collector treats you all as visiting friends. One of the ticket collectors, though, was a rapist, and one day when she was alone with him in the compartment he wouldn't let her get out at the last stop, and in the siding he got what he wanted. "It's no good resisting, I've seen women brought into hospital in an awful state. My skirt was all messed up, a good thing I had a raincoat with me."

She reported the rape to the railroad police but they didn't believe her. "They could see what I looked like—provocative, did you say? O.K., so I looked provocative. They wouldn't have minded having a go themselves; they thought I'd been asking for it." The man didn't work their line after that. Denise found another woman he'd raped, and one day when she and her husband were walking along the platform she saw the man again. She called "That's him!" and her husband caught him. There was a trial, the railroad police suddenly remembered other women complaining so there was plenty of evidence.

"I met him again, years later, on a coal truck. He was dirty and his clothes were torn. God'll get you, make no mistake about it. That's what he said. And he was right, cos here I am."

You can challenge life once too often. Denise had already been in trouble once before. She came off duty, glad to catch the afternoon train home; she bought a bag of new potatoes to give the children a treat and cheese to go with it. Then she ran into an old friend and he took her for a glass of wine. It was a lovely day; they sat outside the café. What's all the hurry? The washing and the cooking can wait. He drove an ambulance, he'd get her to the station in time for the next train. The family was used to seeing her come home late. They had another glass, and then a third; life doesn't go by the rules, the ambulance driver drank as much as she did. Then all at once it was late, a long time to wait for the next train, the children without their supper, the lovely day spoiled. Never mind, a fast ambulance would get her home all right. Off they went, the siren wailing, her driver singing her favorite song, "By the Graveside." He had a beautiful voice. And to the tune of the graveside they left the road and the ambulance somersaulted down a grassy slope to the river, losing Denise on the way, breaking the windshield and twisting the driver's door, but landing on all four wheels again. She gathered up her scattered potatoes and stopped a truck to help get them back on the road, and all would have gone well if there hadn't been a woman cutting grass for her rabbits. She started screaming at the sight of Denise's face, scratched and bleeding, and then, "Just my luck, Eva, the police were there and who should come past but Bartík." Denise never spoke of her husband by his Christian name. "And the inspector called him over, he was a friend of ours. 'You've got a fine wife, Charlie, in such a hurry to get home she's half killed herself,' and Bartík got off his motorbike and looked down at me and then at my friend and just hissed at me: you needn't bother, the kids have had their supper."

The magistrate bawled her out for using an ambulance as a taxi and gave her two months on probation. Denise behaved decently; she'd hurt a kidney and pissed blood, but she didn't let on, or the driver would have had to pay for her treatment and her sick pay. He promised to take her share of the court costs.

"And did he?"

"Like hell he did. Pretended he'd never promised."

"What was his sentence?"

"Not bad, six months' probation. He told them he'd been driving ever since six in the morning and was tired. It didn't occur to the police to give him a blood test; nobody expects an ambulance driver to drink on duty."

"He wasn't much of a friend, though."

"My own fault—I ought to choose them better."

Denise's father was a gravedigger in the village where Denise was born, went to school, got married, had her children, and frequented the pub. Besides serving the world in that way, he also worked in a factory. Her mother was humpbacked and had been afraid to have children. Her father loved and respected her mother, who was a good cook, handy with her needle, and liked knitting. Father was a real man, though, and one day he had a child, a son, in the next village. Father did what he could for the boy, in secret, and mother never found out. It would have killed her. And after all, mother had a child, Denise, as healthy and pretty as mother was sickly. Not only that, Denise was hardworking and knew how to take care of herself.

"What were you like when you were little, Denise? A tomboy? Hot tempered? Disobedient? You must have been more like a boy than a girl."

"No, no, Eva, you're wrong. I was always a hundred percent girl. A bit wild, but always a girl. A girl that liked boys but a girl really, if you know what I mean."

"You mean you go for men. And men go for you."

"You couldn't have put it better."

Denise's first love was her half brother. She was an apprentice in the factory where her father worked—he wanted to keep an eye on her. She didn't become a nurse till later. Earlier, her father had made the same arrangements for his son from the next village; and in the factory brother and sister met—and fell in love.

"There wasn't a boy for miles round that was so attractive, and he said the same about me. He used to take me to the station, and we'd walk along the river together. Then one day father saw us together at the station. 'What's going on between you and Mike?' Well, what if there is? He appeals to me." Poor father had no choice, he had to tell us; first one, then the other, then both together—walking along the river bank. I cried my eyes out!"

"What about Mike? Did he mind discovering he'd got two fathers?"

"Mike's mother was a widow by then, and anyway she was always fair, she never made trouble. Mike was eighteen; he didn't seem bothered. What mattered most was that he had to stop going with me."

Until Denise's mother died, the two met in secret, linked by a bond of real affection. Denise was always in trouble, and Mike helped her out. She had another gallant knight: her father-in-law. Either he was a remarkable man, or Denise was so enchanting that she could tell him all about her loves, and he never got angry with her on his son's account. "Grandad's a real gentleman," and Denise was charming and precious.

Her father did not live long; he had a weak heart. Her mother's trouble were her lungs, overstrained by that crooked back. Mother was taken to the hospital and father had a heart attack soon afterward, but he absolutely refused to go to the hospital. He was going to be at home when his wife was brought back. Her mother was in the ward where Denise worked, and she was always asking anxiously about Father. "It was lucky there was a flu epidemic, so she couldn't have visitors. I don't know what I'd have told her. Sometimes I thought she knew all about it, anyway, and it was a waste of time to tell her lies."

Denise even hid her father's death from her mother, and his funeral. She hoped her mother would get stronger, and then she'd have told her, gently. Her mother died, too.

"It was awfully cold, a real frost, and snow everywhere. I was on afternoons, and took Father his dinner on my way to the train. He wasn't in bed; Bartík had been in to see to the fire. Father was sitting at the table when it happened. I managed to straighten him out, but I had to leave him lying on the floor; it was an awful rush to get to the ward on time so mother wouldn't suspect anything. As soon as I got into uniform I went to see her, as calm as could be. Sister stuffed sedatives into me. I'd let fall to Mother that Father wasn't too well, a touch of flu, nothing to worry about; and then I was glad because she couldn't expect him to come and wave up at her window. She was so close, so dependent on him! Father was everything, she didn't bother so much about me. It was always a wonder to me that it didn't get on his nerves. When she couldn't get her breath, he'd carry her, even to the loo, like she was his third child. Now mother wanted to know all that was going on, at home, what Father had for dinner, for breakfast, for lunch, whether I'd changed his sheets, whether he had enough clean shirts. I used to take his shirts for her to mend, in hospital. She sent him the orange she got as dessert. He had dumplings and sauerkraut today, I lied to her, left over from Sunday, and lean belly of pork. I made a good stuffing, don't worry, I didn't put too much pepper. This evening Bartík'll be bringing him cheese for supper. He didn't eat more than two dumplings, well, it's the flu, he's got no appetite. But the fever's gone, he was O.K. this morning. Eva, can you imagine how I felt? I'd have dropped where I stood. When he was at home father wore a short fur jacket, and when he got up that morning and put the jacket on, it kept him warm. His hands and face were cold, but his body was still warm. Sister was listening at the door, thank heaven, and called me away and I fainted right there. A week, Eva, just think, a whole week! There wasn't a better actress, I'll swear Mother never knew a thing. I had to think up three different meals each day and tell her what he said about them. What messages he sent her. Who'd been to see him. I had to be careful not to think up too much, or she'd have noticed. Poor old dad, that week he lay dead and there was I washing his shirts, seeing he went to the barber's. . . . After the funeral I forgot to change my black stockings, and mother noticed them. Eva, just think, I couldn't even take the three days off I had the right to, for his funeral; mother would have known. She was waiting for me in the corridor, leaning against the wall. Why've you got black stockings? There was a hole in the others, and anyway, it's the fashion. You know I never manage to get my stockings mended! The black go well with my coat, though, don't they? She didn't say yes, just looked at me. Eva, she knew! She knew and all she needed was to make sure. And I lied to her all the time. I'll never forget how she shuffled backward along that corridor. She was trying to get the truth out of me. When she died and lay there, I wondered whether I'd done right to lie to her like that. She didn't live any longer for it, and if I hadn't, we could have cried together. As it was, we were trying to catch each other out."

It was winter, it was freezing cold. Father had been the local gravedigger and there was no one to follow him, no one to dig his grave. The neighbors said I should have him cremated and his ashes put in an urn, but Father always wanted to be buried in the ground. He thought he'd be able to meet Mother again. So then they said I ought to keep the body in a fridge till the spring, for the ground to get soft . . ."

Denise, his daughter, took a spade and a pickax and fought

with the hard ground. You have to know what her hands are like, if you are to appreciate what she did. When she combed my hair her fingertips were so soft, so gentle, I could feel her letting my hair run through her fingers, and yet as her hands touched my scalp there was both firmness and gentleness, like a mother running her fingers over the head of a fluffy newborn baby— like the nurse she was, bandaging painful wounded flesh. How good it must have felt to be cared for by those hands! And there she was, the ground as hard as rock, snow to be cleared off, the ice was biting. They needed a deep hole. Her brother, her husband, her son, and her daughter all helped her dig. A week later, when her mother died, they did the same thing for her.

She said it herself: the men go for me. There were four men tangled in her case. She stole, to be able to help her loved ones. And the details of her thefts were shameful enough. When the grapevine began to condemn her, and sharply, she tried to pretend to the others that she had only shown a deficit in a pub. One of the men she refused to love had informed on her—and when the police caught her, his love was not up to date: what IS, IS, and so he felt discarded. Not only did he tell the police she had stolen for him, his jealousy was so poisonous, he had to tell her next lover, and when everything came to light her family, husband, son, and daughter were all caught up in it. Her husband was weighed down by all the shameful network of lovers, thefts, and deceits that came to light when the police really got to work on Denise. When the case came to court and he was called as a witness, he said he was going to divorce her. At last. And the rejected lover—a fireman—would be one of the witnesses at her divorce. The shame of it! Yes, your honor, she gave me this car radio, we used to go on picnics together. No, your honor, of course it was a gift from her. She didn't have to give me anything, your honor, I'd no idea it was stolen goods, your honor, not until the case came out, your honor, and where would she have got enough to buy such an expensive radio, your honor?

"Half the village will be there to look, Eva, they won't pass up the chance. What a treat I'll give them!" If only they hadn't remanded her; if she were free, outside, she'd manage things, persuade people, smooth things over—that was something she did well. It was the power of her personality that kept all her NOW lives in balance, kept everyone happy. It was her cheerfulness, her bravery, and her extraordinary will for good that kept them all going. And now that she was in jail, her will, her personality could no longer influence any of them: evil must prevail. Her husband would divorce her, her beloved would leave her, the rejected lover would do all he could to damage her, she was so unhappy: "Eva, say something, please, do!"

Denise had got married young, nearly twenty years ago; he was handsome—like his father—and only he could have said what bound him to her when she was so unfaithful. They had two children, but the first child, the girl, was not his. If my calculations were right, Denise must have conceived while her husband was in the army, not long before their marriage. He was still in uniform then, his commander was his best man and the whole unit arrived in an army truck. Denise used to visit her husband, taking a hotel room somewhere near the camp for the night; it was one of those great loves. They got married because she was expecting, although he knew the child wasn't his. Denise never told me who the real father was. Her daughter was a lovely girl, happy and determined, like her mother. The girl lost her job when Denise was arrested, but she didn't mind. She took whatever jobs were going and sent kind letters to Denise in prison. This child caused Denise reproaches from her husband for years, and the girl did not like her father; her relation to her mother was one of quiet conspiracy, such as women know how to spin. It is women's only means of defense, to create a world where man cannot enter. Denise's husband was wildly jealous of her: he was rough, he beat her, he got drunk.

Looking at their relationship from his point of view, I would have to agree that Denise had ruined his life. Yet if she were released she would have him for her own again; she would smile, or she would not, she would talk to him, or she wouldn't say a word, she would cook for him, or she wouldn't bother, she would come home, or she wouldn't—the way women run their men. I love you, I don't, I will let you, I won't, teasing, offering joys to come . . .

Denise was like a crystal: beautiful with its sharp edges, its shining surfaces, its glow. Whatever she longed for, she took. In her defense it must be said that she was always ready to take full responsibility for the consequences. She was estranged from her husband, but it was not only habit, and the fact that they had a son, that kept her in his home. Whatever happened, she still loved him. She was proud that their son took after him. Her love for her husband may not have changed much; her love was as clear as crystal, and from its facets every new lover drew a new reflection. She could have left her husband: her daughter was going to get married and the boy was apprenticed and didn't need her any more. She and her lover had even worked out a plan of escape. Yet her heart would have ached for her husband. They lived poorly enough, no luxury, yet she liked the rooms that used to be part of a monastery, where there **was** no bathroom and the lavatory was outside in the yard. And she liked the secret room in Prague where she and her lover used to meet. It was all part of her innermost, real life.

She understood her husband's anger and suffered for it. She was unhappy to see their unsatisfactory, unsatisfied marriage fall apart; yet the next moment she started worrying about her present love. That she was in prison did not worry her so much as that, being in prison, she might lose her lover. Prison life in itself she didn't find too bad; her day was filled with trivialities wherever she was, so why not in prison? And across the yard she had a friend arrested for bankruptcy; his wife was her best friend and slipped scraps of news about her husband's case into the letters Denise got from her family. She managed to get the same lawyer for Denise as her husband had. All these little things helped Denise to feel at home in jail; she made no effort to resist, she accepted prison, and got used to it. She was happy for the whole day if she managed to catch sight of her friend in the exercise yard. And how happy she was to find a boy from her schooldays among the guards! "That's our Stan!"

Stan gave not the slightest sign that he recognized her, but he took her part at the doctor's when she was asking for the right to lie down during the day. The two were alone in the waiting room for a moment, and he begged her never to speak to him of her own accord. "You've no idea how things work here." That same Stan helped me, too, once, and Denise was happy to hear it. She had the great gift of seeing everything as she saw it herself. That she settled down in jail did not mean that she accepted prison conditions; she simply took whatever came, as best she might. Nor did she ever start blaming others . . . look, here I am in jail, and you've got away with it . . . she was too much of the grandee.

Jaroslav, the last and for the moment the greatest love, had no idea she was getting money like that, and he was insulted when the police investigating her case suggested theft. If he had known, he would have forbidden it! Denise did not blame anyone else. She took all the blame on herself and was not even angry with the jealous, unsuccessful rival for her affections who did her such damage at the trial. She ought never to have started anything with such a weak no-good! She made no attempt to deny her thefts, to lead her interrogating officer up the garden path. What I did, I did, and I'm willing to bear the consequences. All I want is for *him to love me still*. She didn't tell them, at home, that trouble was brewing. For months they'd been investigating, and she waited for the whole affair to break out, ashamed for her children and afraid of what her husband would do. Then the police came to her house to arrest her; there was no hiding her shame before the neighbors in the village. The police searched their home for hours. Yet she did not treat her interrogating officer as an enemy out to trip her up, but as a village friend who knows what is going on. Denise could only send one letter home every two weeks, and because she could not send messages to her lover in letters addressed to her husband, the woman officer in charge of her case offered to act as go-between. Jaroslav's letters were delivered to Denise as official communications, and her letters for him were collected by the officer when she was interrogated, and Jaroslav went to pick them up at the High Court. It was a clever move on the part of the woman officer concerned, but Denise gave no return. It was her character that would not let her deny the truth, and there was no hint of sycophancy in her attitude. She was simply happy to find, in her misfortune, a woman officer who understood her love life and its troubles.

Denise and her lover had a room in Prague, in a flat belonging to a widowed friend. From all she said I soon knew what the house looked like, what the room was like. The weekend hut of their friend and his son flooded that year when the river overflowed, and Denise helped them to dry out all the mattresses and floor mats. And I knew what their window in Prague looked out on, the window box of fuchsia on the third floor, and the Gypsy children begging cigarettes on the sidewalk in front. When they sent me to the prison X-ray in the central hospital, I was driven along those streets Denise knew, and at four in the afternoon there was a traffic jam. As we drove slowly I saw it all: the spot where Denise let a Gypsy child pull at her cigarette; the spot where Jaroslav waited in the rain because he'd forgotten his key and she had mixed up the time of their meeting; the shop where she always bought wine and sandwiches; the spot where she always gossiped with the Gypsies—and anyway, they're better fun than whites, in a pub. When I got back I had to recount every detail of my journey and answer her questions: Who was standing outside their house? Were the house doors open or shut? Which tram went past just then? Were the Gypsies there in front of the pub, from grannies to sucklings at the breast? What was I thinking of as I passed? Was I remembering her? Was the sun shining? Just at four o'clock in the afternoon the sun always shines for a while on the fuchsia in the third-floor window. Then she broke down and cried. I had seen the place where she had been happiest on earth—and she wasn't there!

How difficult it is to keep the present alive in us. It is easier for those who think both of the past and the future in the present moment. Hope is always possible for them. But those who see only what is NOW are worse off, because the force of gravity of what IS destroys hope and all that is left is a fleeting vision and a bad taste in the mouth. The NOW that IS does not know what NOW will be coming next.

For the first two months in jail Jaroslav filled her days; either she was talking about him, or she was writing to him. Her fear of losing him made her sick, nervous even to vomiting. She told us so many tales of their life together; either they went away somewhere so as to make love, or they met somewhere where they couldn't make love. Denise loved everything about Jaroslav, his body, his character, his children, his car, his weekend cottage, his job. The only thing she didn't like about him was his wife, but they were preparing to get rid of her. Jaroslav had made up his mind to run away. And that was what hurt Denise most of all: Where would she not have been if they hadn't arrested her just then? They would have been together in the mountains; Jaroslav would have been working as a lumberman, and she would be waiting for him in their cottage. She wrote him long and persistent letters. When she was taken out for interrogation she had with her all the notepaper she could get hold of, covered from margin to margin in her tiny handwriting. She kept an account of when she wrote and when she could expect an answer, and she wept inconsolably when replies were slow in coming. She worked out her lover's shifts: now he's on the morning shift, then there'll be two night shifts, then he'll have a day off, and she worked out, according to his timetable, when he would have time to write to her, since he had to do it on the sly, mostly on night shifts, and when he could manage to take his letters to her interrogating officer, in the High Court building. When she calculated that a letter ought to arrive, and it didn't, she sat there dully. "Eva! Say something, for God's sake!"

"Don't be so impatient."

"You don't know what I'm like."

Poor Jaroslav! When Denise was arrested it was like being hit over the head. At first he had no idea what had happened, why she had disappeared; he was afraid to go to her home, because her husband had already beaten him up once. Denise did all she could to make sure the first news he got was from her own hand; her interrogating officer gave him a letter soon after she was arrested; it may have been a week later, ten days . . . but by that time rumors were going round the place where he worked, and where she had been employed up to the time she was given an invalid's pension. Unpleasant news travels much faster than genuine appreciation of hard work done. And even if Denise had no enemies—she had so many of them!—and even if nobody spread unkind rumors, the very reason why they arrested her was enough to crush Jaroslav.

"If only you had told me, yourself," he wrote. "You might have let me know what was happening. They'd been watching you for months, and you didn't say a word!"

Denise managed to persuade the officer not to tell Jaroslav the whole truth. The whole, or the almost the whole, truth he learned from the man he had displaced in her affections, and how willingly the rejected lover obliged! There you are, that's women for you, it wasn't only for you that she went thieving, I had my share, as well. And poor Denise was so helpless, shut up in jail with us. She tried to guess from Jaroslav's letters how much he already knew, and what his reaction was, reading between the lines because he was too proud to write what he really felt. And between the lines she might read more than he meant—or less. She could not judge the true state of his feelings, and even if she guessed right, by the time he got her letter he might be thinking God knows what! Oh, dear, what was left to her but to use her only weapon: words. Words on paper, and words she could not write, like how was she to find money for their love life when he had to take his whole wages home to his family, and she couldn't bring herself to rob her family, either? There was rent to pay for the room where they met, there was the occasional meal out, there was petrol to be paid for. She bought a bottle of wine now and again, his favorite cigarettes . . . she bought a secondhand carpet for their room, curtains, a cover for the divan. Only the woman knows that love alone is not enough when you're no longer seventeen, and that it's important to give love the right setting. And there were things that could not be explained without a caressing hand, without a smile, unless they were gazing into each other's eyes. Oh, how gently those hands would have calmed him while she explained that she had *had* to steal for the man before him, and not only for him! How lovingly she would have erased from his mind the image of the unworthy creature she had deserted for him!

Jaroslav did not know what to think; he wrote her in moments of deep emotion, but his letters betrayed the waves of mistrust and doubt that overwhelmed him. Doubt that everybody around him would only too willingly encourage. Why should anybody take the side of a woman in prison? There was no one on her side, on the side of a woman who lives freely, with her own ways, her own victories, no one to stand by her even when they were still free, and what could she expect now? They were all against her, and now she was not there to fight them! The only live link between her and Jaroslav was her interrogating officer; he wept in her office, he waited hours to catch her, crushed, and yet with a grain of hope that the whole business was a dream, that it just wasn't true. Reading Denise's long letters, secretly, and burning them afterward so his wife wouldn't find them, Jaroslav felt terribly alone and betrayed.

"If he loves you like that, he'll wait for you to come out."

"He won't wait. I've told you. You don't know him. He's well over six foot. He used to do muscle training, and when he left off it all went to fat. Eva, he's a mountain of a man, and he's got to have a woman every day, whatever happens." And my little Denise folded her hands helplessly in her lap, so tiny, so virginal, I could not imagine how she had managed to satisfy her giant. Jaroslav's wife was kind, pretty enough, a bit stupid, that wouldn't matter, but she wasn't lively enough. And Denise was just that—not a consuming fire that is soon over, but a flame, a clear, bright flame that was ever ready to light. He would have been scared off by a devouring conflagration! When Denise talked about Jaroslav she was like a pitcher overflowing with the good wine poured into it. So full of happiness that she had to break off, she had to rest before she could go on remembering such happiness. What man could resist such a woman! It would have to be a lazy fellow, one that Jaroslav's wife would be happy with. That she "went for men" was at last appreciated. Jaroslav came to see her every day when she was in the hospital after her hip operation. The surgeon was a friend of his, and he let him take her out into the country every day. Psychological preparation for my operation, the doctor said it was. Even the last day, I was all prepared for operation, all the tests and everything, and he persuaded the surgeon that I'd be best prepared if he took me out. When I'd been operated he just looked in at the door. I had my whole family around me then, then two days later he turned up and said I had to have a bath, and he carried me in his arms, into the bathroom, and locked the door. When we hadn't enough time to go to our room, he would park up in Břevnov, beyond the monastery, there's never a soul there. He valued every minute he could be with me."

"What about Sundays?"

"Eva, use your brains. Why do you think Bartík took to drink?"

"Denise, he'll never find another woman like you."

"What do you think he did before he knew me?"

She was terribly unhappy. But she was Inanna, and she lived for the moment.

Denise had been in Ruzyně for three months. Once again she was writing long letters, such long letters. We had been moved to an older building, where they had made a special women's wing. There were six of us in a cell meant for four, with a low ceiling, and when we set up all six beds you could not get a finger between them. We breathed into each other's faces, stifling in the stink of our bodies. Denise slept next to me, and I would be wakened in the night by the sound of her pencil rustling over the paper, covering sheet after sheet in her small fine hand. We had managed to save a whole roll of toilet paper my husband had sent, firm enough to take the pencil, soft enough to roll up tight, tie with elastic, and let down through the window.

A new star shining in Denise's heaven! If she could get out of jail she would run as fast as she could to her Jaroslav, but it would be a long time before that could happen. Her family, her husband, her children, even her lover, had turned into the motionless background of a renaissance painting, a stage setting that has nothing to do with real faces. They would seem strangely naked against that immovable background. She no longer had any influence on her family or on her lover. Her daughter was getting married to a boy she had never seen, her son had bought the motorbike she had refused to allow him, her husband was asking for a divorce, her lover Jaroslav had not been heard of lately. . . . Life goes on outside, and life must go on inside, as well. Now, at this moment, and for this moment.

Make no mistake about it, Denise was not engaged in a lighthearted flirtation. Our cell was above two smaller ones, with three and four men in them; we had two windows, one above each of theirs, and with the one cell we could communicate by the toilet phone, with the other by shouting into the wash basin. There were seven men, or fourteen, if you count those two floors down, who also called us. Denise unfailingly chose the most decent boy, the most unfortunate, perhaps, in the whole prison just then. He wasn't even twenty, and for his sake she pretended to be younger, and she probably saved his life.

Let's say his name was Jura; he sent his papers up for us to read: he was to be court-martialed for desertion and for preparing to defect. The way he put it, it was all the fault of a jealous woman. He'd been sleeping with the wife of one of his officers, then he didn't want her any more and said more than he should have at their army dance. The lady told her husband, and his friends at the dance gave evidence against him; they were all scared. A soldier on military service had said in front of witnesses that he'd rather get away from the bloody country altogether. Anyway, he was a Hungarian Slovak and he had relatives in Vienna. Besides the charge of preparing to cross the frontier illegally and the charge of desertion, they added a third: preparing to steal arms and other military property, that meant his uniform, because they assumed he would defect just as he was, in uniform. As a Hungarian Slovak, in jail Jura felt alone in the world. He had nobody besides his mother, who spoke no Czech—it took a long time for the prison censor to have her letters translated from Hungarian, before Jura could get them. He had a girlfriend, but she wrote simply that she was dropping him. Wasn't that more than enough for one young fellow?

Prisoners left to their fate, helpless and alone, draw comfort from smuggled letters; it is a bond between one human being and another, a bond that is closer than the spoken word because it is more personal, more intimate. Denise wrote and wrote; and she needed to write, to get her own unhappiness out of her system. She rolled her papers up like a medieval bard; she never showed me what she had written, I knew all about her love for Jaroslav, and perhaps she had some qualms of conscience, but I was careful never to suggest any reproach—she would have been deeply hurt and ashamed—and could never have forgiven me for calling up that shame. Judging by her glowing face, her shining eyes, she was writing love letters to Jura. And she struck a new slogan for our cell: everything for Jura! Persevering, active, inventive—and I accepted her necessity.

Everything for Jura! Our cells had been specially repaired, and the mesh of the window screen was double-thick and covered the whole of the embrasure. The prison authorities never know what to do with a lot of women, how to prevent them contacting the men prisoners, how to keep them isolated. This newly repaired wing was their pride. The Governor's deputy came to inspect all our windows, personally, and wherever he found the tiniest gap he had the trusties in to make it fast. Denise and I had never sent horses before—that was something the young girls did—but now we found ourselves scraping the plaster away to form a gap between the screen and the wall, to get our horse through. It had to be done carefully, because the daily cell inspection might have betrayed us; the girls who were silly enough to break the screen to get their horses out not only had the screens fixed even more firmly but had to pay for the repairs themselves; where the guards found lumps of plaster missing, wires were put in. We used our spoons to wear away the plaster a millimeter at a time, taking turns, and getting our knuckles raw and sore. Everything for Jura! Denise and I had been given new blankets when we were moved, and the stitching thread was the best you could find for horses; we unpicked it carefully; it was good strong thread and long enough for plaiting to make a good rope. Everything for Jura! It was not too difficult to push cigarettes through at the edge of the screen, and letters went all right, too, but we had more trouble with the homemade sausages Jura's mother sent him, and the chocolate liquers my husband sent me. To get a drop of alcohol to those thirsty men! How they rejoiced when one of them got a whiskey, one a rum, and the third a plum brandy! When Denise sent her horse off in the morning, I did my exercises right in front of our cell door, sure of catching the guard's eye if he peeped through the spy hole, and he would not see what she was doing. Our horses and riders made from the cardboard mattresses of our broken-down beds had to be well hidden. They caught us once, and so we had to be doubly careful, but I'm not going to say how we hid them. That is a secret to be given only to other prisoners. Everything for Jura!

Denise rejoiced: "Just look at Eva: she's sending a horse!" That was when she couldn't get a thick letter round the screen, she was angry and frustrated, and I pushed her aside and did it for her. Her horse might have fallen down, the way she was pulling the thread! Everything for Jura! We took turns to stand by the door when she was phoning Jura, red in the face as she got as close as she could to the drain pipe in our oriental loo, so as to be understood in the cell below without shouting and attracting the attention of our guards. Everything for Jura!

In jail, nothing can take the place of genuine friendliness. Hunger and cold, you can stand them; but to feel yourself alone, deserted, that is the worst. It is like winning a lottery to find someone to rely on, someone whose good word, good deed, can help out. That young soldier was trying to think out ways of committing suicide in jail. He was in a state of profound depression, as we heard later from his fellows in the cell. He hadn't eaten for days, hadn't spoken to them. He did not even want to say anything in self-defense at his trial. The whole world is a whorehouse, people are just swine. Why bother? ... When Denise started writing her love letters, Jura had no time left to bother about suicide. She wrote on one side of the paper, and he was supposed to answer on the other, and when the poor boy had nothing left to say, he taught her Hungarian. He was an automobile fan, he knew all the speed aces and their records, and Denise learned a lot from his letters. He was caught, once, phoning with Denise, and so he was punished. He was not allowed to buy anything in the prison canteen, and they even kept back a parcel his mother sent him. . . . What did it matter? He took it all as the price he paid for Denise. He must have been beaten up when they caught him the second time, but it didn't seem to matter. Anyway he could tell Denise about it. . . . The only thing he feared was being moved to another cell. He wasn't worried about his trial, and he thought of mother more than he had before, but not so sorrowfully. His feeling for Denise had brought him back into the world of the living, out of that hopeless emptiness.

Everything for Jura! It was not only the moment, the present. Denise gave herself up once more to another human being, to another flood of emotion. We never had enough cigarettes. It was a big cell, and that means there was always someone new, someone who had nothing to smoke. Denise's share was halved: to me and Jura, and she offered her half share around. How could Jura get along, if he didn't share what she sent him? Denise was allowed a visit by her husband. He told her he wanted a divorce, and one of his arguments was her consumption of cigarettes. Her daughter had lost her job and had to take something that paid much less, he had only his two thousand a month, the boy was getting pocket money but nothing more. Denise's pension had stopped the moment she was arrested. The family couldn't afford her cigarettes! It didn't upset her that her husband calculated how many cigarettes he had given her lawyer, her interrogating officer, how many he had put into the parcels he sent her in jail. It was his right, he was paying. And she agreed, there were really more cigarettes than she could have smoked alone. "We're giving up things so you can have enough—and God knows who you're giving the fags to."

That was a blow below the belt. Who was she giving the fags

to? Jura! She couldn't accept the idea that she was saving smokes for herself while Jura didn't have any. Her family were going short? Her family were far away, Jura was close by. She was going short for Jura, and Jura would do the same for her, if he could.

"He can't help it that they're there and they caught him telephoning so now he can't even buy his own smokes. Eva! Say something. I can't let him go without a smoke, can I?" Selfish? She'd have done the same for anyone in the family, if they'd been at hand. And if anybody in the family, God forbid!, were arrested, she'd have done the same for them. She'd have stolen, to help them. Given her last rag.

Suddenly Jura was taken away. He knocked on the ceiling at a time we weren't used to and said sadly into the toilet phone that he was being moved. He didn't even have time to write a letter. Denise could not grasp the terrible news.

"Be quiet, will you, I can't make out what he's saying." Jura commissioned his cell mate to write Denise and tell her he'd never loved anybody as he loved her. The cell mate added of his own accord that Jura had wanted to kill himself, and it was thanks to Denise that he didn't. We all cried as we sat round our table that night. Denise was slowly beginning to realize that she'd never hear his voice again, never read any more of his letters. At night she lay gazing dry-eyed at the ceiling. We talked, but that kept the others awake. So we wrote each other letters, we each had part of a toilet roll and put down whatever thoughts the day had brought. I wrote about the trivialities of our prison day—anything to keep that empty look out of her eyes. She was amused for a moment, and then she again lay there gazing at nothing. Then she had a brilliant idea: Jura had disappeared into the labyrinth of prison, but she would find him! She engraved his name on all our mess tins—six every morning, twelve at midday, and another twelve every evening.

When she had time enough, she added, "Denise sends her love to Jura!" She hustled us, eat up, do, let's scratch his name before they come around for the tins. We tried to work out how the mess tins might move round the prison: at least one of all those dozens of tins might reach him, if he had lodged an appeal and thus prolonged his remand time. For a few weeks Denise lived on her hopes that Jura would be drinking his tea, or eating his soup, and find beneath the stale crust of other people's food her loving greeting. Everything for Jura!

There is something to add to the Jura story: Denise came into prison with a severe handicap; one hip had been operated some two years earlier, and the other a few months before her arrest. She used a stick to walk, because the operated hip joint was still not firmly healed. They took her stick away from her. She limped, her leg ached, she got cramps, and had to take pills. After a few weeks when she was forced to walk without a stick, even the short distance to the exercise cages, her knee began turning outward, a sure sign that the repaired hip joint was still weak. Perhaps that is the worst thing about prison, that it makes the sick suffer even more. Each time her lawyer appealed for her release on health grounds, the answer was: all her needs are being taken care of. Her needs were so well taken care of that she had to have her pills sent in from outside, otherwise she'd have been without the treatment her operated-on hip needed. Denise was a brave woman; she put every catastrophe away from her, and could not bear anything that humiliated her. I am myself, even if I have to limp! Jealous girls in the next cell, who could listen in on her toilet phone talk, guessed who she was by counting the cells. Although it was true love they were eaves-dropping, or perhaps for that very reason, they warned Jura that it was no young girl he was writing his love letters to, but an elderly woman (everybody over thirty was old to them!) and not only old, but lame as well. He was quick to confide in her, and she wrote back that they had just mixed her up with somebody else. I had to admire her. She did not shrink, she did not get upset, she did not let it throw her off balance: I am myself, and if anybody thinks she's better, we'll see. I might break her nose. Jura may have loved her gentle, velvet voice, her letters, more than he cared for the truth.

When they moved us to this cell we could look out beyond the prison precincts, and I found a spot where I could see my husband. The family began to make Saturday afternoon visits, although all they could see was a white handkerchief tied to a piece of string and pushed out between the wall and the window screen. For them to be sure it was me I would have to have shouted at them. There were two things I could not bring myself to do in jail: to talk into the toilet phone and to shout from the window. It was my own pride that would not let me. I was not going to give my jailers the pleasure of seeing me behave otherwise than I would if I were at liberty. Yet I would have given anything to know my husband recognized that I was waving that handkerchief. Denise followed my insoluble embarrassment and then climbed on to the top bed and did what I could not bring myself to do: she shouted. And how! That clear ringing call of one prisoner to another, every morning and every evening. My husband hung a bunch of flowers on the fence (it was not long before someone stole them) and Denise's voice rang out: "Jirka! I love you! Eva!" The flowers made a tiny red blob of color, so far away, like flowers on a grave, and we were all in tears: we had overcome the feeling of being imprisoned. How disappointed we all would have been the next Saturday if my husband had not appeared with a bunch of flowers. "There he is!" Denise saw him first. And the flowers were at least partly hers.

In that new cell, every evening Denise became its queen. Not during the day, when the guards reign, but in the evening. She knew a sentimental song that was said to be the anthem of the prisoners in Valdice, and she turned it into Denise's song. We all sang it together as our goodnight. We laid out our Gypsy camp, setting up the beds, spreading sheets and blankets for the night, changing into our orange pajamas, folding our brown track suits and gray shirts as the regulations demanded, ready for inspection. We trod on each other's beds because there was not an inch between them and sang:

The sun is setting, the pale moon has emerged from the
   clouds,
The tiny island of Tahiti glows in the afterlight.

A little boat sails away, its captain the king of the seas,
And he calls back to land: I won't forget!

A dark-skinned girl waves him farewell, come back soon,
Come back, my love—I send this pale flower after you.

The sun is setting, the pale moon has emerged from the
   clouds,
And only the tiny island of Tahiti hears the song the dark
   girl sings.

Denise growled out of tune, moved by her song every evening.

Toward the end of my remand period, probably because it had already been decided to release us, I was moved to what had been the hospital wing, with its airy, sunny cells. Probably so I wouldn't get "ideas," other women were moved there with me—three cells in all. Denise was among them, but we were not put into the same cell, and so we could only talk to one another through the windows—and once we met in the bathroom. Then they came and said, "Get your things ready, you're going home." I knocked on the wall to let her know, but there was no time to talk. The guards were at the door. And so I couldn't even say good-bye to Denise.

11

VERA

They brought in a girl with the face of an angel and the body of a young virgin, which only goes to show the tricks reality can play on us. Vera was anything but angelic or virginal; she was a real tough, and Lucy's prediction, "Just wait till you come up against a real tough girl!" came into its own. I would rather have skipped Vera, because I do not like writing about people for whom I cannot find a good word to say. But it happened to be through Vera that Helga worked her revenge on me, and a drama once begun must be taken to its very end.

A real tough girl, so far as I can judge from experience in jail, is one who is unable and unwilling to acknowledge any but her own little world, one who is her own measure and wants to be that for others as well; but since she gives short measure, she soon comes up against them and begins using force to get her way, to stake her claims, to impose her law. There was a real tough girl in the cell next to us who beat up an old woman every day, just because she was old. "She didn't ought to be old, that's all. Can't bear the sight of 'em, they've no right to be hanging round."

Some other real tough girls started to skin a mentally defective girl because she wouldn't give up her place at the toilet phone. Talking to the men was her favorite pastime, and they must have found it too idiotic to listen to. They used their fingernails to scratch the skin off her legs and arms. The poor girl sobbed and screamed and they must have been having a great time. Listening to the sounds, magnified like everything else in jail, we thought some weak creature was slowly being tortured to death. The guards must have heard it too, but it was hours before anybody opened the cell. By that time blood was pouring from the girl and they took her off to the washroom. The real tough girls protect some of their cell mates against others; a tough "king" protects his followers against newcomers.

Vera had grown up in a children's home. All she said about her mother was that she was a deaf-mute; her father, her "old man," was a Gypsy. She was sent back to him at fifteen, neither white nor Gypsy, but with an idea of the world of the whites and their material advantages; that was all she wanted of life, yet she was unwilling to lift a finger to get it. She had failed her apprentice exams in the textile factory where she was learning an undemanding trade. She was utterly ignorant, and yet she raged that they had the cheek not to keep her on; she had counted on starting to earn a real wage instead of the apprentice's pocket money. So she ran away from the home and from the ungrateful factory. In childhood she had learned the law of the jungle: fight to get what you want or use your charms. She could not accept failure. Living in a large group had made her wildly ambitious, and she was convinced there was nobody to beat her. Her stunted emotions had never had a chance, and she was deprived of the tenderness, the devotion, the playful child-like happiness that Gypsy girls have. She only hankered after material things; unlike Lucy, for instance, she didn't care about expressions of affection. The only personal relationship Vera knew was: Will you give, or won't you? Love meant sex and nothing more. She was arid, hard, but not without intelligence, quick to see where advantage lay and seize it. She must have grown up surrounded by proofs that the world goes to the strong and death to the weak. She would only be deflected by someone stronger than she was or by the realization that she was in danger of losing some material advantage.

She made for Prague with a gang of youths; the only girl, she enjoyed a privileged position as the leader's moll and that flattered her. On their way across the country, they stole from gardens along the road. Her lover suffered from an irresistible urge to break into any car that took his fancy and drive away in it. "It was his old man's fault, not letting him drive theirs." Pseudopsychological clichés are a prison commonplace. The father was apparently a doctor and the son a university student. He was arrested in Prague just as he was opening somebody else's car; Vera was a short distance away and managed to flee. After her lover's arrest, the leaderless gang hanging round her became a potential danger, and she dropped out of their sight.

When she was arrested she told the police plenty about her lover; the idea of being considerate, faithful, affectionate, understanding, tactful, or kind simply made her laugh. "What sort of a world d'you people live in?" She took it as a real compliment when Denise said she was a tricky bitch. "You're bloody well right," she answered, and not because she was stupid. I came across at least a dozen girls in Ruzyně who resembled Vera in their background and in their stories; each of them had been arrested in a disco, all of them had been through the closed VD ward, none of them had a job, they all lived by small-scale prostitution and petty theft—and practically all of them came from children's homes. They gravitated to Prague in the hope of adventure and an easy life; and they all kept to that life and its little pleasures, unable to live otherwise—except for Vera. Ambition drove her, and in the three months after she came to the capital she had got into bigger business, making money on black market currency deals and living with a young woman who had contacts with German visitors interested in getting hold of Czech girls on the cheap. We were told the other young woman had a child whose father in West Germany paid her Prague rent and kept her. He was an older man, and he was going to marry her. Vera swore to Denise that the woman was just a friend, and that she was not a procuress. With her connections and her experience, Vera was a cut above those other girls. In Prague she had caught both the clap and scabies, but I would put that down to conceit rather than stupidity; she was so sure it couldn't happen to *her*. She did not intend to give up her career, although she was in Ruzyně, and got me to tell her the German for such phrases as "I've got an apartment of my own"; "Come with me, I'm worth it"; "I take four hundred marks." She wrote the words down phonetically, in a notebook of folded toilet paper, and repeated them aloud until she knew them by heart. That was the only activity that didn't bore her, except perhaps eating.

In everything she was just beyond the limit one could understand and beyond which one becomes watchful. She would not acknowledge anybody who did not admire her. But what was there to admire? To say she had no manners would be putting it mildly. Convinced that she was irresistible, she was utterly uninhibited in her coarseness. She would belch loudly and laugh at a particularly effective performance. She farted deliberately, getting up to wiggle her ass for every raspberry; she thought she was excruciatingly funny as well as charming. But it was her way of attracting attention.

When Denise offered her a cigarette Vera showed her appreciation by blowing the smoke back in her face; it made her feel they were on more intimate terms. She envied us whatever we were eating, watching every mouthful and never omitting to look into our mess tins three times a day, to make sure we hadn't got something she hadn't. We adults treated her more or less as a child, and she naturally was given the best helpings. And of course we shared our parcels with her; neither of us would have dreamed of eating anything from home without offering it around, but Vera took it as an insult that we could even receive something she didn't. That was why she stole so openly, stealing as naturally as she walked or breathed; it was her personal way of righting the injustice of the world. She would have stolen from us in the cell if Denise had not put her foot down.

Vera was unbelievably dirty for an ambitious young girl. She had to be made to wash herself. She never cleaned her teeth because "there was nothing wrong with them"; the track suits we were issued were bad enough when they were clean, but within an hour or two Vera's was filthy with food smears, felt-tip colors, and snot. The radiator in the cell was small, just five ribs, and three times a day let out a faint warmth that had no effect on the cellarlike dankness in which we sat. The prison authorities maintained that the cells were not ventilated properly—which was true of some cells where they couldn't see one another for smoke—and as winter came on, they remedied this hygienic defect by nailing an inch-wide strip of wood across the window frame to stop prisoners from shutting the window. All day and all night there was a chilly draft; as soon as the radiator warmed up a little, Vera sat down on the floor with her back to it, absorbing all its warmth into her track suit and her body.

"Vera, sit next to the radiator, not in front of it, the warmth isn't getting into the cell at all."

"I'm cold."

"We're just as cold," Denise replied with the firmness of an experienced mother.

"You should have got here first and then you'd be warm."

"We wouldn't think of a dirty trick like that, Miss Clever."

"So much the worse for you," she sneered and did not move until Denise threatened to stop giving her cigarettes.

To make herself more interesting, she pretended she was Italian, but we lived too close to one another, and she modestly withdrew the claim. In other cells, though, especially the men's, she was known as the Italian girl. She based her claim on two things: a slight resemblance to Gina Lollobrigida in the placing of her well-shaped cheekbones and big black eyes, although her plebeian eyebrows were too thick—Denise had to pluck them for her—and her hair was typically Gypsy. When Vera began to get fat—because she stuffed herself all day on bread and jam, out of sheer boredom—her features coarsened like those of older Gypsy women, and Lollobrigida and angel-face were gone for good.

Her other bond with Italy was her future: if it was not the first thing she said, it was the second: she was going to marry an Italian. She had been picked up at a disco by a handsome and wealthy young Italian dealer in antiques, who took her to the flat he maintained in Prague. They went there by tram, and he gave her an engagement ring.

"Why doesn't he have a car if he's so rich?"

They went by tram so the police wouldn't notice anything. If her fiancé was as handsome and rich as Vera was Italian, they made a fine pair.

"What's his name?" The practical mother in Denise was aroused.

"Mario."

"Mario what?"

She didn't know his surname, but that did not shake her self-assurance; if she didn't know his name yet, she'd find out later. Mario had gone back to Italy to prepare his mother for the marriage. Wealthy Italian families laid great stress on such things.

"How's he going to find you in jail?" Denise pretended to be anxious.

Even that did not shake Vera. He'd find her, never fear.

"All those girls at the disco," Denise went on. "He'll soon find someone else." She winked at me—now watch me take the mickey out of this signorina of ours. Her teasing was good-natured, for we were both deceived by Vera's angelic virginal appearance and took it for granted that she was a normal young girl who'd got into bad company, and we wouldn't have wanted to push her deeper into trouble by seeming not to care.

"No way. I'm the one he loves. He came to the disco one night, it was before I'd chucked the gang, and Mario was so jealous he got tight and went off in a huff. I wanted to give him his ring back next morning . . ."

"You and give something back! Where is the precious ring, anyway?"

"In the prison safe."

"Sixpenny junk, and in the safe!"

"No way. It was pure gold with a blue stone. I'd get I don't

222

know how many thousand for it. Mario wouldn't take it back; that shows he loves me, so there."

"He must have loved you plenty if he got the clap from you."

"He couldn't get the clap from me."

"Be your age. What did you say you'd been treated for in the VD clinic, the clap or the pox?"

"Clap."

"There you are—and listen to me, Vera. Didn't it ever occur to you that it might have been him told the police about you?"

"Couldn't have been; he was in Italy by then."

"A fine bride-to-be *you* are, getting the clap the minute his back's turned. Haven't you any idea who you caught it from?"

"What's it matter, I'm clean now, aren't I?"

"Hey, Vera," Denise winked at me again, "wasn't it the other way round and you caught the clap from him before he went back to his rich mother?"

Vera had picked up three Italian words, whether from Mario or from somebody else; they formed her entire vocabulary: *pronto, cento, amigo.* "Mario!" she clasped her hands imploringly and looked up at the window (which unfortunately faced north), "Amigo, when are you coming to fetch me?"

"He'll be here pronto, pronto—in cento years." Denise gave her small comfort.

Vera had been cured of the clap, but we got scabies from her. The sores spread over her back and down her legs; she sat on the floor with her legs stretched out and scratched and scratched.

"Don't scratch the sores, Vera, they'll get infected."

"They itch."

"Vera, you've got the itch!"

She was insulted. "Me? Where'd I get the itch, I ask you?"

"Same place as you got the clap."

"I've always had eczema ever since I was little," she replied huffily, "I've got a delicate skin."

She refused to go to the doctor. A young signorina who looks like Lollobrigida cannot have the itch. Her long hard nails with their rim of thick dirt scratched and scratched, and I thought of Andy scrubbing her fingernails white. When lumps appeared on Denise's breast we asked to see the doctor, and Vera withdrew in disgust: "There you are, I got it off you, our beds are close together, and I smoke the fags you give me."

Denise and I were each given a bottle of white lotion to smear on our bodies as a prevention. Vera had been given a zinc ointment that had a foul smell; she stared at us with eyes full of hate as we used our lotion that didn't smell. And then as Denise rubbed the stinking ointment on her sore back, Vera sneered, "You got something better than me and your fingers'll stink just the same."

Vera's father was in prison too, and for the third time, for the same offense: assault and battery. Vera was proud of her father's reputation for brutality and felt even closer to him now they were both in jail. It was her stepmother who wrote and told her that he did not know about her arrest, and she hoped Vera would come home first and then it could be hushed up, not to worry Father. It was a generous letter, and I didn't have the feeling that they were empty words. Vera's stepmother was a non-Gypsy, older than her Gypsy father; she may have had trouble finding a husband, to marry a Gypsy. That takes courage in a small town where everybody knows everybody else, and that courage may come from despair and loneliness. Vera's father married her because she had a cottage of her own, and that made him a gentleman. It was on the outskirts of a town in northern Moravia, where the wife was the district rat killer, employed by the District Office of Public Hygiene to drive around to clean up infested homes and public buildings. Perhaps the two were happy for a few years; she bought beer for them to drink at home, and then he didn't go to the pub and didn't get into brawls. She began to care for her appearance—which roused Vera's jeers—but as it turned out, her Gypsy was happy to have a comfortable home where he was the master. He even started to wash, and he set up a hammock in the garden, where he would lie and be waited on by his wife. A Gypsy baron.

Then sixteen-year-old Vera appeared on the scene. Her stepmother accepted her without hesitation and affectionately; Vera had her own room upstairs; her stepmother bought her new clothes and got a job for her in the local laundromat. Her Gypsy father had scarcely seen her before (How often had he been to visit his child in the home?) and at the side of this lovely girl who admired him to excess he felt less a father than a man, flattered by the admiration of a young woman. After the restrictions of the home Vera felt free to give rein to her wild instincts, to her unlimited curiosity. She had a devouring thirst for unfettered liberty, and her "old man" let her do everything his wife wisely tried to restrain: she used makeup, she smoked, she drank, she was out late. Whenever she thought of her stepmother, Vera's voice became venomous with hate. The only letter she got while she was in jail was from her stepmother—she had nobody else, except her father in prison—and as she read it her face twisted with scorn: "That old cow's not going to tell *me* what to do!" She tore the letter to shreds in a fury and threw it down the toilet. She never wrote home except when she had a parcel permit to send. The "old cow" sent her a Christmas parcel and put into it the cigarettes she had forbidden her stepdaughter to smoke at home.

The rat killer was probably not much to look at, but she must have been a decent woman—and she had come upon Vera in bed with her father. She had not been trying to catch them out, she simply couldn't help discovering them sooner or later. She had begged the girl not to undress in front of her father, not to walk about naked—she would send her up to her room to dress—but Vera could not help teasing the man she had nearest to hand, who happened to be her father. In her conceit she asked Denise how the old cow could have dared to come between them.

Her stepmother tried to hang herself from a beam in her own cottage; Vera's father heard the stool fall as she kicked it away and cut her down at the last moment. Vera talked of the incident as something that hurt *her*. "The old man was wild, wild at her and wild at me. I had to get out that same night and run through the rain to the next village and sleep with friends there. It was so cold! There wasn't time to pack my warm boots, but the old cow will have to give them back. I'm going to write and ask for them the minute I get out."

"You're like a bomb, kid," said Denise. "Everything goes up in the air when you come on the scene."

This affair probably played a part in Vera's decision to run away. Her father began haunting the pub again, and before long he was fighting and landed in jail.

All the girls of Vera's kind are obsessed by sex; dancing, drinking, and sex are their way of evading the boredom of daily life. Yet even here Vera seemed to go farther, to go beyond the normal curiosity of her age, and even farther than her future profession required. She came back from gynecological examination and said despairingly, "There was a doctor there."

"So what?"

"Didn't even touch me, and he could tell I've had it."

Denise and I exchanged smiles. She's repeating what she's heard somewhere. And then, one Saturday, when there is hardly any warmth at all in the cells because the offices are closed for the weekend and why waste fuel on prisoners? I asked the guard on duty whether I couldn't go to the washroom for hot water—I'd got lemons from home—and make us all a hot drink. It was Tony, the fair Helen's friend from her psychiatric days, and while I went to fetch the water he dallied in our cell. Vera was still slim then, and her beauty moved Tony to pity her: "How did you get here, a pretty girl like you?" he asked sadly. "You must have been very, very naughty."

Vera was sitting on a stool by the door and didn't bother to get up as prison regulations demanded. Tony did not yell at her for that offense against discipline, either; he bent over to stroke her hair. He drew his hand back hurriedly and retreated a few paces from our angelic Lollobrigida . . . "But you ought to wash your hair," he said reproachfully.

As he shut the cell door Vera said loud enough to be heard: "I'd let him."

Denise was shocked. "A guard? A bengo? And one as old as that? Only the lowest sluts do that inside."

"Why not? He's the only one who's smiled at me."

"What's that cost him?"

"And he stroked my hair."

"And hurried off to wash his hands," Denise admonished her. "I keep telling you to wash your hair. You can be sure he couldn't wait to get away." Then she went on in a warning voice: "Now you listen to me, Vera, while you're in this cell you don't start any funny business with a guard, or you've had it. Got me?"

Much, much later, when Vera was in the punishment cells and we were free to talk over our gullibility and our flashes of foresight, we congratulated ourselves that we had never allowed her to phone from our cell. Love and sex are the two powerful incentives in jail, both natural and understandable. Few prisoners sink to obscenity. There was a young streetwalker in the next cell, a pretty, good-natured girl, the sort that will put up with anything. She was hard worker and made quite a bit, but she was always as poor as a church mouse and couldn't even take care of her one child—that was left to her mother. Her trouble, and the reason why she was always penniless, were unprincipled friends. She would come off the streets into a café and find them there, waiting for her to pay the bill. If she had any money on her, she'd fork it out straightaway; if not, she'd go out on the streets again to earn it for them. She was kind and sympathetic in prison, too, and provided sex orgies for the men in six cells on the three floors above her; when she took the toilet phone and began to describe the delights of love, they were silent with delight. It was not until she was moved away from our cell that Vera could enjoy this freedom of speech. And then no sooner did they hear her voice than the men on all three floors, in all six cells, pulled the chains to drown her obscenities. Nobody sent her so much as half a cigarette. Nancy, the most womanly of women, whom I shall soon introduce to you, told us how relieved they felt when Vera left their cell for the punishment cells once more.

Denise and I realized, then, that Vera must have been hopelessly bored with the two of us. She couldn't play cards, and stared dumbly as Denise laid out her sets and sequences; she was not capable of reading for any length of time, and there was nothing that held her interest for very long. She dreamily recalled the black marketeers she had met and sat for hours just doodling on old newspapers. She could hear the girls in other cells shouting out of the window, sending and receiving horses;

she listened avidly to their quarrels, their fights. She tried calling under the door in the evening, but she got no reply because nobody knew her. She tried hard to join in the evening concert, singing at the window, but nobody applauded her. She hardly knew a single song, got her words mixed up and went over to la, la, la, halfway through, and her voice was strained and harsh. Even in jail you must show talent if you are to win admirers. She felt terribly alone—and yet she was made for prison life. She began to hate us because we did not admire her. Our grave mistake was to treat her as just one more unfortunate.

On Friday evenings the women prisoners could ask to be sent to the doctor, which then took place on Monday. As the guard came round with the list the call went up; "Ask to go to the doctor's!" The waiting room was the social center of prison life, the place where letter-smuggling flourished, where messages were exchanged, where lovers met, and rivals fought. Some girls went there with letters for the other wing planted all over their bodies. If no other symptoms could be produced, sometimes a girl would have a tooth extracted just to be able to meet someone or hand something over. Lucy lost two teeth that way. There was a girl whose grapevine worked so well that when her lover was in the punishment cells in the basement, she went to the doctor's waiting room on the sixth floor and not only talked to him on the phone but managed to get a horse to him as well.

Helga, proud of her iron constitution, never went to the doctor's. She refused all pills on principle, as a dangerous habit, and would not even take the vitamin tablets I offered her. Yet as soon as she was moved to another cell she became a regular Monday patient. It was Denise who met her first.

"That Helga of yours, Eva, has she got big breasts and a belly that hangs down nearly to her knees? Her track suit stretched tight, and from the back you'd say it was a man?"

"Something of the sort."

"There was a woman like that in the waiting room and she asked everybody which cells they came from. She started talking to me when I said the number, and it was mostly you she was asking about."

"What did she want to know?"

"Whether you were still an informer."

"What did you say to that?"

"I said I hadn't noticed anything like that."

"That was nice of you, Denise."

"Now just you listen to me, Eva, you've got to do something about it. You've no idea how dangerous it's getting. You're running a big risk."

"What d'you expect me to do? Go to the doctor's every Monday and tell everybody I'm not a spy? Or had I better shout under the door every evening: I'm not a spy! If she's so sure, why doesn't she spread it around like that? It's the way you do it here if you want to give someone away. Shout the truth down the corridor and that's the end of her. D'you want me to challenge Helga to a duel? Go and start a fight in the waiting room?"

"I know, it's bloody silly."

"There's nothing I can do about it, Denise, nothing active, that is. She knows that very well, and she knows I know it too. It's a clever way of getting her own back."

"If you're sent to the same camp she'll have a start on you, and the informer story will be there before you are."

"Can't be helped, but I hope the women in camp make their own judgments and aren't likely to fall for what someone like Helga makes up."

"It's a good thing for you she doesn't look trustworthy. An old floozy."

Then Vera came across Helga at the doctor's. When she came back to the cell she didn't say anything at first, just looked me over thoughtfully. Then she said, more to Denise than to me, "There was a woman there with big breasts, she was asking about you. I didn't know it was you she meant, she said you're a writer. Is that true?"

"Of course she is," Denise answered for me.

"That fat woman told me to watch my step, you're a spy."

"Then you'd better watch your step, hadn't you?"

"Eva, stop it," Denise interrupted. "You're just egging her on. And you just have nothing more to do with that woman, Vera."

"She told me you always said you'd been taken for questioning and it wasn't true, you'd been informing."

"Vera, be a good girl and if you must talk nonsense do it by yourself in a corner, O.K.?"

This was Vera's first time in prison, and something told her it wasn't going to be the last. She was learning the ropes, and she could see I got very different treatment from hers. Her envious little soul could not help noticing that I had privileges the common criminals didn't have. They were at the mercy of the prison authorities, while the State Prosecutor's Office kept close watch on the political prisoners. Like our lawmakers, Vera made no distinction, and so when the office sent someone to ask whether I had any complaints about my treatment in jail, she pouted and said she'd like to be asked if *she* had any complaints. We were allowed to write home once a week, as the Governor's deputy came in person to tell me—in front of Vera.

Our families were allowed to visit us several times during the year they held us on remand, while common criminals, unless the investigating officer makes special arrangements (for some purpose), have to wait until they have been sentenced before they are allowed visitors, and then only if the judge explicitly says so. Even then, it is a rare occurrence, because it makes more work for the officials and so the authorities simply put the date off. The convicts' families then have to travel all the way to the work camp to see them. It was not we who had won the privilege of these visits, but our families outside. Just before Christmas my husband was allowed another visit, and so our cell enjoyed real Christmas fare.

Denise was delighted: "Did you guess I like fish best of all?" My husband had sent the traditional carp and Vienna steak, ready fried, potato salad, chocolates, Christmas biscuits, halva, nuts, oranges, and bananas. There were no bananas to be had in the shop, but as he passed a milk bar he noticed chocolate-covered bananas in the window. So he went around to the back, where girls were decorating dishes of trifle with slices of banana, and told them: "My wife's in jail for writing books, and she's innocent. Would you sell me a banana for her?" They sold him three, and so we had one each.

Denise told Vera, "Eva and I have been more than decent to you, Vera; we share everything we get with you though we could just as well have left you out."

And what did Vera reply? "Why shouldn't I take what I get? I didn't ask for anything, did I? I don't want anything off you."

"Vera, don't make me mad. You don't want anything off us, O.K. Just say you don't want any more cigarettes off me—and you stop smoking from that moment."

"You don't have to take it out on me. You shouldn't have given me smokes if you want to take it out on me afterward."

"Nobody's taking anything out on you, you dope. People who take it out on you aren't the ones to give things away, if you haven't noticed that yet. All I want to get into your head is that if someone behaves decently to you she expects decency in return. If you behave like a son of a bitch nobody's going to bother two hoots what happens to you."

"You expect me to fall for bloody fool talk like that?"

Christmas Eve was spent playing games and giving each other presents. Denise had made her little Christmas tree out of breadcrumbs, and Vera gave us a piece of chocolate each, under the tree. On Christmas Day they brought clean laundry round, and we each got a bundle: a sheet, pajamas, pillowcase, and towel; the trusties made up the bundles and I took the clean things in while Denise handed over the dirty washing. And Vera said: "You've got a better sheet than me, like last time."

Sometimes the sheets were dreadful, badly washed, with smears of blood that hadn't soaked out, filthy patches, tears, and holes. The trusties gave the more respectable things to cells where they got fruit or cigarettes in return. "We've all got decent sheets, Vera. Denise gave the trusties ten cigarettes."

Vera stood by her bed and made no move to lay the things out; she still held the bundle in her arm, hadn't even looked at it and couldn't possibly know what her sheet was like, but she repeated: "You've got a better sheet than me and I want yours."

My sheet was already stretched over the mattress. "Don't be silly, Vera, we can't start quarreling about nothing. I looked the sheets over when I took them in, and you've got a clean one that isn't torn. I'd have asked them for another if it hadn't been O.K. Just look and see."

She stood there cradling the bundle in her arms and said in a low voice full of hatred: "You cunt!"

For the first moment I didn't realize the word was meant for me and was going to defend the trusties in my unthinking amazement. Then the personal pronoun she had used struck home. For me filthy language was worse than cold or bad food; there was only one thing that troubled me more, in prison, and that was when letters from home were held up. I sometimes wondered how I would ever get rid of the filth I heard round me every day. And here was a little guttersnipe using that word to me!

"Never say that again, Vera. I can be tough, too, so watch your step." She laughed scornfully. "If someone behaves decently to you, it doesn't mean she's soft or that she's afraid of you."

Vera said it again, and stronger: "You spying cunt!"

And so it had to happen. Don't worry, I didn't hit her. She had the advantage of the first word and the first blow, the advantage of the aggressor. She knocked me over. It all happened so quickly that I cannot remember when she started tearing my hair out or when her long dirty nails went for my eyes. Nor can I remember when Denise sprang at her. My memory only retains the moment when I was lying across my bed while Denise was holding Vera down on hers with all her strength, with the whole weight of her body. Vera was kicking and struggling to get at me again, and Denise was shouting: "Vera! Stop that! Stop that!" Her shouting probably did the trick.

Later on, we laughed together because Denise hadn't had time to push her chair back *like this* before she flung herself at the strapping filthy-minded girl raring for a fight. That Denise fought for me when her hip was still troubling her was an act of great courage as well as a kind deed. She certainly saved me from something horrible. Vera did not stop trying to get at me until a kick caught Denise on her painful leg and she cried out with the pain. Then Vera went and sat at the table with her back to us, burying her head in her hands. We could see the muscles of her back twitching like those of an overexcited horse. Denise caught sight of her eyes, bloodshot like she'd never seen before.

They say that horses' eyes get full of blood, like that, when they are driven mad.

Vera was in the cell with us for almost a week after that. At night she stayed awake on purpose to scare me. "You can't sleep, can you? Scared, aren't you? Scared to death of me." Strangely enough, I was not afraid; the outburst had cleared the air and I no longer felt any obligation to be considerate and understanding. I did not speak to the girl again, acting as though she was not there. When I walked across the cell from the door to the window she had to get out of my path. I combed out the handful of hair she had torn from my scalp, joking grimly with Denise: "I don't have such a job combing my hair now there isn't so much of it." Vera sniggered, ready to share the joke and make friends again—and was astonished that neither of us would take her back. She simply could not imagine that anyone could ignore her existence. "That's how we should have treated her from the start," said Denise.

The fight had a traumatic effect on Denise; she watched Vera's every movement, every word, every cough, every disgusting thing the girl did. Denise felt sick at the smell of her and stopped eating; that week was a torment to her. She did not want to let go and storm at her, and she knew she would find it difficult to control herself. And it hurt her to think Vera had been taking advantage of her kindness. And because Denise would not side with her, Vera played her a nasty trick. In her locker Denise treasured a newspaper clipping showing her daughter selling Christmas carp at a stall in the street. She had even rescued it when our cell was searched and the clipping thrown out among the rubbish in the corridor; she had demanded and got it back. Vera was always doodling on our newspapers; she took the cutting, doodled all over it, and threw it away.

Denise and I decided that I would put in a complaint. While the fight was on Denise had noticed the spy hole open a fraction. There was a guard not far off when the trusties were handing out clean laundry, and she must have heard Denise cry out, even if she took no notice. I waited until the senior officer was on duty; it was New Year's Eve, and she asked where I'd got the scratches around my eyes. I showed her the handful of hair Vera'd torn out, and she took the girl off to the punishment cells for three days. That was more than I would have asked for her. How happy we were, though, to be alone. Vera was getting ready to celebrate the New Year by shouting out of the window and under the door. Denise was unhappy because it was the sad time of Christmas and New Year in jail, and she wanted to sleep and be quiet.

We heard Vera often enough, after those three days, and Denise was particularly sensitive to the sound of her voice. Later, Nancy told us how Vera's filthy language disgusted the girls in the next cell she was put into, and before long she was on her way to the punishment cells again, because she was caught telephoning. The guard was outside the door listening to her; Vera was still kneeling over the drain when the woman opened the door, and yet she denied it to her face. She started arguing that she couldn't be punished for something she hadn't done. It happened to be a decent guard, who would have let her off if she'd said she was sorry; but Vera made her so mad that she handed out punishment. Then Vera refused to go, crawling under the table and then under the bed, kicking whenever anyone came near. So they used tear gas and the whole cell suffered. In the end two more guards had to come and take Vera away in handcuffs. As they went down the corridor we could hear her complaining, but that was the last we heard of Vera.

12

HELGA (3)

Helga could rejoice—and all my enemies with her—that I'd got what was coming to me, in jail; a beating. Now it's time to say farewell to Helga.

Halfway through January the women prisoners were moved to the fourth floor of the old prison building, and the guards took the opportunity to search all our cells. We had made our things into a careful bundle, tied up in our blankets so we could carry them safely, and we were barely out of the cell when we were told: bundles on the ground and spread them out. There were a dozen or so guards, and the floor of the corridor was covered with letters, underwear, bits of paper, plastic bags, food, spoons, tubes of pills—and filth, where puddles of our breakfast acorn coffee were trampled about.

"We have to sleep under the blankets," I protested, for there wasn't a dry clean spot.

"Get a move on, you're not the only women we've got to deal with. Hurry up!"

There were two guards to each cell; both of them set on my bundle, and I never saw such busy fingers. There is skill, there are busy fingers, of all kinds. Knitting, for instance, making neat parcels, typing; but this was the skill, the busy fingers, of thievery. They poured my sugar out of its bag; plastic bags are forbidden—the women block the drains with them. There was sugar all over my blanket, among my letters, everywhere; I shook it out on to the floor. They tore my absorbent cotton out of its packet; I had to argue that it was unhygienic to have it lying about loose. And when we got to the new cell I discovered that while I had been arguing with one guard about hygiene, the other had thrown away a little plastic vase with artificial flowers in it that my husband had sent me. It was Scooter who did that; she must have found the flowers I had in the cell too much for her.

Off we went, with our bundles badly made up again and hard to balance. When we came to the iron grille we were joined by others, among them Helga. She had already been convicted and was waiting for transfer to a work camp when fate brought us together again. By the door of the guard's office lay an unclaimed bundle; its owner had been taken to court. The guard told Helga; "Pick it up, you're the strongest around here." Helga pretended not to hear. We were being hustled through the gate, the bundle was still lying there, and so the weakest of us all picked it up: Denise.

"You're mad, Denise. You can hardly manage your own."

"Somebody's got to take it," she said angrily. It was not so much out of kindness that she had acted, as out of obstinate pride. It was also a gesture of defiance toward Helga, and toward the guard who had thrown her letters about and poured sugar all over her things. She dragged her two bundles up the stairs and down a long corridor before I managed to get the unclaimed bundle from her. Helga watched us with a sneer.

"I don't do other people's work for them," she said contemptuously. Denise just shrugged; the effort of carrying the bundles had cooled her anger.

It is strange how soon one can swallow humiliation inflicted by the guards. For a moment you gasp for breath; you have felt something you would not have believed possible: for instance, pouring sugar over blankets. Did the fool think anybody would use it after that? She might just as well have thrown the sugar away. But no, she had to let it trickle all over our possessions. And how she enjoyed doing it! It can drive you to fury—and then you draw a thick line between what *they* did and what it means for *you*—and you can laugh at them. Because Helga did not pick up that bundle she had put herself on their side of the line, away from the rest of us struggling up the stairs with our load. To be generous to other prisoners, and to ridicule the guards—those are the two crutches prisoners have to lean on in their stumbling, hustled life. The nicknames they think up for guards are always apt and often inimitably offensive. Moll Doll, Potato Face, Country Boy, Horse Face, Gestapo, Scent Bottle, Scooter, Georgie. Country Boy was partly an expression of sympathy, partly a warning not to fall for his tricks. He looked intelligent and was said to have been a teacher; he was the only guard who could catch even experienced convicts sending a horse from cell to cell. He took a horse away from us and confiscated the cards we'd made, too. Horse Face was both stupid and cruel. Potato Face just plain stupid. The Gestapo woman was unadulterated cruelty. Scent Bottle was a conceited fool; Georgie quite a decent chap. It was Andy Rum Candy who gave us the most effective weapon against the rough ways of the guards: one of them came around shouting his head off one morning, and she watched him quietly and then said; "Poor thing, his wife wouldn't let him." That helped us, and as soon as the shouting started we'd look at each other: of course, he had no luck last night; he can't help it.

In our new cell I could not believe the change that had come over Helga. We hadn't made our beds, we hadn't put our things away in the lockers, we hadn't looked around and agreed who would sleep on which bed, and Helga was already at work with a rag, mopping the water out of the toilet to phone.

"Hello there! This is Emmy," in a sweet little girl voice. "Who's that?" she asked hopefully, a princess waiting for her Prince Charming. In this cell the toilet was the European kind, and Helga had to press her chest up against the bowl, her head down inside. She gave out that she was seventeen, in jail for murdering her auntie, a joke she sniggered at endlessly. "But I'm a pure little girl, no man has ever been near me." Her story was a mixture of naivety and obscenity, but it did its job. She had been gone three days, and there were still men asking to talk to her.

Helga had just come from a big cell, where she invented Emmy to keep herself amused. She shared it with a couple of lesbians, beat them up when they started making love, and then managed to have them moved away. She described the scene to me with indignation. I was expected to admire her moral stand, but I did not feel that by beating up lesbians she became any better herself. Then Gypsies were put in with her, and being outnumbered, she beat them up before they could start on her.

"Any nigger that got in my way got kicked—and I've got plenty of strength in my legs. And my hands. When they'd had their ears boxed, they took care to keep out of my way." She gave the Gypsies cigarettes and they did all her work with the bed, washed the floor for her, cleaned the toilet, and wiped the soles of her shoes when they came in from the exercise yard. There were two tables in the cell, and on one she put a notice: WHITES ONLY. About Christmas time the balance of numbers was such that she had that table to herself while seven Gypsy girls were squeezed around the other.

"What did the guards do?" The cell was opposite the guard office and they must have heard the blows and scuffles.

"A guard came running the first time I beat one of them up, then they let me do as I liked so long as I kept order in the cell."

Helga, who would have vomited if she'd been asked to put her head down to the toilet phone in our old cell, had become Emmy. It was really shocking to see the one-time magistrate and patriotic goddess of vengeance as she knelt over the toilet with her head down inside, pouring out Emmy's silly filth. The woman whose bundle we had brought up, when she came into the cell later that day and heard Emmy talking, was horrified. She had been in the cell next to Helga and said Emmy talked such filth you couldn't listen to it; the men thought she was a seventeen-year-old cretin and took her as a joke. With me, in the new cell, Helga spent her time working out details of the "auntie's" murder.

Helga looked terrible. Coarseness, no longer restrained, is bound to settle in the features, in the voice, in the manners and the movements of the body. Helga had always been resolute in her speech, repeating after every pronouncement her favorite: "Well, I'm right, aren't I?" When I took no notice of her resolute tone she found ways of retreat. Here she took no notice of anybody, like a tank with no brakes and no steering gear. She did not kick anyone in my presence, although we did have a Gypsy with us in the cell. She took the first bed and thus the first turn at cleaning the cell, and nobody did it for her. But the place was full of her and her noise. I'm first, wherever I am—but first by what means, for heavens' sake? She made a great to-do, for instance, telling us how she'd lost her hair. I had spent hours on it when we were in the first cell together. It was such fine, thick, bushy hair, and at first she had worn it high on her head like a crown, dyed blond, and with a fashionable style. Once she came back from questioning, almost in tears. "You'll be in jail till you turn black," the officer had threatened her. He meant it one way—till you give in; but she took it literally (and Bessie swore that when they showed Helga on TV she had fair hair). Perhaps she had dyed her hair to cover her tracks? Now the blond had almost all disappeared, and she wore it in a bun—looking simply like a woman who hasn't time for such vanities.

The evening before her trial she put paper curlers in her hair, as she used to in our old cell. The girls warned her that the guard on duty didn't allow it, so she got written permission from the day guard, saying that she was allowed to curl her hair before going to court. The Spaniard woke her in the night, the guard she used to show off her bosom to—and perhaps seriously, perhaps in the spirit of their flirtation, told her to take the papers out of her hair. In the same spirit she showed him her written permission to curl her hair.

"I give orders round here," said the Spaniard, "and you'll get those curlers out."

The Spaniard seemed quite out of place among the other guards, both in appearance and in his manners. He wore a romantic little beard and dark glasses with gold rims. To me he looked less like a Spaniard than the American film idea of a South American. His voice was vibrant and his smile mysterious. The jokes he made were intelligently contemptuous. One Saturday evening he came round as the trusties were ladling out the inevitable borsch, the horror of all prisoners, and said to me: "I've tasted it myself and can recommend it."

"May I invite you?" I'd replied, "I'd gladly give you my share."

"No thank you, not on your life."

"Not even after you've recommended it?"

"Not if I was starving," he answered with a smile that he thought gentlemanly.

The girls said he was a bachelor, a woman-hater who'd been cruelly deceived, and so he took it out on the women prisoners. He bred Russian wolfhounds and was interested in criminals even outside his job. Once he was very kind to Denise and me, although like everything in jail his kindness turned out the reverse. It was Christmas Day, and after we went to bed he opened the door (he was one of the few guards who were not content just to spy in on us) and said, "Are you being good?" What does that mean, in prison? That we weren't planning to hang ourselves? To slash our wrists? We said nothing and the Spaniard, instead of switching the strong light over to the weaker night bulb, put the light out altogether. The cell was plunged in darkness. It was a Christmas gift. We were so unused to the dark by then that we could not sleep.

To continue the story of Helga's curls. "That's not fair," she told him, "the men can have the barber, why shouldn't the women curl their hair? You wouldn't make a man go to court unshaven."

"Would you like the barber?" he asked. "You can have him if you want."

"Yes I would," Helga replied, still in that flirtatious mood that did no good for her, because he was the jailer and she the jailed.

That was the sort of joke he enjoyed. He had the barber awakened and sent round. He was the man who shaved and cut hair and need no more have been a barber in civil life than the men who worked in the kitchens had been cooks. Helga sat down on her stool, the Spaniard and the Gypsies looking on, and had her hair cut.

"Have you seen what you look like?"

"No, and I don't care," she replied with the conceit of her kind. "It's good enough for prison. They'll cut my hair in the camp anyway, so I've got it over with."

Jagged edges, some short, some long, and the color going from black to pepper-and-salt, she looked a real convict. And putting on that little girl voice, she called down the toilet: "Hullo there! This is Emmy, can you hear me? Auntie was so unkind to me. I had a little white basket and Auntie wouldn't let me go out, so I stuck a knife in her. Wouldn't you like a nice little prick?"

She still had her mission, though; I thought it was hardly a coincidence that we were put together again just before she left. Blah, blah, blah, and here and there a name dropped, "Georgina," Třešňák, Lasička, what did I think of this and that? Three days later she left; she hoped it would be for office work since she had such a beautiful hand and liked domineering. She had been given five years in a Grade I prison; she'd been in remand prison for over six months, so that in less than two years she could get her remission. God and sharp wits defend all who come her way!

13

NANCY

"**N**ancy!" that trumpeting voice still rings in my ears, "Nancy, love!" Annie was an outlandish young woman, a lesbian of about twenty-five who had come to try her luck in Prague after a not very successful début in East Slovakia. Nancy was over thirty-six. "Nancy!" Annie's voice was both tempting and threatening. "Come on!"

Annie's lust was awakened every evening when we started making our beds. Hers was by one wall, Nancy's on the opposite side, and between them we set up the other four beds, which had been piled to one side during the day: at night they took up the entire floor space of the cell, their metal frames touching. The only way Annie could reach Nancy was across our beds. The mattresses were laid over moldering, disintegrating sheets of cardboard that gave way wherever she put her foot down. We tried to keep her off, for our bodies would be sagging to the floor through the holes she made.

Nancy fended her off with shrieks of horror, "No, Annie,

no!" as she shrank in her corner trying to change as fast as possible from one set of rags to another, from gray prison shirt to orange prison pajamas, quick, quick, before Annie got to her across our beds, hindered by her sinking feet. Her eyes were fixed on her victim who was trying to show as little of her naked body as possible, before slipping under her blanket, drawing it up to her chin and round her body until she was no more than a mummy wrapped in prison gray.

As she crossed the treacherous ground of our beds by leaps and bounds Annie's resolution began to flag; and by the time she reached Nancy's bed, bruised by the iron frames she had knocked against, her lust had subsided. With half her ass on Nancy's bed and the other half on the toilet seat, she would no longer have touched so much as a toe. She simply gazed with longing, admiring eyes at the object of her love, her salvation, the only thing that lifted her above the purgatory of prison. Her lust waned not because she knew that any lesbian love-making would provoke physical punishment from at least one of the other four women in the cell, but because Annie was a tough, aggressive conqueror of women's bodies in words, but not in deeds. In this case her infallible instinct told her that Nancy was easy game, that she was Only-a-Woman, one who could not resist any sexual offer or attack. If the two of them had been alone, if Annie's advances had not been so pressing, if she had crept up under the cover of night, if she had begged for it, Annie would have got what she wanted. Nancy knew it, and that was why her terror as she huddled under the gray blanket was quite unfeigned. "No! No, Annie, no!"

While she squealed her rejection she smiled, the confused, vague and tempting smile of those who take refuge in Only-a-Woman. Some nights Annie would dare to go a little closer, to leave the edge of the toilet seat and settle comfortably on

Nancy's bed, happy to be so near her idol. From time to time she
even got a kiss, for Nancy was incapable of refusing outright
and protested only so long as she didn't hurt Annie's feelings.
Once in every ten days, when we all stripped naked in the
shower room and Nancy had to reveal that girlish body that
seemed to deny she could ever have given birth to three children, she felt defenseless. Pointing out politely that there were
only four showers for six prisoners, Denise held Annie back
firmly so that Nancy could wash herself in peace in the opposite
corner. The air was always chilly, and the water from the
showers, though not as warm as we would have liked, soon
formed clouds of steam. The women were only vaguely visible,
and Annie could not enjoy more than an occasional glimpse of
her prey. "What you want to protect her for?" Annie complained, "just one taste of love with me and she'll never want
anything else."

Nancy was thirty-six, and had already fulfilled all the hal-
lowed functions of womanhood prescribed by custom and by
life itself. She had been Daughter, Wife, and Mother; yet each
had been no more than a bypath she followed with womanly
patience but no sense of satisfaction at heart. That's the way the
world goes: you are born to someone and then you beget or bear
someone else; what can you do but submit? Nancy did not rebel
against her mother so openly as to be called an ungrateful
daughter; she loved her three children tenderly yet felt more
like their older sister; and she came to hate her marriage
because she found her husband repulsive and was afraid of him.
Yet she was unable to do anything against him except on the
superficial level of running away. Nancy's own nature was to love
someone tenderly and happily, always ready to serve him with a
clear, sensual, affectionate woman's heart. Her husband was a
dolt, and so she felt driven to get away, to find out whether,

somewhere else, there was not a spring from which she could drink long and deep. Maybe she wasn't exaggerating, maybe she'd really have gone crazy if she hadn't let herself go. "Just imagine, I thought it'd pay him back! Can you believe anyone could be so naive? I wanted to pay him back and he's got me into prison, as easy as that."

When Nancy set out to see what the world had to offer her, her husband filed a suit for nonpayment of maintenance for their three children. It did not upset her that her flight had ended in jail: prison was another world, filled with interesting characters, and far preferable to the dark, chilly, loveless cave that her marriage had become. And in Ruzyně she was safe from her husband; so long as she was in jail, he could not get at her. Nor did her womanhood feel neglected there, and that not only on account of Annie's lesbian yearnings.

Prisoners due to appear in court are taken there by bus, handcuffed, with a guard to each prisoner and two for dangerous criminals. Whatever the time your case is expected to come up, you are driven off first thing in the morning. Nancy's case was heard about midday, so that she spent the whole morning in a cell in the court building, and since she was not fetched back until evening, she spent the whole afternoon there too. When she got back she said nothing about the three-months' sentence that had been confirmed; she talked about the cell; she was the only prisoner for Ruzyně (it was a local court) and so she was alone with the guard all day. The moment he took charge of her she could sense it: he had the hots for her. "It was dreadful! I can tell 'em a mile off. I didn't know what to do. All those hours alone with him, he didn't lock me in, I s'pose the key would make a noise if he kept locking and unlocking, he was coming and going all the time, offering me cigarettes and tea and coffee and talking about my case. He said I shouldn't appeal, I've nearly done three months already, on remand, and if I appeal they might double it, but I was so nervous all the time, you know what I mean. He had that naked look in his eye and I was terrified I wouldn't be able to say no, and he could tell what I was thinking and he must have thought I wanted it as well. So every time he came and said something I answered at the top of my voice, shouting like a moron 'cos I thought there might be another office beyond his, and if there was anybody there they'd hear me. He jumped when I shouted, and told me not to make such a noise and went back to his side of the door. He did it at least twenty times, you could see he was scared. When he went to the john he said he'd leave the door open, I wasn't to get into mischief, though, and he must have thought I was wrong in the head, asking him to lock me up so nobody could get at me. A half-wit *asking* to be locked up! When he came close I squeezed up against the bars. There was nowhere to run to except his office, and I kept on yelling Yes sir, No sir, Yes sir, like I'd gone out of my wits. Just think, I was too scared to say I needed to go to the john. I couldn't have mentioned such a thing, so now just let me go before the worst happens."

Nancy was sweet, submissive, kind, amusing, gracious, tolerant, charming, refined . . . and after she'd been with us a few days we were at our wits' end. The first time in a new cell, most prisoners have told you all about their case within a day or two; it's a relief, they and you know where you stand, and after that they only talk about themselves to a chosen confidante. Even Denise, who had quietly taken on the role of Nancy's protector, was driven to shouting wildly: "For God's sake, Nancy, shut up! Stop chattering. Cool it, woman, my head's in a whirl! Try to keep quiet for ten minutes. Would you like us to get the cards out? Don't you want a nice book? Eva, lend her that Hemingway. She's got to leave us alone for a bit. Nancy, d'you feel like a biscuit? A bit of sausage? Eva, have we still got those good chocolate cookies? Let her have a couple to keep her mouth busy with something else. That would be a godsend. Nancy! Stop talking and eat. Eva! You tell her off, she'll take more notice of you."

Nancy smiled vaguely, acknowledging the truth of what Denise said, and feeling guilty. She tried to keep quiet, but she just couldn't. They started a game of cards, Nancy was winning, she cheered up and Denise and I exchanged glances: blessed peace! Then those irresistible words came to the surface again. She jumped up from her stool and started pacing the cell once more, her right hand thrust out in a dramatic gesture. At night she fell easily into quiet and dreamless sleep; Andy was the only one I ever saw sleep so silently, curled up like an animal and seeming not to breathe at all. In the morning Nancy looked round her from the iron bedstead or the already warmed toilet seat, her eyes still heavy with sleep, then realizing where she was and remembering what lay in store for her, she opened the floodgates and the neurotic torrents of words poured out once more, spewing out her fear, her powerlessness, her frailty, and her suffering. Her pilgrimage had come to a dead end, and her Only-a-Woman quiescence could never break out of the vicious circle, never take decisive steps to reach happiness. Her womanliness was what made her tick, but it was also her curse.

She had left her husband, yet nobody but her husband would be waiting for her outside; she was the defeated, he the conqueror, with all the authorities behind him, and with the attributes of true womanhood at his side—to wit, Nancy's mother and Nancy's children. Her sentence was a trivial one, and it was neither the sentence itself nor the odium attached to it that upset her. You can do three months, as the saying goes in jail; sitting on razor blades. She had been so long on remand that her time was almost up, anyway; the day when she would be free, outside, was not far off, and that was what worried her most. She would lose the protective barrier of the prison walls. She recounted her case from the beginning, from the end, from the middle, as though desperately hoping it would vanish if she got it out of her system. It would cease to exist and she would miraculously find herself in another world, one where her children would be with her, where she could even bear to have her mother around, but where a man who could send the mother of his children to prison would be forbidden entry. It would be a world of cheerful happiness and friendly affection, maybe she wouldn't have all the love she would like, but she would be cosseted and protected. Nancy was intelligent enough to know that she was talking nonsense, and in the torrents of unbearable chatter and the violent eruptions of words, she ridiculed herself and laughed. That was an agreeable trait and one that always won forgiveness. "All right, all right," Denise shrugged resignedly, "go on, tell us what happened next, if you must."

"Now, isn't that unnatural?" We had finished breakfast, leaving one table in the middle of the floor where it could be seen from the spy hole—that was where they played snakes and ladders—while the other was pushed up against the wall by the door, out of the guards' line of vision; that was where we played our forbidden card games. Nancy was pacing the cell, her body bent forward, her right hand thrust out dramatically in a gesture Denise liked to make fun of.

"Well, don't you call it unnatural for a man to sit there in front of the telly, as naked as Adam, and sit there scratching himself all over? Eva! Denise! Now isn't that unnatural?" We were careful not to reply, to make her even more insistent.

"Just keep quiet whatever she says," was Denise's prescription, "it may be a delusion, an obsession."

Nancy spoke of her husband as a hateful monster arousing fear and repugnance. She called him by his surname if she named him at all, but mostly he was Smugpot. She never called him any other names; indeed she never used bad language at all, and fluttered her eyelids delicately at the filthy expressions that flew round prison like ineradicable black moths. She was helpless in the face of coarseness, but in her definition a smugpot was a stupid, unnatural, coarse smart aleck out for his own advantage, and a coward to boot, and she had no use for him. A woman of delicate beauty, and precious for not losing that delicacy in evil company nor among cynically cunning fools, she paced back and forth across the cell, and sometimes as she ended one reproach flung at the indifferent world, and before she began another, she ran the fingers of both hands through the fine soft graying hair that framed her well-shaped head. That was another of her typical gestures. Her hair had once been coal black, but now the gray predominated; she said that was in the last few months, and Denise and I both agreed we had grown gray in prison. "There he sat, stark naked, the children were at school but they might have come in at any moment. That didn't bother him at all and he didn't care what I felt about it, either, just sat there staring at football on the telly and scratching and scratching. For hours on end. Eva! Denise! On my word of honor. Hours and hours. One day he had to repair something in the box, he'd got a screwdriver in his hand so he scratched himself with that. After that, he always had the screwdriver when he sat down to watch. Stark naked, and I could hear him scratching himself with that screwdriver as far away as the kitchen."

For a year or two after she left school Nancy had been happy. Her final exam results were excellent and she got a good job, in charge of the milk deliveries to a dairy. She had a little office in the yard and when the trucks drove in she took down the quantity delivered, the tested quality, and calculated how much the supplier would be paid. She was independent, living away from home and out of her mother's reach—a heavenly time, but she did not know, then, that she was Only-a-Woman. She did not tell us why she got married. Once there was a hint in her torrent of words that she had to get married because she was expecting a baby, but other times she said her husband was not much good in bed and that she was still a virgin four months after their marriage. The latter account seemed more likely, judging from the ages of her children. Undoubtedly the urge to get away from a mother who did not love her was a pressing one.

She never knew her father, not even his name, unless "the Russian" will do, or even less specifically, "the soldier." A soldier in the liberating Russian army marching across Slovakia in the spring of 1945 got her mother in the family way and marched on, to live or die, nobody knew; but he was never heard of again, nor did her mother try to find him. She married a Ruthenian and they moved as far away as possible from where her disgrace was public, right to the Sudeten border in the west. They had two children. Nancy got on well with them and with her stepfather, who treated her as his own. Either her mother resented this living evidence of her shame, or perhaps Nancy reminded her too much of "the Russian." She herself assumed that she resembled her father, because she was not at all like her mother. Her face did have something Russian about it, though not strikingly so; she had honey-colored eyes with full, heavy lids and short thick lashes, reminding one of Siberia and its ancient tribes, and her cheekbones were broader than we are used to. Her lips were firm and well-shaped, hiding strong white teeth, and her nose was neither snub nor retroussé, but something in between.

After her marriage Nancy had three children in quick succession, a boy and two girls who loved their pretty, happy, delightful mother. The boy was already beginning to understand how she felt in the home, and he was the only one who wrote to her. "My dearest, dearest Mum, come home soon, it's sad here without you." A childish letter for a boy of thirteen. He had drawn lines on the paper and formed his letters carefully, saying that he was writing in secret and so could not finish the letter all at one go, and would Mum forgive him if some of the lines looked different. He had to mail it secretly, too: "I cannot mail this until tomorrow when we have games. Granny does not go as far as the playing field to meet me. Other days she does the shopping when I am coming out of school, on purpose. I cannot write more now, Mum."

The boy had not only got hold of her address which the grownups had hidden away, but also knew that he had to put her date of birth on the envelope or else it would not be delivered in prison. "Isn't that a lot to burden a child with? Writing to his mother and he has to put my date of birth on the envelope. The shame of it! The immorality. I'd rather he didn't write at all. What's his innocent mind going to think? What about the damage it'll do to his soul? What is his mother going to mean to him now? At that sensitive age! He'll remember it as long as he lives! If he knows he's got to write the date of birth as well as my name, he's bound to guess that whatever's happening to me isn't nice. I expect they told him I'm in the hospital, Granny certainly said I'm in the hospital; it's just the sort of hypocritical thing she would say. What if he doesn't believe her? No, that's wrong, I know what happened: Smugpot told them; he told them everything. He sat down and started weeping and said, my poor little children, I've landed your mother in jail. He can go to the devil, Smugpot can, but what am I going to tell my children when I get back?"

She tortured herself with the thought of this crime against the innocent soul of her boy, whose image of maternal purity and honor was being destroyed when he had to write her address according to prison rules. Then this thought became too painful and she gave it a new twist—against Smugpot. "It wasn't like that at all, it was quite different. It must have been Smugpot who made Stan write. He's quite capable of a dirty trick like that. How could the child find my address unless the grownups wanted him to write?" She was pacing up and down the cell again, her right hand stretched out in front of her with all the urgency of Rodin's John the Baptist. "That's just like him to use my children to force me to go back to him. He knows very well that I wouldn't lift a finger if he wrote to me himself. But he thinks if the children write I'll come running back asking for forgiveness. That's how it was. He's a disgusting blackmailer. He said write to your mother, Stan, look, here's the address, and line the paper so you'll write straight. That was always what *he* did, drawing lines on the paper because he wanted to be sure he'd write straight. It doesn't matter much what he writes, so long as it's neat and straight. Maybe Stan did write in secret. He's not a boy to lie, but then he only had to keep it secret from Granny, he lives with her, and then he took it to the post secretly, I believe that too, but it was Smugpot who arranged it all. And it was Smugpot dictated my date of birth after the name, the child must have felt so ashamed, can't you read between the lines how ashamed he felt? And he doesn't say anything about his father, that means his father read what he'd written. And Smugpot couldn't care less about the child's feelings, all that matters to him is getting me into a corner. I'm married to a sniffing bloodhound. Married to a wolf that wants to drive me back into the fold. And he'll do it by destroying the souls of my children. What can I say to the poor children? How can you tell your children that their father's a sniffing bloodhound?"

At first she was too young, too innocent, and too ignorant to stand up against him. Then she had three children one after the other, and that took all her energy and all her time. "He only had to have me once and I'd a bun in the oven." Since she had only three children, the first coming two years after their marriage, she could not have got much fun out of her husband. He was an officer in the regular army, and they moved from one garrison town to another as he was transferred, and in each new place she felt lonelier and lonelier, more and more powerless, and more and more firmly tied to him. She avoided the other officers' wives, describing them to us as narrow-minded and dull, quarrelsome and backbiting. Nor did they stay long enough in any place for her to get to know anybody better. While the children were still small, the narrow confines of home were broad enough to occupy her mind, and when they got bigger and started school, with outside lessons and hobbies, she began to peep over the fence of the marital fold. Then she saw that she had been short-changed in her husband, that other men were more honest as men, and better as human beings. Her children no longer filled her life completely, and she found herself in no-man's-land. She struggled against the feeling, because she thought it was immoral and she didn't want to be immoral, she didn't want to be unfaithful to her husband, that would be despicable, and it horrified her to imagine herself carrying on like the other officers' wives.

"I started going to the cinema a lot, I read a lot of books, I even started embroidering to fill in the time." And it was all this, her unexpected experience and above all the loneliness she felt, her discontent and sense of humiliation, that awakened in her the Only-a-Woman. The woman in her was waiting to seize her chance.

Then her husband was discharged and Nancy lost the only form of excitement she had, that of change and the moving from one place to another. They settled down in one place and the emptiness of her life stared at her nakedly from all sides. "Nothing but curtains, carpets, shirts, socks, plates, pots and pans. Pots and pans, plates, socks, shirts, carpets, curtains. By then I was so unnatural, I'd keep wishing the children would fall ill. I was happy when they were sick, it gave me something to worry about, something to occupy me. They didn't need me much, otherwise; they were quick at school and didn't need help with their homework. The three of them were company for each other, and I was stuck with the pots and pans, the shirts and socks." She was still young, she was lovely, and she longed for love. Her husband spent all his time getting ready to take exams, he was doing an extension degree so as not to have to sink to the bottom of the working class after he'd been an officer, almost a gentleman. For Nancy his starting to study was a betrayal, the expression of his male egoism.

"Why shouldn't he be a worker? He'd have earned more and he'd have had more time for the children. Just when they needed him most, he was buried in his books and we had to be quiet and take care not to disturb him. When they moved him from one place to another, we had to follow. When they threw him out, we had to follow. He spent all Saturdays and Sundays cramming, and the children had to be as quiet as mice."

Nancy found a lover. It may not have been love, but simply someone she could feel respect for. He was one of those innu-merable hangers-on employed in the film studios, name-drop-ping as though they'd just got over the hangover from last night's star party, but that was not what attracted Nancy; she was too intelligent and subtle for that. She was profoundly happy to love someone who loved her. "Johnny had a fast car. Men are silly about things like that, about drinking real French cognac, or having an American car. We used to go to our weekend chalet, I stole what time I could from the children, going out there when they were in school and didn't need me. The chalet's at the far end of the hamlet and we used to drive through fast so nobody would see me and give me away. Nobody could see us once we were inside, it's at the end of the road with only a drop into a quarry. I wasn't doing any harm to anyone. I kept the apartment in better order than ever and the children were happier because I was happy and cheerful. To salve my conscience I spent more time with them than before, we went for walks together and went swimming and to the playground. The children were better off because of Johnny. And Smugpot didn't know a thing. He was always busy with his computers and when he got home it was late and all he did was bury himself in the newspaper or scratch himself in front of the telly. A pity it didn't last; we were all getting the best out of it."

Her husband was not as indifferent as she imagined. He watched her, putting bits of the jigsaw puzzle together, drawing his own conclusions. One Saturday when he said he had to go to a training session for those computers, and Nancy had sent the children over to her mother's, he drove out to the chalet to catch the lovers red-handed. To catch them . . . well, he saw the Saab outside and so he hid behind the bushes, and when the lovers drove off to do some shopping he skipped into the chalet and hid in the bedroom.

"I went to get my dressing gown and there was Smugpot sitting all hunched up among my clothes, but it didn't upset me. How could Smugpot be hiding in there when I knew he'd gone to that training session of his? I'd been looking forward to that weekend for so long! I couldn't let him come and spoil it. I shut the door on him and ran to tell Johnny. Johnny, could Smugpot possibly be hiding in my wardrobe? Tell me it's only my nerves and I'm having hallucinations, because if he's really there I'm going out and jumping from the top of that quarry. And Johnny said, of course it's just your imagination. You can't get him out of your head, now try and forget him and don't be a spoilsport, and we sat down and had a glass of wine."

Alas, her husband really was in the wardrobe, and when he emerged at the right moment and started calling his wife names, he got a good thrashing. "Johnny nearly knocked the life out of him and I did nothing to stop him. It was worth watching Smugpot getting his desserts for once. Then Johnny threw him out of the door like a puppy. It was wonderful, let me tell you what was the best: Johnny came back inside, dusting his hands as though he'd just finished a dirty job, sat down and poured another glass of wine. Now you can forget him, Nan, he said, but I knew Smugpot was there. I could feel him sitting in the bushes and snooping. I didn't enjoy the wine; I couldn't enjoy anything. I kept running to the window to see if he was there and looking at the door in case he came in. The weekend was spoiled, and Johnny said it's no good, we'd better go back home. Smugpot was nowhere to be seen as we locked up, but just as Johnny opened the car door the creature dashed out of the bushes and knelt down in front of the car. It's a terribly narrow path between the steep hillside and the edge of the quarry, there's only a little room in front of the chalet where a car can turn, and most people prefer to back up there. Johnny couldn't move down the path, there was Smugpot on his knees with tears running down his cheeks, begging me not to leave him. He wasn't going to get up unless I promised to stay with him. I wouldn't get away from the place with that man except over his dead body. If we didn't want to run over him we could throw him down into the quarry, but he couldn't live without me. He wasn't going to get up unless I swore to be faithful. I can see you're laughing—and I can laugh at it now—but what would you have done with that Smugpot kneeling there in tears?"

Nancy went to her husband, set him on his feet, brushed the knees of his trousers, led him to one side, and the offended lover drove away.

Now she could no longer have a lover, because Smugpot watched her closely and would have spoiled any affair she started. She began to wander about. During the day, when Smugpot was at work and the children in school, she would set out as if to go shopping, and in a derelict tumbledown part of the town she would go from one pub, one cafeteria, to another. Sometimes she would slip out in the evenings, while Smugpot was watching the TV; she took a beer pitcher with her so he wouldn't start tears again. She was hungry for human company, eager to talk to people, and the pub is the best place for that. Anybody who has had a few beers or a glass of rum is ready to listen to your troubles. Nancy breathed in the smell of cheap goulash and stale beer, mingled with the stench of vomit and filthy lavatories, and felt it was rebellion. She had to be careful with the housekeeping money to save enough for the odd glass of beer or rum.

"Weren't you scared, going to that sort of place on your own?"

"They looked after me."

"Who did?"

"I didn't know for a long time they were from the underworld. They called me Amulet. They were really nice lads. They never took liberties, and so I usually sat at their table. And if a stranger came in and looked as though he was going to annoy me, they'd throw him out of the place."

I believed her, because her trusting frailty was a good protection. Only-a-Woman always rouses the protective instinct in her men; and Nancy knew how to listen, and she was no spoilsport. She threatened nobody's interests, encroached on nobody else's rights—not even those of other women. She neither admonished nor condemned. She had a tender smile, a touch of the hand—don't drive me away; I'm one of you. She was like that with us in the cell, too, friendly, never creating conflicts, understanding. She did not look out of place in those low-down haunts, in dress or in ways, nor did she look at home there. She was not coarse, she did not get drunk, she was not provocative. She was what is called a good sort in every walk of life.

And she enjoyed herself! For the first time she was really finding life good fun. Each of the figures around the beer-stained, goulash-spotted table had something individual about him, something unusual. One was dreadfully ugly—scrawny, with mousy hair and a badly sewn harelip. She liked him, and he talked to her about his mother, how she'd died and how lovely she looked in her coffin. He used to go and light the little lamp on her grave every evening, because she was afraid of the dark. And there were unhappy women there, trembling bodies and sorry lives, who'd go with a soldier for five crowns and then not get it off him; and there were beauties who wouldn't take less than two thousand and got it every time. This was a hundred times more exciting than reading novels or watching films: this was life. At last she could laugh her scorn for the dream of all would-be almost gentlefolk, a three-room apartment in a high rise, where you can hear all the others at their excretions and ablutions, where every family sits down to table in the same spot determined for them by the architect, where they all sit down to watch the TV at the same moment, and all drag their sleepy children to nursery schools and day-care centers at the same time in the morning—that scrubbed and constricted life her husband was so proud of leading. The friendly company of down-and-outs and the wayward fringe is a well of muddied water, but it is a deep well and one that never dries up. Hi there, Nan! Have a beer with me? They drink their beer and say nothing, or else they listen while you tell your latest troubles. Their social interests go no farther than the next soccer match. They don't spend time worrying about where to get hold of a chandelier for the living room or a carpet for the bedroom, and they never get across the boss because of their ambitions. All this was a relief to Nancy, and before long she had fixed it up with two of them to give Smugpot a thrashing.

"We had it all worked out. The children were at my mother's and I'd given those two lads my keys. Smugpot was supposed to think it was me when they opened the door, and they were supposed to take him by surprise, watching the telly. They wore stockings over their faces so he wouldn't recognize them again, and so he'd get a real fright. And he got the better of them after all, Smugpot always gets the best of everybody because he's cunning, he's not only a coward. I gave them a hundred crowns and they promised they wouldn't kill him, only knock him about so he'd have something to remember. It all worked out as I said. He was sitting watching the telly and the two of them wanted to start in on him, only he edged backward into the bedroom and ran round the bed, and before they could hit him he was out of his dressing gown and lying on the bed stark naked, with his toes stretched out like a ballet dancer. You're a good pal, Nan, they told me afterward, but we couldn't start hitting a man when he was lying on the bed naked. We wanted to help you out, but that was more than we bargained for, and they gave me back the hundred."

"What good did you think it would do for him to get a thrashing?" Denise asked her.

"I wanted to scare him. I thought if he got scared he might go off and leave me. I thought he'd guess I'd given them the keys, because it was my keys they used to get in. Then he'd be afraid it might happen again, and leave me."

Smugpot did not leave her, he came home day after day, determined not to relinquish his family life, although it could not have been much of a life. And so Nancy let herself go. "I decided I'd be really bad, and then he'd be glad to leave me."

"That was real clever of you, Nancy," Denise said, and whispered to me in an aside: "I hope you don't believe half of this, Eva. Nancy's good fun, but you're too inclined to take everything people say seriously."

Nancy had made friends in the pub with a man who traveled back and fore to Slovakia on business, and had told her he liked it there. He was married, but not very satisfied with his life as it was. He and Nancy got on well together, so well that when she decided to see what it was like to go burgling, he said he'd go with her.

"You wanted to go stealing?"

"Not really stealing. I didn't need to do that; I'd got all I needed. I just wanted to know what it feels like to be a burglar. I thought it must be exciting."

They decided to try the nearest weekend chalets, picking the biggest because they thought the bigger it was, the harder it'd be to get in. It was a moonlit night, their shadows were long and dark behind them and they couldn't see what was hidden in the shadows ahead, but it all added to the fun. Every twig that snapped underfoot, every stone that rattled gave them a little thrill of fear. They'd had just the right amount to drink, the fun became a thrill and the thrill became the fun of doing wrong.

"You can't imagine how long it takes to climb over a low barbed-wire fence without making a noise. First one leg, then the other; the wire catches your pants, your windbreaker, there's nowhere to get a foothold. And the noise it makes in the night, when you try to force the lock on the door! Every tap like a rifle shot. I was crouched down in the garden watching. And if you're scared the time just seems to stand still. Everything takes so long. I was really depraved though, because I wanted us to get caught. That would have been something for Smugpot to live down! Look at him, his wife goes burgling!"

Quietly, and with the shutters fast, they lit a lamp and opened and ate a tin of meat. They ate it with their fingers, not wanting to add insult to injury by leaving dirty cutlery behind them. Then they tried to make love but it was no good; the fright they'd been enjoying was too much for her companion and he was shivering with cold. They just warmed each other and then ran back toward the town, leaving the chalet unlocked. Then her friend took Nancy off to Humenné in East Slovakia.

"Why there, of all places?"

"Why not? If he'd said Košice, I'd have gone to Košice—anywhere, so long as it was far enough away from Smugpot. Maybe the name of the place made me think it was close to Russia."

"To Russia?"

"I found a photograph of some Russian soldiers in Mother's things, not the Russians in sixty-eight, those in 1945. Their tunics were all crumpled and they'd got forage caps over one ear and lots of medals. Mother wouldn't tell me which one it was. I suppose she was afraid I'd try and look for him."

"You didn't expect to find him in Humenné, surely?"

"I didn't think anything, really. You don't have to think when you decide to do something. Humenné was just luck. I went to see him off at the station and when I asked where he was going he said Humenné, I liked the sound of the place and so I said take me with you, and he said O.K., so get in. I climbed into the train and before we'd had time to work out whether it was a joke or whether we meant it, the train was moving. I hadn't got anything with me, not much money either, when I paid the ticket collector in the train I'd only got forty crowns left, but I'd got a big piece of meat. It was Tuesday, they get it fresh from the slaughterhouse on Tuesdays. I always buy my meat on Tuesdays and that day I went to see him off, so I'd got the meat with me."

"Didn't you think of the children? What were they going to do when they came home from school and found you gone?"

"I didn't dare to think of the children. I'm telling you, you don't have to think when you decide to do something."

"Did you think you were running away to freedom?"

"I had the feeling I was running away. Something snapped inside me, something broke, and I was going far, far away in a train. It was the feeling you get when you are just happily drunk, not too much, not too little, just enough to make you light-headed and happy."

"Would you have run away on your own? I mean, if your friend hadn't happened to be going to Humenné and hadn't taken you with him?"

"No, I wouldn't have been capable of doing that. Not then. And you may not believe me, but it was easier because of that shopping bag. I kept saying to myself: you're just going shopping, that's all, you're just going shopping. The train was on its way and I was still thinking, you've been shopping and you're taking the meat home, only it's a bit longer way round than usual. It seemed funny to be going all that way round."

When they got to Humenné they parted on the platform and Nancy set out to live her own life. Humenné did not live up to what its name had seemed to promise, but Nancy was not made to live her own life in Humenné or anywhere else. "Never go to Humenné, it's a dreadful hole. A pitiless hole. A high rise suburb, a café, an army barracks, and one or two decent old houses. And plenty of brutes about."

She found a room with an elderly couple in an old cottage; they treated her almost like a daughter. Sometimes they gave her something to eat, and they didn't press her for the rent. She gathered sloes out beyond the town, to be able to prove some means of subsistence. "The sloes growing there, the place was blue with them! I was careful not to lose the purchase slips, and so I was able to produce them in court. It wasn't much, but they couldn't get me for living off anybody." ("No means of subsistence" is parasitism, the Czech authorities' term for prostitution.)

The couple she lived with sent her to a village where there was a pig-killing, to help out. It lasted three days, the whole village in an orgy of pig-killing, at least twenty families. The butcher drank his plum brandy straight from the bottle; he could hardly stand on his feet, but his hands were sure enough. One of the men was so drunk he couldn't hold the pig properly and the animal got away and they all had to chase it. She got a taste of the plum brandy too, so she tasted all the good things of village life, but the other women were sipping sweet drinks. She told us how the whole village admired her, and especially the good wives. "I didn't mind any job they gave me, even stirring the warm pig's blood with my hands. It smelled awful and made a thick black line just below my elbows. They didn't have running water, it all had to be carried from the well, and I did all that. It was freezing and I kept slipping and spilling water over my feet, and it froze on my stockings and in my shoes." But she was given her share of the meat, enough food to last her a month. "I'd have liked to stay there. There was a young chap who didn't have anyone; it would have been a good thing, life's simple in the country, you know what's what."

In town she sat in the café all day, where it was warm, sipping the one cup of black coffee she could afford. She had no trouble getting into conversation with men; she looked a cut above the local women, but all the men she found were boring. In the pubs things were gayer, but the fuzz was closer. The first time they arrested her, a fuzz took her to the station and made her buy a ticket for Prague. She was so terrified by this first encounter with the police that the fuzz believed her promises and did not wait to put her in the train himself. She returned the ticket—it represented all the money she had on her—and slipped out the back way. For a while she spent all her time gathering sloes for the market, to be sure they couldn't get her as a "parasite." The next time she was held, the fuzz was wise to her; he took her identity card off her and threatened to have her sent back to Prague under police guard. It was late in the evening, and the two were alone in the police station. It was like any other office, with desks, chairs, telephones, and dirty curtains; the only difference was that he was in police uniform. He was young and rough-mannered. "The only thing that saved me was that I gave him what he wanted. It was dreadful, conscience struggling against necessity, that really tears you apart. He was shouting at me, he was going to lock me up and send a report to Prague, and I'd have hated to be sent back just then, and I didn't want to go to jail either. He was flicking at my card with his fingers, I could tell I wasn't going to get it back all that easily. If only I hadn't had it on me! As a rule I only carried the purchase slips from the market, so they couldn't get me that way, but just that day I'd had to go to the post office for something and so I had my identity card as well. What would I do if he really didn't give it back? Any bit of fuzz could pick me up on the street and lock me up if I couldn't prove who I was. Everything was stacked against me, it was dark, we were alone in the place, somebody'd turned me in. It's woman's eternal question: Shall I let him or not? He wasn't too bad to look at, not tall but quite well built. It didn't matter that he was shouting at me, it takes some of them that way. I knew one who had to pretend he was dying, none of them know how to put it straight to the woman they want. But this was fuzz! Can you see my dilemma? The shame of it, going with a fuzz. On the other hand, I thought, what sort of a woman are you to refuse? It's our fate, we always have to take them when they want it. That's what we're made for. Of course I felt ashamed because it was the fuzz, but how can a woman avoid her fate?"

She didn't want to be driven out of the town just then, because she had found a lover. He was a draftsman in a building firm, an amusing, agreeable chap, one of the "Slovaks who come out right." He was married and lived high up in a high rise apartment with his wife and the inevitable three rooms and a kitchen with the cheapest equipment, built-in cupboards, bathroom walls of cardboard, and a narrow balcony with a view of the balconies opposite: just what Nancy had left behind in Prague. His wife went out to work and he would take Nancy home whenever he could get away from the office; sometimes the marital couch was still warm. Her lover fed her, let her shower, and wash her hair, rinse out her underwear. He was always giving her little presents. Perhaps it was admiration, rather than love; she was his little miracle, the lady from the café.

It was quite a long time before kind neighbors told his wife what was going on. Then she stormed into the nest the intruder had defiled, flinging open the door and finding Nancy clad only in a slip, standing by *her* bed, on *her* carpet, admiring herself in *her* mirror. She flung herself at Nancy, who ran through the apartment. You could go all around it in a circle, through the kitchen, the hall, the living room, the kitchen, the hall, the living room. Only the bedroom lay to one side. Nancy slammed the doors behind her as she ran, one so violently that the glass panels shattered. The wife was determined to exact the final penalty—she opened a window and started pushing Nancy out.

"Her eyes were popping out of her head, her hair falling down, she had one of those built-up hairdos and it slipped over one ear, and she was screaming, screaming dreadfully. I couldn't make out a word. It was really absurd. I wasn't trying to protect myself, what I minded most was her seeing me almost naked, I didn't have a bra on, nor panties. It was her husband had given me that transparent slip and I was just trying it on when she rushed in. It was really absurd, and as I ran round the place I kept my hands over my breasts and my back to her, I was ashamed for her to see me and that's how she caught me." It was her husband, Miro, who prevented the defenestration of Humenné, grabbing Nancy away from his furious wife and locking her in the bedroom out of the way. The wife went to the police, and Nancy paid for her escape by being arrested.

And so the time had come to move. "I was getting a bad reputation in Humenné." Her friendly policeman took her to the station; this time he waited to see the train safely out; he did not return her identity card, though, saying he had to send it to

Prague, but he assured her he was sending it as "lost and found"
and not making any report. He told her where to go and get it
back. She didn't believe him and didn't go to the office where,
as she learned later, it really was lying innocently waiting for her.
Her husband had twice sent money to Humenné for her fare
home. I do not know how he found her address, unless she had
written to her mother when there was no other way out. The
first time, she spent the money on food and paid the rent for her
room in the old couple's cottage; the second time she bought the
ticket, but she did not go home. At the Prague Main Station she
turned her steps toward Václavské náměstí, not knowing what
she would find to eat or where she would find a place to sleep.
She could not go to her mother's because she would be forced
back to her husband by that loyal woman—and not only out of
loyalty, but because her mother would be glad to get rid of the
children. Nancy did not yet feel like going back to her children,
either; she missed them, but not fiercely enough; the woman in
her was not yet satisfied. Then, too, she had got used to living
without responsibilities. In any case, she was afraid to go home.
You could believe her as she told how she hated reproachful
scenes, the endless repetitions she would have to endure. Nancy
seemed to be forced to carry on as she was, until somebody else
took over; she was incapable of changing direction herself. If
her husband had been waiting for her at the station, I am sure
she would have gone home with him. But he was not there, and
so—all the wiser for her experience in Humenné—she went not
to a pub, not to a café, but to a cake shop. She thought that only
respectable men would be met with in a cake shop.

She sat sipping a cup of coffee, fingering the last ten crowns
she had in her pocket to pay the bill. She need not have worried;
three not-so-young lady-killers soon invited her over to their
table. Once again she could be sociable, witty, and feminine, the

way she enjoyed being in the company of men. It was less for the delight of three elderly gentlemen that she was trying out her charms in a cake shop, though, than for her own self-assurance; she needed to recover from the after effects of Humenné, and that was what happened, in the vanilla- and coffee-scented air and the warmth. The humiliating domination of the fuzz, all the unpleasantness of Humenné, was far away.

Prague was a better place than that pitiless hole away out in the steppes. Better because there were more people around, and one sheep wandering from the fold could hide more easily. The three gents invited Nancy for a homey evening: we're getting on so well together, wouldn't it be more comfortable at my place? Evening was drawing on, and she had to find some-where to go; she dared not risk being picked up at the railroad station by a police patrol. They took her by car although it turned out to be just round the corner, to a prosperous town-house with tall mirrors in the hall, not even cracked; she could see that the wide staircase was paneled in marble, and the elevator they went up in was an old-fashioned ornamental cage for six, polished and gleaming. The fourth-floor flat was a bachelor's apartment with a big window looking on to the park, a kitchenette, and a bathroom. They had invited her, a lady, home, and so she could not very well ask to have a bath after her train journey, but she got a good look at the place: there was a little divan in the kitchen which looked just right for her tired body, and she would gladly leave the soft bed with its camel-hair blanket and decorative cushions to her host.

The lady-killers were charmed by her, listening to her tales of her travels, looking at the shopping bag she produced as Exhibit Number 1, but having learned her lesson in Humenné, she gave a false name, a false itinerary, and a somewhat expur-gated version of her adventures. They made her at home, asked her to pour the cognac—she glimpsed another five bottles lined up in the sideboard, all good Georgian cognac with the white peak of Ararat on the label. The refrigerator was packed with ham, Ementhal cheese, and Hungarian salami; there was a rosy leg of pork in the freezer, along with ruddy steaks. She liked the little apartment, it was clean and pleasant; her host had a rather pompously loud voice, but who's to say that everything in the garden has to be lovely? After a cold snack they asked her if she'd mind making coffee.

Wiser after Humenné, she first closed the kitchen door firmly, and then softly opened it a crack. The lady-killers were arguing about who would have first go: "I'm not having her after you've finished."

"You don't think I'm going to wait till you've had your go, do you?"

"You think I'm going to hang round waiting for an hour, just watching you at it?"

"I invited her up here so I get first cut."

"It's my cognac and my ham she's been stuffing down."

"Now then," the third intervened, "she looks the right sort. She can give it the two of you at once. You only have to decide the details in advance."

She had to admit that the flat wasn't worth all that much. She slipped out of the kitchen into the hall, and *very much* wiser after Humenné, drew the key out of the lock, went quietly out, and locked the three old gentlemen inside.

It was a bunch of keys; the car keys were on it, too. It was raining, and she had no more than a light jumper. In Humenné she'd had to sell her coat. The first thing she had to do was get rid of the keys in a safe place, and rub her fingerprints off them, too. She ran through a couple of streets to get well away from that prosperous place and found herself in a broad covered way, with garbage cans lined up waiting, spilling over. That seemed a good place; the light went out, so she looked for the switch, and when it happened again she saw she was being watched. By a handsome young man. Why is it that when Only-a-Woman gets into trouble, there's always a handsome man in the offing? This one appeared to be rather drunk; after watching her clumsy antics with the keys—wiping them with the hem of her skirt: as she wiped off the prints of the right hand she imprinted those of her left—he said: "D'you happen to know where those keys belong?"

"I certainly do," she said, "but I haven't the slightest desire to go there and use them."

The handsome young man was wearing shabby jeans with a leather patch at the crotch, a bedraggled sweater and sandals, not the best way to be dressed in April weather. He hadn't shaved for about three days, but there was a happy light in his eyes, the light that always signaled a soul mate to Nancy. His nose was delightfully turned up at the tip, too. He was certainly the kind to turn to in trouble, and she ingenuously told him the story of the keys.

"Look here, Nan—you said you're Nan, didn't you? Look, Nan love, I've got a bloody good idea, Nan, darling, suppose I sort of stole the keys off you? A bottle of cognac wouldn't be a bad idea, Nan, now, would it, my love?"

"For Heaven's sake, no! Be sensible, do, there were three of them and they'd be sure to recognize me again. I need to get away, not to go putting my head in there again. I haven't even got my identity card, the fuzz have got it."

The handsome young man's name was George and he behaved like a gallant knight; he gave up on the cognac and took the keys and threw them down the drain. So simple a solution would never have occurred to Nancy! They laughed together at the thought of the three old gentlemen banging on their locked door. George put his arm round her shoulder—she was wet through—and took her home with him.

George lived with his mother, who was poor and honest and earned her living as a cleaner; his last wife had left him when he failed to go free from the courtroom. Without a word his mother provided Nancy with a blouse and skirt, and put water on the stove to warm. They lived in one of the old houses with an open gallery from which you stepped into the kitchen, and through there to the only room; there was a toilet at the end of the gallery, common to all the tenants. It was plenty big enough: George and Nancy slept and made love in the back room while his mother lived in the kitchen, where she cooked, slept, and took in washing and mending. George's love-making was child-like, subtle, and delicate—they could have played at love in front of mother. He was the joyful type—but only up to the moment when his obsession took hold of him. He had just done two years for theft and was required to report at the police station every week. He was a fitter, and worked at the railroad station; Nancy looked after him properly, and besides helping his mother she spent the whole day near the station so that George could find her if he needed to. When she drank with him he never got too drunk, but if some ruffian got hold of him before she got to the bar, and they started drinking together, she had to drag him out from under the table and get him home. She took good care to see he reported to the police, because that was the only way to keep clear of them. It was not a great love, but an affectionate, comradely sort of life, with its joys as well as its responsibilities. She did not talk about him much, but when she did it was in a kindly way. She was proud that for several months she had brought him home every day in such a state that he could get up and go to work next morning.

And then everything collapsed.

Nancy began to long for her children and went to see them at her mother's. It was a terrible meeting, her mother storming at her: What sort of a mother are you? You don't take after me, that's sure. I never had a husband but I didn't desert you, you've got everything a woman can want, a husband, a nice home, a car, a weekend chalet, and you're not grateful for any of it. I'll take care of the children for him, I'm willing to do it for him, but not for you. Don't you forget it. I'm not going to look after your children so you can go on the streets like a whore. Nancy foolishly told her mother where she was living: Mum, please, if anything happens to the children, let me know, if they're ill or if they miss me too much, write and tell me, promise me you'll write. Her mother gave the address to Smugpot, and he came along the gallery one Saturday afternoon when all the tenants in the old house were home from work. Fortunately George's mother had gone to take flowers to the cemetery and the kitchen door was locked. Nancy and her lover were asleep, and heavy blows on the door woke them up. Open this door! I know you're in there. If you don't come out I'm going to get a divorce and you'll never see the children again. Open up or I'll fetch the police. Nancy was trembling and clutching George, who had a hangover and wanted to go and kill Smugpot for waking him up. It was a long time before Smugpot went away, and the neighbors told George's mother that there were tears streaming down his face when he went along the gallery and down the steps to the street. His lawyer told him it would be wiser not to ask for a divorce but to file a suit against his wife for neglecting the children and failing to contribute to their maintenance. Nancy's mother added her evidence, and when they drew up his complaint Smugpot worked out to the last penny how much money he'd sent her to Humenné—bringing the postal receipts to prove it.

Smugpot was having his revenge. Nancy kept getting threatening letters from his lawyer, and George was falling back into his old ways. His eyes grew sharp and lost their happy glint. He beat her and shouted at her; his mother borrowed a camp bed and Nancy slept in the kitchen with her. George would disappear for days at a time and come back drunk and battered; once a couple of prostitutes brought him home. In the good months that they'd had together, they made a date for five o'clock every afternoon at the smaller of the two Prague stations, unless they had other plans. This Central Station is the main refuge for down-and-outs, hoboes, petty criminals, easy girls, and homosexuals looking for a chance partner. The normal traveler notices nothing as he hurries through the hall, stops for a hamburger or a beer, and goes on to find his train. But if you know the place, you can get involved in a brawl, mixed up with gays and pimps, or talk to the dirty old man masturbating under the filthy tablecloth at the corner table in the station restaurant. All the girls with no place to go in Prague knew the Central Station as a place where you may have good luck—or bad. Nancy went there every day, without revulsion and without fear. Once again she did not look out of place, nor did she look at home there. And she kept on meeting their five o'clock date even now when George was sick again. It was a Tuesday, the day when he ought to have reported to the police, and if he didn't the fuzz would be looking for him at home. It was already afternoon and George had not been seen there all day. Maybe they've locked him up, a train worker she knew suggested. And so she needn't drink the bad beer at the bar while she waited for George, he said he'd make her a cup of coffee in the den. The den was an old railroad coach where the workers sheltered, played cards, and took their girls. It was by the den that Nancy was arrested. She had no identity card with her, but a warrant was out for her not paying maintenance, and so she landed in Ruzyně. George's mother wrote and told her he was in Ruzyně, too, but Nancy had neither the energy nor the will to try and find him by shouting his name, or smuggling letters.

I was awakened one morning by something tickling my neck, and my fingers caught something. I woke Denise who confirmed my suspicion. Lice! I only had that one, perhaps because Denise dyed my hair for me despite strict prohibition in jail; I found plenty of the creatures on her head. We woke the others up; Annie, Denise, me, Mrs. Vacková, Fanny, Nancy: we all sat there in our gray blankets, our heads heavy with the fetid air and our minds shocked by that awful discovery. Nancy was the worst off: the lice had wormed their way under the skin and her neck, beneath the hair, was a mass of moving painful lumps. There was no point in trying to work out where the pests had come from; when we reported the calamity the guard acted as though it was all in the day's work. We understood then why Nancy ran her fingers through her hair so often: her head was itching intolerably, but she didn't think it worth mentioning, it was only the dust from her blanket that had got into her hair. And if she did think anything of it, she wouldn't have said so because she'd have been ashamed and waited for it to blow over somehow. That's what you have to pay for behaving decently in a place so far from decent.

We were in despair. The next day Nancy was due to be transferred to a prison camp, and old hands had told us that when a convict arrives with a head full of lice, instead of cropping her hair they just shave the whole head. Our guard confirmed this; instead of changing the pillow cases and giving out ointment, like in Ruzyně, they make short work of the lice — and the convict. Nancy was due to be released in two more weeks, and we begged the guard to leave her with us that night, we'd take turns to keep awake and clean her head with ointment. They wouldn't come for her till morning and could just as well take her from our cell as from the transfer cell in the basement.

"Just you get your things ready," the guard replied, "we couldn't care less. The camp officers are always complaining we send them women with filthy heads, anyway."

Nancy's hands were shaking so she couldn't tie her sheet into a bundle, so we did it for her; she had nothing of her own, nobody had sent her anything while she was in prison. We collected whatever we had between us; maybe good soap or chocolate would be enough to bribe the camp guard to leave her hair. She took nothing but a couple of cigarettes. "You'll be here for ages. I've only got two more weeks."

"Bye, Nancy, my love." Annie turned her back so we couldn't see her tears. She gave Nancy a long kiss on the lips, and her idol smiled vaguely. Denise pressed her head against Nancy's. You've got lice? What's it matter, I'll have them too. And then we sat there sad and humiliated because we'd been able to do so little for her.

We went on picking out our lice, and Denise suddenly told me to put the biggest and fattest into an empty pill tube the guards had forgotten to take away. Since they were more interested in their regulations than in cleanliness in the cells. The tube was half full when they came to take Denise to the doctor's; she could not take it with her, it would be seen, and so she took as many of the fat, egg-rich lice as she could hold between thumb and forefinger, careful not to squash them. She let one drop on to every uniform she passed on the way, and the last she saved for the nurse whom she particularly hated. It was one way of avenging poor Nancy's graying hair.

14

ANNIE AND
FANNY

"I'll get yer!" ... the girls were kneeling on their stools round the snakes and ladders board open on the table; Annie had thrown a six and her man was on the move. "I'll get yer yet." Another six, another frenzied yell. She chased the other men, hopped over them, slid them down snakes, not really aware who was winning and who losing; there was no strategy about her playing, the main thing was to yell: "I'll get yer!" Annie yelled when the others threw sixes, as loud as for her own. Yelling relieves pressure, and making snakes and ladders frenetic was a good way of letting off energy. Annie's shouts drove them all to throw the dice feverishly, as though their lives depended on the result. "Got yer!" The colored men seemed seized by the same frenzy as they hopped home. The game is far too simple to arouse the passionate absorption these girls display; but they are so hungry for excitement, for thrills, that they find them in the most trivial things.

When the game begins to pall, they can always fall back on a scuffle or at least a loud quarrel. Then they are quiet for a while. In jail there is a constant inner vibration running through women and girls, a real physiological tremor than can be seen if you watch closely enough: muscles, internal organs, nerves, all are pulsating even in sleep. All women in prison are neurotic, subject to outbursts of violent temper, of weeping, of aggression. When men prisoners were out in the exercise yard all we heard was the hum of low voices and the shuffling of feet, broken by an occasional shout from the young men, but on the whole it was a soothing sound. When women are taken out it sounds like a wasps' nest that has been disturbed. Their emotional energy has no outlet and turns to restlessness. Annie whipped up the passions of everybody in the game although she herself rarely won and did not even seem to be playing to win, or for the fun of the game, but for those hectic noisy moments followed by a pleasurable numbness.

"I'll get yer!" Annie was still shouting, but her passion was abating and she followed the men with dulled and apathetic eyes. Those who are losing are the most pertinacious; as her physical need subsided, Annie always gave up the game.

Annie came from Košice and had come to Prague to work, some years ago—exactly how many years that meant we never managed to work out. Annie did not confide in us, but sometimes as she recounted incidents she would let something drop. She loved describing things that had happened, but they were isolated events, not the story of her life. In that way she could conceal whatever she wanted to hide, and she did it so expertly that Denise and I were surprised when the young woman who took Annie's place in our cell told us she had known her in a prison camp. Annie already an old hand? It could have fitted in to the time scale, but not to her own account; she took great care to act as though she was in prison for the first time. She worked in a chocolate factory with the older woman who had brought her to Prague and knew her way around the capital. It was a good start: they were paid a bonus by the factory and had rooms in the factory hostel where there was a canteen, a cinema, and of course a TV on every floor. Annie could have lived happily there for years, and she regretted that she hadn't. She loved the smell of candy that pervaded the factory workshops, the corridors, the stores; she had a room to herself in the hostel, and the chocolates she ate! They could eat as much as they could digest of what the factory produced—within its walls, that is—and she praised the canteen cooking, too.

The only thing she didn't like was the job she was given, that of trundling the caramel mixture to the filling machine. The machine itself fascinated her and she could describe its automatic working in detail. It was pushing the cart along that bored her. She would have liked to work on the new German automatic lozenge machine, but you have to do the worst jobs before you can graduate to the better ones in a factory, and Annie hadn't the patience.

And so Annie tried other ways of conquering the capital. She told us that her friend had persuaded her to try seasonal work in the sugar beet campaign, but it was probably under police escort from the work camp, and not just with her woman friend, that she arrived at the Pardubice factory every morning. Her next step from the chocolate factory had been prison.

And now she was in Ruzyně. She took up her place in the corner where she felt safe from all sides and watched us; not too obviously though: her head was bent and she only shot a quick glance at whoever happened to be speaking. She did not let on what she thought of us. Her eyes had that darkly knowing look of people who have seen more of life than the rest of us and feel marked by it. She did not seek the favor of any of us, nor to distribute her favors, except to Nancy. She was not given to the easy friendships most girls covet. She had nothing of her own, nothing but the official prison issue. She didn't worry her head about getting hold of anything. She ate what we were given, whether it was eatable or not; and if she'd been given nothing she would just not have eaten, without comment. There was nobody outside to send her anything, and she did not have the money for cigarettes. When the prison officer in charge of our floor told her she'd be working in the cleaning squad, she thought it over for a long time and only agreed when she was told sharply that she had to contribute to her child's maintenance and so she'd got to earn something. She accepted a cigarette, a slice of meat, a chocolate, pleased when we offered; if we hadn't, she would have noted the fact but said nothing. She was indifferent, but it was a broad-minded, not an apathetic, indifference. Annie was an unusual and original person. She asked me one day:

"What are you reading all the time? It's enough to drive you crazy."

"You mean it's driving you crazy to watch me?"

"No way. It's you'll be off yer rocker, not me. There was a nutcase in the village, a teacher he was, reading and reading till he went bonkers. I know what I'm talking about."

"I'm sure you do. There are people who've gone mad from reading."

"What d'you have 'Doctor' on your envelope for, yesterday? You a doctor or something?"

"No, not a doctor, I got a degree in philosophy."

"What's that supposed to be, philosophy?"

"Annie," Denise intervened, "don't pretend to be sillier than you are."

"I can ask, can't I?"

"People have always wanted to understand what the world's all about and worked out different answers."

"There you are, I told you it'd drive you crackers."

"It wouldn't be easy to explain what philosophy is, Annie."

"Haven't you had enough if it got you in here? There's still the loony bin if you don't stop in time. Come on, let's have a game and you leave that damn fool stuff alone."

One day we got *For Whom the Bell Tolls* from the prison library and a Gypsy girl who had learned to read really well in a children's home was turning the pages when she came on a dirty word. She giggled and showed the page to Annie. "Now I know why you've always got yer head in a book," she said. Looking for more dirty words, she read the whole novel. She retained all that is essential in the story and joined in our discussions about it.

"There you are, Annie," Denise commented.

"Who said I was a moron?"

"And don't tell me you've never read a book."

"You think I'm as dopey as that? Reading books like I'd nothing better to do? I'm bored in here, that's all."

"Didn't you read books when you went to school?"

"School, phew! What's so good about school? Forget it."

"You're having us on, Annie."

"There's a book I've read," Annie replied, "that you've never even dreamed about."

"Go on! What's it about?"

"Now don't you go pretending you've read it, though," she warned me, then added mysteriously: *Kamasutra*. She gave me a look tinged with barely hidden and slightly scornful triumph. "D'you know it?"

"Where did you get hold of it? When *Kamasutra* was published it was sold out immediately. It's a real rarity."

"I've got it, though," she said proudly, "I bought it, keep it locked in my case."

"Why lock it up?"

"You'd know why if you'd ever seen it."

"It was written by a monk, Annie."

"A monk! You don't say!" and she laughed joyfully.

"He was a very learned monk. *Kamasutra*'s an ancient Indian book that teaches all about love."

"That's what it says, anyway, you don't have to believe it," she told me loftily and began to tell us what the book was really about.

Nancy put in, "I once saw a photograph of an Indian temple, the walls all round were covered in carvings showing different positions for making love."

"A church?" Annie was amazed. "Indians are as good as all that?"

"They used to be, long ago."

"You mean they showed all the positions there?"

"Well, plenty," Nancy said, "enough for them to be all there are."

"Did they show two women together?"

"Annie! How can you?" Nancy was shocked.

Annie and her friend had read the book in secret, with unholy relish, in their hostel room by the chocolate factory. Two girls from East Slovakia and the *Kamasutra*. Look what treasures you can find in Prague! What the monk Vatsyayana had to say about "the delights of love" had nothing in common with

MY COMPANIONS IN THE BLEAK HOUSE

Annie's own experience. At one and the same moment she was deflowered and impregnated; her child was conceived on the way home from a village dance, and her seducer was not a seducer: Annie loved him, but he didn't want her. "He was drunk," she said, "and the child was born an idiot."

Annie felt no fondness for her idiot child; the birth was a hard one and nearly cost her life. The child was put away in an institution, but it was not so easy to forget her unhappy love and disastrous first sexual experience. The man married her when she found she was pregnant, but when everything turned out so badly, her love and her child, he became set against her and his mother turned her out of the house. He got a divorce. They shouted abuse at each other at village dances; never again did he take her home, even when he was drunk—she had to watch him taking other girls home. Her sorrow, her loneliness, her fury rose up in her and she broke all the windows in her mother-in-law's cottage. She did it in broad daylight; the whole village gathered to watch her getting a pile of stones ready and then relentlessly, wildly shatter the windows one after another, screaming abuse. That didn't help to get her husband back; he married another girl. Annie could only beat her head against the wall and later, in Prague, learn from the *Kamasutra* that her husband was nothing but a coarse brute. She was glad to discover that fact, though not even that exorcised her love. Abused and deserted, she spoke of him with furious hatred, but where there is hate, there was once love. Cauterized by her painful experience with one man and one birth, instructed in theory by *Kamasutra*, and perhaps in practice by the morals of a women's prison camp, Annie embraced lesbian love. Not as readily accessible as heterosexual love—that is to say, less accessible outside but predominating in prison—she found it sweet and gentle. "Just one taste of it," went Annie's favorite axiom, "and you'll never want anything else."

The other great moment in Annie's discovery of Prague was the revelation of the "great world." Which world is "great" and which is not? Annie gave me a good lesson in the relativity of scales of values. The cafés, the discos, the cheap dance halls where she went to hops, that was all on her own level; interesting, but nothing out of the ordinary. The Central Station, as she saw quite clearly, offered a gathering place for people of her kind, and then the dregs of society found a refuge there, people she could feel herself superior to. She talked as simply and openly about that railroad station as a village grandmother describing comings and goings on the village green. She sat there drinking beer and got into fights, watched the black market in operation, got to know burglars and other professional thieves, watched the filthy old man jerk off. The Central Station is an information center, a place to meet people, the place for meetings, the place to go back to; her first errand after release will be to that station. But it's not the "great world."

The most aristocratic creature Annie met in Prague was the Countess; she talked about her, dreamily, dazzled. She was silently and hopelessly in love with the Countess. The Countess, a well-known figure around Prague, is over seventy now, indeed a good deal over seventy. She used to be a dancer, and her husband owned what is now one of the wine bars with the worst reputations, in the Old Town. The wine bar is in a street where prostitutes walk their beat, and there's a police car parked on the corner all night. It's a rowdy place, that wine bar, a place where strangers are not welcome and are taken care of by bouncers. It's down a long flight of stairs, and the steps are usually pissed on from top to bottom. When the regulars get warmed up, it is said that you can even see some fucking on the crowded dance floor, in the shadows of the intimate lighting effects. The Countess has her table there (and her account) and arrives about half past eight every evening; then she invites whoever takes her fancy to sit with her. Sometimes she brings a girlfriend with her. After a substantial supper the Countess starts to dance. Slim, supple, well-proportioned, she is a good dancer and in spite of her age will join in rock 'n' roll. She dresses extravagantly and wears a selection of youthful-looking wigs, of which the most familiar gives her long fair hair. It is not until she washes the makeup off that her real age shows up. Elegantly scented, she takes a different young man home each night. Her own taxi driver comes to fetch her home although she lives only a few streets away. She is never drunk, just in a happy mood, and never drinks beer or spirits, only wine. Her manners are perfect and she knows how to keep her distance. In any case, should anyone try to bother her, he'd find himself being carried out to the street. Annie hinted that she knew where the Countess lives; she was invited to her table one evening; the Countess had ordered trout, her beringed fingers hovered lightly over the plate, long gold earrings swaying, a heavy gold chain round her neck. Annie longed almost romantically to be chosen by the Countess instead of those green boys she habitually favored. Just one taste of it . . .

Annie's knowledge-ignorance, presented with such assurance, was touching; what a long way she had come, to find the "great world" embodied in the Countess! She is hardly likely to have won the lady's favors, or she would have boasted of it. Annie hadn't much chance as a "chick" because she was not attractive. She had a lovely head, with thick black hair, great dark eyes with long lashes, beautifully arched brows, an aristocratically aquiline nose that was not too big, and a firm well-shaped chin. If the head were all, Annie would have been a real beauty, but her body was unnaturally out of proportion, looking either prematurely aged or childishly immature. Drooping shoulders and a potbelly that began at the childishly undeveloped breasts and spread sideways and downward like an enormous drop that cannot break free from the tap; that belly was her worst feature, hanging down over her private parts to reach her thighs. It was not fat—nature had played an unkind trick on Annie. "My Gran looked just the same," she said, but Gran had never set out to conquer the capital. Gran enjoyed great respect in the family; she gathered and dispensed herbs, and was something of a clairvoyant. To her oddly proportioned body Annie had been given short arms and legs, while her hands were tiny, with smooth palms and baby fingers. We were all looking at the lines on our hands, telling our fortunes, one day, and Annie held hers out too. There was nothing to be read there: her palms were bare, smooth, with one deep furrow dividing the fingers from the palm and thumb. Don't monkeys have hands like that? We were not sure, and Annie was proud of being different.

Annie exercised her own judgment, although to the conventional she might seem stupid and certainly was bizarre in her ideas. She was an individualist, not of the common herd. She had always suffered for her individuality and always would. She was not particularly bright at school, although she had great talent—her lively, colorful tales! She told us how she'd been seduced on the way home from that dance, in a couple of sentences; and yet I can still see vividly the tree they were lying under, the blood-spattered grass and the black sky far above. I'm not embroidering: Annie even remembered a cricket that was tirelessly and annoyingly trilling nearby. Annie had only to look at a face and she knew what was behind it; it was a skill inherited from her clairvoyant Gran, no doubt, but one that did not help her in life. She had her own decided ideas on what was right and what was wrong about the way the world went. She wore her unusual traits of mind and soul as she wore her strange physical self, as a matter of course and not at all provocatively.

Annie was aware that she was different but was not upset by the fact, although it brought her nothing but trouble. The good and unusual characteristics that she possessed (and used) seemed only to hinder her in her efforts to get what she wanted. Her surroundings always took it out of her; at home in her native village they thought she was crazy and a nuisance. Had she said too soon and too openly what she was after? That she wanted the man she loved even if he scorned her? That she wanted a lovely, healthy child, although she nearly died in the attempt and ended up with a physically and mentally deficient one? And that she wanted to live where she was born? So long as her parents were alive, and her Gran, Annie was protected. Gran died and then her parents; her brother built himself a cottage and then sold the old one, Annie's only home after her mother-in-law turned her out. He did it deliberately and cunningly; the moment he sold the cottage and deprived Annie of a roof over her head, he got the local committee to drive her, his only sister, out of the village. I do not know how he managed it, and Annie did not understand it either. She was simply told to go. And how could she stay, when she had nowhere to live? Annie did not tell us why her brother and the village authorities were so anxious to get rid of her. Was it because of those broken windows? Because of the abuse hurled about at their village dances? The rows and scenes? She went first to Košice and then to Prague. Since then she had been back home once, taking presents for her brother's children. They would not let her into the yard and refused her gifts. That was after she'd been to prison for the first time.

Annie was a rowdy; she had become violent from so many desperate failures. After all she had been through—a ruined marriage, ruined motherhood, driven from home, ostracized, ending up in jail—she turned her cleverness to creating a protective camouflage; she disguised her powerlessness under a mask of assumed force. When she came to our cell her first words were: "Watch out! If you get in my way you'll feel these fists." And she described, with appropriate action, how she had fought a boy stronger than herself and drawn blood at the Central Station. That was when they arrested her. "Let'em lock me up," she couldn't care less, Annie the terror of the pubs. O.K., we took the hint: Annie was not to be trifled with, we would be careful not to irritate her. She was impetuous, always ready for a quarrel, and we tried to smooth things out, not to give her an excuse to start a fight.

Every morning she woke up in aggressive mood, heavy-eyed, murderous. She refused to fit in with our early morning timetable—something that is important in such crowded quarters where we each had to perform our bodily functions; wash, clean our teeth, change into day clothes, pile our beds up one on top of the other, take turns to wipe down the floor and set up the table and stools ready for breakfast, with the shutter of the spy hole opening all the time as guards looked in, and with somebody getting ready to smuggle a letter and somebody else to phone before they brought breakfast round.

"Leave me alone. I'm going on lying here." We tried to cheer her up, to get her moving slowly and gently—not because we were really afraid of her little fists, but because every open conflict has a depressing effect, it takes a long time for the mood in the cell to get back to normal calm. During the day, once she had got over her morning handicap, Annie was a cheerful, agreeable girl. And in jail it is not difficult to work out why the morning mood is so murderous. When an explosion seemed imminent, Nancy would say, "Annie, stop heating it up!" That was the severest step we ever took; Annie would always listen to Nancy.

One morning as I was doing my daily dozen (something Denise stoutly defended my right to, making my bed for me so that I had time to do the exercises that were good for my aching back), swinging my arm back where I expected nobody to be, I hit Annie, who deliberately got in the way because the sight annoyed her. It annoyed most of the women, and only the very decent few would refrain from smoking; the others smoked like chimneys and screeched when we opened the window. Annie got in my way on purpose, the morning being her time to go looking for trouble. I did not hit her hard—my arm had gone full circle and slowed down—yet the slight blow knocked her to the floor. She lay there helplessly and we could not understand why she had fallen. She got to her feet clumsily, and we felt her all over to see if there was anything wrong; her eyes were confused and ashamed. Suddenly we felt ashamed, too: it dawned on us that not only was she no rowdy, no aggressive fighter, not only was she not strong—she was weak! Her un-developed body was weak, and her verbal violence was the mask behind which she hid her weakness. That was the dark knowl-edge that lay in her eyes, the knowledge that she was powerless against force. She knew no other way of fighting force than by force, and so she pretended. The strange thing was that this realization did not bring us closer together, now that we knew her raw spot; she seemed to draw farther away, as though she looked at us from beyond the pale.

After she was released from the prison camp Annie worked in the largest Prague laundry, a modern, newly equipped workshop, and the way she described it, it was a slave's life. No machinery? Of course, and all automatic. But the links between the machines were human beings. Mountains of linen were spewed out by the washing and drying machines, Annie collected it, faster, faster, but taking care not to mix the batches up. It was work for quick hands, careful eyes—sheets, pillowcases, it all passed through her little hands, and after eight hours of hot white ironed linen her hands were burning, weak, and slack, her attention failing. It was so hot in the laundry that the women worked practically naked. Were she Jack London, it might have made a writer out of her, but as it was, she simply ran away. When they caught her, she'd missed so many work days they took her to the VD ward, found she had the clap, and brought her to Ruzyně. She was a recidivist, and the fact that she wasn't paying for her mentally defective child in the home was probably brought against her, too.

When you are living as we were, body to body, breath to breath, you learn not to romanticize. An ugly duckling was dropped into our cell one day; from southern Slovakia, half Gypsy, half Hungarian, and Annie, who had made us feel ashamed because she was afraid of us, at last had a victim. The weak creature found one even weaker, on whom she could take her vengeance for what the world had done to her. The ugly duckling spoke only a little broken Slovak, enough to cope with everyday things like sleeping, washing, eating; she looked half-witted, with a silly smile, and she was ugly and starving. She jumped on all the leftovers, cleaned all our mess tins out, ate everything we refused to eat, and seemed to be trying to catch up on a long period of hunger. Perhaps when we offered her all we could, it helped her not to feel ashamed of her hunger, because we did not laugh at her for stuffing herself. She began to get fat and to look even more stupid than before. She was called Fanny.

There was a barrier between us, the barrier of language and that of shyness, the shyness of a little animal cast upon the unknown world. She sat on her stool, realizing quickly that nobody would take that from her, sitting close to the door where she was least in anybody's way, rocking from side to side and humming softly to herself. She longed to be understood, though, longed for a kind word, and her plain little face with its spotty complexion smiled at us hopefully. Bit by bit, with the help of one of the girls who spoke a little Romany and a few words of Hungarian, we learned her story. Brought up in a children's home where her parents put her because they already had too many children, she went back to them at fifteen, ready to join the labor force. They lived in a village in the fertile plains, on a prosperous cooperative farm where Fanny worked in the pig sties. She had a little boy, not long ago. She was just over eighteen, and her husband was doing his army service.

She was inveigled into coming to Prague by a woman friend from the village, a Gypsy who had settled in the capital. She sold poor trusting Fanny, getting seventy crowns a time from her customers and not giving Fanny a penny pocket money. Wasn't she keeping her, giving her board and lodging and all those customers? Fanny was picked up in a police raid, sent to the VD clinic where they found she had the clap. They couldn't charge her with anything; she was a married woman with a young child and not required to show she was employed. She told them she had stopped off to see a friend in Prague, on her way to visit her husband in the army. When she was cured of the clap they told her to go back home, which she was doing when the Gypsy woman caught her at the station and said she'd kill her if she didn't stay. Fanny knew something of what went on in those circles, and although she may have feared for her life unnecessarily, she went back with the Gypsy procuress. The second time she was caught they sent her straight to Ruzyně. She was shocked and terrified. She had never envisaged prison, and the longer she stayed on in the capital, the more obstacles arose in the way of her return home; a mountain of fear and guilt was building up between Prague and that south Slovakian village. During the next few days we realized that she was heavily infected with the clap. She knew it but was afraid to say so. My neighbor in the next bed just then was a pleasant, well-built woman nearing sixty, a warm-hearted village housewife. She had tried to help her son build a house of his own, by falsifying wage slips to pay herself from cooperative funds. She had the countrywoman's native honesty and had started defrauding partly because it was so easy and they needed money, partly because the trend in society today is to take what you can from the state. She was not a cunning soul; her crime was motivated by love for her family and the fact that everybody around her was stealing as well. She passed through Ruzyně with a ten-year sentence already pronounced. She was only waiting for them to decide which camp to send her to, and Fanny's clap was her first real glimpse of the depths to which she had fallen.

Fanny had the next bed to hers, and the poor woman was so shaken that during the night she instinctively moved over onto my bed, even in her sleep, and her face was wet with tears. They left Fanny in our cell (the clap is not contagious without more intimate contact), but we must watch our towels so as not to infect our eyes! That was a week later, when our towels had been hanging side by side according to regulations. We watched over

Fanny, making sure she took her antibiotics regularly and washed her panties and her own towel every day—now hanging segregated from ours. The poor girl was shrinking before, but now she would have been happy to disappear altogether.

Annie hated her, the symbol of her own weakness and powerlessness; she sat watching her rocking on her stool, the murderous hatred of the weak for the weaker in her eyes. One of the laws of prison life: hit everyone weaker than yourself, a cheap way to be thought powerful. It was not only stupidity, ugliness, and now the clap that made Fanny such a likely victim: she snored unbearably. She had polyps in her nose, and the sounds she emitted were horrible. If you did not fall asleep before she began to snore, there was no hope unless you took a sleeping pill or by strength of will made her snores your lullaby. We all hurried to fall asleep first. Fanny slept soundly, the deep sleep of a healthy young creature, and one who had eaten up every scrap of bread and wiped up all the horrible jam before going to bed. She looked forward to sleep, her release from a hostile world. When she snored we tried to wake her, shaking her, holding her nose, turning her over, but all in vain; she snored as loudly when she lay on her belly or her side as when she was on her back. The sensible women shrugged and let her be. If you can sleep, O.K.; if you can't, just your bad luck. Fanny smiled uncertainly, unable to help us. Annie hated Fanny for that snoring because she could not fall asleep; and in the morning, with murderous hate in her eyes, she was preparing to beat the poor girl up. Annie needed to let off steam in the mornings.

"Stop heating it up, Annie."

"She can't help it, she's got polyps."

"She can't help having the clap, either?"

"Take it easy, Annie, you've had the clap too."

"Not here, though, I was in the clinic. And I'd see to it I got cured in here, too. I wouldn't go round with dirty black pants."

Fanny was prepared for an assault sooner or later; she was used to being knocked about. I couldn't understand how she managed to keep that good-natured smile on her face all the time. She did not understand what Annie was saying, but she got the sense of it all right, and she must have felt afraid. She was neither embittered nor self-pitying; that's the way the world is, her smile said, and I can't do anything to change it. There was something very good in her, so good-natured as to be stupid, but deeply rooted.

When Nancy was transferred, Denise took over the task of protecting Fanny, not out of sympathy, but on principle: if anybody's going to hand out thrashings in this cell, it's going to be me! One morning Denise was taken to see the doctor and the ugly duckling sat on her stool with downcast eyes. What had to happen would happen; there were never enough people to protect you all the time. The two other girls, Gypsies both of them, sat down on my bed like spectators waiting for the bull-fight to begin, impatient and tense. They did nothing to egg Annie on; their silent anticipation was enough. Get her! The air grew so heavy with expectation that my nose began to itch.

"Fanny, let's have a game of cards, O.K.?"

"Since when d'you play cards?" Annie snapped at me.

"From this moment. Wouldn't you like a game as well, Annie?"

"What? Play cards with that filthy snoring pig?"

"Don't bother, the two of us can play alone."

"What are you getting mixed up in this for? why d'you bother about her?"

"I wouldn't get mixed up in it if she were strong enough."

"What yer mean?"

"She's weak and she's afraid of you. Just look how scared she is. So I'm going to fight on her side."

"You fighting?" Annie found that excruciatingly funny. "You'll get sent down to the black hole."

"Annie, it's not fair to hit someone weaker than yourself."

"Ha! So you think I ought to hit women stronger than I am?"

"If you dared."

"You can't win if the other's stronger. Can't you see that?"

"It's shameful, hitting the weak. If you want to beat her up you'll have to beat me first."

Her dark unhappy eyes looked me over; it was sad to see how any obstacle was enough to deflate her angry passion. "I told you so," she said scornfully, "those books've turned your head."

All the glory of the ugly duckling's good nature was revealed when we found lice in our hair. One after the other Fanny examined us, sitting on the piled up beds and taking our heads on her lap. We each sat in front of her on a stool, and laid our face on her knees. She deloused with such professional skill that our initial panic subsided. If anyone can help us, it's Fanny. She did not reproach us for having shouted at her when she had the clap. Gently she took strand by strand; the experience of life in a children's home came in useful—what experience doesn't? I learned from her that you have to look most carefully around the ears. It takes the most humiliating circumstances to teach one how unimportant is the outward social mask. I can still feel her quick fingers taking each strand of hair firmly at the roots and slipping on down, I and the ugly duckling, both stinking of jail, and able to exchange happy smiles when she declared my head clean. In misfortune people draw closer to one another, and even Annie had to let our ugly duckling delouse her.

Fanny believed it was polite to do so, and when she was

interrogated she nodded agreement with all that was said: "Igen, igen." She did not understand a single word and was simply anxious to do what the interrogating officer wanted. She even signed the formal report of the proceedings, which was written in Czech and of which she again understood not a word. She was charged with "parasitism," with spreading venereal disease, and with some kind of black market dealings. She had been in the procuress's apartment when she was arrested, and her "friend" seems to have given something away and blamed Fanny. She herself said nothing about the woman's customers; she was not able to say anything in Czech, and in any case she was terrified of the woman. She really believed the woman would be able to have her done away with. When Fanny received the court's notice of remand, and the charges, one of the girls who knew a little Hungarian helped me to write a letter returning the document to the court and asking for it to be translated into Hungarian. Fanny carefully and fearfully copied out those few Hungarian sentences and signed the letter. It is a scandal that nobody advises these girls about the implications of these (for them) mysterious proceedings, or about their rights. They had a vague idea of what the interrogating officer was getting at, and what the judge was for, but their understanding of trial procedure was such that they confused the prosecution with the defense. Every remand prisoner has the right to borrow the penal code from the prison authorities, but how many can understand the legal language? Most of these young girls, with no money behind them, never saw their defense lawyer in prison, and often he did not even bother to attend their trial. The prison officers in charge of each floor were originally, perhaps, supposed to protect and guard over the helpless prisoners, but what has survived of that humane intention? The law lays down the right of every prisoner to be interrogated and tried in his mother tongue; Fanny smiled incredulously when I told her she had the right to ask for an interpreter. She was nearer to the truth than I was. For who would bother over the rights of an ugly duckling who did not know how to defend herself and said "Igen, igen—yes, yes," to everything?

The prison officer doubted the authenticity of the letter and brought it back to the cell. She was a decent woman; many of the others would simply have thrown it into the waste paper basket. I assured her that the girl really did not understand Czech, and the officer really sent the letter. And then things began to happen! Fanny was taken for interrogation again, and a lawyer who spoke Hungarian was present. When she came back to the cell, where was our ugly duckling? A transformation had taken place: no longer the long-suffering creature who would let you cut her head off without protest, but a sweet, happy, lively girl. No sleeping princess, indeed, but not nearly so plain as she had seemed. She eagerly described what had been going on and flapped her hands impatiently when we could not understand her Hungarian. That evening, so happy because her mother tongue had restored her humanity to her, she organized a ball after supper.

It was that festive March 8, when our guards celebrated International Women's Day by having a thorough cell inspection. Fanny dismissed our objections with a wave of the hand. She took all the arrangements on herself, the music, the dancing, and the need to placate any guard who might object to the noise. She got everything ready herself, without talking, since we were too boneheaded to understand her Hungarian, and only indicating with a movement of her chin when she needed something done. We pulled the table to one side and arranged our stools round the free space in the middle of the cell. Then we sat down, like girls waiting to be taken onto the floor at a village hop. Annie came from the same cultural background as Fanny, and she was given the role of the band—to tap out the rhythm while Fanny herself sang the czardas. The two Gypsy girls started delightedly dancing and when Fanny saw that neither Denise nor I knew the steps, she insisted that we learn. So now I can dance the czardas.

After this wild beginning our ball quieted down a little, Fanny sat us all down again, and then led me out to dance a stately waltz. It was an honor and my reward for the idea of writing that letter. Then we went on singing, stamping, and shouting, leaping in the air and whirling round, sliding in a tango and hopping in a polka. We were making an incredible noise, and the guard came along twice to see what was going on, but she neither sent for reinforcements nor took us off to the punishment cells. Our cell had the reputation of the best-behaved lot on the corridor, and her benevolence may have been a reward. Or maybe she thought we were celebrating International Women's Day. What we were celebrating was Fanny's victory over illiteracy. Fanny was the second girl, Andy the first, who had made me forget my sadness and truly rejoice. I do not know how her trial turned out; the last time I saw her she was out in the exercise cages with another cell. It was about five days after our ball, and Fanny looked content.

15

THE SPIRITS
OF THE DEAD

At the beginning of March, quite unexpectedly, the officer in charge of our floor moved us and the inmates of two other cells from the fourth to the sixth floor, to what used to be the sick bay; it was rarely used, and then only for a night at a time, as transfer cells. We were moved on a Friday afternoon, the least likely moment for such an event. Our jailers must have received sudden orders that took even them by surprise. By Friday afternoon any prisoner who is leaving has already gone, while new arrivals are not brought in until Monday morning. The officer said they were pressed for room, but as she took us along to the showers I could tell by the names on the doors that not all the cells were full. If only they had waited until Monday! I was expecting my husband's regular Saturday visit at the end of the street—and it was his fiftieth birthday, a very special day for me.

The sixth floor cell was airy, with windows barred but no wire screen over them; it faced south, and for the first time in nine months I saw the sun and even felt it on my face for a while. It was snowing outside. If I pressed my cheek to the bars I could just see, beyond the prison, a corner of the White Mountain Park and the little houses on the slope, looking so innocently normal. It was a warm cell, with the outside wall open to the sun, and there were only four of us in it. I was put with three women each from a different cell, but all three charged with misappropriation of socialist (that is, state) property. The women accused of this offense were usually respectable, quiet, and well-mannered. One of my new companions had worked out with her husband a method of robbing public telephone booths; her husband laid all the blame on her, got away with a trivial sentence, and then divorced her. One had fallen in with a gang that robbed the Metro turnstiles. The third had committed the "crime" of buying in the better supplied Prague shops the goods that her country customers wanted but could not get in her village shop. She had resold them at the official price and made no profit, but this meritorious service contravenes the law on retail trade. For the first time in nine months I could enjoy not just an occasional moment of peace and quiet, but hours and hours while one of my companions was drawing, one writing home, and the third reading. They never all spoke at once; they did not seek quarrels; each respected the habits of the others; and no voices were raised. In jail the simplest good behavior becomes a precious gift. But alas, when I was rid of the wild young toughs who made life so difficult—that was probably what the move was all about—I also lost Denise. We begged in vain to be left together.

The food for all three cells was brought up to the sixth floor in the elevator, on a special trolley, by the cook himself. It was the same old prison food, but (at least for our cell) there was always a second helping and the bread was fresh and soft every day. Down below, it depends on the trusties and their whims whether you get fresh or stale, hard bread. We no longer had to get up at six, because there was no loudspeaker on the sixth floor; and we often did not wake until the guard came round with breakfast, especially on Saturdays and Sundays. That was at eight, and instead of yelling she just laughed to see us still in bed. The prison officers and even some of the guards came up to see whether we were satisfied with prison conditions at last. "You've plenty of air and sunshine up here," Scooter said to me—an unheard-of comment.

One of my new companions had worked for a few months in the team that cleans the prison premises and moves all over the different wings. The "shampoo girls," as they are known, have quite a few privileges, but she had never seen anything like the comfort we now enjoyed. Under the impact of these incomprehensible changes in their lot, my new friends agreed that it could mean nothing less than an amnesty. They eagerly checked on conditions in the other two cells, comparing details of all the cases, and refused to admit that an amnesty could not possibly apply only to the inmates of three cells. An amnesty is a gift from the gods, something as unfathomable as prison itself, and therefore logic has no place in it. Amnesty is the prisoner's last hope, and whenever anything out of the ordinary occurs, amnesty is the first explanation that springs to mind. At least once a month the rumor runs through the prison that an amnesty will be promulgated on such and such a day; prisoners are not interested in politics, but they know very well which dates might serve, either for topical reasons, or as a commemoration. Indeed, they are more aware of these occasions than are those with the authority to decide. Prisoners are even sure they know which categories will be covered by the supposed amnesty. But as a rule, the only grounds for their certainty are that someone, some time, some place—in the central prison hospital or whatever—heard someone tell somebody else . . .

It is part of prison psychology that nobody ever believes the official explanation of anything (just as we did not believe that we had been moved because of overcrowding); rarely do prisoners think of the worst eventuality, either. The first thing they seize on is the hope of freedom. Personally, I did not believe an amnesty was imminent, but neither did it occur to me that the changes might have been made on my account. The authorities had apparently already decided that I and the others arrested on the same charge would be released without being brought to trial (though not with the charges dismissed). When my husband saw me last, at the beginning of March, he was horrified at the condition I was in. That was when we were trying to cure Fanny's clap; we all had lice, and the four wild young toughs in our cell, three of them Gypsy girls, yelled and screamed and fought all day long. You could not hear yourself speak, and it was a struggle to hold your nerves together, not to speak of maintaining civilized standards. I must have been in a sorry state.

My husband took energetic steps, and I think it was after this that somebody higher up decided that it would be better if I did not leave jail looking like a bundle of shattered nerves. And if this *is* what was behind our move, I am glad to think that on my account another eleven or twelve women benefited from the change at least for a couple of weeks. The guards were so kind that they took us down and back from the exercise yard in the freight elevator, every day! The fact that the way we were treated was such a rarity brought it home to me that imprisonment need not be the cruel and humiliating experience they make it; and that when forced to do so, prison officers are capable of acting differently.

The incomprehensible nature of the change, of our new conditions, raised questions which could only be answered by the spirits, since human logic failed. Superstition is rife in prison at all times and the magical rituals are handed on by personal example and experience.

One of my new friends, Zdenka, like Helga before her, told our fortunes from the cards. Helga spun endless tales from what she read there (and from her tales, I could deduce what she knew about me that she could not have learned from me). The favorite way with the cards was the cross: what you don't know, what lies in wait for you, who is thinking of you, who loves you, and who hates you. I always drew the king of spades and the king of hearts, rarely the ace of spades but always the ace of hearts. I was considered a happy woman, with love and hate fighting over me. Fortune-telling from cards is too arbitrary, though, and your future too dependent on the imagination of the fortune-teller. In prison the spirits are always being called upon. It was not the first time I had taken part in a seance, but up there on the sixth floor, shaken out of our accustomed attitudes by unexpectedly decent treatment, the need to call upon other worlds became an obsession. Not an hour passed without the presence in our cell of some spirit from the beyond. Tired, all our questions exhausted, we pleaded over and over again: Why are we here? Shall we be going home? When will that be?

As I write now, I can smile skeptically, but there, and then, the dark powers of magic made my flesh creep. We used a book to call up the spirits of the dead, probably a reminiscence of the missal used in black magic; but for us it did not matter what book it was. It was merely the instrument, but it had to be a fairly light and fairly thin book. You counted the pages and then inserted the handles of two toothbrushes exactly in the middle of the book; the handles had to be flat and straight, and the brush end stuck out at the top and bottom of the spine, bristles upward. They formed the axis from which the book (held shut by a rubber band) hung, and on which it could turn. Two women sat facing each other with the book between them; one was there to address the spirits, the other to help her. Each of them supported one of the brushes on the last joint of her right forefinger. When the spirit had entered the book and began to answer our questions, the book turned smoothly on the taut skin of our fingertips, moving to the right if the answer was YES, to the left for NO. When there was no answer because the spirit was annoyed by the question or did not know the answer or because the question was not put properly, the book remained motionless.

I myself never called up a spirit from the dead; the idea of arousing forces in which I do not believe, and which must therefore be hostile to me, had no appeal. I prefer to guide my life by my own experience, my own actions. I often took the part of the helper, however, and can state in all seriousness that nobody ever manipulated the book; it did indeed move to the left or the right on our two fingers, and it did so only after the spirit had been asked a question. The book was obviously waiting to hear the question before reacting. Nor were the answers always what the questioner would have liked; often the reply went dead against what she wanted to be told. There is another fact that I can state authoritatively: everyone who questioned the spirits, every single one of them, had an icy cold forefinger after the book—her physical contact with the spirit—had turned a couple of times. The helper, holding the book in exactly the same way but not in direct contact with the spirit, had a forefinger as warm as her other nine fingers. This phenomenon could be tested on one and the same subject: while she asked questions her forefinger was icy, and when she changed roles and became a mere helper her finger was warm again. On the other hand, I must bear witness that the spirits were often wrong in their predictions; to err is human, and we were calling on the spirits of human beings. It did not occur to us to call upon gods or demons.

I can smile at it all, now; inside I was absorbed by the whole ceremony, and although I was not ready to surrender my disbelief, my skepticism was to say the least subdued. I gave myself up to the experience of the moment as wholeheartedly as those who did believe. I trembled all over just as they did; I felt the tension mount as the book turned, manifesting the presence of the spirit; I was moved and spellbound by the ritual. Thinking back to those moments, though, it was perhaps the women themselves who were so moving, rather than the presence of spirits in the cell. Try to imagine them: a cell, grim and gloomy, a comfortless world, indeed a dead world. Homeless souls with the last flicker of hope dying in them. A handful of women, as neat as they can make themselves in their gray rags, sunken eyes with the light extinguished in them, in gray, tired faces. They huddle together in the one corner that is not readily visible from the spy hole. In our atheistic and unspiritual prisons, it is strictly forbidden to have commerce with the spirits. Four, five, six women, six minds each burning not with ten or twelve but a hundred different questions. Raw, aching questions. About lost hopes, broken loves, inaccessible opportunities. About lives that are ruined—as they know too well—and the dead, empty years ahead that are part of no life at all. Is it any wonder that they yearn to find a thread of assurance, of truth, of hope? Who can they turn to for reassurance that all is not lost, however grim the future seems? Who would dare to give a prompt and unequivocal answer to their fears? The living are either inaccessible, or they have already turned their backs. And so these unhappy women call upon the dead.

"Spirit of Václav Vojtíšek, I call you up from the kingdom of the dead. Come and be here with us."

There is a moment of tense silence, and then the book moves—hesitantly and then decidedly—to the right.

"Spirit of Václav Vojtíšek, are you here with us?"

The questioning voice trembles a little; the book confirms the spirit's presence.

"Spirit of Václav Vojtíšek, thank you for coming when I called you."

The book is still, waiting. It is a good thing to be very polite to the spirits, and indeed the ceremonial form of the questions is laid down.

"Spirit of Václav Vojtíšek, will you answer my questions?"

The book does not move.

"Spirit of Václav Vojtíšek, I am asking whether you will answer my questions?"

The book moves hesitantly to the right.

"Thank you, spirit of Václav Vojtíšek. May I put my first question?"

Conversation with a spirit is a ceremonious affair. The book answered again by moving to the right.

We sat in silence, motionless, listening anxiously to the questions. They had to be put clearly; the spirit heard them, and so did we. It was like eavesdropping at the confessional, for each asked about the things that troubled her most deeply. The questions had to be honest and sincerely meant; you can play about with human beings, but not with the spirits of the dead.

We sat huddled together, living through each other's moment of truth. Strangely enough, none of the secrets revealed in these tremulous moments was ever used as a weapon in quarrels. Even the toughest girls knew that what went on then was sacred, and it was an article of faith that the spirits would take vengeance on anyone who abused the ceremony.

This dark ritual was a plea for mercy, a tempting of fate; but first each woman had to put herself on trial, to clear her own conscience. Would her dead mother come to her inside? Or, wounded in her respectability, would she refuse to come? Would father answer all the questions she wanted to put to him? I have seen a father's spirit answering only some of his daughter's questions, refusing to reply where he would have hurt her. Dad, are you angry with me? No answer; the book did not move. The grandmother of another girl would not answer questions relating to the divorce she disapproved of when she was alive. Granny, we didn't have time to get married. Will Karel stand by me now? Silence; the book did not move. Granny, I asked you about Karel. Is he going to drop me? No answer. One girl, fearful of such family situations and the unhappiness they entailed, would only call up the spirits of strangers. In a daredevil spirit, one day she called up the ghost of Adolf Hitler, and then Hitler refused to leave our cell and return to the kingdom of the shades. He resisted all our pleas: spirit of Adolf Hitler, go back to the world of the dead! The book was unmoved. When that happens, the one who called up the recalcitrant spirit has to take the book to bed with her and sleep with it. Who can tell what a spirit like that of Adolf Hitler may not do during the night? We were careful not to offend him. In the morning the girl said she could tell he had gone, because we were all relaxed. The spirits behave in very different ways, some coming readily as soon as they are called, others needing persuasion; but all without exception are extremely sensitive to ridicule or offense. If you do not believe in them you had better not call on them, or they will have their revenge. Helga was scornful of this commerce with the spirit world, and not one of those she called ever came to the cell. The book simply refused to budge for her, although it was the same book that a little later turned for one of the other girls. A spirit that has a friendly relationship with you can help you a lot, and a spirit you are careful not to offend will try to protect you.

We huddled together, encouraging each other and prompting the right formulation of the ceremonial questions. We put a positive interpretation on negative answers, deciding together which questions to ask to make things clearer; positive answers cheered us all up. The tensions between us disappeared, our disagreements faded, and we were considerate toward one another. Other people's questions were ours too, and we were as concerned over their answers as our own. The spirits certainly made for better interpersonal relationships in the cells.

Will my trial be soon? In March? In April? Shall I get the hardest sentence? The shortest? Something in between? A year? Five years? Seven? Shall I be sent to a work camp? Shall I be allowed a visit before I'm transferred? Will my husband come to my trial? Will Mother come? Will Karel desert me? Will Jan desert me? Will mother look after my little girl? Will they take my apartment away from me? Will they confiscate my savings? Will my husband give evidence against me? Will he divorce me? Will they take the children away from me? Will my children turn against me? Will they stop having anything to do with me? Will the family leave me to my fate? Shall I end up all alone? Shall I have a home to come back to? Shall I ever get home again? Won't I fall ill? Won't I die? Will mother survive the shock? Shall I end up like a stray dog, dead in a ditch somewhere? Will my lawyer manage to deal with the chief prosecution witness? Will my husband put up money for bribes? Will my boss remember what he promised to do for me? Will my family stop trying to do me down? Shall I get a parcel? Tomorrow? Next week? Shall I get a letter? Will my lawyer come? Shall I be taken for questioning again? Have they got any more witnesses against me?

The questions had to be clearly put, so that the spirit could answer YES or NO. They varied from individual to individual, case to case. Some were roundabout questions, edging into details; others went straight to the point, however painful. The intelligence of the questioner played its role, too; but all questions worked toward one final subject: amnesty. When everything else had been dealt with, interrogation, trial, family relationships, there came the inevitable question: Will there be an amnesty this year? In May? (May is the obvious month, with the anniversary of the liberation as well as May Day.)

Spirit of Václav Vojtíšek, will there be a general amnesty? Will it be an amnesty for some crimes only? Will it cover what I'm in for? Shall I be in a work camp by then? Shall I still be in jail? Spirit of Václav Vojtíšek, where shall I be when I'm released? The spirits were generous, they always said YES to an amnesty—if not a general amnesty, then at least for some categories. The book turned to the left, to the right. At times it seemed to hesitate, but sometimes it reacted sharply, answering so vehemently that it fell to the floor.

Denise used to call on the spirits, and because she could not bear me not to know what the future held for me, the spirits she called up were asked about my fate as well. They always answered that I would not be sent for trial, but they could not tell me when I would be sent home. Sunday was the first day of spring, the sun was shining on deep snow that had fallen during the night, and the horizon glittered. I wrote a long letter home. On Monday we were released. When Jiřina and I embraced in the corridor, she said, "And only yesterday I finally got reconciled to the idea of conviction." She expected to get eight years, I expected three or four.

Spirits of my dear departed, come to me now and answer my questions:

Are my friends still living?
Are they sick?
Are they feeling cold?
Are they hungry?
Have they been given thankless jobs to do?
Do they earn a decent wage? Enough pocket money?
Are they allowed to boil water for tea?
Can they buy a bit of sausage to liven up the food?
Do they cheer up sometimes?
Does anybody beat them?
Do they feel forlorn and deserted?
Have their children stood by them?
Do their husbands and lovers still love them?
Are they allowed visits?
Are they allowed to write home?
Do they get letters from home?
Are they in the punishment cells?
Do they get parcels?
Has anybody stolen from them?
Can they overcome their despair?
Can they overcome their loneliness?
Are they holding out against filthy ways?

Can they defend themselves?
Have they lost hope?
Are those who have already gone home happy?
Have they got into trouble again?

Spirits of my dear departed, do my friends think of me sometimes?